RAVES FOR SUE MARGOLIS'S NOVELS

SPIN CYCLE

"Rachel [Katz] is a first-rate comic, and this delightful novel is filled with more than a few big laughs." —*Booklist*

"A funny, sexy British romp ... Margolis is able to keep the witty one-liners spraying like bullets. Light, fun ..." —*Library Journal*

"Warmhearted relationship farce ... a nourishing delight."
—*Publishers Weekly*

NEUROTICA

"Screamingly funny sex comedy ... the perfect novel to take on holiday." —*USA Today*

"Cheeky comic novel—a kind of *Bridget Jones's Diary* for the matrimonial set ... Wickedly funny."
—*People* (Beach Book of the Week)

"Scenes that literally will make your chin drop with shock before you erupt with laughter ... A fast and furiously funny read."
—*The Plain Dealer* (Cleveland)

"Taking up where *Bridget Jones's Diary* took off, this saucy British adventure redefines the lusty woman's search for erotic satisfaction.... Witty and sure ... A taut and rambunctious tale exploring the perils and raptures of the pursuit of passion."
—*Publishers Weekly*

"Splashy romp ... giggles guaranteed." —*Daily News* (New York)

Also by Sue Margolis

NEUROTICA

SPIN CYCLE

APOCALIPSTICK

SUE MARGOLIS

DELTA TRADE PAPERBACKS

A Delta Book
Published by
Dell Publishing
a division of
Random House, Inc.
New York, New York

This is a work of fiction. Names, characters, places, and incidents
either are the product of the author's imagination or are used fictitiously.
Any resemblance to actual persons, living or dead, events, or locales is
entirely coincidental.

Copyright ©2003 by Sue Margolis
Cover design by Lynn Andreozzi

All rights reserved. No part of this book may be reproduced or
transmitted in any form or by any means, electronic or mechanical,
including photocopying, recording, or by any information storage and
retrieval system, without the written permission of the Publisher, except
where permitted by law.

Delta® is a registered trademark of Random House, Inc., and the colophon is a
trademark of Random House, Inc.

Library of Congress Cataloging-in-Publication Data

Margolis, Sue.
    Apocalipstick / Sue Margolis.
      p. cm.
    ISBN 0-385-33656-X
    1. Women journalists—Fiction.   I. Title.

PR6063.A635 A6 2003
823'.914—dc21

                                                    2002071586

Manufactured in the United States of America

January 2003

RRH 10 9 8 7 6 5 4 3 2 1

For RW, who might laugh more than most

APOCALIPSTICK

Rebecca was fiddling with the tuner button on the car radio. She'd been sitting in the monster traffic jam on Camden Road, engine off, for the best part of fifteen minutes. For the last two she'd been trying and failing to find some traffic news that might explain what was going on.

"...still offering huge discounts on our exclusive range of *Lazee Dayze* recliners..."

Fiddle:

"Here's Brotherhood of Man, with *Save All Your Kisses for Me*..."

Jab this time:

"...and my Alan was just lying there, completely limp—not even the faintest sign of life. So, I did what anybody would do. I got down on the floor and started giving him the kiss of life."

Rebecca found herself stopping to listen.

"And isn't that a cheery, feel-good story to brighten up this drizzly A.M. in the capital? Jacky from Borehamwood, there, talking about her house fire and how she successfully resuscitated Alan, her iguana."

Her nose wrinkled as she imagined puckering up to some slimy reptile. Not that she hadn't puckered up to one or two in the odd drunken moment. The only difference was, her reptiles had worn tight leather pants and called her "babe."

Fiddle:

"...so best to avoid the Camden Road area if you can. More traffic news in the next hour. Caroline Feraday, 5 Live Travel..."

Rebecca Fine, newly appointed beauty columnist of the *Daily Vanguard* Saturday magazine, now let out a tiny yelp of frustration and switched off the radio. The monthly beauty, fashion and lifestyle meeting was due to start in half an hour, and unless the traffic freed up in the next few minutes, there was no way she was going to make it on time. It was her first meeting and she'd been so anxious to make a good impression. Her only hope was that other people would be driving in from north London and they would be late too. For now, all she could do was sit it out. She picked up her bag, which was lying on the passenger seat, and went rummaging for her lipstick and mascara.

She was staring into the driver's mirror, finishing her lashes, when the car behind her let out three long blasts of its horn. The first made her jump so violently that her mascara brush shot upward, leaving a gash of black from her eyebrow to her hairline, which made her look like some kind of unihorned devil. As the honking continued, she saw what had happened. A broken-down lorry, which had been causing the holdup, was now being towed away and the traffic was moving. Clearly the driver of the car behind her was more than a tad put out that she hadn't noticed. Her hand flew to the ignition, but the car refused to start. Honk. Honk. A twenty-yard gap had opened up in front of her.

2

"All right. All right." She was getting flustered now. Looking down, she saw the automatic gear lever was in drive. She shoved it into neutral. Honk. Honk. Honk.

As she turned the ignition key a second time, her eyes darted back to the rearview mirror. The honker was some guy in a flash sports car. No surprise there. Before she had a chance to move, he began pulling out to overtake her. He couldn't get up any speed because he was squeezing between her and the oncoming traffic. As he drew level with her, he leaned across the sports car's passenger seat and lowered the window. Rebecca lowered hers.

"My apologies for disturbing you," he smirked. Plummy voice, expensive suit, floppy Hugh Grant hair. Posh estate agent, probably. "It's just that some of us have jobs to go to."

"Look, I'm really sorry, but there was no need to blast me like that…"

Just then her mobile started ringing.

As she picked it up off the dashboard and pressed OK, the sports car roared off.

"And it's Mr. Subaru Turbo," she said in a singsong voice, "who wins the award for the smallest penis, this drizzly A.M."

"Hi, Becks. It's me," the voice on the end of the line giggled. "Listen, have I disturbed some kind of intimate moment? I mean I can always call back."

It was Jess.

"No, you're fine," Rebecca said, her tone brightening. She put the phone between her shoulder and chin and asked Jess to hang on while she pulled away. It was a difficult maneuver, since all the cars behind her had followed the Subaru and nobody was allowing her to rejoin the stream of traffic. Finally somebody let her in.

"God, he'd have thought twice about intimidating me like that," Jess said when Rebecca had finished telling her about the hooray honker.

"He would?"

"Too blinkin' right. You see I've got this brilliant new bumper sticker that says: 'I'm out of estrogen and I've got a gun.' "

Rebecca burst out laughing. "So," she said, "how's the baby?"

"Oh, you know," Jess said with a sigh, "fine, but knackering. In the two months we've had him I don't think either of us has had more than three hours' sleep on the trot." She paused. "Then there's my Bagpuss."

"Oh, sweet. Bought it for the baby?" Rebecca asked, assuming quite reasonably that her best friend had been to Toys 'R' Us and bought the furry TV character for the baby.

"No, you dope, Diggory hasn't got it."

Diggory. Jess adored the name. And since Rebecca adored Jess, she pretended to love the name, too, but secretly she worried that the poor child might grow up to become a bearded botanist in a cardigan.

"What, so you bought it for you? Getting in touch with your child within. Nice."

"Oh, God. Becks, listen. I haven't *bought* Bagpuss. I've *got* it. Let's put it this way, since giving birth, my pencil-gripping days are definitely a thing of the past."

"What? You could do that?"

"I don't know. I never tried. But if I could, I wouldn't be able to do it now. And I know Ed's noticed. Why else would we have only done it twice since the baby? The second time it took him ages to get a hard-on. He doesn't fancy me anymore. I just know it."

"Oh, come on," Rebecca soothed, "Ed's crazy about you. Always has been. He's not going to go off you simply because you've gained a millimeter or two in the pussy department. You've got a new baby. He's exhausted like you are, that's all. Sex is hardly going to be what it was, not for a while anyway. You of all people should know that."

Jess was the agony aunt at *Femme* magazine. It always amazed Rebecca how she seemed able to get a handle on everybody else's problems except her own.

"Just keep doing the pelvic floor exercises," Rebecca went on, "and I'm sure everything'll spring back into shape."

"Yeah, you're right," Jess said, cheering up. "Look, you don't fancy popping round tonight, do you? Ed's got to work late on the news desk and I'll be all on my own with the Digsbury. I'm longing to hear how the new job's going."

"Great," Rebecca said. "I'll bring pizza."

The moment she hung up, her mobile went off a second time. She pressed OK, desperate for whomever it was on the other end to be one of her few friends who wasn't pregnant or recently delivered and with whom she could still have an above-the-waist conversation.

"...still leaking when she sneezes...Hello? Rebecca?"

Rebecca's brow furrowed.

"Gran?"

"Sorry, darling, I've got Esther here. We're off to the sales. I was in the middle of telling her about my cousin Doreen's bladder operation. I didn't think you'd pick up so soon. So, did you see it?"

"What, cousin Doreen's bladder operation?"

"No, silly. The e-mail I sent you."

Grandma Rose was a Net head—a "silver surfer" who had forced herself to come to grips with new technology when she realized how much cheaper it was to e-mail her brothers and sisters in Miami and Sydney, not to mention her cousin Doreen in Montreal with the leaky bladder, than phone. With time on her hands, what had begun as a money saver had become a hobby verging on an obsession.

"No, sorry, I haven't had a chance to check my e-mail. I was out till quite late last night."

"Ooh, somewhere nice?"

"Just a bar in town with a few friends."

"And you ate?"

"I ate."

"So, what did you eat?"

"We all went out for sushi afterward."

"What? A few bits of raw fish? You'll fade away. You'll turn into your great-aunt Minnie. The woman ate like a sparrow. If it wasn't for her nose she'd have had no shape at all."

From the moment Rebecca's mother died ten years ago, her adoring, devoted Jewish Grandma Rose had taken it upon herself to worry, fuss and kvetch about every aspect of Rebecca's life. "Not that I want to meddle, but..." became her mantra. This of course was the surest sign that she was about to do precisely that, on a scale unsurpassed since Hitler meddled with the Sudetenland.

Top of Rose's causes for concern list was Rebecca's lack of a husband. This was closely followed by her granddaughter's health, which naturally included her eating habits. God forbid she should mention the gut pain she'd had last week after a dodgy prawn bhuna. Rose would have her off to a gastroenterologist before she could say barium enema.

"So," Rose continued, "did you, er, you know, meet anybody nice?"

"Gran, believe me, the only man I went to bed with last night was Jerry Seinfeld."

"Ooh, do I know him? You've never mentioned him. Well, I hope he took precautions."

Rebecca decided against teasing her grandmother further and explained that she'd been watching the TV show. (*Seinfeld* being her absolute, all-time favorite sitcom. Last night The Paramount Channel had been showing twelve episodes back-to-back. She'd managed to stay with it until just after one, before finally dropping off.)

"So, Gran—the e-mail."

"Oh, right," Rose said cheerily, clearly over her disappointment that Rebecca wasn't going out with Jerry Seinfeld. "Well, I was surfing yesterday afternoon and I came across this lonely hearts Web site. Listen, have I ever got a fella for you."

"Gawd."

"OK, get this: 'Orthopedic surgeon, Jewish. Midthirties. Looking for love.' Doesn't he sound just perfect?"

Rose was positively squealing with delight. " 'Dark. Six two. Lean, masculine guy. Not hairy chested.' Personally I like a man with a bit of chest hair, but never mind. Goes on to say he's got a mustache…You know, I think that Clark Gable look's definitely coming back…and that he's passive and very versatile. What more could you want? A man who doesn't argue and can turn his hand to anything. Then it says he likes to give O…I'm not sure what that last bit means. Maybe he donates to some orthopedic charity or something. My God, a philanthropist as well. So what do you reckon? There's an e-mail address."

"You sure that's all it says?" Rebecca said with faux casualness.

"Yes, except for some initials I don't understand at the beginning."

"What initials?" Rebecca asked. She knew precisely what was coming.

"G.W.M. Actually, thinking about it, I reckon that must mean good with money."

"Gran, it stands for gay white male."

Grandma Rose missed a beat.

"You sure?"

"Positive," Rebecca declared.

Another beat.

"Esther," Rose hissed, "Rebecca says he's gay."

Rebecca could hear her explaining about G.W.M. A few moments later she was back on the line.

"Esther reckons it might be worth contacting him anyway. She says perhaps he's not *very* gay. She could be right. It's possible he's just confused. So many young people are these days. You could help him sort himself out. What else have you got to do? After all, you haven't had a date for nine months. Why you had to finish with that Simon beats me. He sounded so nice. Two weeks you went out. How can you expect to get to know a person in two weeks?"

"Gran, you can't be a bit gay. It's like being a bit dead. And I've told you before, it just didn't work out between me and Simon. I know you worry, but I'm doing fine on my own, honest. And it's not like I don't have friends. Look, I gotta run, I've just pulled up outside the office and I'm running late. I'll speak to you later. Love you."

She was grateful for an excuse to get off the phone. There was no way she could ever tell her the real reason she ended it with Simon.

The truth was that Simon, an exceedingly cute stand-up comic and ventriloquist, had been just a tad off piste personalitywise. But not in a trendy, cool way—more in a weird, *Star Trek* convention kind of way. For a start, his hobby was wood turning and polishing. On their second date he presented her with an exquisitely finished mug tree. On the third, a newel!

What was more, he insisted the dummy—a pint-size football hooligan with a rictus grin, two earrings and a Tommy Hilfiger tracksuit—accompany them on all their dates. At first Rebecca thought this was a hoot, since Wayne (the dummy) would often pipe up with the odd witticism. The real problem—and the reason she finally ended it—began as soon as she and Simon started having sex. Whenever Simon came, the omnipresent Wayne would yell at the top of his voice: "Back of the net! Back of the fucking net!"

Apart from the occasional till-dawn-do-us-part relationship, there hadn't been anybody since.

"You know what you should do?" Grandma Rose had said soon after she finished with Simon. "Pack up and move somewhere where the men outnumber the women."

Rose immediately went on the Net to gather statistics. It turned out Rebecca's choices were the Shetland Isles, Qatar or Tower Hamlets.

Occasionally she found herself sharing Rose's pessimism about her lack of a man. She was thirty-two; if she wasn't careful her life was going to end up on the remaindered table along with all the Anthea Turner biographies. It was always Jess who brought her to her senses, made her see that playing the field could be just as much fun as being in a relationship. She'd done it the other night when she popped in for a quick chat (having left Diggory and a bottle of expressed milk with Ed), only to discover Rebecca sitting in her PMS dressing gown, drowning her sorrows in Baileys and Marshmallow Fluff sandwiches.

Jess spent ages doing her sympathetic but sensible agony aunt bit, reminding her that a relationship did not guarantee happiness. "I mean Liz Hurley had to put up with Hugh's antics. Mick constantly cheated on Jerry."

"Yeah, you're right," Rebecca said, scraping around the inside of the Marshmallow Fluff jar with her finger and starting to cheer up, "and some poor woman somewhere must have been Mrs. Pol Pot."

Rebecca charged out of the lift and into the office, rubbing at the remainder of the mascara gash with a tissue. By her calculations she had about three minutes before the meeting was due to start.

"It's all right, don't panic." It was Snow, the fashion, beauty and lifestyle assistant—painted-on freckles, pigtails, spiky dog collar choker. "Lucretia's just rung in to say she's going to be ten or fifteen minutes late. She's only just left Sorrento."

A fully functioning person who hadn't stayed up until past one, watching back-to-back episodes of *Seinfeld*, might have suggested to Snow that it was highly unlikely that Lucretia Coffin Mott, the magazine's haughty, razor-cheeked fashion, beauty and lifestyle editor, would make it from the Bay of Naples to Farringdon in ten or fifteen minutes, but since Rebecca wasn't fully functioning, she didn't.

"Thank the Lord for that," she said, slapping her hand to her chest with relief. Snow smiled and began heading back to her desk.

"So," Rebecca called out after her, "you told Justin how you feel about this name thing yet?" Justin was Snow's fiancé. He was the old-fashioned traditional type who insisted she take his surname once they were married.

Snow shook her head. "I don't want to upset him. I mean maybe I could learn to live with being Mrs. Snow Ball."

Rebecca shook her head. Snow was a kind, sweet girl, but she allowed people to walk all over her—especially Lucretia.

As she reached her desk, Rebecca did a cartoon double take. All her stuff had gone. Her computer, her notebook, her ceramic arse full of Biros and emery boards, the mass of freebie cosmetic samples sent in by publicists desperate for publicity, not to mention three pairs of windup walking sushi, had all vanished.

But the desk wasn't empty. A sleek, brushed aluminum laptop now sat dead center. A matching PalmPilot lay to one side, a brand-new yellow legal pad to the other. Lying across this, bisecting it diagonally into two precisely equal halves, was a painfully fashionable Plume de Ma Tante fountain pen. Sitting at a safe distance was a Starbucks cappuccino.

"What the …?" She stood frowning and looking for Snow to ask what was going on. But she'd disappeared.

"I don't suppose anybody's seen my stuff, have they?" she asked nobody in particular. The three or four people sitting close by staring into their screens looked up briefly to smile and shake their heads.

Her eyes shot round the huge open-plan office. Nothing. For one dreadful moment it occurred to her that after only a fortnight on the *Vanguard,* she'd been sacked. But why? She'd done two beauty columns so far and there hadn't been even a sniff of a complaint from Lucretia. In fact only yesterday she'd made a point of coming over to her and saying how much she'd enjoyed the one on nasal waxing.

Finally she located her possessions piled up on the floor beside the fire escape. Next to the pile was a desk. On it was her computer. She knew it was hers because the screen was covered in Post-it Notes.

Suddenly everything became clear. Rebecca's original workstation was directly next to the *Vanguard's* news desk and the office of its editor, Charlie Holland. Obviously, he had just taken on some new hotshot hack (and an anally retentive one at that) whose worth he considered to be far greater than hers. As a result she'd been banished to the far side of the office, to fire-escape purdah.

She trudged toward her new desk. By rights she had no cause to feel so put out. As a freelancer whose only contribution to the *Vanguard* mag was a weekly column that took her no more than a day and a half to write and that she could quite easily knock out at home, she had no real claim to a desk at all, let alone one in a prime location. But Lucretia, in a rare moment of generosity, had insisted she have one. And positionwise—being right on top of the proper hacks as opposed to being with the girlies on the magazine—it couldn't have fitted Rebecca's needs more perfectly.

The truth was that from a journalistic point of view, her interest in cosmetics was limited. Not that she didn't adore buying them—at the last count she owned nine lipsticks, all in the same shade of neutral—and not that she wouldn't happily have supported any move to make Bobbi Brown a dame of the British Empire. It was just that in her opinion, there was only so much a person could write about a tube of concealer.

Over the years she had also become pretty skeptical about the cosmetics industry. Whereas she could see the point of spending a fortune on velvet-edged cardigans with little pearl buttons and having her roots tended by Camp David, he of Antoni e David on Berkeley Street, she could see no reason to slap on fifty-quid-a-tube gunk every night when hand cream probably worked just as well.

Jess, on the other hand, had virtually no interest in makeup beyond a superficial coat of mascara and lip gloss. This was partly because she remained almost untouched by postfeminist thinking and still clung to the quaint notion that makeup enslaved women. But mainly it was because she didn't need it. Jess was a natural beauty with perfect skin, a mass of gleaming shoulder-length curls the color of toffee apple and deep blue almond-shaped eyes.

Rebecca had only one professional ambition—to become a successful investigative reporter. In the eight or nine years she'd been in newspapers she'd had her fair share of decent stories, but nothing big, although she supposed the Belfast women's group story and the one about chlamydia looked pretty impressive on her CV. The thing about doing investigations as a freelancer was that they took so much time—years, often. Occasionally she would get lucky and a story would be commissioned rather than her having to do it on spec and submit it when it was finished. Then a features editor might give her some expense money up front to keep her going, but more often than not she was forced to finance her own investigations.

She'd been working on a story about a company that seemed to be making huge amounts of money selling meat intended for pet food to butchers (her bank balance getting redder by the day) when her friend Nat, the heavily pregnant beauty columnist on the *Vanguard* mag and an old mate from their early days on the *Rotherham Advertiser*, suggested Rebecca fill in for her while she went off on maternity leave. The struggle to make up her mind—which centered on the loss-of-dignity issue versus the increase-in-cash issue—lasted no more than three seconds. She spent the next couple of days mugging up on her liposomes, ceramides, lotions, potions and glowtions as if she were studying for her finals, convinced Lucretia Coffin Mott that she was a veritable Elizabeth Arden of cosmetic knowledge, and got the job.

The next day when her dodgy meat story collapsed, due to a consignment of pet food meat that she was assiduously tracking turning up at, er, a pet food factory, Rebecca realized she needed to find another big story, preferably a genuine one this time, to avoid imminent penury. So when Lucretia phoned to offer her a desk, which turned out to be just a few feet from the news desk, she was ecstatic. It meant that when the journalists were at the editor's daily conference or at lunchtime when they were in the pub, she could answer the phone and maybe, just maybe, a proper, grown-up story might just land in her lap.

Now she was sitting by the bloody fire escape, however, and she'd feel far too conspicuous walking past the subs and advertising people to answer the phones.

She picked up a pair of windup sushi, the ones with halved and flattened plastic prawns on top, wound the mechanism and sat watching them lumber across the desk. At the very least, she thought, somebody might have told her she was being moved. Apart from anything else she was now miles from the kitchen and the loo. There weren't even any people from the magazine sitting nearby. Just Dennis Eccles, the local government reporter, who bleated on constantly about devolution for Lancashire, and was so boring he'd been consigned to the fire escape too.

Rebecca decided to have a hunt around for Snow. It was half past ten and she wanted to know if Lucretia had arrived yet.

The male voice came from behind her. "Love the sushi," it said.

She spun round. It was the Hugh Grant hair she noticed first. Good God, it was him—the honker with the small penis. What was he doing here? For one mad, irrational moment it occurred to her that he had somehow heard her make the small penis remark or even lip-read it in his rearview mirror. Having followed her to work, he was now about to have the most almighty go at her in front of the entire office.

"I just wanted to come over," he began, his manner disarmingly polite and charming, "and apologize about all this—you being forced to move."

Hang on, Rebecca thought, *this* was the new bloke Charlie had taken on? Pretty certain now that he wasn't about to berate her about her small penis remark, she felt safe to go into affronted mode regarding his behavior on Camden Road—not to mention the small matter of her being turfed out of her desk. She shot him a thin, tight-lipped smile. Then she bent down and began gathering up papers.

"Thing is," he continued, clearing his throat, "there wasn't a lot I could do, I'm afraid. Charlie insisted. The girl with the freckles— Snow I think her name is—was supposed to explain. She did, didn't she?"

Rebecca straightened and put the papers down on the desk. "Actually, no. Snow hasn't said a word," she replied frostily.

He was tall with broad shoulders. The navy suit was Kenzo, maybe Paul Smith. Underneath, he was wearing an Italian cotton shirt in a slightly lighter blue, with a matching tie. Brand-new shoes, she noticed. Expensive black slip-ons. Unquestionably overdressed—certainly for the *Vanguard,* where all the blokes wore Dockers, open-neck shirts and sensible shoes.

Clearly fancied himself, she decided.

"Sorry," he said. He was looking at her, his head tilted slightly to one side, "but have we met?"

"Briefly," she said, "and I have to say it was a total blast."

He gave her a look of total noncomprehension.

"Camden Road. Half an hour ago. I was the woman in the blue Peugeot."

"What, the one doing her makeup?"

She reddened. "OK, I admit, it may not have been the most sensible thing I could have been doing, but you didn't have to be quite so bloomin' rude."

He looked distinctly sheepish. "No, you're quite right," he said. "What can I say? You must think I'm a complete prat."

"Well, I have to say my thoughts were veering in that direction." She was *so* enjoying getting her own back.

"Look, I'm most terribly sorry. Thing is, I was in a bit of a state this morning. My car got pinched from outside my flat."

Her enjoyment instantly turned to guilt. "God, I'm sorry," she said.

"Yeah, not the best way to start your first day in a new job. By the time I'd sorted everything out with the police, I was running severely late. I tried calling a cab, but there weren't any. Anyway, I was just leaving to get the tube when I bumped into the guy from downstairs who I know pretty well and he offered to lend me his car. I'm thinking great, problem solved. Then I hit the traffic on Camden Road."

"Oh, right. So the Subaru isn't yours?"

"Good God, no. Bit flash for my taste. Plus I always think blokes who drive cars like that are out to prove themselves in some way, don't you?"

"Maybe," she said, casually turning back to organizing her papers. "Never thought about it."

"Really? I thought most women loathed blokes who drive flash cars. Anyway, look, I know I was appallingly rude, but please could we possibly start again?"

She swiveled round to face him. He was smiling at her, but it was an uneasy, slightly diffident smile, she thought. He was also fiddling with the loose change in his pocket. Maybe she had misjudged him. Perhaps what happened this morning really was nothing more than an aberration brought on by stress. She decided to give him the benefit of the doubt.

"OK," she said. "Let's start again." She extended her hand and introduced herself.

"Max Stoddart," he said, taking her hand in his. She couldn't help noticing how big and warm it was. "I'm the new science and environment correspondent."

Of course. The *Vanguard* had just poached him from the *Independent,* where he'd won the Listerine award for an investigation into hospital superbugs.

"Look," he said, "let me help you pick this stuff up."

"No, I'm fine, honestly."

But he bent down anyway. She was now acutely aware that her hair, which always took on a life of its own whenever it was exposed to the damp and drizzle, was probably sticking out all over the place. God, she must look like she spent the night under a helicopter rotor blade.

"By the way," he grinned, "nice bum."

"Er, excuse me?" she shot back, thinking maybe she shouldn't have given him the benefit of the doubt after all.

"The pot thing," he said, pointing to the ceramic arse. He picked it up and handed it to her.

"Oh. Right. Yes." She put it down on the desk, next to the papers.

"Before I forget," he went on, "I found a few more bits and pieces in your desk drawer." He put his hand into his jacket pocket and took out a box of TheraFlu and her ChapStick.

"Oh, thanks."

"Hang on," he said, "there's something else."

His hand went back into the pocket. The next second it had reemerged holding what looked like a tube of something wrapped in a paper tissue. He passed it to her. Then he said he'd better get going as the editor's conference was due to start any minute.

Once he'd gone, she unwrapped the tube. It was her Monistat. In order to spare her blushes, he'd wrapped her thrush cream in tissue. Max Stoddart might fancy himself, she thought. He might even lose it under stress, but he wasn't without sensitivity.

"Lucretia's on her way up." It was Snow calling to her from the other side of the office. "Planning meeting, two minutes."

Rebecca picked up her notebook and headed off toward the magazine conference room.

She was almost there when she saw Lucretia step out of the lift.

Sorrento? Rebecca thought to herself. What *had* the ditsy Snow been on about before, with her "Lucretia's going to be ten minutes late on account of her only just having left southern Italy"?

Lucretia was wearing a heavily embroidered black silk kimono, white toweling turban and satin mules.

Rebecca stood shaking her head with confusion and amusement. Maybe the Turkish baths were having a formal night. It was only as she carried on watching Lucretia sashaying toward the main office, Snow a respectful couple of paces behind holding a suit carrier, a plastic container full of salad leaves and two liter bottles of Lucretia's fashionable Kaballah water, that Rebecca noticed something even odder about Lucretia's appearance.

Her skin—at least the bits of it Rebecca could see—looked dreadful, not in an "Oh, dear, did we forget to clarify, tone and moisturize last night?" sense, but more in an "Oh, my God, the woman has clearly suffered some kind of catastrophic dermal eruption, which has left her smothered in a crusty, lumpy lava, the color of Marmite" sense.

Rebecca screwed up her face. What on earth was wrong with her? Maybe she was suffering from one of those appalling flesh-eating diseases. That would explain the kimono. The soft light silk was probably all she could bear next to her skin.

A few of the journalists gave Lucretia a quick smile or said hello as she passed, but mostly people carried on working. For the life of her, Rebecca couldn't work out why, when the fashion, beauty and lifestyle editor was clearly rotting and decomposing before their very eyes, nobody seemed even remotely bothered.

2

OK," **Lucretia said** briskly, using two menstrual red
talons to pincer off a cruddy brown bit from her
wrist, which she then crumbled into the ashtray. "So far this month
we've got Sheherazade's feature for the health page—'Stars and Their
Scars.' Fashionwise it's Madonna, Calista and Gwyneth on 'Pleats in
My Life.' Beauty—we've decided lips are still in. Oh, and I don't want
a repeat of the faux pas we had last week with the evening wear
shoot. There was a definite trace of nipple on one of the models."

Lucretia was a contradiction. She was elegant and glamorous—
sexy in a postmenopausal Barbie kind of way—but she was also a
prude. She was famous for it and made no apologies. She flinched
at the mere mention of the word *sex* and had stopped going to
the movies and watching TV on the grounds of the "execrable filth"
being shown. She loathed anybody in the office talking about their
sex life or telling an even remotely risqué joke around her—although everybody did, especially the blokes, just to wind her up.

It was all very odd, since Lucretia, who was expelled from one of the top girls' boarding schools after being caught at age fifteen with a gardener in her bed, had begun her career in journalism working on porn mags. By the midseventies, she was editing one called *Tongue*. She shot to fame when the magazine was unsuccessfully prosecuted for seditious libel and blasphemy, and each day she turned up at the trial dressed in a skimpy black rubber minidress and thigh boots. Spurred on by winning the case, she then stood as a candidate for the Party Party in the 1992 election (manifesto commitment: bondage gear on the National Health Service). Naturally she lost her deposit. After that, she set up her own magazine, *Suck*. Then, suddenly, in the early nineties, she had a religious epiphany, which she described in her biography *Out of the Blue*.

She was alone in her office at *Suck* editing a piece called *Around the World in Eighty Shags* when she heard God speaking to her and telling her to give up her life of debauchery.

"The Lord explained my mission," she wrote. "I was to go out into the world and, through my writing, save the souls of fat ugly women with no fashion sense. I was to preach to them about the sacraments of waxing, exfoliation and laser dermabrasion, teach them they were doing the devil's work by wearing Miu Miu over the age of twenty-five."

A year after her visitation, the rubber bondage gear had gone and she emerged as a self-appointed fashion and beauty guru. By coincidence the *Vanguard* had decided to start a Saturday supplement aimed at women and they took her on to edit it.

"Right," Lucretia continued. "Any more thoughts?"

As the writers and features editor continued to put up ideas, Rebecca turned to Snow, who was sitting next to her at the far end of the conference table.

"Isn't Lucretia just so brave?" she whispered.

"How d'you mean?" Snow mouthed.

"You know, her skin. Is she in terrible pain?"

"What, from the Sorrento?"

"Sorrento?" Rebecca said. "What's Sorrento got to do with it? It's January. Even in southern Italy, she couldn't have gotten sunburned."

Snow did her best to stifle her giggles. "She didn't *go* to Sorrento. She went *for* a Sorrento."

Rebecca gave her a quizzical look.

"She has it once a fortnight," Snow explained. "It's a fake tan. Right mess it makes 'n all. They cover you in this muddy gunk that gets left to dry. You can shower it off at the salon after about half an hour, but Lucretia likes to leave it on because the longer you leave it, the deeper the color. She'll pop to the office shower just before lunch. I can't believe you haven't heard of it, what with you writing a beauty column."

Rebecca gave Snow a sheepish smile and immediately looked round with a start. Lucretia was saying her name.

"Er, Rebecca, if you'd care to join us."

"Sorry, Lucretia."

Suddenly Lucretia turned to Snow. "God, I nearly forgot. Did you pick up my cans of oxygen from Harvey Nicks?"

Everybody was used to seeing Lucretia gulping pure oxygen from what appeared to be empty drink cans. The idea was it energized and revitalized the entire body. In Lucretia's case she took such huge amounts that it was as much as she could do to stop from keeling over.

"No, Lucretia, not yet," Snow said meekly. Rebecca wished that just once, Snow would pluck up the courage to tell Lucretia to go to hell.

"Well, I suggest you go now. And get me a large half fat decaf cap on your way back."

Snow stood up, head bowed ever so slightly, and walked to the door.

"Right, Rebecca, as I was saying," Lucretia went on, "I've got this brilliant idea for your column this week. Tonight is the Mer de Rêves Winter White Party. *Le tout Londres* will be there. Bound to make great copy. It was dazzling last year ..."

"God, yeah," Sheherazade butted in, stubbing out her fag. She was a vague, grubby Sloane with lank hair and permanently dilated pupils. "I mean, like, all the food was served by these like cute little guys in white sequinned G-strings. Not one of them was like more than three feet tall."

Lucretia grimaced—at the mention of men in G-strings, Rebecca presumed, rather than Sheherazade's limited eloquence.

Rebecca moaned inwardly. She couldn't bear the thought of another cosmetics company bash. Another night of air kissing X-ray celebs, fashion and beauty hacks, most of whom were about as deep as a worm's grave. Plus she owned nothing white. It looked dreadful on her. It wasn't just that it instantly added ten pounds to her hips and made her look like a bandaged Anne Widdecombe. It also drained every ounce of color from her face, leaving her with the complexion of an anemic geisha.

It was Sheherazade who, seeing her expression, nudged her and whispered that there was loads of white gear in the fashion cupboard. "Take what you need. The rest of us do. Nobody minds."

"Right," Lucretia said, "any other ideas before we wind up?"

"Well, I thought we could do a piece on ways to ring the changes with bottled water." It was Butter. She was from L.A. "I mean water cocktails are just so right now. Personally I'm into two parts Evian, one part Volvic."

"Brilliant. Absolutely inspired," Lucretia declared, making a note. "Right, that it?"

"Well," Rebecca piped up hesitantly. This being her first fashion, beauty and lifestyle planning meeting, she was feeling distinctly nervous. "I thought maybe we could do a hard-hitting feature on wrinkle creams. I mean everybody buys them, but we all know they're a con and chip oil's probably just as good. Then there's all the meaningless made-up vocabulary the manufacturers use. I mean, who are the people who sit round all day thinking up words like *lyposculpt*? Anyway, I thought we could get women to test a load of creams—maybe pay a dermatologist to write a report. It would cost a bit, but..."

The room fell deathly silent. Rebecca found herself wondering if she'd farted without realizing.

"Rebecca," Lucretia said, her expression and tone equally scathing, "I have one word to say to you—advertising. How on earth do you think the magazine makes money?" She began gathering up her bag and notebook.

Rebecca colored up. "Oh, God. I didn't think."

"Clearly." Lucretia stood up to go.

It was obvious to Rebecca that the fashion, beauty and lifestyle editor was doing her utmost to dispense an acrid smile, but was having some difficulty making her mouth obey her brain. It took her several seconds before she remembered what Snow had told her about Lucretia's lust for rejuvenating (mostly freebie) facial procedures and realized there probably wasn't a muscle left in her Sorrento-ed, wrong-side-of-forty-five-year-old face that hadn't been frozen with Botox.

The moment Rebecca got back to her desk, the phone rang.

"Hi, Max darling, it's me," the young woman's voice purred, before Rebecca had a chance to speak. "Just wanted to check everything's OK for tonight."

"Sorry," Rebecca said, "but I'm afraid you've come through to the wrong extension." She transferred the woman back to the switchboard. Twenty minutes later another woman called for Max. Again Rebecca transferred her back to the switchboard. Realizing the switchboard had gotten hold of the wrong end of the stick regarding the Max/Rebecca desk situation, she complained to the operator, but it did no good. Ten seconds later the caller was back. Rebecca offered to take a message, but the woman said it was personal and she'd try him on his mobile. Half an hour went by and a third woman was on the line—another personal call. Each of the callers had been young and sexy-sounding—confirming Rebecca's growing suspicions that Max Stoddart was something of a babe magnet. Not that his private life was any of her business. As far as she was concerned, he could have hordes of naked women chasing him down Farringdon Road after work every night, so long as they didn't call him on her extension.

By the time the fourth woman rang, Rebecca had had enough. OK, she decided, indignation and sense of mischief rising, if she'd become Max Stoddart's messaging service, she might as well make a decent job of it. She picked up the phone.

"Hello," she said in her best breathy siren voice, "you've reached the Big Max Hot Line. To find out Max's star sign and favorite pizza topping, press one on your telephone keypad now. To hear an inspirational spiritual message, press two. To check his current availability for dinner, theater and bar mitzvahs, press three. To leave a message, press the star key at any time."

"Max?" the woman's voice piped up. "It's Beth. What's going on? I take it this is one of your daft jokes. I'll speak to you later. Anyway, for now I have one word to say to you—fireworks. With a bit of luck, tonight is going to go with such a bang." Then she giggled and hung up.

Rebecca snorted with laughter. Her "Big Max" epithet was inspired, she thought.

As she turned back to her computer she realized she hadn't told Jess she couldn't make it to her place tonight on account of the Mer de Rêves do. She picked up the phone and punched in Jess's number.

Jess didn't seem too bothered about Rebecca's not coming round, since Diggory had started dropping off for a few hours round about nine and it would give her a chance to get some extra sleep. Rebecca promised to pop in for tea the next day instead. She had two days to write the column, so could easily afford to take an afternoon off.

"Oh, by the way," she said, "you'll never guess what happened with Small Penis Guy from this morning..."

She recounted the story, ending with her fake messaging service performance.

Jess roared and agreed the "Big Max Hot Line" was, indeed, inspired. "Mind you," Jess said, "if he's as good-looking as you say he is, he's bound to have loads of women after him."

"I guess."

"Ooh," Jess came back, "do I detect the slightly maudlin tone of a woman who'd hoped she was in with a chance of a leg over?"

"Don't be daft. He's not my type. Too posh. Too smooth, and I could never go out with a bloke who spent more time in front of the bathroom mirror than me."

Jess gave a small laugh. "Right, if you say so."

After half an hour rummaging through the fashion cupboard she finally came up with some beautifully cut white hipster flares and a matching satiny blouse. When she looked in the mirror, even she had to admit the outfit wasn't entirely unflattering.

Her newfound confidence in her ability to wear white was, however, short-lived. She arrived at The Sanderson to find everybody dressed in black. How could she have been so stupid? She might have known Fleet Street's fashion and beauty queens would refuse to be cowed into abandoning their regulation uniform—even by an edict from the director of Maison Mer de Rêves, Coco Dubonnet du Sauvignon.

Only a handful of people had made the effort—mainly Mer de Rêves employees and those who could carry it off, like Jerry Hall—who was all golden mane and white cashmere legs, looking, Rebecca thought, like an exquisitely coutured Palomino—and

Vivienne Westwood, who had come as a bride. Fergie's attempt to get into the spirit of the occasion had been less successful. Her weight had clearly taken a turn for the wurst and the layer upon layer of sticky-out white tulle she was wearing did nothing to disguise the fact. The words *Sugar Plump Fairy* were being bandied about by the gay waiters who were wearing ironic white polo necks over the tightest leather hot pants.

Since she couldn't take refuge with the photographers, who were all in the street waiting to snap the stars as they got out of their limos, she decided to take a wander round the room, writing down names of celebs, whom they were with and what they were wearing.

She'd been doing this for a few minutes when she suddenly became aware that somebody was following her. Each time she turned round the same woman, about her own age, a Mer de Rêves employee or publicist she assumed since she was wearing white, was hovering a few feet behind. The woman followed her to the bar and a few minutes later into the ladies' room, where she took the next-door cubicle. As Rebecca sat peeing she couldn't make up her mind whether she should be worried about this person trailing her or dismiss the whole thing as meaningless coincidence. She decided on the latter. As they stood washing their hands, Rebecca smiled at her through the over-basin mirror. The woman returned it briefly and opened her mouth as if she were about to say something, then, clearly thinking better of it, she made a beeline for the door, her hands still dripping wet.

Rebecca shrugged. Then she picked up one of the small linen towels and dried her hands.

Back at the party, she decided to go up to Fergie—whom she'd interviewed at a couple of charity dos and rather liked—to see if she could get a quote for her column. She greeted Rebecca warmly and swore blind she remembered meeting her. Rebecca couldn't help feeling flattered. They'd been standing chatting about what

Fergie described as the "dazzling decor" (vast potted trees sprayed white, their branches laced with tiny white fairy lights, ten-foot ice statues, a purple-draped ceiling twinkling with stars) and the food, which was equally "dazzling," when Rebecca realized the woman was still watching her. Feeling slightly spooked by now, she decided to go over and say something. Just then Victoria Posh came over and collared Fergie, enabling Rebecca to make a discreet exit.

She was easing her way through the crowd when she felt a hand on her shoulder. She turned. It was Guy Debonnaire, whom she knew from her days on the Sunday *Tribune* "Zeitgeist" section. He was one of those men who gloried in being referred to as a "straight gay," because it had been fashionable for a while in the nineties to fop around like one of Louis XIV's wig bearers while secretly being totally straight—which Guy most definitely was, since he had been trying to get inside her knickers for years. Moreover, Guy was a drunken bore. Totally off his face now, he stood swaying in front of her.

"Ah, the sublime, refined and utterly divine Ms. Fine," he proclaimed, saluting her so majestically with his kir royale that he spilled most of it down his maroon Thai silk suit.

Rebecca rolled her eyes.

"Oh, come on, Becks, don't be like that," he slurred, doing his best to steady himself. "Do you know underneath these clothes I'm completely naked?"

"No, but if you hum it, I'll sing along."

He gave her a wounded look. "Please, Becks. Please come out with me. We could go and see a film."

"Sorry, I've seen it."

"Oh, right. Shame. I like films, though. Don't you? Especially film noir. Have you ever thought, though, how odd it is that the Elephant Man never did anything else?"

"Guy," she said wearily, "you're slaughtered. Go home."

As she squeezed past him, he lunged at her. Being so pissed, his aim was less than perfect and his mouth ended up connecting with her left ear. As she heaved him off, he lost his balance for a moment or two and spilled even more kir royale. Having regained it (his balance, not the kir royale), he winked, made two loud tongue clicking sounds and staggered off.

As she stood wiping Guy's slobber out of her ear with a tissue, she looked across to where the woman had been standing, but she'd vanished.

Rebecca had planned to take a taxi home and charge it to the *Vanguard,* but by the time she left, it was snowing, and there wasn't a yellow light to be seen.

Although it was late, the pavements were still pretty crowded. Even so, Rebecca couldn't help feeling uneasy. Every few yards, she would stop and look to see if the woman was following her, but there was never any sign of her among the scores of bent-over pedestrians battling against the driving snow. She checked again as she stood on the platform and once more in the train carriage. Nothing. By the time she got back to her flat just after half past eleven, she'd dismissed the woman as a harmless weirdo and pretty much put her out of her mind.

She took off her coat, breathed heavily onto her red, frozen hands and flicked the switch on her answer machine.

"Hi, Becks, it's Dad. Listen, I know it's short notice, but could we meet for a bit of lunch tomorrow? I've got some great news. I'm on my way out now. Phone me first thing."

Under normal circumstances she would have stayed awake for hours, wondering what on earth her father's surprise could be, but because she'd gone to bed so late the day before, she drifted off almost as soon as her head hit the pillow.

The next she knew it was half past seven. She decided to wait until eight to call him. Maybe at long last he'd found himself a girlfriend, she thought as she stood soaping herself in the shower. But she knew full well the idea was ridiculous.

In the ten years since her mother, Judy, had died, Stan hadn't shown even the remotest interest in dating. Naturally Grandma Rose had done all she could to remedy the situation. She would invite her son over for Friday night dinner and arrange it so that one of her friends' divorced-and-desperate daughters would turn up unexpectedly. Over the years, a string of women had presented themselves at Rose's on a Friday night—all of whom, according to Rose, "just happened to be passing." Even the ones who lived in Birmingham and Leeds.

Rose had also posted Stan's personal profile on the *Lonely Jews* Web site and signed him up to countless dating agencies without telling him. Each time he found out he was furious, but when she finally resorted to employing Minnie Mann, an octogenarian matchmaker from Stamford Hill who turned up at his house unannounced carrying a rolled umbrella, a Gladstone bag and an album full of photographs of ultra Orthodox widows in wigs, he didn't speak to his mother for a month.

Stan always said that his twenty-five years with Judy had been the happiest of his life. When she was killed in a car crash, his world fell apart. Afterward he simply threw himself into his business. Stan owned a chain of lingerie shops called Lacy Lady. He and Judy had set up the first one in the seventies. Today there were twelve. While his female staff and managers served the customers, he took care of the business side. Lately, though, Rebecca had noticed him coming out of himself a bit more. He had joined the gym and a book club.

"But, you know," he often said to Rebecca as they took one of their Sunday morning strolls, her arm through his, "that feeling of loss never goes away. You just learn to live alongside it."

Of course, he wasn't telling her anything she didn't already know.

"So, Dad, come on, what's the deal?" she asked excitedly the moment he picked up the phone. "I know, you're floating Lacy Lady on the stock market?"

He chuckled. "I wish. No, it's nothing like that."

"OK, you're in the England squad for the World Cup?"

"That goes without saying. I'll tell you the real news over lunch."

They arranged to meet at Zilli's in Soho at one.

She stepped out of the lift—carrying a cappuccino from the place over the road—just as Max Stoddart was about to get in. He was wearing chinos and a lightish blue open-neck shirt. He'd clearly adopted the *Vanguard* dress code.

"Hi, how are you?" he said.

She smiled, told him she was fine and asked if the police had found his car yet. He shook his head.

"Oh, I'm sure it'll turn up," she said.

"Hope so. Bit of a day yesterday," he went on. "If getting my car pinched wasn't enough, I was up to my eyes finalizing arrangements for this big night I had on."

"Yes, I know all about it," she said.

"You do?"

She told him about the switchboard mix-up and the women being put through to her by mistake.

"Oh, God. Once again, I can only apologize."

"I've had a word with the switchboard," she said, "but I'd really appreciate it if you could, too—just to make sure they know your extension. It did get pretty irritating after a while."

"I can imagine. I really am sorry."

"Not to worry," she said, giving him another smile. Despite her protestations to Jess yesterday, she suddenly realized how un-speakably fanciable he looked. She was suddenly imagining him tonguing her in the fashion cupboard.

"Anyway," she said, finally coming back to earth, "I must get back to work. Got a column to write."

"Mind if I walk with you?" he said. "I was going that way."

"But I thought you were about to get into the lift."

He shrugged. "I can take the fire escape stairs just as easily."

"Look," he said when they reached her desk, "I don't suppose you'd let me take you out to dinner to make up for being so rude to you yesterday?"

"Oh, that's kind of you, but there's really no need. And judging by all those calls, your social life seems pretty packed right now."

He reached across her desk, picked up a pair of the windup sushi and began winding.

"Not really. I mean I had my parents' do last night, but I've got nothing on for the rest of the week."

"Parents' do?" she said.

"Yes, it was their ruby wedding. It was my sisters you spoke to on the phone yesterday. I assumed they'd explained."

"Sisters?" She cleared her throat. "Er, no. They didn't say anything."

"I've got four. All older than me and exceedingly bossy. They put me in charge of the booze, the music and the fireworks. For the last couple of days they've been on the phone constantly, checking up to see I had everything under control. Lord knows why they didn't just do it themselves."

So, he had a party last night. That would explain the posh suit.

"Oh, so the fireworks were real?" she said.

He gave her a puzzled look. "Yes. What did you think they were?"

"Oh, no, nothing. Doesn't matter."

"Anyway, you have to believe me when I say the calls that came through to you were a mere fraction of the number I got." He paused. "So, will you have dinner with me? Please?"

"I'd like that," she said.

Clickety-clack. Clickety-clack marched the sushi across her desk.

When she arrived at Zilli's, Stan was already there, sitting at a table by the window. The first thing that struck her was his hair. Usually the first thing she noticed about him was the lacy bra or knickers sample sticking out of his jacket pocket (she'd lost count of the times he'd had to explain to people—waiters, her teachers on school open nights, rabbis—that he worked in ladies' underwear). Today there was no lingerie, just the hair. A week ago it had been gray, now it was a dark, bottled reddish brown. He'd also brushed it forward so that there was a strange kind of early Beatles fringe thing going on. The effect was made particularly hideous by the yarmulke-shaped bald patch he had, right in the middle of his head. The upshot was he didn't look so much John Lennon as Little John.

The moment he saw her he stood up and held out his arms to greet her.

"Wow, Dad," she said, giving him a kiss and a hug, "great hair."

"You mean that? I just thought it was time for a new look. You don't think it's too much for a man of my age?"

"No, I love it. It really suits you."

The waiter came over to take their drink order. Stan ordered a bottle of champagne "because this is a celebration," but it was as much as she could do to stop herself from saying, "Oh, and innkeeper, my father will also have a tankard of your best mead."

"And what do you think of the slacks?" he said, half standing again. She hadn't noticed until now. He was wearing cargo pants. With a tweed sports jacket. And shoes with Velcro fasteners. "Personally I prefer something with an elasticized waist, but I thought I'd give them a go. Apparently they're very with-it."

"Yeah, they're great. Very now."

She reached into her bag and pulled out a paper bag. "Before I forget, I found this in the secondhand bookshop at the end of my road. Thought you might like it."

Stan collected bizarre books with equally bizarre titles. He had over fifty. Her favorites were *A Study of Hospital Waiting Lists in Cardiff, 1953—1954; Who's Who in Barbed Wire* and one from the 1930s called *Games You Can Play with Your Pussy.* Whenever she saw something she thought he would like, she bought it. This one was a Western from the fifties.

"*Tosser Hitches His Wagon,*" he guffawed. "Brilliant. I love it. But you shouldn't."

"Yes, I should," she said, smiling. "So, Dad, come on, you've got me all excited. What's the big surprise?"

He reached across the table, took her hand in his and squeezed it. "You know I love you, don't you, sweetie?"

"Of course I do. And I love you, too."

"And you know that nobody could ever replace your mother."

Could this possibly be going where she hoped it was going?

"You've met somebody, haven't you?"

He nodded. "Her name's Bernadette," he said, beaming. "We're getting married."

"Omigod!" she squealed, getting up to hug him. "I can't believe it. After all these years, you've finally gone and done it. But you never said anything."

"I—that is, Bernadette and me—we wanted to be certain."

"Yeah, it's a big step. I can understand that." She went back to her seat. "So c'mon, dish," she said, taking his hand again, "tell me everything about her. How did you meet? Where does she live? Does she work?"

Stan said they met at his book club, that she lived in Muswell Hill, just a few streets from Rebecca, and that she owned her own beauty salon.

"And what, she's about your age?" Rebecca said, imagining a slim, beautifully preserved woman of about sixty.

"A bit younger."

"What, fifties?"

He gave a little shrug.

"Forties?"

He shuffled uncomfortably in his seat.

"Dad," she said, beginning to feel anxious now. "Exactly how old is Bernadette?"

He cleared his throat. "Thirty-two."

"Ah."

She leaned back in her chair and sat processing this information. "Omigod. I'm going to have a stepmother the same age as me."

This could take some getting used to, she thought. But at least now she had an explanation for Stan's new look.

"I know this has come as a bit of a shock," he said, "but Bernadette and I just don't think about the age thing. When you're in love, a few years is neither here nor there."

The waiter arrived with the champagne and began filling their glasses.

"But, Dad, it's not just a few years," she said when he'd gone. "It's over thirty years. What do you have in common? What are you going to talk about? You remember rationing and Glenn Miller. Her idea of rationing is probably a Miller Lite."

"I know, I know, but we just think stuff like that's funny. We are just so happy. She makes me feel like a teenager again."

She took a long, slow breath and looked into his watery brown eyes with their droopy lids. His face always reminded her of a King Charles spaniel. She could see how desperate he was for her approval. Despite her reservations, she at least had to pretend it was fine with her.

"Well, Dad," she said, her face breaking into a smile, "if it's what you really want and this Bernadette makes you happy, then I'm happy, too."

Stan patted the back of her hand. "You don't know how much I was hoping you'd say that. By the way, don't say anything to your grandmother. I haven't mentioned any of this to her yet. Apart from the age thing, Bernadette's not Jewish. She's Catholic."

"No kidding."

"Might take your gran a while to come round."

Rebecca nodded. Then they clinked glasses and toasted the future.

"And guess what," he said afterward, lowering his voice, "I had my vasectomy reversed just after Christmas—during those two weeks you were away."

Rebecca almost choked on her champagne.

"We don't know if it's worked, but I've got my checkup this afternoon. I can make a start on your book in the waiting room."

He began flicking through the first few pages of *Tosser Hitches His Wagon.*

I'll **have you** know, young man," Lady Axminster was bellowing down the phone, "that I have spent the last half hour shoveling three feet of 'dry and partly cloudy' off my daughter's front path."

Rebecca, who had been shown into the kitchen by Jess's elderly maid, Dolly, shot her friend an amused, quizzical look.

"Oh, Mum's just having one of her rants. Apparently the BBC got the weather wrong again and forgot to mention the snow."

Rebecca nodded. She'd known Marjorie Axminster almost as long as she'd known Jess. Over the years she'd grown accustomed to her rants. Once, when she'd been staying with the two of them at the Axminster pile in Slapton Gusset, her ladyship had spent several hours each day on the phone to the emergency help-line at the rural district council demanding something be done immediately to halt the dawn chorus. It had been starting an utterly unacceptable two hours before sunrise and disturbing her sleep.

"It's all these agrochemicals the birds come into contact with," she'd railed at some poor minion. "They're making the poor creatures hyperactive."

Jess swiveled back round on her chair to face Diggory, who was sitting in his little bouncy cradle, looking exceedingly cute in the Gap tracksuit Rebecca had bought him just after he was born. In her hand Jess had a stack of what appeared to be printed postcards.

"OK, darling," she cooed, holding a card about two inches from Diggory's nose. "Now come on, concentrate for Mummy. Spitsbergen, Arctic country. Edvard Grieg, Norwegian composer, 1843 to 1907. Wrote *Peer Gynt*. Kemal Atatürk, reforming Turkish president. À la Florentine, a dish with spinach."

"Jess, what on earth are you doing?" Rebecca asked.

"Showing him flash cards. According to this book I've been reading on the development of human intelligence, you can't start exercising babies' brains too soon." She chucked her son under the chin. "And we don't want you turning out to be an ickle Dignoramus, do we?"

"But with all due respect to my godson here," Rebecca said, bending down to give Diggory a kiss on his scurfy head, "babies this age aren't much more than glorified plants, are they?"

"Well, that's just where you're wrong. Apparently they start absorbing information virtually from the moment they're born. Look, I know it seems harsh, but you have to remember he's got his preprep entrance exam in less than three years. The competition's horrendous."

"But I thought you disapproved of private education."

Jess had rebelled against her privileged background as a teenager. Ever since Rebecca had known her she'd been a card-carrying member of the Labour Party. Two years ago she married Ed, a reporter on a left-wing tabloid, and moved to oh-so-egalitarian Archway.

"Oh, I do. I do," Jess shot back, her eyes gleaming with sincerity. "Ideologically. The problem is the state schools round here are just so dire. You know the kind of thing—they reach sixteen and can't even write a business letter. Best they can manage is a formal collage."

Rebecca smiled and supposed she couldn't blame Jess for wanting the best for Diggory—although she still had grave doubts about the flash cards. If Jess wasn't careful, the poor mite would be burned out before she had him on solids.

She pulled out a kitchen chair and sat down at the long, grease-smeared farmhouse table that was littered with dirty dishes and cups, baby clothes and a couple of sodden Pampers that were starting to smell. At the far end, the cat—a lardy ginger tom—was sprawled out over a plate of dried-up egg, sniffing and licking Diggory's pacifier.

One aspect of her background Jess hadn't been able to shake off was the traditional upper-class penchant for domestic disorder and chaos. Although scrupulous about her personal hygiene (un-like her mother, who always had a niff of damp Labrador about her and who would arrive home after an afternoon out with the Slapton Gusset hunt and get changed for a ball without showering first), she shunned household cleanliness with an energy most people reserved for depleted uranium. To her, a skid mark-free lavatory bowl was just one step away from a home gym and a cock-tail cabinet that played *Greensleeves*.

Jess's lack of hygiene about the home was nothing compared to her grandfather's. In the twenties the then Lord Axminster (vir-tually the only member of the upper house who believed Mrs. Simpson would have made an excellent queen) had ordered a uri-nal to be plumbed into the dining room at the house in Slapton Gusset so that he could break off for a pee during dinner and still carry on a conversation.

It was Ed, who had been brought up by a lorry driver and a school dinner lady in a thirties terraced house in Chingford, who insisted on getting a housecleaner. But as far as Rebecca could make out, all Dolly seemed to do for eight hours a week was re-arrange the dirt.

"And you with knobs on," Lady Axminster boomed, slamming down the phone.

Looking every inch the queen at Balmoral (green padded jacket, tweed skirt, pearls), she strode over to Rebecca and greeted her with a perfunctory, rather distracted double kiss. Yep, definite doggy smell, Rebecca decided.

"Hi, Lady A. How are you?"

"Well, if you must know, Rebecca..." Her accent couldn't have been more cut glass if it had been made by Waterford. "I am fed up to the back teeth with being patronized and whined at by ignorant nincompoops with degrees in Estuary English from the University of Haringey."

"And I'm not so bad either, thanks," Rebecca said, and at the same time happened to notice Lady Axminster's earrings.

"Gosh," she said peering at the clusters of diamonds and pearls, "those are exquisite."

"Yes, they are rather stunning," Lady Axminster said, allowing her face to break into a smile. "They were given to my mother when she came out."

At this point, Dolly the cleaner, who until now had been supposedly vacuuming upstairs, walked back into the room, carrying a pile of Diggory's dirty clothes.

"Ooh," she said, opening the washing machine door, "we 'ad a coming out party for my mum once. She went down for soliciting on the Whitechapel Road. Same wi' yours, was it?"

But Lady Axminster wasn't listening. She'd noticed Jess's computer, which was sitting at the far end of the table next to the ginger tom, and had begun reading from the screen.

"Good Lord, Jessica," she said, "this is revolting, utterly revolting. I cannot believe you get paid to write filth like this."

(Since having Diggory, Jess was writing her magazine advice column at home. She was in the middle of replying to a chap desperate to find a cure for his premature ejaculation.)

"What filth?" Jess came back, feigning offense and nudging Rebecca.

"You know—words like that," she tapped the screen.

"Like what?" Jess insisted, teasing.

"Stop it, Jessica. I will not be bullied. You know precisely what I mean." Rebecca smiled to herself. Although they weren't even remotely alike in any other way, Lady A reminded her of Lucretia.

"What? Words like penis, erection, come?"

"Oh, please, no, not that last one." Lady Axminster looked as if she'd just been offered a plate of whelks.

Jess turned to Rebecca and grinned. "What you have to understand," she said, "is that the sexual revolution never quite made it to Slapton Gusset. People there don't say 'come.' They prefer to announce that 'one has arrived.' "

Jess and Rebecca collapsed.

"Now you're just being silly," her ladyship said huffily. "It's just that when I was growing up, sex was a personal affair. Men and women never talked openly about their private parts. In my day, one's husband kept his scrotum firmly under his hat."

More snorts from Rebecca and Jess.

"Quite right, yer ladyship," Dolly said, heading back upstairs, a duster in one hand, a can of Pledge in the other. "When I was a girl we had no time for sex. We were too busy having babies."

Lady Axminster merely arched her eyebrows in disdain. Then

she bent down and dabbed at some fresh sick that had begun trickling down Diggory's chin.

"That's a dear little outfit he has on," she said, regarding Diggory's Gap tracksuit, "but do you mind telling me why everything people wear these days has to have a brand name emblazoned across it? And it's not just clothes. TV programs, public buildings, sports stadiums—everything has to have a sponsor. I swear it's only the royals who have any dignity left."

"Not for long, Mum," Jess said. "You know they're always pleading poverty. Pretty soon we'll have the All Bran Queen proceeding down the Andrex Mall with her son the Tampax Prince of Wales to see the Changing of the Durex Featherlite Guard."

Lady Axminster gave a theatrical shiver. A moment later she was picking up her gloves and Burberry handbag and announcing she had to get home (to the Chelsea pied-à-terre) to change for a charity do.

Jess always said it was her mother's good works that had kept her sane since Lord Axminster left her ten years ago for a high-class Spanish call girl half his age. The day after he was famously caught by the paparazzi drinking champagne from the woman's evening shoe, Lady Axminster was quoted in Dempster, saying, "I hope the swine catches athlete's tongue." From that moment she rarely mentioned or spoke of him again. Arranging charity fundraisers became her therapy. As far as the do-gooding members of the upper classes were concerned, her organizational skills were second to none. Within twenty-four hours of any earthquake, hurricane or interesting new disease being announced, Lady Axminster would be putting on a ball.

The moment Lady Axminster left, Diggory started to squawk. Before Rebecca could stop her, Jess had leaned across the table, picked up Diggory's pacifier from beside the cat and shoved it into his mouth.

"OK, do I have news," Rebecca said as the baby sucked quietly on the cat-lick-smeared teat.

"Oh, God, you're not."

"What?"

"Up the spout."

"No. I am not up the spout," Rebecca shot back indignantly. "What I am, is about to acquire a stepmother."

"What? Stan's finally getting married? That's great."

"Yes. Except she's thirty-two."

"Oh, my God," Jess cried, "he's done exactly what my father did. Except Dad and Bienvenida aren't actually married. And she was a prostitute, of course."

"And I bet your dad didn't start dyeing his hair and wearing cargo pants. He's even had his vasectomy reversed."

"His vasectomy reversed? Jeez, him and the kids'll be in nappies together." Jess paused and took a deep breath. "I dunno, when does maturity finally set in for a man?"

"About six months after death, I reckon," Rebecca replied, making her friend laugh.

"So, come on, joking aside," Jess said, getting up, "how do you really feel about your dad and this woman?" She flicked the switch on the kettle.

Rebecca said she'd only tell if Jess promised not to make fun or say she was stupid.

"Hey, c'mon, I'm your best mate. As if."

"OK. I know it's daft, but I feel jealous of her. I mean Bernadette's my age. What if she's really gorgeous?"

"You mean you see her as some kind of rival?"

Rebecca nodded. "Plus she's taking my dad away. I never thought I'd feel like this. I mean, I've been praying for him to get married again, for years. But now I'm starting to realize how much

I've enjoyed having him to myself. And what if she takes the whole stepmother thing to heart and starts trying to boss me about? Then if they have kids…" Her voice trailed off.

"Your dad may not want you anymore."

"God," Rebecca said, "I sound like an insecure eight-year-old, don't I?"

"Yeah, but it's perfectly normal. I loathed Bienvenida until I discovered she couldn't have children and had a face full of moles."

She began pouring boiling water over tea bags. "Look, Stan worships you. That won't change. And the chances are this Bernadette'll turn out to be dead ordinary-looking and really nice."

"Yeah, you're right. I should stop worrying."

Jess brought the mugs of tea to the table. Rebecca asked how the pelvic floor exercises were going.

She said she was persevering.

"I read in one of the mags it can take a few months for things to get back to normal, you know."

"Yeah, I know. I probably wrote it. It's funny, you spend your life reassuring other people. It's so different when it happens to you. It feels like my entire body has gone to pot post-Diggory. Ed won't even look at me."

Rebecca took her hand. "Look, you are one of the most beautiful women I know. Plus you're clever and funny. Ed knows how lucky he is to have you. You just think he doesn't fancy you because your self-esteem is a bit low just now."

"But I reek of milk the whole time. And I leak over the bed. Who could blame him for going off me? And why else would he come home late every evening? I mean take last night. He came to bed stinking of booze, barely said two words—admittedly I was feeding the Digperson and at the same time going through the French verbs that take *être* in the perfect tense, but he just turned over, fell asleep and started snoring. God, why do men snore?"

Rebecca took a sip of tea. "It's when they lie on their backs," she said. "Their balls fall over their arseholes and the air pressure just builds up."

Jess couldn't help laughing.

"Oh, by the way," Rebecca said, "Max Stoddart asked me out."

"And of course you said yes."

"What makes you so sure?"

" 'Cause you fancy him something rotten. Go on, you do, don't you?"

Rebecca reddened.

"Aha! Told you. Told you," Jess chanted. "So, when you seeing him?"

"Tomorrow night. We're having dinner at Le Poussin."

"Wow. Posh. What are you going to wear?"

Half an hour later, when the assistant in Hampstead Whistles declared that the strappy blue silk, calf-length dress with the draped neck Rebecca had on would look even more sensational in a smaller size, she was convinced she could hear harps playing and birds singing.

But when she tried the ten, it was fractionally too tight round her middle.

"We could let it out," the assistant suggested. "It would be ready by tomorrow afternoon."

"No, I'll take it," Rebecca shot back. "It's perfect. Absolutely perfect." There was no way she was about to allow her joy at discovering she was a size ten be diminished by having the dress seams let out.

She patted her stomach. "Bit of water retention, that's all. Time of the month."

Five minutes later she was in Boots buying Slim-Fast. There were three meals between now and tomorrow night. Plenty of time to lose the bulge.

By the time Rebecca got back to the flat she was starving. She immediately made up the vanilla shake. She had to admit there wasn't much of it. She'd down it in three or four mouthfuls. And all she'd eaten today was a tuna salad with her dad and a couple of sips of champagne. She knew there was some ice cream in the freezer. How many calories could there be in a couple of tiny scoops? It would just bulk the Slim-Fast up a bit, that's all. Plus it was her firm belief that food consumed in private had no calories (along with food licked off spoons when cooking and anything consumed at the cinema, which was part of the entertainment package and didn't count).

She poured the shake into the blender and began chipping away at the Cherry Garcia Ben and Jerry's. She looked at the fruit bowl, where a speckled overripe banana was just crying out to be eaten. She unzipped it and threw it in too, along with an inch of full-fat crème fraîche she had left in the fridge. It seemed a shame to waste it. She blended the whole thing up and stuck her finger into the mixture. Not bad. But it could do with something to counteract the sweetness. A bottle of Bacardi, left over from Christmas, was sitting on the counter. Perfect. It would also give the whole thing a bit of a kick into the bargain. After all, she'd had a shock today, a bit of alcohol would be medicinal. She reached for the bottle and sloshed a couple of inches into the shake. But by then the bottle was virtually empty, so she added the rest. She blended the whole thing one more time and poured it back into the glass. There was still masses left in the container. She would finish it later.

She went into the living room and sat herself down on the sofa. As she sipped her "Slim-Slow," she looked round the room and thought about how much she loved it. With the help of the *Changing Rooms* CD-ROM, the Ikea catalogue and an oversize, over-the-top crystal chandelier that Lady Axminster had found when she was clearing out her attic at Slapton Gusset, she had created a twelve-by-fourteen monument to what she liked to think of as funky minimalism.

She'd moved in six months ago and had spent virtually every weekend decorating. She'd steamed off the ancient mint green woodchip, lined the walls and painted them white, sanded and polished the floorboards. The only time she'd needed professional help was when it came to hanging and wiring the chandelier. All she needed now were blinds. Roman, she'd decided—in a slightly milkier shade of white. But not so milky that it would clash with the white marble of the fireplace, which had a slightly grayish tinge to it. On the other hand, if she went too gray it wouldn't work against the rich yellow-gold floorboards. Best thing would be to go to John Lewis, get some swatches and stick them to the walls and floor. One was bound to speak to her.

"But, Becks," she could hear Jess say the moment she saw the swatches. "They're all identical. White is white is white."

Then she'd beg her to go for a more practical color that didn't show the dirt, like maroon.

Although she adored the marble fireplace, what Rebecca loved most were her sofas. She had two—bought on credit from Ikea. One was very long, low and bright pink. The other—black leather with stainless steel legs—was equally angular and self-consciously trendy, only smaller. Right now, she was sitting on the pink one. She closed her eyes, rested her head on its unyielding back and began caressing the soft woolen pile. Like all her girlfriends, she recognized there comes a point in a woman's life—round about when she discovers the Naked Chef and acknowledges Tom Jones may be cheesy, but has a really great voice—when seating gets sexy.

Her friend Mad, who was doing a fine-art course, had provided paintings. She specialized in huge, highly abstract nudes and had given Rebecca two as a flat-warming present. She'd hung one—a bloke with a triangular head, whose pubic hair was made up of thousands of lowercase letters—over the mantelpiece. The other, which was at least six feet by four feet and which Rebecca had leaned against a wall, thinking this looked supremely arty, was of a chiseled angular woman wearing a hat made of equally angular fruit. She was lying on a bed, her hand draped between her legs. Mad, who wasn't without pretension when it came to her work, called it *Plaisir et la Femme*. Jess called it *Woman Wanking*.

Rebecca took another sip of her shake and wondered if she should have a wank, too—not because she particularly fancied one, but because she thought it might help her lose weight. She'd read somewhere that a few minutes snogging used up sixty-four calories. An orgasm had to be worth a couple of hundred. Maybe more. She could usually manage three on the trot with this brilliant new vibrator she'd just bought.

A few months ago, she and Jess had been out shopping for baby stuff and Jess had forced her into this trendy, upmarket sex shop in Covent Garden, where all the sex toys looked like they'd been made by Alessi.

"So what do you fancy?" Jess had boomed across the packed store, sounding like a younger version of her mother. "A basic dildo, one with rubber spikes and an anal attachment or something battery operated with detachable heads?"

Mortified, Rebecca shot over to where Jess was standing, next to a glass bowl of what looked like sequins.

"Will you just shut up," Rebecca hissed. "Now the whole bloody shop thinks we're a pair of lesbians."

"No, they don't. Stop being so sensitive. I bet nobody even heard."

Rebecca grunted, then began trailing her fingers through the sequins.

"Clitoral bindis," Jess giggled, digging Rebecca in the ribs. "They're called 'clindis.' "

By now Jess was bending over another glass bowl, full of tiny ornamental rubber dinosaurs. "Oh, and talking of lesbians. These are meant to be lesbian dinosaurs." She burst out laughing. "Look at the name underneath."

"Lickalotopus," Rebecca said tonelessly. "Brilliant. Now please can we go?"

But Jess refused to budge. She'd gone back to the vibrators and was busy reading the blurb on the Vibroclit—the stainless steel one with the detachable heads.

"You just have to buy this. It guarantees you'll come within five minutes. God, maybe I should get one too. I take so long with Ed, he gets repetitive stress injury in his tongue."

Realizing buying the thing was the only way she'd get Jess out of the shop, Rebecca took the Vibroclit from her and marched over to the counter. They were leaving the shop, Rebecca dragging Jess out by her coat sleeve, when they heard some bloke say to his mate: "You know, I've always wanted to watch lesbians do it. Haven't you?"

Rebecca didn't forgive Jess until the following day—after she'd tried the Vibroclit and it had made her come in less than two minutes.

She was just about to get in the bath, before having an early night with the Vibroclit, when the phone rang. She picked it up off the coffee table.

"Hi, sweetie, it's Dad. Listen, I hope my news didn't come as too much of a shock today. I just wanted to check that you were OK."

"Well, I have to admit it was a bit of a surprise, but I'm fine with it now."

"Really?"

"Honest."

"So how would you feel about meeting Bernadette? I thought

after I've broken the news to your grandmother, maybe the four of us could go out for dinner."

She said that would be great.

"Oh, and by the way," Stan continued, "I forgot to tell you, Bernadette says she thinks she knows you. I had no idea, but the two of you were at the same school."

"Really? What's her surname?"

"O'Brien."

"O'Brien? You're kidding, right?"

"No. Why should I be kidding? So, you remember her, then?"

Suddenly, everything became clear. Her father had always been a bit of a humorist, and now she realized the whole story of him getting married was just one of his jokes. Of course. It was just like the time he'd been having a spat with the Inland Revenue and had rung the local office to say he was from British Telecom and they were testing the lines by sending a blast of hot steam down the wires. She could still hear his voice.

"And I would strongly advise your staff to wrap their phones in towels to avoid the possibility of being badly scalded. There's a BT van outside full of towels." He insisted that for legal reasons he needed to stay on the line and listen while they made the announcement. Which they duly did.

She should have realized that the whole story, the marriage, the champagne, the "don't tell your grandmother," was nothing more than a huge windup. And she'd fallen for it.

Marrying Bernadette O'Brien, yeah, right.

"Becks, you there?"

"Yeah, I'm here," she said, laughing. "Very funny, Dad. You know you really had me going for a while."

"I did. How? I don't get it, what's so funny about me marrying Bernadette?"

"Oh, come on, you know. She was ..."

She broke off. It suddenly occurred to her that Stan seemed

genuinely confused. In a horror-struck instant she realized that this was no windup.

"Dad, you're serious, aren't you?"

"Of course I am," he said with an uneasy, slightly confused laugh.

She swallowed hard and raked her fingers through her hair.

"So, come on," he repeated good-naturedly, "what's so funny about me marrying Bernadette?"

There was, of course, nothing even remotely funny about him marrying Bernadette. On the contrary. It was one of the most hideous things she could imagine. But she didn't dare tell him that. How could she? He was happier than he had been in years. She couldn't hurt him by telling him the truth. Instead she had to backtrack. Fast.

"Sorry, Dad, I think we've been at cross-purposes. I was confusing Bernadette with another girl called O'Brien. This other one had buck teeth and terrible BO. I couldn't believe you'd fallen for somebody like that."

He laughed, obviously relieved. "So, you remember Bernadette now?"

"Of course I do," Rebecca said, desperately trying to force some enthusiasm into her voice. "Who could forget Bernadette?"

"Brilliant. I'm sure the pair of you will have loads to catch up on."

"Can't wait."

She put the glass to her lips and downed the remainder of her "Slim-Slow" in one gulp.

4

Rebecca **found the** Crouch End High official school photograph (summer 1986—she was sixteen) rolled up on the top shelf of her wardrobe, along with a whole load of other memorabilia she didn't have the heart to chuck out. This included copies of three pop numbers she'd written during her adolescent songwriting phase and sent to Wet Wet Wet—she was still waiting for a reply—and her Blue Peter badge from 1979 (for her poster promoting road safety).

She spotted Bernadette immediately with her doe eyes, perfect figure and mass of bleached Kylie hair, pouting and posing in the back row. (The year before, she'd been crowned Miss East Finchley and it had gone to her head big time.) The lapels on her school blazer were turned up, the sleeves had been pushed to her elbows—*sooo* eighties—and her skirt was just a millimeter short of her knickers.

She was easily the most beautiful girl in the school, but although there were tons of boys and fawning Bernadette wannabes who hung around her, not everybody liked her. She had an aloof, sneering manner and made no secret of the fact she thought she was better than everybody else because she was pretty. On top of that her parents were well-off—at least by Crouch End High School standards. They owned a chain of betting shops. Rebecca remembered seeing them show up at the school summer fête one year in their metallic gold Rolls; him chewing on a fat cigar, her face caked in UltraGlow. But although they were a bit flash, they were big-hearted, salt-of-the-earth types. Completely different from their daughter.

On the day of the fête, Bernadette's mum had been in charge of the lucky dip and she'd spent the entire time laughing and joking and letting the first years have extra goes for free. As a result the stall was permanently mobbed. Three times, she had to ship Bernadette's dad off to Woolies to buy more prizes. Even back then Rebecca used to think how funny it was that somebody like Bernadette O'Brien should have a nice mum.

Everybody knew Bernadette's parents spoiled their only child. Girls who'd been to her house said she had two wardrobes stuffed with clothes. She also had a twenty-quid-a-week allowance and a pony, which was kept stabled somewhere in Hertfordshire.

If money and beauty weren't enough to separate her from the Crouch End High rabble, in the second year she received yet another boost to an already grotesquely inflated ego. Her cousin became a roadie with Kajagoogoo. In her eyes, not to mention the eyes of everybody in the class who clamored for the free tickets she could now get to any gig anywhere in the country, this catapulted her to star status. Consequently most of the class went into permanent suck-up mode and Bernadette took to swanning round the place, looking down her nose like Christie Brinkley in Argos.

She started wearing makeup to school in the third year—thick black eyeliner and equally thick purple frosting on her lips. From then until she left school at sixteen, she was continually being sent home by the aging spinster head, Miss Titley, for coming to school "looking like a harlot." She'd relent for a few days and then go back to makeup. The boys started calling her Lipstick or Panda Eyes, but it was Lipstick that stuck. Pretty soon nobody called her Bernadette anymore. Snotty as she was, she didn't seem to mind. In fact, she seemed to rather like the idea that she had been singled out for a nickname. It clearly made her feel even more important.

But Lipstick wasn't simply a stuck-up tart. She was also a bully. Swots were her main target—girls like Rebecca who were much brighter than Lipstick, who worked hard and handed their homework in on time. Of all the swots, she picked on Rebecca the most. She singled her out because she was small for her age and at thirteen, going on fourteen, she was virtually the only girl in the year not wearing a bra. ("Oi, Fried Eggs, here's some cotton wool" ... and she would try to stuff it down Rebecca's shirt front.) Rebecca also had braces ("Oi, Tin Grin, give us a smile"). Each time, the rest of the class—apart from Rebecca's small but loyal gang of mates— would snigger. Lipstick was never threatening or violent, just relentlessly taunting and bitchy.

Rebecca didn't merely dislike Lipstick. She loathed her. She never mentioned Lipstick's bullying to her mother, because she knew she would go marching up to the school, which meant Rebecca would get a reputation for being a mummy's girl and Lipstick would pick on her even more.

There were a couple of examples of Lipstick's nastiness that Rebecca would never forget. First there was the art lesson in the fourth year when Lipstick purposely smeared red paint on the back of Rebecca's skirt, so that it looked like she had her period and was leaking. Even now she could hear the boys chanting "Rebecca Fine's on the blob."

When Judy found out she was livid and it was all Rebecca could do to stop her phoning Lipstick's parents.

"Mum, you can't," she'd pleaded. "You'll just make it worse. I'll deal with it. OK?"

And she did. By then, she was older, more confident, and people were beginning to stand up to Lipstick. Rebecca and her posse took their glorious revenge the next day. They went to Lipstick's locker, where she kept her packed lunch, pried it open with a screwdriver and spread Head and Shoulders inside her cheese and pickle sandwiches. Even in the sixth form—after she'd left—people were still telling exaggerated tales of how Lipstick had run red-faced and screaming from the school canteen, yards of bubbles streaming from her mouth.

But the most hurt she ever caused Rebecca was just before the fifth-year prom. Although Rebecca's tits had arrived by then, so had her acne. Acres of it. Her face was a mass of blackheads, boils and those hard painful lumps that refused to turn into actual zits. Even the unaffected skin was flaky and red raw, through too much washing and overuse of the Retin-A the doctor had prescribed.

"Dunno why you've bothered to come, Spot," Lipstick had sneered, all purple frosting and thigh-high side slits. (By now Lipstick was seeing a twenty-five-year-old bloke called Craig, who had George Michael hair, drove a Ford Capri and was rumored to be Duran Duran's record producer.) "Nobody's going to want to dance with you."

And, of course, nobody did—despite the fabulous Laura Ashley taffeta ball gown Judy had bought her. For most of the evening Rebecca sat with Roger Shakelady, the class saddo, who wore knitted school sweaters and had been infamous when they were all at primary school for sitting in the playground licking moss.

"And my dad's about to marry this appalling, stuck-up tart," Rebecca wailed on the phone to Jess.

"Oh, stop it," Jess came back. "That was years ago. You were kids. She won't still be a tart. Or even remotely appalling or stuck up."

"OK, I expect she probably isn't a tart anymore. She was a snob and she'll have gone all sophisticated by now. She's probably got entire rooms full of Prada and Gaultier. But she'll still be horrible. I guarantee it."

"Look," Jess said, "your mum was one of the kindest, most down-to-earth people I've ever met. Stan would never go for somebody who wasn't like her."

"I wouldn't be so sure," Rebecca said. "All men lose the plot when beautiful women start paying them attention. Particularly beautiful younger women. She'll have conned him—made out she loves him when all she's after is his money. She's just the kind of cold calculating type who'd do that."

"But you said her family was rich. She doesn't need money."

"They had money and they were flash, but they weren't rich rich. Anyway, she's the type who could never have enough."

"Sorry, but I can't see it," Jess said. "Your dad has spent ten years waiting for the right woman to come along. He is not going to make a mistake like that. You told me the other day you'd feel threatened if Bernadette turned out to be beautiful. Well, she is and here you are, jealous as hell."

Rebecca didn't say anything for a moment. "She's also successful," she muttered, eventually.

Jess laughed. "Come on," she said gently, "I bet Lipstick's really sweet."

"I dunno," Rebecca said. "I can imagine Lipstick being a lot of things, but sweet ain't one of them."

Rebecca fell asleep—having completely forgotten about her date with the Vibroclit—and dreamed her stepmother-to-be had two really ugly grown-up daughters and that all three got to go to the annual Press Awards ball and dance with Max Stoddart, while she was forced to stay at home stitching endless Bagpuss pajama cases.

* * *

The next morning, the bulge was still there. She decided it was a toss-up between starving all day, doing five hundred stomach crunches or going on her date with Max wearing her M&S control pants. It was no contest. Starving herself would only make her feel sick and lethargic and probably have no effect on the bulge. Crunches hurt and although she fancied Max Stoddart, she didn't fancy him enough to slip a disk for him. The pants, on the other hand, would cure the problem instantly—even if they were the size of the Balkans and so tight they cut off the blood supply to her head and turned her bum into a mass of taut, unyielding flesh that gave a whole new meaning to the phrase tight-assed. She would just have to hope he didn't try to stroke it.

She decided to finish her column at home and e-mail it to Lucretia. That way she could spend the afternoon titivating. Her bathroom shelves were stacked with freebie tubes, jars and gadgets. Cynical as she was about the beauty business, it seemed a shame to let them go to waste.

By half past five she'd cleansed, toned, exfoliated and moisturized to such an extent that even she had to admit her skin felt as soft as an Hermès scarf. She was sitting on the sofa watching *Neighbours* and sanding the Parmesan buildup on her feet, when the phone rang. It was Rose.

"Darling, I was wondering if you could do me a favor. I forgot to pick up my prescription for my blood pressure pills today and I've run out. Do you think you could possibly pop round to the doctor before the office closes and collect it? I wouldn't bother you if it weren't really urgent. You see the moment I stop taking the tablets I start getting these pounding headaches." Pause. Cue weak pathetic voice: "Apparently they can be really dangerous if they go untreated."

Rebecca couldn't help thinking that her grandmother should have been a travel agent for guilt trips. "OK, don't panic," she said kindly. "It's no problem. I'll be as quick as I can."

She threw on a pair of trackie bottoms and a fleece. It wasn't six yet. She wasn't meeting Max until half past eight. There was just about time to get to Hendon and back.

But the rush-hour traffic was hellish. On top of that, the doctor hadn't printed out the prescription and she had to wait. Then there was a twenty-minute queue in Boots.

By the time she pulled up outside Rose's it was nearly seven. She decided to ring Max to say she was going to be a bit late, but there was no reply from his home phone, his mobile or his office line. Since he was clearly not at home or at work, she left a message on his mobile.

Rose opened the door dressed in her best suit—the imitation Chanel she'd had ever since Rebecca could remember. It was navy with gold buttons and cream edging around the jacket. These days the skirt was a bit stained and a couple of the buttons were missing. She'd also painted her nails. Badly. But the clumsily applied scarlet provided the perfect accessory to the wobbly red on her lips and the dollops of sky blue on her eyelids.

Rebecca kissed her hello and remarked on how glam she was looking.

"So, what's the occasion?"

"No occasion," Rose said casually. "I just felt like giving the outfit an airing, that's all."

Rebecca handed her the Boots bag, said she was sorry that she had to dash and that she'd catch up with her at the weekend.

"But you can't go," Rose insisted. "You only just got here. Come in. Sit down. Have a cup of tea."

"But I can't. I'm meeting some friends for dinner and I'm already late." She didn't dare say she had a date. Rose's interrogation would be endless.

"Five minutes, that's all I ask. What difference can five minutes make? I hardly get to see you these days."

"But I came for dinner four days ago."

Rose pulled one of her lonely neglected old woman faces.

"OK. Five minutes," Rebecca said firmly.

She followed Rose into the kitchen and sat down at the old blue Formica table. Rose started faffing around making tea. Every so often she would stop to peer shortsightedly at the kitchen clock.

"You sure you're not expecting somebody?" Rebecca asked.

"Who should I be expecting?" Rose sounded distinctly edgy, Rebecca thought.

"Dunno. It's just that you keep checking the clock."

Rose's tea making seemed to take forever. Rebecca kept expecting her to bring up the subject of Stan and Bernadette, but she didn't. Clearly Stan hadn't plucked up the courage to tell her yet.

Once she'd poured the tea, she couldn't find the biscuits.

"Gran, I don't need biscuits. I'm going out to dinner. Look, I really should get going."

"No, you can't go." The edginess had turned to pure anxiety. She fell theatrically onto a kitchen chair. "Ooh," she said, breathing hard and tapping her chest, "I just went a bit dizzy there for a second. Darling, do you think you could fetch me my pills and a glass of water?"

"'Course," Rebecca said, jumping up. She went over to the sink and picked up a glass from the draining board.

"Gran, you OK?"

Rose was rubbing her forehead. "Don't worry, I'll be fine."

"But I am worried. Perhaps I should phone the doctor."

"No, no, it's nothing. It'll pass as soon as I've taken my tablets."

Rebecca handed her the box of pills and the glass of water. Rose pushed two tablets out of the foil and knocked them back.

Just then the front doorbell rang. As if by magic, the tension left Rose's face and her mouth turned smileward.

"Oh," she said, "that must be Warren. He's Esther's nephew. The picture's gone fuzzy on my PC. She said she might send him round to take a look at it. Apparently he's a wiz with computers. Lovely boy. Oxford degree. Very brainy."

As she toddled off on her short bandy legs to answer the door, Rebecca tried Max's mobile again. Still no answer. She left another message. After two or three minutes, Rose returned.

"Look, Gran, I'm really sorry, but I just have to go. I've got to have a shower and get changed."

"OK, but you must come and say hello to Warren. He's in the living room with the computer." She cleared her throat. "Be rude not to."

"All right, but it'll have to be a very quick hello and good-bye."

"Hi." Rebecca waved tentatively from the doorway. "I'm Rebecca, Rose's granddaughter."

Rose pushed her so hard from behind that she nearly fell into the living room. She turned round. Rose was making shooing motions with her arms, urging her granddaughter farther into the room.

The penny finally dropped inside Rebecca's head. She turned to glare at Rose, who was still busy shooing and pretending not to notice.

Warren stood up. He was tall and stooping, with masses of wiry ginger hair.

He gave her a nervous smile and introduced himself. Rebecca couldn't work out if he had been expecting to meet her or had been set up, too.

"Why don't I take your coat," Rose said.

Underneath he was wearing a red Alan Partridge V-neck with snowflakes all over it.

"Your grandmother tells me you're a journalist," he ventured. She nodded. "What about you?"

She was guessing something in environmental health.

"Local government," he said.

"Which department?"

"Planning and urban traffic calming."

She smiled to herself. OK, not quite environmental health, but it wasn't far off.

"Oh, right. Must be interesting. You working on anything in particular at the moment?"

"I'll say he is," Rose butted in eagerly. "Warren's planning a whole new road system for the center of Chalfont D'Arcy, aren't you, Warren?"

"Yes. But it's all a bit hush-hush at the moment." He tapped the side of his large, pointy nose and began rocking back and forth on the balls of his feet. "I'm working on this neotraditionalist road-growth paradigm based on grid street networks. Wouldn't want the press getting hold of it."

"God, no," Rebecca said. "I mean the *Sun* would seize on something like that in a flash. Anyway, it was great to have met you, but I really must get going."

"But I've made a lovely supper," Rose pleaded. "Look at the table. Look at all the trouble I've gone to. It would be a crime to waste it."

Rebecca turned toward the dining room table at the far end of Rose's through lounge. Her grandmother couldn't have found room for another platter or serving bowl if she'd tried.

"It's your favorite," Rose said to Rebecca. "Poached salmon. I even got those baby corn you like." She turned to Warren, who was still rocking and looking stupid. "Ever since she was three years old, she's had a thing for baby corn."

"But, Gran, I have to go…" Rebecca whispered, giving her grandmother a how-could-you-do-this-to-me? scowl.

Rose responded by letting out a soft moan. Then she closed her eyes and began rubbing her forehead. "Oooh, the pain." She gripped the back of the sofa and started to wobble.

Much as she adored Grandma Rose, Rebecca also knew she could be as manipulative as a two-year-old when she wanted something.

"Sorry, Warren," Rose said in a small, breathless voice, "you'll have to excuse me. Sometimes my blood pressure shoots up. The doctor says that at my age and with my blood vessel history, I can't rule out the possibility of a stroke."

Rebecca rolled her eyes. She was almost 100 percent certain Rose was putting on an act, but she couldn't be sure. She put her arm round her shoulders and gently guided her to the armchair.

"All right, Gran." Rebecca smiled, realizing she had no choice but to stay and keep an eye on her. "Of course I'll stay for dinner. Just let me make a quick call."

She went out into the hall and dialed Max's mobile. Once again all she got was his voice mail. She explained about Rose, left profuse apologies for standing him up and said she hoped they could arrange another date.

When she came back into the room, Rose was yakking away to Warren, nineteen to the dozen.

"Of course the doctor thinks I should change my diet—you know, start eating health foods—but I keep telling him that at my age I need all the preservatives I can get." With that she began shaking with laughter.

"So, feeling a bit better, Gran?"

"Maybe a little. I think perhaps the pills have kicked in." She tapped the photograph album sitting on her lap. "I was just showing Warren the picture of you when you were bridesmaid at your cousin Valerie's wedding. Look, you'd just gotten your new braces."

Rebecca gave Warren a weak smile.

"Now then, why don't we all go and sit down," Rose said.

As they made their way to the table, Rose gave a little tug on Rebecca's fleece. "Couldn't you have worn something a bit smarter?" she hissed.

"So, Warren," Rebecca said, offering him a bread roll from the basket, "tell me all about this new road layout of yours."

"Well," he said, reaching for a roll, completely unaware that he was dragging his sleeve through the potato salad, "my plan is a reaction to the arterial-slash-collector road system we have at the moment, which essentially supports urban sprawl. You see, road networks don't have to be like that. I mean, take Peninsular Charleston in South Carolina. There you have a perfect example of a vibrant, eclectic, profoundly inspiring urban village...."

Even though she'd finished her column, Rebecca decided to go into the office the next morning. She had some research to do for a profile she was writing on some new girl band, which the *Mail* had commissioned. She could see no point staying at home and paying for phone calls when she could make them at the *Vanguard* for free. On top of that there was always the possibility—albeit un-likely—that a major investigative scoop would come her way.

When she arrived just after ten, there was no sign of Max. She guessed he'd gone off on a story. Her phone must have rung half a dozen times that morning. Each time—assuming it was Max—she'd snatched it off its cradle and purred a deep, sexy hi into the mouthpiece. The first time it was Rose phoning to find out what she thought of Warren.

"Very sweet, but not really my type," Rebecca said diplomatically. She decided that getting cross about last night would only send Rose's blood pressure up again.

"You know your problem, don't you?" Rose said in a gently

scolding tone. "You're too fussy by half. Take my word for it—wait much longer for your boat to come in and you'll find your jetty's collapsed."

The rest of the calls were from beauty company PRs looking for publicity for new products. The last one was from Mimi Frascatti at Mer de Rêves, who had been phoning every couple of days to try and persuade Rebecca to do an interview with the director of Mer de Rêves, Coco Dubonnet du Sauvignon.

Rebecca, who had about as much interest in Coco Dubonnet du Sauvignon and her doings as she did in those of Sven Goran Eriksson, had repeatedly made "I'll mention it to the editor"—type noises and promised to get back to her. Of course she never did, which meant Mimi was forever on the phone nagging.

"Now, I even have a brilliant peg for the interview," Mimi had trilled a few minutes ago. "Mer de Rêves is about to launch a new antiwrinkle cream—Revivessence. But unlike all the other wrinkle creams, this one really does work."

"Right," Rebecca said, with the same kind of enthusiasm with which she greeted her dental hygienist.

"No, honestly. It really does work. You see it contains this miracle ingredient, which dissolves wrinkles in a matter of days—completely organic, of course. Unfortunately we can't let you have a sample yet because it's all deeply under wraps until the official launch. But we'd adore some prepublicity—you know a *Hello!*-type interview with Coco looking gorgeous, sipping Taittinger at her rustic gîte in the Périgord."

Rebecca made the point, as tactfully as she could, that without a sample to try out on some willing guinea pigs, there really wasn't much of a story.

"Right," Mimi said, going into flounce mode, "I desperately want to give it to you as a world exclusive, but we have got *Vogue* and *Elle* snapping at our heels."

"You must do what you think best," Rebecca said, in little doubt that Mimi had already tried *Vogue*, *Elle* and very likely the *Romford Recorder* too and met with the same response.

She'd just gotten rid of Mimi when the phone rang again. Once more she tried the sexy voice, only to discover yet again a woman's voice on the end of the line.

"Hello," it said in an anxious nervous whisper, "you don't know me. My name's Wendy. I saw you at the Mer de Rêves party the other evening."

A cold chill shot down Rebecca's back. She knew at once it was the creepy woman who'd been following her.

"I tried to speak to you then," she went on, "but I was too scared."

Rebecca frowned. "Scared? Of what?"

Pause.

"Them."

Them. Rebecca groaned inwardly. Why was it that wherever she'd worked the switchboard always sent her the paranoid, gibbering schizos convinced they'd seen Stalin in the Asda parking lot with a cart full of Vienettas?

"Look, can you just tell me what this is about?" Rebecca said kindly. For some reason she decided to persevere with this one.

"Well, until yesterday I worked at Mer de Rêves as a personal assistant. But I was sacked."

"Oh, I see," Rebecca said, relieved. "Look, if you're after publicity for an unfair dismissal case, I'm not really your person. You should talk to—"

"No, no. It's nothing like that. I mean, I was unfairly dismissed, but that's not what I want to talk to you about. You see, I have some information about the company you might find interesting."

"What sort of information?"

"I can't say. Not over the phone. Could we meet?"

There was no way Rebecca was going to meet up with a possible nutcase until she had something more to go on. She pressed the woman for more information, but she refused to say another word.

In the end Rebecca's curiosity won out over common sense and she agreed to meet her for coffee the next morning at Salvo's, the sandwich bar across the road.

When two o'clock came and Max still hadn't called, she decided she'd definitely blown it. Having gathered most of the information she needed for the girl band piece, she decided to work on it at home.

She was halfway there when she decided that as she hadn't had lunch, she'd stop off at Jess's for a quick sandwich.

Dolly answered the door in her hat and coat. As Rebecca stepped into the hall, she could hear Jess and Ed rowing upstairs. Dolly rolled her eyes.

"Been going at it all bleedin' morning," she announced. "Right, that's me done for the day. I'm off."

With that she picked up her shopping bag from the hall table and disappeared out the door.

Rebecca hung her coat on the end of the banister.

"So who is she?" Jess was shouting. "Come on, Ed, who have you been sleeping with?"

"For Chrissake, you know there's no other woman on the planet apart from you."

"So, what are you telling me—that you've been sleeping with an alien?"

Silence followed by a door slamming.

"OK, fuck you," Jess screamed.

The next moment she was charging down the stairs, her face

red and puffy from crying. "Becks," she said, sniffing, "I didn't hear the bell."

"Hi, babe." Rebecca smiled. "Look, I can go if you want."

"No, stay. I fancy a talk."

Rebecca followed her into the kitchen, where Diggory was fast asleep in his pram. She stood with her back to the sink. Rebecca sat down at the table.

"We tried to do it again last night, but this time Ed couldn't get it up at all. My body clearly repels him. Becks, I'm really starting to panic. I think he might have found somebody else. We've been rowing ever since."

"Come on, Jess," Rebecca said, getting up to give her a hug, "most blokes get a touch of willy-nilly from time to time. It doesn't mean he's having an affair. I'm sure it'll pass. What the pair of you need to do is sit down quietly and talk about what's going on. I mean have you thought that perhaps you're so taken up with Diggory at the moment that he feels a bit pushed out?"

"Yeah, it did occur to me. God, I'm an agony aunt, for crying out loud. Why am I handling this so badly?"

"The reason you're handling it so badly," she said, "is because you have a new baby and you're severely sleep deprived. Exhaustion does your brain in."

She sat Jess down and put the kettle on.

Just then Ed appeared. Tall, blond, boyish freckles. Most women thought he was dead cute, but although she thought the world of him, lookswise Ed was just a touch too Hitler youth for Rebecca's taste.

"Right, I'm off," he said to Jess. He shot Rebecca an awkward smile. There were dark shadows under his eyes.

"I've got a going away party tonight," he said to Jess, "so I'll be back late."

Jess ignored him and looked straight ahead, grim faced.

"Jess, come on," he pleaded, bending down and giving her a kiss on the cheek. She looked up at him. Rebecca could see she was doing her best to fight it, but a moment later her face had broken into a weak smile.

"Oh, look, no milk," Rebecca piped up, sensing she should make herself scarce for a few moments. "Perhaps it's still on the step."

She made a swift exit into the hall and stood listening.

"Love you," she heard Jess say. "Look, I know there's nobody else. I'm just being paranoid. Sorry."

" 's OK. I love you too. So we friends again?"

"Friends," Jess said.

Eucch. Snogging noises.

Rebecca counted to ten and went back into the kitchen. Ed was putting his PalmPilot into his Eastpak.

"Oh, look," Rebecca said, picking up the carton of milk from the table, "there it was all the time."

Ed winked at Jess, gave Rebecca a tiny wave and left.

"So," Jess said, "how was the hot date?"

Rebecca explained. "I've blown it, haven't I? I mean why else wouldn't he call? Oh, God, please tell me I'm not going to end up married to a stupid town planner with a head full of ginger pubes."

Jess laughed. "Why don't you call him?"

"Who? Ginger pubes?"

"No, you dope. Max."

"I called last night," Rebecca pronounced. "Now it's his turn."

Her friend snorted with impatience. "Oh, for Gawd's sake get off your high horse. Just phone."

Jess handed her the phone and she rang his mobile. When she got his voice mail, she tried the office. He picked up immediately.

"Hi, Rebecca—God, synchronicity. I've just this second walked in. I was about to phone you. Look, I am so sorry about last night. I hope you can forgive me."

She frowned. "Forgive you?"

"Yeah, I left messages on your answer machine—just after six last night. You know, about being stuck in the biodiversity meeting."

God, she hadn't played back her messages.

"Oh, yes," she said brightly, doing her best to disguise her unease, "of course you did."

"In the end I didn't get home until three in the morning. Then when I got in I realized I'd had some problem with my mobile and I can't access any of my messages."

Her face could have lit up a small town.

"Look, these things happen," she said, her voice oozing understanding. "Please don't worry about it."

"So," he said, "what are you doing tonight?"

5

Hideous as they were, the huge, industrial-strength control pants provided her with a positively prairie-flat stomach. If Max made a move, she would simply say she had a strict no-sex-on-the-first-date rule. This was true, although in Max Stoddart's case, she had been prepared to make an exception.

Her cleavage came courtesy of a wondrously sexy, ninety-pound La Perla bra. (She'd justified the expense on the grounds that spending money was her only extravagance.) A pair of Kurt Geiger killer heels gave the illusion she possessed ankles. These had cost even more than the bra, but, as she kept reminding herself, Cinderella didn't flirt wearing Birkenstocks.

Thanks to La Perla, Herr Geiger and the pants, the blue dress looked and felt fantastic.

As she waited to be shown to Max's table she slipped off her pashmina (thereby offering him an eyeful of her gorgeously sexy shoulders and cleavage as she walked in). Then she turned to face one of the restaurant's mirror-covered pillars so that she could touch up her lipstick. She lifted her hand to her face and froze. Armpit stubble! Four days' worth, at least. And it was flecked in deodorant. She screwed up her face in horror. She'd shaved her pits less than an hour ago—in the shower. She lifted the other arm from her side. Depilated to perfection. She immediately realized what had happened. She'd been so engrossed listening to *PM* on Radio 4 that she'd lost concentration and shaved one pit twice. By now sweat had started breaking through her expensive freebie foundation.

She took a deep in-through-the-nose, out-through-the-mouth yoga breath. OK, she could handle this. She would just have to keep the pashmina on. Bummer. Now he wouldn't get to see her shoulders and cleavage. And there could be no question of a good-night kiss. The moment she put her arms round his neck, he was bound to notice the fuzz.

Max was sitting at a table by the window—gray suit, purple open-neck shirt—stirring the ice in his Scotch. Her heart rate picked up. He stood up the moment he saw her. She gave him a tiny wave and quickened her step toward him, unaware that the waiter was leading her in a completely different direction.

The next thing she knew she was lying on the floor, her head pounding and spinning. Max and the waiter were helping her up.

"Rebecca, you all right?" Max said. His face was full of concern. Despite the pounding and spinning in her head, she managed to register how sublimely sexy she found this.

"Yeah," she said, "just a bit dizzy, that's all."

The waiter disappeared to get her some water.

"God," she said, brushing some flecks of dirt off her dress, "what happened?"

"The wall's made of mirrors," he said. "You were waving at my reflection and you ran into it. You've cut your forehead. Let's sit you down and take a look at it."

It was only now that she realized her pashmina had come off in the fall and was lying on the floor. Even with her left arm clamped to her side, she could see the little tarantula legs sticking out. If she wasn't careful, he'd see it and think she was a member of some weird cult that only shaved one armpit. How she was going to get the pashmina on again with only one arm, she hadn't the foggiest. But before she had a chance to try, Max had picked it up and draped it round her shoulders.

As Max guided her to their table, she could feel warm blood starting to trickle down her forehead.

Once she'd sat down, he crouched in front of her and gently lifted her fringe. She got the faintest whiff of expensive aftershave.

"It's not huge, but it's pretty deep," he said, dabbing at it with a napkin. "I think we should get you to the ER. You might need a stitch in it. And there's always the possibility you could have concussion."

"No, I'll be fine," she said, still shaking. "Tell you what, though, I wouldn't mind a vodka and tonic."

She wondered if it was possible to be concussed while at the same time as horny as a herd of rampant rhinoceroses.

When Rebecca's head was still hurting two vodkas later and the bleeding was refusing to stop, Max absolutely insisted on skipping dinner and driving her to the hospital. (He'd gotten his car back that morning. The police had found it abandoned in Ilford minus only its CD player.)

She spent most of the journey apologizing and remembering to dab at the cut with her right arm.

The ER was pretty empty, but the electronic notice board was indicating a two-hour wait. The TV was blaring in the corner (*BallyK*) and they sat on red plastic chairs eating salt-and-vinegar-flavored Monster Munch, which was all the machine had left.

"At least you're a cheap date," Max said, smiling.

They passed the time talking about work. She told him how she was just doing the beauty column to pay the bills. "It's not really me," she said, "I'm desperate to get stuck into a proper story."

"You shouldn't knock the beauty," he said. "Great stories often crop up where you'd least expect them."

"Funny you should say that." She told him about the weird phone call from the woman who got sacked from Mer de Rêves. "I've agreed to see her, but she's probably just some nutter."

"Maybe. But you never know. You could be on the verge of a huge beauty industry exposé."

"Yeah, right," she said, laughing, "I can see it now: 'Rebecca Fine peels off face mask of lies and deceit in deep cleanser scandal.' They could call it exfoli-gate."

"You know, you're very funny."

She could feel herself going red. "So," she said, "tell me a bit more about this French story you said you were working on."

He explained that just over a year ago a partly British-built nuclear power plant eighty miles east of Paris had come within minutes of blowing up. Had it happened, it would have left a radiation cloud over the whole Paris region and part of southern England, too.

"Apparently the workers were having a Christmas party and nobody noticed the radiation leak. Of course..." he lowered his voice to whisper, "the French government and ours have been trying to cover it up. At least two people who've tried to tell their stories have been bumped off."

"Blimey. Aren't you scared that they could do the same to you?"

"A bit, but it's unlikely."

He explained that the moment he'd uncovered the story

(which had come via a physicist he'd known since his post-grad student days at the Sorbonne), the *Vanguard* had insisted on sharing it with *Liberation* and a French TV company, as well as Channel 6.

"The plan is to release the story simultaneously. It's all about safety in numbers." He started grinning. "If the French government finds out we're on to them and tries to stop us, there'd be a heck of a lot of people to kill."

"But they could still try."

He shrugged. "I try not to think about it."

How could he be so cool, so laid back? She hadn't felt so horny since that bit in *Braveheart* where Mel Gibson saves his wife from being raped.

Her head X ray was clear, but the harassed junior doctor said the cut was deep and needed a couple of stitches.

Rebecca was no coward. On a school Outward Bound trip to Wales when she was sixteen, she'd rappelled down a forty-foot rock face and canoed through rapids. On holiday in Corfu a couple of years ago she'd had a go at paragliding. Despite her undoubted bravado, she couldn't bear the thought, let alone the sight, of needles.

"Can't you put one of those sticky tape things over it?" she asked the doctor, having explained about her fear of needles.

The doctor said he wouldn't advise it as the wound would only open up again. When he offered her a couple of Valium to calm her down, she agreed straight away.

She started to feel woozy almost immediately. It was probably made worse by the two double vodkas she'd downed on an empty stomach.

While the doctor fiddled around with surgical gloves and tools, she could feel herself getting more and more relaxed. She barely flinched as he injected the area round the cut with local anesthetic. Max was looking down at her.

"You all right?" he asked gently.

"Couldn't be better," she said with a drunken, and drugged to boot, giggle. She paused. "Has anybody ever told you how incredibly sexy you are?"

Max reddened and exchanged a glance with the doctor, but Rebecca didn't notice. "Doctor," she carried on, "don't you agree that this is one of the sexiest men you have ever seen? I mean I know you're a bloke and everything, but I reckon even blokes know when another bloke's sexy."

Then she must have drifted off.

"Right, that's it. All done," the doctor announced as she started to come round again. He snapped off his gloves.

She was aware of Max sitting at the end of the cubicle. He was sipping coffee, but so Valiumed-up was she, that she was convinced he was licking ice cream from a cornet.

"God, I bet you give the best oral sex," she said woozily.

The doctor suggested they leave her to sleep off the effect of the Valium for a half hour or so. When she woke up, she still felt pretty doped and had no memory of what she'd said. Max insisted on driving her home. They stopped off at a drive-through Burger King. She had a veggie burger because they were less fatty than meat burgers, which tended to give her indigestion.

"Look, I am just so sorry for the way tonight turned out," she said as he pulled up outside her flat. "I ruined everything. Do you forgive me?"

He didn't answer. Instead he cupped her face in his hands and drew her toward him. Then he kissed her lightly on the lips. Oh God, she wanted his head between her legs and she wanted it now.

"Just to show you how much I forgive you," he said, "why don't you let me cook you dinner tomorrow night?"

"That would be lovely," she said, running her hand through her hair and realizing too late that her underarm fuzz was on full view.

OK, **there has** to be a catch," Rebecca said to Jess the next morning, as she lay on the sofa in her Angelica Rugrat PJs, cordless to her ear. "No man is this perfect. Not only is he gorgeous, intelligent and kind, but he is risking his life for the sake of justice and truth."

"Divorced, beheaded, died. Divorced, beheaded, survived."

"What?" Rebecca said.

"Sorry. Diglet and I were in the middle of our history lesson when you phoned. We're doing Henry the Eighth. Why on earth should there be a catch? You're being paranoid. Maybe that bump on your head was more serious than you thought."

"Don't be daft. I'm fine. No, there has to be something wrong with him. I know—I bet he's a veggie. God, yeah, that's bound to be it."

In Rebecca's book real men ate food that had parents. Veggie blokes on the other hand had lifetime membership to the

National Trust, ran like girls and wore prosthetic sympathy stomachs when their wives were pregnant.

"What's the betting he goes on Tyrolean walking holidays?"

Jess laughed and told her to stop being so stupid.

"So how are things?" Rebecca asked.

"Nightmare. Ed still can't get it up. 1535, dissolution of the monasteries begins and Thomas More is executed....Says he doesn't know why. Swears he still adores my body."

"See, what have I been telling you?" Rebecca said.

Jess didn't say anything.

"Jess, you there?"

"Yes, yes I'm here," she said, her voice suddenly brimming with excitement. "God, I think the Digman just said 'Papal Bull.' "

"Jess, he's two months old. He was probably bringing up some wind."

"Yeah, maybe." She paused. "Becks, tell me honestly, do you think I control Ed too much?"

"What, like the other day when you told him to stop breathing because it was getting on your nerves?"

"No, I was thinking more of the way I choose all his clothes."

"Can't see anything wrong with that. Loads of women do it. It's 'cause we have the more sophisticated style gene. It's thanks to us that the entire male population isn't swanning around in Aussie ranchman hats and espadrilles."

"But maybe I'm undermining his self-esteem," Jess said. "Perhaps he feels emasculated. That would explain the willy-nilly. I'm wondering whether I should stop telling him what to wear, hand over all the financial decision making to him and become a surrendered wife. I read somewhere that subservience is the new pashmina."

"The financial stuff I can understand. It's a pain in the arse. I'd love some bloke to do it for me. But handing over sartorial responsibility to a man." Rebecca breathed in sharply through her teeth. "We are talking major risk here. I mean suppose he came home one night with a mullet or vinyl trousers? Or even worse— what if he grew a beard and no mustache?"

"Oh, come on," Jess laughed. "I've taught him everything he knows about style and fashion. He wouldn't do anything like that. I know he wouldn't."

When Rebecca arrived at Salvo's, Wendy from Mer de Rêves was already there, sitting alone at a table for four. She was wearing a denim jacket over a bright pink polo neck. A funky multicolored woolen hat was pulled down over her dark bob. She looked far prettier than she had at the party and not in the remotest bit mad or threatening. Nevertheless, Rebecca still felt wary.

The moment their eyes met, Wendy stood up and smiled.

"Hi," she said, extending a hand. "Thank you so much for coming. I can't tell you how much I appreciate it. Particularly after my behavior the other night. I'm sorry if I scared you."

"That's OK," Rebecca said, shaking her hand and returning the smile.

As they sat drinking cappuccino, Wendy explained that she'd been with Mer de Rêves for five years. It was her second job since leaving school and she'd worked her way up to personal assistant to one of the managing directors.

"I'd always been really happy there. Then over the last year or so the atmosphere changed. I can't quite put a finger on it, but suddenly this air of secrecy sort of descended. Everywhere I went there were executives whispering in corners. My boss would break off in the middle of a telephone conversation the moment I came into his office with a cup of coffee."

Rebecca suggested he was talking to his mistress.

"No—he's divorced. Then about six months ago they stopped me taking the minutes at board meetings and began holding them in private. Anyway, I'd gotten so curious about what was going on, that a couple of weeks ago I stood outside the door and listened. I know I shouldn't have, but I just couldn't help myself."

"So did you hear what was being said?"

"Bits and pieces. From what I could make out, they're about to put this new wrinkle cream on the market that contains some wonder ingredient."

Rebecca instantly remembered her conversation with Mimi Frascatti. "Yeah, I know about this," she said, seriously intrigued by now. "It's called Revivessence."

"That's it," Wendy said. "Well, the thing is, I think it may be dangerous."

"In what way? The PR I spoke to said there was a secret ingredient, but it was entirely organic."

"Then why did I hear them referring to 'the chemical'? And why were one or two of the directors dead set against it? They kept going on about the risks and that the company would never get away with it. Anyway, then it got really heated. Everybody was talking at once and I couldn't follow what they were saying. Of course by then I was convinced there was something illegal going on. I thought about it for a few days. Then I decided I just had to go to the papers. I mean, God knows what this chemical's going to do to people. I knew there'd be journalists at the party. I recognized you from your picture at the top of your beauty column. But I lost my nerve. My boss is a pretty scary guy and I knew I was putting my job at risk. Then the day after the party I was made redundant. The letter from personnel said the company was cutting back. But as far as I know they haven't sacked anybody else."

"Do you think somebody saw you listening outside?" Rebecca asked.

Wendy shrugged. "Possibly."

"So, you're sure that's all you can remember. There's nothing else? No clues as to what this chemical might be, or its effects?"

Wendy shook her head. Rebecca turned to a clean page in her notebook and wrote down her home and mobile numbers.

"If anything else occurs to you," she said, "or anybody from the company starts threatening you, please just pick up the phone."

"Do you think they might?" Wendy said uneasily as she wrote down her own number and handed it to Rebecca.

"It's possible. They might want to warn you off talking to the press." She patted Wendy's hand and said she should try not to worry. "Meanwhile," Rebecca said, closing her notebook, "I intend to find out precisely what's in this cream."

"I wish you luck. I know for a fact that until the official launch it's being kept under lock and key at the factory in France. Although I think there's also some at the Mer de Rêves office in Paris. The lab is there. It's where they develop new products."

It wasn't until after they'd said their good-byes that Rebecca allowed herself to get excited. Of course it could all come to nothing. Wendy could still be a delusional nutter, but Rebecca didn't think so. God, now she could show off to Max about having her own Deep Throat. He was bound to be impressed. Although she supposed that since this was a cosmetics story, Wendy was more of a Smooth Throat.

She spent the rest of the morning working on her girl band story. She looked for Max, but he wasn't around. Then she remembered him telling her he had a meeting at Channel 6 with the director of the documentary that was to accompany his French nuclear story.

At lunchtime she took the tube to Selfridges. She'd decided to buy the matching pants to the La Perla bra on the off chance that

Max turned out to be carnivorous (therefore still fanciable) and made a move on her. After last night's wondrous snog she was pretty sure he would.

Once again she spent ages getting tarted up. Only tonight it took longer than ever. This was on account of her fringe, which refused to stay put and cover up the cut on her head. In the end she smothered it in so much wax, it virtually stuck to her skin. On top of the fringe problem she couldn't decide what to wear. She wanted sexy, but casual. Definitely not trousers. Not if there was any possibility of sleeping with Max. She hated all that endless farting around to get them off because they were so bloody tight. Then there was the embarrassing hosiery issue. How many times had she ended up on some bloke's sofa—having been finally divested of her trousers and knickers—starkers except for her flesh-colored M&S Knee Highs?

In the end she decided on her purple satin A-line skirt with a matching lace-edged cardie. The skirt made her hips look big. On the other hand the cropped, low-cut cardie more than compensated because it showed off her tits and offered just a hint of midriff, which was still vaguely tanned from last summer.

She was just about to put on her makeup when she decided to try the sample of freebie lip plump, which she'd been sent a few days ago. Of course, it was bound not to work. On the other hand, if by some miracle it did, she had to admit she rather fancied the idea of an ever so slightly fuller, more sensuous pout.

After half an hour her lips looked no fuller, more sensuous or poutier than usual. No surprise there, then. What she hadn't bargained for was her lips starting to go dental anesthetic numb. She tried speaking. Definite slurring. Panic rose inside her. She was due at chez Max in Highgate in less than an hour. Considering and immediately rejecting the possibility that he might have a thing for palsied women, she phoned Jess for advice.

Jess assured her the numbness would wear off after a few minutes.

"How d'you know?" Rebecca asked, enunciating as best she could.

" 'Cause it'll be the same stuff I used. Take a look at the tube. Does it say 'Luscious Lip for Lady Woman'?"

Rebecca looked. It did. "Oh, God," she moaned. "It's only made in Kowea."

Rebecca hadn't so much as glanced at the tube before she tried the lip plump. She'd just assumed it was a posh European or American make, along with all the other samples.

"I knew it was a con," Jess said, "but that manky chemist at the end of my road had it on special offer. Turned out to be totally useless, though. My labia are just as shriveled and wrinkly as they always were."

But by the time she arrived at Max's flat there was still no improvement.

He opened the door wearing jeans and a baggy T-shirt. He also had bare feet, which she found particularly sexy. The first thing he did was give her a hello kiss on the lips. She tried to pucker up to return the gesture, but couldn't.

"You OK?" he said, clearly sensing her unease.

She decided to tell him she'd just gotten back from the dentist. "Had a fiwing this afternoon," she said, rubbing the side of her mouth. "Stiw a bit num."

"Oh, I hate that. Always end up biting chunks out of my cheek when I eat."

As he led her down the hall toward the kitchen he asked after the cut on her head. Then he told her how beautiful she looked.

" 'hanks," she said, blushing with pleasure and at the same time sniffing the air for signs of meat. There were hot oveny smells, but nothing that actually shouted animal.

The kitchen was tiny, with eighties orangey pine units, beige wall tiles with dirty grouting and a bare frosted window over the stainless steel sink. The mixer tap was crusted with lime scale. It was lit by a single fluorescent strip. Rebecca was reminded of a kitchen in a slightly seedy holiday cottage somewhere like Great Yarmouth.

"You'll have to excuse the place," he said. "I've been here a year, but I still haven't got round to doing it up. Apart from the bedroom and bathroom, everything needs ripping out."

"Reawy?" she said. "I hadn't noticed."

He poured her a glass of wine. She took a sip.

"Whoops," he said, grinning. A moment later he was dabbing wine dribble from her chin with a napkin. He did it slowly, looking into her eyes all the time. She thought he might kiss her, but he didn't.

She sat down on a kitchen stool and they chatted while he made salad dressing. Gradually and to her huge relief, the numbness began to wear off.

She told him about her meeting with Wendy.

"And you think she's on the level?" Max said.

Rebecca shrugged. "I think so."

Just then the intercom buzzer went.

"Oh, that'll be my sister," he said, putting down his wineglass and heading toward the door. "She'll only be a minute. She popped round earlier on to borrow my laptop and my little nephew left his blankey thing here. Won't go to bed without it."

A few moments later he was back. Behind him were a slim pretty woman with expensive Fulham highlights and a rather tearful-looking boy of about four, dressed in a Thunderbird outfit.

"Rebecca, this is my sister Beth."

Beth? Rebecca did a double take. Oh, God, Beth was the sister who had heard her Big Max Hot Line performance.

"Hi," she said, taking Beth's hand, "pleased to meet you."

"And this," Beth said, "is one extremely overtired and miserable Jake. Look, I'm so sorry to barge in like this, but he gets hysterical if he hasn't got blankey at bedtime."

Rebecca turned to the little boy. "Wow, great costume," she said. "So which Thunderbird are you? Don't tell me. Scott Tracy."

"I'm Vergil," he said grumpily, looking at her as if she were a complete fool. "Scott wears a yellow sash."

Beth rolled her eyes and told Jake to stop being so rude. "Sorry," she said to Rebecca. "He should have been in bed over an hour ago."

Max crouched down so that he was on a level with the boy. "Hey, Jake. Come on, cheer up. Remember what we say."

Jake gave a self-conscious grin.

Max's hand went to his head in solemn salute. His face became grave. Jake followed suit.

"OK," Max said, "let's see if you remember how it goes: All hail the *goosenflappers,* masters of the park, lords of all things that flap ... come on, you have to say it, too."

Max began again. This time Jake joined in, between giggles.

Rebecca shot Beth a quizzical look.

"Sometimes Max takes him to the park on a Sunday morning so that his dad and I can have a lie-in. A few months ago they saw a huge flock of geese. Max invented this daft ritual and it just stuck."

By now Max and Jake were in stitches. Rebecca couldn't help registering that Max seemed to be a bit of a natural with kids.

Max turned to Beth and said he'd take Jake into the living room to look for his blankey.

"Always had a bit of a weird sense of humor, my brother," Beth went on. "You should hear his mad voice mail message at the office. He's only got some sexy woman telling callers they've reached the Big Max Hot Line. I keep meaning to speak to him about it. God only knows what people must think."

"Oh, don't worry," Rebecca shot back. "He got rid of it. He was just messing about and forgot to erase it. I don't think too many people heard it."

"Well, thank the Lord for that. I was beginning to think he'd completely flipped. So, Rebecca, how long have you been at the *Vanguard*?"

They'd been chatting for a couple of minutes when Max appeared carrying Jake, who was clutching an ancient and rather grubby-looking blue cot blanket.

"Mission accomplished," Max announced. "It was under the sofa."

Beth took Jake from him. "Come on, Vergil, let's get back into Thunderbird 2 and leave these people to their dinner. Sorry again for intruding."

She turned to Rebecca and waved.

"Nice to meet you," she said.

"You too."

"She doesn't seem even remotely bossy," Rebecca said to Max after Beth and Jake had gone.

"On her best behavior, because you were here." Max grinned. "Plus Beth has never been quite as scary as the other three."

He topped off her wineglass. Then he turned to look at the oven timer.

"Right, I think we're almost ready to eat. Why don't you take the salad next door and I'll be with you in a sec." He bent down to open the oven. She was desperate to find out what was inside, but she thought it would be rude to hover.

The large living room was similar to hers before she decorated. It had yellow anaglyphic walls, faded green velvet curtains on a mahogany pole and a gas fire with a seventies teak surround. She assumed the black ash wall unit, matching table and gold Dralon sofa were his. Her heart sank. She'd assumed by the way he dressed he would have good taste in furniture. She was clearly wrong.

As she put the salad bowl on the table, she noticed a brown envelope. The bird motif caught her eye and she picked it up. Across the top it said Royal Society for the Protection of Birds. Inside there was a newsletter and a glossy brochure advertising Twitcher Weekends in the Chilterns…"to include nightly lectures from the award-winning thrush expert Dr. Finn McGwerter." She put the brochure back and dropped heavily onto one of the black ash chairs. She would just eat and make her excuses.

"Chili con Quorni," he announced, putting the serving dish down on the table.

"Oh, wow," she said, hoping she sounded sufficiently enthusiastic. "Smells great."

He disappeared and came back with the wine bottle and their glasses. "Mind the table. It's a bit wobbly. I bought all the furniture along with the flat. I'd lived in a furnished place before, so I've got nothing of my own apart from a bed, CD player and TV."

"Oh, so none of this is yours?"

"What? Good God, no."

Her spirits lifted, but only slightly.

"Oh, there's something I want your advice on," he said, spooning chili onto her plate. "You know my sisters and I had this anniversary party for my parents?"

She nodded.

"Well, we haven't gotten them a present yet. Mum and Dad both love the countryside and wildlife, so I thought about sending them on a bird-watching holiday. What do you reckon?"

Her eyes shot to the envelope. "Oh, right." She started giggling. "For your parents?"

He gave her a bemused frown. "Yes."

"Fabulous. Wonderful. I can't think of anything more perfect."

"Great," he said, "I was hoping you'd say that….So, Rebecca, how long have you been vegetarian?"

She didn't say anything for a second. "Me, a vegetarian?"

"Yes. Yesterday, on the way home when we stopped at Burger King, you ordered a veggie burger. I just assumed..."

She burst out laughing, only just avoiding spraying him in chili. "The only reason I eat veggie burgers is because they aren't quite as fatty as the meat ones. Bit lower on the old cholesterol. But I adore meat."

He looked at her, clearly relieved. "God, you had me really worried last night. I thought you were going to turn out to be terribly self-righteous and fart a lot."

She made a mental note not to tell him about the effect Brussels sprouts had on her.

They started eating.

"God, this is crap," he said after a mouthful.

"No, it's lovely," she lied. "Quorn's got a really interesting texture."

"Yeah, right, so's barbed wire," he said, picking up her plate. "How's about I order in a curry absolutely stuffed with dead animal?"

It may have been the Fleurie, or Frank Sinatra playing on the CD player, but before she knew it, she was telling him about having lost her mum and how much she missed her. She hadn't cried over Judy in ages, but now tears came rolling down her cheeks. He took her hand and squeezed it.

"What happened?"

"Car crash. Drunk driver shot through a red light and plowed straight into her."

She took another sip of wine.

"So," she said, anxious to lighten the mood, "tell me a bit about you."

He told her his father had been in the RAF and that he'd been sent away to boarding school at eight.

"Rough," she said.

He shrugged. "It was the same for all the forces kids. You got used to it."

"So I guess the military background and boarding school would explain your obsessively tidy desk."

He reddened.

"So, was he pretty senior, your dad?"

"Air vice marshal—retired a couple of years ago."

Blimey. He was even posher than she thought. She'd never been out with anybody really posh before. Except Jess.

They'd almost finished eating when Rebecca noticed a pile of videos next to the TV. "My God," she said, reading the felt-tipped labels, "you like *Seinfeld*, too."

"Love it. I don't think there's a show I haven't got on tape. I've gotten to the stage where I can recite whole chunks off by heart."

"I know. I'm the same. So, come on, which is your favorite episode?"

"'The Baby Shower,'" he said.

"That's one of my favorites, too."

"I love that bit where Elaine and Jerry are talking and she says her friend has Lyme disease in addition to Epstein-Barr syndrome."

"Yeah, she goes: 'It's like Epstein-Barr...' "

" '... with a twist of Lyme disease,' " Max joined in, bursting out laughing. "Brilliant. Just brilliant."

"Isn't it?" Rebecca said. Only she wasn't simply referring to Jerry Seinfeld.

After dinner they went to sit on the sofa. There were a couple of framed photographs sitting on the side table. One was a wedding picture. Rebecca picked it up.

"The bride is my sister Kate," he said.

She was pretty, like Beth, but a bit darker.

"And these are your parents?" she said, pointing to the reedy, distinguished man and the elegant woman in pale lavender.

He nodded.

"Your dad's still very handsome. You look just like him."

"Really?" he said, clearly enjoying the compliment.

The other photograph was of a little girl—about two years old, Rebecca guessed. She was naked and splashing in a plastic paddling pool.

"Wow, gorgeous child," Rebecca said, picking up the photograph to take a closer look. "Look at all those red curls."

"I know." He smiled. "She gets them from her mother. Of course, that picture's ages old; she's a teenager now."

"Who is she?"

"Amy," he said. "She's my goddaughter."

Rebecca insisted on washing up to say thank you.

She was standing at the sink rinsing plates when she felt his arms round her waist.

"Leave it," he whispered, starting to kiss the back of her neck.

She closed her eyes and felt herself start to tremble. "But it'll stink by the morning."

"Don't care," he said, turning her to face him. She was still holding the squeegee mop. He took it from her and dropped it into the sink. Then he brushed the back of his hand over her cheek.

"How did somebody get to be this beautiful?"

"Cod's roe," she said.

"Cod's roe?" He hesitated. "What, you put it on your face?"

"No," she laughed. "You eat it. My mum swore by the stuff. All I ever got for my school lunch was cod's roe sandwiches. She reckoned fish breath was a small price to pay for great skin. Not sure it really worked in my case, though."

"Oh, believe me, it did," he said, drawing her toward him. He brushed his lips lightly across hers. This time she felt every delicious, stomach-quivering sensation. As he parted her lips with his tongue and she felt him deep inside her mouth she put her arms round his neck and breathed in his deliciously warm, slightly boozy smell. He ran his hand over her bottom. She moved her pelvis toward him and felt his erection hard against her. By now she was feeling distinctly wobbly and leaning against the kitchen units for support. As their kissing became more and more urgent, he put his hand up inside her skirt. He ran his fingers along the inside of her thighs. When he began gently stroking the flesh between her stocking tops and her pants, she thought she was about to pass out with delight.

Without saying anything he led her to the bedroom. She stood in the doorway.

"Max. This is beautiful."

Every surface was covered in candles. There had to be dozens, their flames dancing in the dark, casting long shadows against the roller blinds. Musky, exotic perfumes she couldn't identify hung in the air.

"You did this for me?"

He grinned. "I thought you'd like it."

Like it, she adored it. The most romantic thing Simon the ventriloquist had ever done when they were going out was getting Wayne the dummy to sing "Strangers in the Night."

In the candlelight he looked sexier than ever. He guided her to the bed. It was low, Japanesey and covered in brand-new white linen. They stood beside it and kissed again. Taking his time, he began undoing her cardigan buttons. Afterward he pulled down her bra straps and planted kisses on her shoulders and over the tops of her breasts, chasing the goose bumps that were racing over her. When he began running his tongue over her neck, she threw back her head and let out a tiny whimper. She felt him unzip her skirt.

Once she'd stepped out of it, he stood looking at her, running his hand over her stocking tops, fingering the lace of her bra. He reached behind her, unhooked it and pulled it away.

"Wow," he said. Then he took each of her nipples in turn and began sucking them until they were long and erect. He pushed her gently onto the bed. Her head and shoulders sank into the huge square pillows. As she inhaled more of the joss-stick aroma, she felt herself starting to float. He started kissing her stomach and licking the insides of her thighs. By now her breathing was slow and deep.

As she floated somewhere between northwest London and heaven, she was vaguely aware of her pants being pulled off. Then suddenly his head was between her legs. She cried out as he opened her and his tongue began flicking her clitoris.

By now she was begging him to make her come. He responded by slowing down, lightening the pressure so that she could barely feel it. The more she begged him, the more he teased her. Only when she was quiet again did he give her what she wanted. The quivering inside her started to build up almost immediately. Then he stopped again, moved up and began kissing her on the mouth. Their kissing was frantic, frenzied. By now she was desperate to feel him inside her. She reached for his jeans belt. He knelt up, let her undo it and unbutton his fly. She pulled his jeans and his boxers over his thighs, releasing his long, thick erection. She kissed his taut stomach, traced the line of dark hair that ran down from his navel.

As she covered the end of his penis with her mouth and began running her tongue over it, his head slumped forward and he dug his fingers into her shoulders.

"Bloody hell, you're good."

She kissed him on the mouth, pushed him gently onto the bed and went down on him again. He screwed up his face in delight as she ran her mouth back and forth over the shaft.

"I want to come inside you," he said finally.

Before she knew it, he was pulling her by her ankles to the edge of the bed. He made her bring her knees up to her chest. Kneeling on the floor in front of her, he started probing her again with his tongue and fingers. Finally, he began to concentrate on her clitoris, stroking it gently at first, then rubbing it in a firm, circular motion. Once again the quivering began to build up inside her. She took hold of his erection, and guided him toward her. As he entered her she let out a tiny moan. His thrusts were slow and deep, the pleasure so intense she was sure she was about to pass out. She came almost immediately.

Afterward he lay beside her trailing his finger over her breast.

"You know, I've often wondered what those small bumps are round women's nipples."

"It's Braille," she said, keeping a perfectly straight face, "for 'lick them ever so lightly with the tip of your tongue.' "

He was laughing and moving in on her left nipple when her mobile went off.

"Fuck," she said. "I'd better get it. Might be my gran. Her blood pressure's been playing up and she's all on her own."

"Don't worry, I'll get it," he said, leaping off the bed.

He was back in a second. "Text message," he said.

"Probably Lucretia. She's always texting me with ideas for the column. You read it. What's it say: 'CRIMSON MSCARA HOT ACCRDNG 2 NY TIMES 2DAY. U CHECKIT SOONEST'?"

"No, it says: 'IN MY ABC I'D PUT U AND I TOGETHER.' Do you think maybe Lucretia's developed a lesbian crush on you?"

"Very funny," she said, looking puzzled as he handed her the phone. She read the rest of the message with Max looking over her shoulder. " 'TCKTS STARLIGHT XPRESS 2MORROW. FANCY IT? I'M HOT 4 YOU, WARREN.' "

"So," Max said, "who's Warren?"

So, you phoned this Warren bloke," Jess said, scooping a dried-up cat turd out of the tray with a garden trowel, "told him he's a lovely bloke, *Starlight Express* was a sweet thought, but the chemistry between you wasn't quite right. Then you sent him on his way."

Rebecca hesitated. "Pretty much."

"How d'you mean, 'pretty much'?" Jess said, carefully balancing the turd on top of the pile of rubbish spilling out of the pedal bin.

"I said I was in Greenland."

"Greenland."

"Yeah. I told him I was spending three months there researching a feature on the body-painting rituals of the Inuit and that I'd give him a call when I got back."

"But why couldn't you just be straight with him?"

"Dunno," Rebecca said as Jess put the trowel back on the floor next to the cat tray. "I felt sorry for him, I s'pose. I wanted to let him down gently."

"So you made up some daft story? I mean, like the Inuit even have body-painting rituals. They're wrapped up in furs for eleven months of the year, aren't they? Warren may be a bit pathetic, but from what you've told me he's not stupid. There's no way he'll have believed it."

"Yes, he did," Rebecca said. "I turned on the hair dryer and held it over the phone, made out I was getting blown to bits in a snow-storm. He totally bought it."

"But that means he'll keep on phoning you."

"He won't. I told him I could only be reached on a satellite phone at five pounds a minute."

"So, how did he get your number in the first place?"

"At first I thought it was my grandmother, but it turned out to be some temp at the office."

"And what about the Max factor? What if he believes there's something going on between you and Warren?"

"I explained everything. Told him about Gran's matchmaking. He thought it was really funny." She let out a long sigh. "You know, Max could be the one. It sounds sloppy and romantic, and I hardly know him, but I think I may have found the man of my dreams."

"That's how it goes," Jess said wistfully. "You marry the man of your dreams and a couple of years later you find yourself living with a sofa that farts."

Jess poured more coffee into Rebecca's mug. They'd just fin-ished lunch. Dolly had taken Diggory to the park in his pram.

"Come on, don't go all cynical," Rebecca said. "Be happy for me."

"Oh, God, I'm sorry." Jess reached out and squeezed her friend's hand. "This no sex thing is really getting to me. I am happy for you, hon, really I am. Max sounds wonderful. I can't wait to meet him."

"You'll love him." Rebecca's eyes started to glaze over. "He's warm, romantic. All those candles. And did I tell you he likes *Seinfeld*?"

"Only seventy-nine times," Jess said, thumbing through Dolly's

Mirror. "Bloody hell, I bet if I looked like her, Ed'd have no trouble getting it up."

She was stabbing at a picture of some Teutonic superwaif wearing a PVC triangle over her nonexistent tits and Madonna hipsters that showed off at least three inches of bum cleavage.

"Look, just stop it," Rebecca said. "You know how ..."

"...beautiful I am. Yeah, yeah." She paused. "Listen, I've been thinking. It's Ed's fortieth next week. Why don't I throw him a huge surprise party? Might really cheer him up. And afterward we could spend the night at some obscenely expensive hotel. Mum can hold the fort Diglington-wise. I'll leave her a load of expressed milk. A night away with a couple of bottles of Krug and me in something crotchless might just do the trick. What do you think?"

"I think it's a great idea," Rebecca said warmly. "What have you got to lose? Things between you and Ed could hardly get any worse."

"So, Stanley," Rose said, peering at her son over her reading glasses and taking in the black suit jacket with the mandarin collar, "where do you think you're off to? Nehru's funeral?"

Rose, Stan and Rebecca were sitting at a table next to the gents at La Belle Epoque in Hampstead, waiting for Lipstick. It wasn't the table Stan had booked. He'd specified one by the window for this meet-the-family dinner for Lipstick, but the moment they sat down Rose started complaining about the draft.

Of course there was no draft. Just like there had been no smear on the wineglass she'd sent back. It was all part of Rose's campaign to make sure Stan knew precisely how much she disapproved of Lipstick. First there was her age.

"Twenty years from now," she'd said to Rebecca on the phone earlier, "when she's off out with her friends, he'll be keeping in touch with his through the obituary columns."

Then there was her religion. Apart from all the obvious objections Rose had to her son marrying out, she had a particular grievance against the church of Rome. Ten years ago, the Blessed Virgin down the road held a bingo session to which elderly members of her synagogue had been invited. To this day, she swore blind the priest called out the numbers in Latin so the Jews couldn't win.

Rebecca patted her dad on the knee and told her grandmother she thought he looked great in the suit. In fact, she was less than keen, but anything was an improvement on the cargo pants he had been wearing the other day. She thanked the Lord his hair was back to normal. The dye must have been a rinse.

Rose said she still thought the suit looked ridiculous, to which Stan replied that ridiculous was a pierced scrotum. The suit was merely trendy. Rose told him to stop being vulgar and picked up the menu.

"So, what are we all having?" she said.

"Mum, we have to wait for Bernadette."

"She's late." Rose tapped her watch irritably.

"Only a couple of minutes," Rebecca said.

She felt the need to be generous for her father's sake. Deep down she thought it was typical of Lipstick to keep everybody waiting. Twenty minutes from now she'd come swanning in wearing some itsy-bitsy floaty Voyagey thing, making it clear she was doing them a huge bloody favor by deigning to turn up at all. Rebecca looked down at her trousers, which were straining over her newly rebulged, post-last-night's-curry stomach and winced. This was partly with revulsion and partly because the fabric was cutting into her. She slipped her finger between the waistband and her skin and felt the indentation it had made. There was nothing for it. She undid the front zip.

"But I have to eat," Rose moaned. "If I don't eat my blood sugar gets low and I get these spots in front of my eyes."

"So, have you seen a doctor?" Stan said, spreading inch-thick butter onto a piece of bread stick.

"No, just the spots." Rose was on her second sweet sherry.

"Look, if you're feeling hungry, eat this." Stan held out the piece of bread stick, smeared in butter.

"What? Are you joking? Butter? I can already feel my left ventricle slamming shut."

"Oh, no. Please, Mum, not the angina monologue."

Rose glared at him. "And have you looked at the prices they're charging here?" she said. "Six fifty for fish soup. What do they put in it? A whale? I remember when you could get a bowl of soup in a restaurant for ninepence."

Stan shot Rebecca a look, making it clear he wished his mother's left ventricle would slam shut for a bit.

"Of course, you know where we should have gone," Rose continued, "the China Garden down the road. I like it there. They do a wonderful omelette. But my friend Millie says nobody goes there anymore—apparently it's gotten too crowded."

Suddenly Stan's face broke into a smile. "She's here."

Rebecca and Rose looked up.

"Where?" Rebecca asked.

"There," Stan said, getting out of his chair.

The only person Rebecca could see was a plumpish, blonde woman about her own age, carrying a vast bunch of yellow carnations.

"Oooh, sorry I'm late, everybody!" the woman cried out as she came bustling toward them. "Traffic's bloomin' murder."

Rebecca blinked.

"Isn't she beautiful," Stan whispered.

Rebecca nodded. There was no doubt she was still beautiful. The blue eyes and cheekbones hadn't changed a bit. Unlike the rest of her. If ever there were a perfect antithesis of itsy, bitsy and floaty, it was the new Lipstick. Gone were the tiny waist and endless legs. Instead, she had thighs that were positively careering toward chunky and forty-inch hips. Oh, and tight leather trousers. Peach-colored ones.

Clearly this wasn't the threatening vision in Voyage she'd been expecting. Ashamed as she was to admit it, this fact was causing Rebecca to perk up considerably.

"You must be Rose." Lipstick beamed, extending her arms before virtually squeezing the life out of her prospective mother-in-law. "These are for you." She handed Rose the flowers. "Stan said they're your favorites."

Despite herself, Rose's face broke into a smile. "They're wonderful. You really shouldn't have."

Stan put his arm round Lipstick, pulled her to him and kissed her on the cheek. "And here," Stan announced, "with her trousers undone, is Rebecca."

Rebecca turned bright red as she yanked up the zip.

"Rebecca," the woman exclaimed, apparently oblivious to Rebecca's frantic zip pulling.

"Bernadette?" Rebecca whispered. As she took in the sun bed tan, the truth dawned. Lipstick had simply turned into her mother—she of the caked-on UltraGlow. Mrs. O'Brien had been a bit on the heavy side, too.

"Omigod, it's so lovely to see you." She hugged Rebecca as if they were long-lost sisters.

"I cannot believe the two of you went to the same school," Stan said, laughing.

Rebecca was positive that for the briefest of moments the smile left Lipstick's face. Did she remember what had happened between them at school?

"So," Lipstick continued, a tad uneasily, Rebecca thought, but back on full beam, "here's me in the beauty business and you with a makeup column. Can you believe we've got so much in common, Becks? You don't mind me calling you Becks, do you?"

"Er, no, that's fine." Rebecca gave her a weak smile.

"Come on, Rose," Lipstick chivied merrily. "Shove up and make room for a little 'un."

Still smiling, Rose shifted along the banquette. Lipstick squeezed in after her.

"Now then, Stan," she said, "don't just stand there. Find a waiter and order some champagne."

Once they were all sitting down Lipstick reached into her handbag and pulled out a gift-wrapped parcel. She gave it to Stan. "Guess what, I found another one of those bizarre books you like."

Smiling, and saying how much Bernadette spoiled him, Stan pulled off the wrapping. "Oh," he said, "*A Farewell to Arms.*"

"Yeah," Lipstick said. "Isn't that just the greatest title for a diet book?"

Stan roared.

"What?" Lipstick said. "What's so funny? Come on, I've got hold of the wrong end of the stick again, haven't I?"

"Don't worry," he smiled, "I'll explain later."

"So," Rebecca said, "Dad tells me the two of you met at a book club."

"A friend persuaded me to go," Lipstick confided. "I don't read much as a rule. I'm more of a miniseries person really. But they were reading this great book about this woman called Jane Eyre. I was just transported to another world. I could just see the movie in my head."

They sat drinking champagne, Rose getting more and more tipsy. Rebecca asked Lipstick about her business, which turned out to be called "The Face Base and Talon Salon."

"You must come in. I'll give you a treatment on the house." She lowered her voice. "You know, I have a friend who used to have your kind of eyebrows until she came to me."

Rebecca's hand shot self-consciously to her eyebrows. They'd always been a bit heavy, but until now she'd always thought they made her look like Sophia Loren.

Finally the conversation got round to the wedding. Stan said they were thinking about arranging it for sometime in April.

"So, Bernadette," Rose said, "Stanley tells me you're Catholic."

Rebecca held her breath. Stan held his head. Lipstick nodded.

"Although I don't go to Mass as often as I should. My family's quite religious, though. Back in Ireland I have a cousin who's a priest."

By now Rose was rubbing the left side of her chest. "Omigod, you're not thinking of getting married in a...?" Rose couldn't bring herself to finish the sentence.

"No, we thought a registry office would be best," Lipstick said gently. "But look, Stan and I have been thinking. We've decided that when we go on our honeymoon, you must come with us. It's my way of saying thank you for producing this wonderful man."

Rose's face could have lit up Brent Cross.

Rebecca started breathing again. Stan let go of his head. If Rose had any remaining doubts about Lipstick, they had clearly disappeared there and then. Rebecca could just see her gassing on the phone to her friends, showing off about how her son and daughter-in-law thought so much of her, they wanted her to come on their honeymoon with them.

To her credit, Rose patted Lipstick's hand, thanked her for the wonderful offer and said she wouldn't dream of inflicting herself on them like that. Stan's relief was palpable, but only Rebecca noticed.

"You know who's a great man?" Rose said.

They all looked at her.

"The pope. He speaks Polish, you know."

"Gran, the pope *is* Polish."

"Yes," Rose said, "but it's a very hard language."

Ordering was a fiasco. Rose kept changing her mind and demanding to know precisely how everything was cooked. Salt was bad for her blood pressure. Cucumber gave her heartburn. It was the skin. "The tiniest morsel and I'm pacing all night." Ditto anything fried. The waiter did his best to keep his patience.

"OK, maybe I'll have the veal. No, on second thought, change that to the *poussin*. Tell me, how do you prepare the chicken?"

"Don't worry, Mum," Stan said, "they tell it straight out it's going to die."

Lipstick roared and said one of the reasons she'd fallen for Stan was because he made her laugh so much. She told them about the time they'd gone into a restaurant where breakfast could be ordered at any time and Stan had asked for kippers in the Renaissance.

Everybody laughed except Rebecca. She sat looking at Lipstick, trying to make her out. Of course people's personalities changed and mellowed as they got older. Take her own for example. Only a few days ago she'd caught herself in a lift humming along to the *Mull of Kintyre* Muzak. But this warm, up-for-a-laugh, salt-of-the-earth Lipstick seemed just too far removed from who she used to be. The Lipstick Rebecca remembered had about as much charm as Mrs. Satan the day before her period. On the other hand, Lipstick had come to look like her mum, so maybe over the years the rest of the maternal genes had kicked in and she'd taken on her personality, too. Then again, this new persona, along with the flowers for Rose and the offer to take her on the honeymoon, might be nothing more than a cynical schmoozing exercise. A way of wheedling her way into Stan's affections before fleecing him. Maybe her first instincts about Lipstick had been right after all.

It was while they were having coffee that Stan turned to Rebecca and said he and Bernadette wanted to ask her a favor.

"Ask away," Rebecca said brightly.

"Well, the thing is, Bernadette's just bought a new flat and it's being renovated—you know, new wiring, central heating—so that we can move in straight after the wedding. There's going to be so much mess and upheaval. Plus she's going to have no heat while they fit the radiators...she really could do with somewhere to stay for a few weeks."

What? He wanted Lipstick to move in with her? Rebecca could feel herself starting to panic. How could Stan land this on her, out of the blue? He should have spoken to her in private, given her some time to think. Then again she could see how excited he was about getting married. He just wasn't thinking straight. The point was, she didn't know Lipstick. She was still struggling to come to grips with the prospect of having a stepmother her own age. She wasn't even remotely ready for them to live under the same roof. But, above all, she didn't trust her.

"Under normal circumstances she could have moved in with me," Stan went on, "but I'm not going to be around. The manager of Lacy Lady in Manchester has just left without giving notice and I really need to go up there to straighten things out. And anyway my place is too far from Bernadette's salon. So, we were wondering if you'd mind putting her up."

Lipstick must have seen the expression on her face.

"Look, Becks," she said, "I know it's a cheek asking and I'll totally understand if you say no."

Rebecca hesitated, desperately searching for an excuse. Then suddenly it occurred to her that having Lipstick come to stay might not be such a bad idea after all. That way she could watch her and maybe find out what she was up to.

"'Course it's not a cheek." Rebecca smiled. "I'd be delighted."

"Oh, Becks," Lipstick squealed, "we are going to have a great time getting to know each other. I can't wait."

Lipstick moved in two days later with five suitcases, a tanning bed and Harrison Ford.

"Isn't he just gorgeous?" she drooled as they sat in the kitchen drinking the Lambrusco Lipstick had brought to say thank you for having her. "Come on, tell me he isn't gorgeous."

Rebecca looked at Harrison Ford, who was still wearing his Burberry mac, and agreed he was indeed gorgeous.

"And he's got a wonderful *pawsonality*," she said, chucking him under the chin and nuzzling him. "But most important, he's completely house trained. The only time he's ever left an ickle pressiewessie for his mummy was when he was a baby and he had a poorly tum tum."

"Look, the thing is, Lips—I mean Bernadette…"

Lipstick laid her hand gently on Rebecca's arm and said they should get one thing straight from the off. She loved being called by her old nickname. "You know," she said, "my mates from school still call me Lipstick."

"OK, if you're sure."

"I am. Promise. You know, Becks, I have to tell you I felt really weird finding out I was about to become a stepmother to a woman the same age as me. I wasn't sure how you'd take it."

"Well, I have to admit it was a bit of a shock at first."

"I really hope we can be friends." Lipstick's face broke into a grin. "I promise faithfully I won't lock you in a kitchen full of pumpkins."

"OK, and I promise always to be home by midnight."

"Deal," Lipstick declared.

They both started laughing. Despite Rebecca's ongoing suspicions about Lipstick, she couldn't help quite liking her.

Rebecca wondered whether now was the time to clear the air about what had happened between them at school, but she thought it was probably too soon. They needed to get to know each other better. Instead, she thought she'd tackle the dog issue.

"The thing is," Rebecca began tentatively, "about Harrison..."

"I know—you're worried about what to feed him. Well, don't even think about it. Every Sunday I cook up a week's supply of heart and kidney. That's your fayvwit, isn't it, baby?"

"Excellent," Rebecca said. She cleared her throat. "But you see, I'm not really much of a doggy person myself, and I've just bought these new sofas."

"Oh, but Hawwison's not a dog—are you, Hawwison? Hawwison's a Bichon Frise. And does he ever have a pedigree. If Hawwison could talk, he wouldn't be speaking to either of us."

"Yes, but I'm just a bit concerned that Hawwison—I mean Harrison—is going to leave hairs all over the furniture and disturb the neighbors with his barking."

Lipstick assured her the only place he ever sat was his basket and that he barked only if he was frightened.

When Lipstick disappeared to the loo, Rebecca got down on all fours and stared directly into Harrison's sickeningly appealing, chocolate-box-brown eyes.

"Right, you froufrou little mutt, make one mark on my sofas, leap up at me with your muddy paws and you are dead. Do we understand each other?"

Harrison clearly got every word because he let out a pathetic little whimper. Rebecca sat down again, told him to stop being so bloody manipulative and that there was no way he was getting round her.

"Just because we've been forced to live together, it doesn't mean we have to be friends."

He looked up at her, a picture of doggy pathos. She refused to meet his eye.

"Oh, for God's sake," she said eventually, taking a dog biscuit out of the packet Lipstick had left on the table and throwing it to him. He gobbled it up.

When he finished he came toward her, stood on his hind legs and laid his head in her lap. She screwed up her face and patted him as if she were patting the head of an Ebola carrier.

As she was throwing a biscuit to the other side of the kitchen to make him go away, she remembered she hadn't checked her answer machine for a day or so. She picked up her wine and went into the living room. There were nineteen messages.

"My God," she said as Lipstick came into the room, "I've never seen so many. Somebody out there wants me."

"I think you'll find they're mine," Lipstick said, shoving her hair extensions into a scrunchie. "I hope you don't mind, but I had my calls forwarded. It'll be clients. I always tell them in case of an emergency—you know, a sudden bikini line crisis—to try me at home. I'll listen to them in a sec."

"Right," Rebecca said sweetly, giving no hint that she was a bit hacked off at Lipstick clogging up her answer machine without asking if it was OK.

Lipstick began looking round the room. "I can see you're almost there," she said, surveying Rebecca's monument to minimalism. This was considerably less minimal than it had been a few hours ago, on account of Lipstick's tanning bed taking up nearly half the room. "All you're short of really is a few knickknacky things. Some bits to make it more homey. An arrangement of silk flowers on the mantelpiece, maybe. Or what about a pine Welsh dresser full of novelty teapots. I love those."

Rebecca smiled and said she'd think about it.

Eventually, Lipstick's eyes alighted on *Woman Wanking*. Rebecca watched her as she stood considering the painting. She kept craning her neck this way and that, as if any second—once her head reached the apposite angle—the penny would drop and she'd get it.

"Well, it's different. I'll give it that. Wouldn't you have preferred a nice landscape? Or some framed photographs?"

Apparently she was planning to have this photographer in Friern Barnet do a studio portrait of her and Stan.

"He's got all these different costumes and backdrops to choose from. At the moment I'm torn between 'On Safari' and 'Victorian Tourists in the Fjords.'"

They spent the rest of the evening looking at Harrison's christening photos.

This was followed by two albums of pictures of him when he was page boy (blue velvet breeches, white silk shirt, lace collar) at his doggy best friend's wedding. After an hour or so, Rebecca said she hoped Lipstick didn't mind but she was knackered and had to crash.

She arrived at the office the next morning and immediately went in search of Lucretia. She knew she was going to have an almighty job convincing her to let her start investigating the Mer de Rêves story because the company was one of the paper's main advertisers, but she was determined to try.

She'd spent most of the drive working on her pitch. In order to sell the idea to Lucretia, it had to contain the two ingredients she considered staples for a magazine aimed at women: glamour and intense personal suffering.

"Lucretia," she heard herself saying at one point, "I've found this great story—it's sort of Oskar Schindler meets Pussy Galore." God, no. That wouldn't work. She couldn't possibly say "Pussy Galore" to Lucretia. The woman would have a baby.

Lucretia's office was empty. Snow was nowhere to be seen either. She went back to her desk to find Max waiting for her with a present of cappuccino and an apricot Danish.

"Oh, Max, that is so sweet. Thank you."

"I just wanted to say," he whispered, brushing his fingers against her cheek, "you know, how much I enjoyed the other night."

"Me, too," she said, holding his hand against her skin for a moment. Then she reached up and kissed him quickly on the lips.

"Listen," she said afterward, "you don't know where Lucretia is, do you?"

"Ah, you obviously haven't heard?"

"Heard what?"

"About Lucretia's call from the producers of *Watching You, Watching Me.*"

"What?" Rebecca laughed. "That new *Big Brother* rip-off?"

"Yeah, apparently they're kicking off with a celebrity edition. Shooting starts tomorrow. But last night Anne Robinson went down with some bug and they asked Lucretia to step in. She said yes, only if she could bring Snow."

"Hmm, to do all her chores while she sits around refurbishing herself all bloody day, presumably."

She asked him who had taken over as she needed to get the go-ahead for the Mer de Rêves story. He told her Charlie Holland, who normally edited only the main newspaper, was filling in.

"Which is brilliant news," Max said. "There's no way Charlie would let a bit of advertising revenue get in the way of a good story."

He kissed her and gave her bum a quick squeeze. "How's about lunch?"

She nodded. They arranged to meet in the lobby at one.

Max was right. Charlie Holland, DFC—who had seen action in the former British colony of Aden in the sixties before going to Oxford and eschewing the military for Marxism—leaped at the Mer de Rêves story.

"OK," he barked, picking up a rubber band from his desk. "So, what's your MO?"

"MO?"

He rolled his eyes and began stretching the rubber band.

"Your modus operandi. Your game plan."

Champion of the poll tax rioters he may have been, but Charlie had never quite managed to shake off the gung-ho fighter pilot thing.

Rebecca cleared her throat nervously. At no time had he asked her to sit down. She felt like she was up before the wing commander for going AWOL.

She told him she was planning to take up Mer de Rêves's offer of an interview with Coco Dubonnet.

"The PR wants me to do it at her place in the country, but I'm hoping I can convince her to let me come to the company's offices in Paris. My plan is to convince Coco to let me see the lab where they make this cream and somehow get hold of a sample for analysis."

He let go of the rubber band. It snapped back into shape. "OK. Carry on," he said, "but make sure you keep me briefed at every stage."

She nodded.

"And, Rebecca," he said, "on no account fuck this up. We don't want you splattered against the wall in some St. Valentine's Day mascara."

He cracked a smile. She only just managed to resist saluting.

As Max had a telephone interview with one of his French contacts arranged for two o'clock, they decided to grab a quick bite at Nick's, the Greek place a couple of blocks away.

As soon as they sat down, Max handed her the Marks and Spencer bag he'd been carrying. "Another little thank-you for the other night," he said.

She opened the bag. Inside were four videocassettes.

"Copies of my top *Seinfeld* episodes," he smiled. "Sorry I didn't have time to wrap them."

"Omigod. Max, you shouldn't. This is fantastic. Must have taken you ages. Thank you so much."

She began reading the sticky labels on the cassettes. "Ooh, it's got 'The Ex-Girlfriend.' The one where Kramer becomes obsessed with cantaloupe. I love that one. You are kind."

"Next time you watch it, you can think of me."

"Oh, I will," she grinned. Then she reached across and kissed him.

They both ordered the stuffed red peppers. Rebecca told him about Lipstick moving in and how she was worried that she might be planning to do the dirty on Stan. "Plus she is driving me mad. For a start she's so bloomin' upbeat and cheerful all the time. It's like living with an escapee from the *Brady Bunch*. If this is all an act, it's bloody good." She told him about Harrison and the novelty teapots.

Max laughed and said at least it was only for a few weeks.

When they'd finished eating, Max told her how gorgeous she looked and how he really fancied her. He beckoned her toward him. She leaned across the table.

"OK, he whispered, "slide down in your seat."

"Why? What for?"

"Just do as I say." He grinned.

"But I don't get it."

"Just do it."

She did it. "OK," she said, "what now?"

He mouthed at her to open her legs.

"What?" She immediately sat back up again.

"Come on. Open them."

"Max, we're in a public place. Behave."

She watched him lean down and take off his shoe, then his sock. His bare foot was forcing her knees apart. Giggling, she slapped his wrist with her hand, but he carried on pushing.

The place was packed. She looked around to see if anybody was watching. They weren't. And they wouldn't see a lot if they were. The table was covered in a long white cloth.

Hiding her giggles with her hand, she slid back down again and did as he asked.

"I hope you've cut your toenails," she said.

He grinned and assured her he had.

A moment later it was all she could do to stop rolling her head in sheer delight.

"Aah. Oh, my God," she whispered.

She wasn't even vaguely aware of somebody coming toward the table.

"Ees everything all right for you?"

It was Nick, the restaurant owner, but since Rebecca was way past the point of no return orgasmwise, she didn't care.

"Yes, great," Max said to Nick.

"Aah, ummm."

Nick frowned.

"The lady. She's OK? She look a beet flushed maybe?"

Rebecca's head was now in her hands as she tried to prevent herself making eye contact with Nick.

"No," Max said, "she's fine."

"Tell you what, I got some freshly baked baklava. You want to try some? Look, eet's over there on the counter. Just look at all that honey just oozing out. Mees, you sure you all right?"

"Oooh. That's it. Yeah, there. Just there. Keep it there. Just like that."

"We'll just have the bill, please," Max said.

"No baklava?"

"No baklava."

"What about some halva? I got some wonderful chocolate halva."

"Nope. No halva. Just the bill."

Just then Nick's wife started calling him. "Neek, are you coming?"

"Yes," he said irritably, "I'm coming. I'm coming." He started to walk away.

"Oh, God! Oh, God, me too!" Rebecca cried.

Nick swung round.

"It's OK," Max said, "I think maybe the stuffed peppers disagreed with her."

Rebecca spent most of the journey home on the phone to Jess telling her about Max toe-fucking her. Afterward she wished she hadn't.

"Great," Jess had said, "you're getting toe-fucked while I have to make do wanking with an electric toothbrush and end up flossing with my pubes."

Then, when Rebecca asked her how the surrendered wife thing was coming along, Jess said fine, except Ed had just come home with one of those leather, fleece-lined airman's hats with earflaps and booked them a weaving activity holiday in the Shetlands.

Rebecca commiserated and said if the no sex thing carried on much longer she'd go back to that sex shop in Covent Garden and buy Jess a Vibroclit.

The first thing Rebecca saw when she walked into the living room was the treadmill. Lipstick was standing next to it wearing a Day-Glo pink silk kimono and matching face pack. On it, scampering for all he was worth in gray tracksuit bottoms and a sweatband round his head, was Harrison. *Star Trek* was on in the background.

"Things are getting so busy at the salon, plus I've got all the workmen to check on at my flat, that I just haven't got time to take him walkies. So I ordered the treadmill and I've put a dirt tray out on the balcony. Hope you don't mind."

Rebecca's stomach turned. Her mind went back to Jess and the cat turd. "Well, to be quite honest, actually I do . . ."

But Lipstick wasn't listening. Some alien had just bought it on *Star Trek.* "You know," Lipstick said, "I think it's so lucky the ray gun was called the ray gun. I mean the gary gun just wouldn't be the same, would it?"

Rebecca said she had a couple of phone calls to make.

"Fine," Lipstick said. "Dinner'll be ready in twenty minutes. I've made a shepherd's pie."

Rebecca's face lit up. She suddenly felt guilty about getting worked up over the dirt tray. "Wow. You didn't need to go to all that trouble."

"Oh, it was nothing. Except you didn't have any mince. By the time I got to the butcher's it was nearly six and he was closed. So I improvised with baked beans and cheese on top. Hope that's OK. My mum used to do it all the time when we were kids, if she'd forgotten to go shopping."

"Yummy," Rebecca said. "Can't wait."

She went into the bedroom and dialed Mimi Frascatti, the Mer de Rêves PR. She'd been in a meeting all afternoon and was due out around now. She picked up immediately.

Rebecca told her the *Vanguard* had been having second thoughts about her offer of an interview with Coco Dubonnet.

"Oh, really?" Mimi said, her tone decidedly cool, which Rebecca supposed was understandable bearing in mind the way she'd given her the bums a couple of days ago. "Well, I'm afraid you're too late. Coco's in Mustique until the end of the month. She's back in Paris for two days."

"Ah, well perhaps I could see her then?"

"Sorry, she has meetings the entire time."

"I wouldn't want long with her," Rebecca said, going into her very best sucking-up mode, "twenty minutes tops." Pause for effect. "The editor would make it the cover story."

"No can do, I'm afraid. She's going to be tied up both days. Then she's off skiing in Morocco. She won't be back for at least another six weeks."

Rebecca put down the phone. "Bugger."

Then she thought for a moment. No, not bugger. She would try the Paris press office. She looked at her watch. It was past six. They would have left for the day. She'd try them in the morning. Maybe they would be more accommodating.

She was just about to ring Max to tell him she'd managed to get tickets for *Art*, which he'd been desperate to see, when he rang. "Rebecca, do you know anything about spots?"

"A bit Doris Day, I always think. Mind you, I think you could just about carry off polka-dot pedal pushers."

"Very funny. No, I mean real spots."

"What, as in zits?"

"No, as in disease. I'm covered in them. They look like tiny blisters and they itch. I can't stop scratching. And I've got a temperature."

"I'll be there in ten minutes."

She couldn't get over how cute and childishly pathetic he looked in the spots.

The emergency doctor said it was chicken pox and that he needed to rest, take plenty of fluids and keep the spots covered in calamine. Rebecca went straight out to Boots and came back with four bottles. "I remember getting through stacks of this stuff when I had chicken pox as a kid."

She made him take all his clothes off and spent ages dabbing him. Of course she spent longer dabbing certain bits of him than others. When she'd finished, she made him a mug of TheraFlu to bring his temperature down. Then, fully clothed, she climbed into bed with him. Soon they were snuggling under the duvet, him telling her a whole string of daft schoolboy jokes. Where he was finding the energy to do this, she had no idea. Either his temperature was making him delirious or the TheraFlu had kicked in and he was feeling better. She decided it was probably the TheraFlu.

"OK, what's yellow and swings from cake to cake?"

She was already giggling.

"I don't know. What is yellow and swings from cake to cake?"

"Tarzipan!"

She couldn't help shrieking with laughter. "Max Stoddart," she declared between snorts, "you may be at death's door, but you still make me laugh more than anybody else I've ever met."

He propped himself up on his elbow and kissed her.

"Do you want me to stay, just to keep an eye on you?" she said. Her offer wasn't entirely altruistic. She would have done almost anything to avoid Lipstick's baked bean shepherd's pie.

He thanked her but said he just wanted to sleep and would prefer to sweat it out on his own.

When she got back the lights were off. Lipstick must have gone to bed. She took off her coat and headed for the kitchen, contemplating Lipstick's shepherd's pie. How mean would it be to throw it away and pretend she'd eaten it? She opened the door. Uuurgh. Bloody Harrison was sitting on the counter. She began making frantic shooing motions.

"Oi, gerroff you filthy …"

As he jumped down she saw the Pyrex oven dish and realized what he'd been doing. Lipstick had left her the remainder of the shepherd's pie to heat up in the microwave, but Harrison—probably suffering from an attack of the late-night munchies—had gotten there first.

"Oh, who's a good boy, then?" Rebecca said, her face lighting up. "Who is a good boy? You know, Harrison, if you play your cards right I can see the two of us starting to get on."

The ensuing head pat, although faltering, wasn't entirely without affection.

9

As she climbed the stairs to Max's flat carrying the bowl of frozen chicken soup (it was either freeze it or have it slop all over the car seat en route), Rebecca could hardly believe what she was doing.

As far as she was concerned, it was OK for a bloke to cook for a woman early on in their relationship, because that was sexy and new mannish (assuming his repertoire was limited to guy things like curry—or in Max's case chili con Quorni. There was no way she could shag a bloke with a goatee who filed his herbs alphabetically and spent the evening fiddling with his ravioli.). On the other hand, a woman cooking for a man when they hadn't known each other very long sent out all the wrong messages. It screamed desperation.

God, why didn't she just go the whole hog and take him to Ikea to look at shelving systems?

It had been Jess's idea to make Max chicken soup. Rebecca was convinced the suggestion wasn't unrelated to her friend's still hanging on in there with the surrendered wife thing (despite Ed having come home the night before with a green corduroy trench coat). Naturally Rebecca had said all the stuff about desperation and Ikea shelving systems, but Jess insisted that taking Max Factor chicken soup when he was ill was an affectionate, caring gesture that would ensure he fell in love with her there and then and had nothing whatsoever to do with desperation.

Rebecca found herself bouncing Jess's theory off Lipstick. Even though she was struggling to work out how a person could adore a pooch quite the way Lipstick adored Harrison, Rebecca was continuing to warm to her. So much so that she'd decided that maybe having the heavy conversation about what happened at school wasn't really necessary. Her personality appeared to have done a complete about-face since school. What was the point of upsetting her? On top of that Stan had phoned the night before to see how the two of them were getting on and he'd told her how much he loved Bernadette.

"I know she's a bit over the top," he said, "and a bit tactless, maybe, but apart from your mother—and you of course—Bernadette is the sweetest, most gentle woman I've ever met. And don't underestimate her. She's far brighter than you think."

Lipstick said she'd never had a problem cooking for boyfriends. She'd cooked for Stan on their second date and it certainly hadn't scared him off. Apparently he'd particularly enjoyed her apricot fool.

"And if you can't find apricots—"

"Don't tell me," Rebecca cut across her, "herring works just as well."

"Herring?" Lipstick screwed up her face. "Don't be daft. I was going to say peaches."

Rose had sent Rebecca to Geoff's Kosher Meats in Hendon for

the chicken. "And make sure you ask for a boiling fowl. You don't want a roaster. You don't get the flavor with a roaster."

When she got home she followed Rose's cooking instructions to the letter. She even remembered to leave the skins on the onions "to give it color."

Rose didn't stop going on about how happy it made her to see Rebecca starting to take an interest in her culture.

"Tell you what," she'd said, "next I'll teach you to do klops."

Rebecca's knowledge of kosher cookery being sketchy at best, on account of Judy having been not so much a Jewish mother as a Jew-ish mother, she assumed this was either a Dutch folk dance or some form of bowel disorder.

Rebecca had almost reached the top of the stairs when she saw Max's front door open and a woman come out. She instantly clocked the gleaming shoulder-length black curls, the treacle eyes and full crimson-stained lips that would never require "Lip Plump for Lady Woman."

Rebecca suddenly became acutely aware of her eyebrows. Since Lipstick's comments these had now—in her mind at least— assumed Noel Gallagher proportions.

Rebecca knew she recognized the woman, but it took her a moment or two to place her. Then she got it. Lorna Findlay. She presented *Tonight,* the heavyweight, up-its-own-arse, late-night news program on Channel 6. Five nights a week, the formidably brainy Findlay, whose interviewing skills were such that she made Peter Jennings look like Barney Rubble, threw intellectual googlies at government ministers, reducing them to stammering, sweating— and on one memorable occasion with Anne Widdecombe— weeping wrecks.

Lorna turned to shout, "'Bye, wish you better." Then she closed the door and began walking briskly toward the stairs. The two women passed on the landing, Lorna shooting Rebecca a brief, rather standoffish smile.

Although Max was up and dressed and pretty much on the mend, he was still covered in pox.

He couldn't get over her having made him chicken soup. "You know, Rebecca," he said, hugging her to him, "that is possibly the most thoughtful thing anyone has ever done for me."

"Really?"

"Really." (OK, she owed Jess one.)

He smiled at her with his pathetic scabby face. Soon they were kissing. Rebecca was vaguely aware of his hand disappearing down inside his joggers and moving briskly up and down. She pulled away, half frowning, half laughing.

"Don't mind me," she said. "I mean if you'd rather be alone."

"Oh, God, I'm sorry," he said, his hand still going at it like mad, "but I've got this really humongous pock on my right ball. The itching's driving me insane."

"So," she said, doing her best to sound like she didn't care, "what was Lorna Findlay doing here?" She turned to face the kitchen counter and began taking the plastic wrap off the soup bowl.

"Oh, you saw her?"

"We passed on the landing."

By now she was chipping away at the frozen chicken soup with a bread knife. Every so often she would spoon up a few meager ice shavings and drop them into a saucepan.

"Lorna and I are working on the nuclear story together. The idea is I'll write the piece for the *Vanguard,* she'll front the documentary....Rebecca, you're being incredibly violent with that knife."

"I am?" she said. "I hadn't noticed." There was no way she was going to admit she was jealous of Lorna Findlay.

He asked her if she was OK.

She explained about her conversation with Mimi Frascatti. "Tried the Paris office this morning. Still no joy. I've got to come up with some way of getting into the Mer de Rêves HQ."

He kissed her again and said he was sure she'd work something out.

When he saw she wasn't making much headway with the chicken soup he suggested leaving it to thaw and that he'd have it for supper.

Max made tea, which they took into the living room. They sat on the hearth rug, him stretched out, his back against an armchair, her with her knees drawn up under her chin. As they sipped their tea they talked about nothing in particular—family stuff, places they'd been, places they wanted to go, books, films.

"So," Max said, "if you had to come back as an animal, what would you choose?"

She said a Siamese cat. "What about you?"

"Aardvark," he announced.

"Why on earth would you want to come back as an aardvark?"

"Easy. I'd be first in the jungle telephone directory."

There were two things they disagreed on. The first was global warming. Max said there was quite a lot of reputable scientific evidence to support the theory it was all rubbish. The second was how to eat a Kit Kat. Rebecca was a firm believer in splitting the foil carefully down the middle with the fingernail of her right thumb and then slowly and meticulously biting off the chocolate to reveal the wafer. Max simply ripped off the packaging and demolished the entire thing in a couple of mouthfuls. She said he was missing out on the "sensuality of the Kit Kat experience." He accused her of being far too la-di-da. Of course the debate came to good-natured blows. He hit her with a cushion. She bashed him back, making him spill tea on the hearth. As she took a tissue out of her pocket to help wipe it up, he took hold of her arm and drew her toward him, holding her gaze in his the entire time. He stroked her face and pushed her gently down onto the rug. That kiss, as they lay stretched out in front of the fire, was the most sublime Rebecca had ever known.

He was trailing a finger over her cheek, when she felt a hard sharp object under her head. She reached back and picked it up. It was a CD cover. A moment later she was roaring with laughter.

"I may be too la-di-da by half," she said, "but at least I have slightly more adult taste in music than you. *Shaggy*? Max, how old are you?"

"Very funny," he said, taking it from her and tossing it onto the sofa. "It's not mine, though. Belongs to Amy, my goddaughter. She was round at the weekend."

"Oh, right—so you two are pretty close, then?"

"Yeah. Pretty close," he said, planting a tiny kiss on the end of Rebecca's nose. "Listen, you know what I fancy?"

"I think I can guess."

He smiled. "OK, we could do that," he said, "but what I feel like even more right now is some fresh air. I haven't been out for days. How's about we go for a walk in Highgate Woods before it gets dark?"

"Great," she said. They were about to go and put their coats on when she noticed *The Little Book of Hugs* lying on the kitchen table.

"Not quite your style," she said, picking it up.

"Lorna got it for me as a daft get-well present."

"Regular Florence Nightingale," she said, forcing a smile.

He was in the hall by now and didn't see her casually slide *The Little Book of Hugs* along the counter. Nor did he see it fall off the counter and into the pedal bin, which she'd just happened to open.

* * *

It was bitter out. He put his arm round her. She snuggled up to his shoulder. As they headed off down the main road, Rebecca realized this was the most relaxed and at ease she'd felt in ages.

"So, how's the French story going?" she asked.

He said it was tough, but moving ahead pretty well. She was squeezing his arm and telling him that with a story like that, he could easily win the Journalist of the Year award, when she noticed a tall loping figure in the distance, coming out of a coffee shop. She stopped.

"What?" Max said.

"I think there's somebody I recognize."

She carried on peering down the street. It was definitely him. Only he looked completely different. The wiry ginger hair had been cut into a fashionable crop and although he was still quite a way off she could see he was wearing a rather cool black leather jacket.

"Shit. Max, quick, cross the road."

He looked at her, confused. "Why?"

" 'Cause I don't want him to see me."

"Who?"

"Warren." She tugged at his arm. "Come on."

"Oh, what, the *Starlight Express* guy? Why don't you just go up and say hi?"

"You know why," she hissed. "I told you on the phone the other night. I'm meant to be in bloody Greenland with the Inuit."

"Ah."

She dragged him to the edge of the pavement. The traffic was fast flowing and heavy. Try as they might, they couldn't get across the road.

"OK, hide behind this tree until he's gone."

Looking distinctly bemused, Max went along with it. They stood there, he shaking his head and telling her she should go and talk to him and come clean about her deception or say it was a joke, and she hissing, "Has he gone yet? Has he gone yet?"

Max poked his head out from round the tree and said he couldn't see him. Rebecca decided he'd probably gone by.

"OK, let's go," she said.

As they crept out, Rebecca virtually collided with Warren.

"Hello, Rebecca," he said. On closer inspection the jacket was Prada. They'd featured it in last week's *Vanguard* mag. Overnight, he'd gone from geek geek to chic geek. "I thought it was you. So, how was Greenland?"

"Oh, you know. Cold."

"And the Inuit?" She was picking up definite hostility.

"They're fine. Send their regards."

She saw him looking at Max.

"Oh, sorry, I should have introduced you. Warren, Max. Max, Warren."

The two men exchanged nods.

Rebecca cleared her throat and turned back to Warren. "Max is my...er...my...chiropodist. Yep. Best chiropodist in London. Bunions, corns, verrucas, athlete's foot—Max is your man. Do you get verrucas, Warren?"

"Actually, no."

"Lucky you."

Max nudged her. A woman had joined them and was looping her arm through Warren's. She was tall, over six foot and beautiful. Correction. Lorna Findlay was beautiful. The creature standing in front of them was in a different class. She was utterly, gobsmackingly gorgeous. Rebecca stood there taking in her gazellelike legs, her waist-length blonde hair, her turquoise eyes, the wondrously applied Nefertiti liner.

"This is Fabergé," Warren announced. "She models for Valentino."

So she was clearly responsible for Warren's makeover.

"Sorry to have been ages, babe," she said, kissing his cheek, "the news agent didn't have any change." She popped a piece of gum into her mouth. Then she turned to Rebecca and Max.

"Hi," she simpered, giving them a tiny wave. Rebecca couldn't help noticing it was a few seconds before Max stopped gawping at Fabergé and returned the greeting.

"So," Rebecca said, once she'd finally retrieved her jaw from the floor, "how did you guys meet?"

"Oh," Fabergé began, between chews, "I went into the town hall planning department to complain about the bypass they were proposing and Warren just happened to be there. He came flying to my aid and sorted the whole thing out. Didn't you, babe?"

Another kiss. Babe blushed.

"Come on, we have to go," she said to him, "or we'll be late for tea." She turned to Rebecca. "I'm taking Warren home to meet my parents. They're getting on a bit. Hate to be kept waiting."

The four said their good-byes.

"OK," Rebecca said when Warren and Fabergé were out of earshot. "Do you mind telling me how in the name of buggery he managed to pull her?"

Max shrugged. "Maybe she suffers from low self-esteem?"

"Yeah, right. Good one."

"Then it has to be the Woody Allen thing. I guess some women just can't resist those geeky Jewish blokes."

"S'pose," Rebecca said. "But can you believe the cheek of the man, messing around like that the moment my back's turned?"

When they got back from the park, Max tried to get her into bed, but she said she had to go home and get changed for Ed's surprise party.

"You sure you don't want to pop in—just for an hour or two? Jess is dying to meet you."

But his hand was already back down inside his trousers.

"OK, perhaps not," she said.

* * *

On the way home she phoned Jess, ostensibly to ask her if there was anything she'd forgotten for the party and wanted picking up. After Jess had thanked her and said everything was just about under control, she brought up the subject of Lorna. Jess said she didn't have much time to talk because she was up to her eyes in canapés, but made it perfectly clear that if Rebecca got jealous of every beautiful woman Max Factor came into contact with, their relationship was destined for disaster.

"You know we're far too hard on beautiful women—always assuming they're preying on our men. Lorna's probably lovely and perfectly harmless. I mean, look at Lipstick. I was right about her, wasn't I?"

She got home just after five. When she went into the living room, Lipstick was standing at the window on a stepladder. Her bum was stuffed into crimson hipsters with gold studs running down the outside leg. Over these she was wearing a shiny mock snakeskin crop top. Bulging out between the two was her considerable midriff. She was hanging blinds. Austrian ones. In cream and olive-green Regency stripes. With a frill at the bottom.

"Ta-dah!" she proclaimed with a flourish.

Rebecca blinked.

"What do you think? Aren't they brilliant? Ready-mades from Laura Ashley. You attach them with Velcro. So when you want to wash them, all you do is pull them off...like so. I thought they were just what you needed. They give the room a much softer, feminine feel, don't you think? And look, I managed to find the cushions to match."

Rebecca looked at the striped cushions sitting on her black

leather sofa. Then she swallowed. By now the color had completely drained from her face. "Lipstick, this is very kind, but…"

"Oh, you don't have to thank me," she said, getting down from the ladder. "I just wanted to get you something to say how much I appreciate you taking me in like this. I don't know what I'd have done without you."

Just then the phone rang. Rebecca reached to pick it up, but Lipstick had gotten there first.

"Bound to be a client," she said, pressing the green button. She nodded to indicate she'd been right.

Rebecca decided the only way she was going to calm down was with a glass of wine and a hot bath.

She went into the bedroom to get undressed. On the dressing table stood a huge turquoise silk flower arrangement thing. On the bed, Harrison, dressed in khaki cargo pants and a T-shirt that said "Doggy Style," was chewing on a dried pig's ear and drooling over the duvet.

"She has to go," Rebecca said, knocking back her second Shiraz. "I know my dad loves her, but she just has to go. She's completely taking over. When the phone goes it's only ever for her. And you should see what she's done to the place. She's talking about getting somebody in to paint a mural in my bedroom. At the moment she's thinking frolicking nymphs and satyrs. God, Jess, the place is getting so camp I feel like I'm flat-sharing with the entire cast of *La Cage aux Folles.*"

Jess laughed and told her to calm down. "Look, it's only for another couple of weeks. As soon as she moves out, take the blinds down."

"But what do I do when she and Dad come to visit? I can't

keep hanging them back up. And what if they drop in unannounced?"

"Then you say you got burgled by this bunch of gays who just went for the extra-virgin olive oil and your soft furnishings."

Rebecca managed a smile. They were sitting at Shazzer's, the wine bar round the corner from Jess's, waiting for the rest of the party guests. The idea was they'd have a quick glass of bubbly there before heading back to Jess's to wait for Ed to get home from work.

The people who'd arrived so far were hacks mainly, most of whom Rebecca knew. Then there were some couples Ed and Jess had met at their National Childbirth Trust prenatal classes, and four or five of Ed's university mates.

"Oh, my God," Rebecca said, noticing a familiar and distinctly unwelcome face, "I cannot believe you've invited that Guy Debonnaire creep. He's always hitting on me. He actually tongued my ear at the Mer de Rêves do."

Jess pulled a face. "I know, he hits on everybody. But I didn't invite him. Somebody from the Sunday *Trib* must have brought him."

Rebecca said she was going to disappear to the loo before he came over and started tweaking her nipples. She stood up and headed for the ladies' room, past the members of the NCT brigade who were deep in conversation about the state of their postpartum perineums and loft conversions.

The moment she came out she walked straight into Guy, who was drunk as usual.

"Hi, Becks."

"Hi, Guy," she said wearily.

He started nuzzling her. He stank of booze. She pushed him off.

"Oh, don't be like that. You wanna come back to my place? I've got an electric blanket."

"Tell you what, Guy, how's about you come back to mine. I've got an electric chair."

He stood in front of her swaying and looking puzzled.

"Rebecca," a voice boomed from behind them.

It belonged to Lady Axminster. She looked distinctly flushed. She'd clearly had a few gins. Rebecca greeted her with a double kiss and introduced Guy.

"Good God," Lady Axminster gasped, "you're not Johnny Debonnaire's boy, are you?"

"The same, fair lady, the same." He took her ladyship's hand and slobbered over it. She looked as if she'd just been presented with a dog turd.

"Johnny courted me many moons ago, you know," she said, wiping her hand with a lace handkerchief. "Hope you don't take after him. Chap had the smallest winkle in Gloucestershire."

His crest may have fallen, but only for a moment. A second later he'd spotted Jess.

"Hey, Jess," he called out, "how's about ditching that husband of yours and coming back to my place for a Bacardi and grope?"

Thirty of them, including Guy, trooped back to Jess's house. By now Lady Axminster had sobered up (for which Jess was hugely grateful since her mother was due to pick Diggory up from Dolly's in a couple of hours and take him home with her).

When they got to the house the curtains were drawn, but there were chinks of light coming from the living room.

"Oh, my God," Jess wailed, "Ed's home early. He'll have seen all the food and drink laid out in the kitchen. And the balloons. And that huge 'Happy 40th' banner I got. This is a complete mess. Shit, what do we do?"

Rebecca told her not to panic. "Look, first, he may not have seen it. The front room's his study. Maybe he came straight in and decided to get on with some work. I reckon if he'd seen it, he'd have phoned you by now. Let's just go in as planned and surprise him."

Jess wasn't convinced, but agreed they had no option. She got out her key and silently turned the lock. The door squeaked open. Everybody flinched. Then, stifling giggles, people began piling in.

"Go on, then," Lady Axminster whispered to Jess, "open the door."

Jess hesitated for a second. Then she threw open the door that led to Ed's study. Thirty voices yelled, "Surprise!"

Which it certainly seemed to be for Ed.

His head shot round to face them, his face etched in terror. Jess screamed and slapped her hand to her mouth. Without saying a word Ed leaped off the sofa, where until that second he had been lying facedown, his pants and trousers round his ankles, on top of a plastic inflatable woman. Beside her was a pile of porno mags. Rebecca put her arm round Jess. Guy Debonnaire, who somehow had made it to the front and was standing with Rebecca, Jess and Lady Axminster, yelled:

"Oi, give us a go after you, mate."

There was a lot of nervous shuffling and coughing from the rest of the guests. A few people started giggling. Ed pulled up his pants and looked pleadingly at Jess. Then the people still standing in the hall, who hadn't seen what was going on, suddenly broke into "Happy Birthday." Rebecca yelled at them to stop.

Calmly and without saying anything, Jess went to Ed's desk, picked up his fountain pen and stabbed the doll with the nib. The air shot out in a loud hiss. The doll folded in on herself. Jess turned to look at Ed.

"How could you humiliate me like this?" she said softly, a single tear trailing down her cheek. "How could you?"

"Just come into the kitchen and talk. Let me explain. I didn't mean to..."

"We've been talking for weeks and this is where it's gotten us. I need to do some thinking. You can stay here for the time being. Diggory and I are moving in with Rebecca."

She then pushed through the crowd of guests and ran upstairs with Ed right behind her, begging her to listen to him.

While Rebecca stood there, trying to absorb the enormity of Jess's final statement, Guy Debonnaire was kneeling beside the shrinking inflatable woman, attempting to give her the kiss of life.

Hang on, where was I?" Lipstick, who was giving Jess a man-icure, stopped filing for a moment and attempted to gather her thoughts.

"Your grandad's funeral," Rebecca chipped in, without taking her eyes off the TV screen.

"Oh, right," Lipstick said. "So in the end it turned out to be really expensive. They had to bury him in a hired suit."

Jess burst out laughing and once again she and Lipstick were cackling like a pair of off-duty hookers in a Dickensian knocking shop. Rebecca, who was sprawled on the sofa engrossed in one of her *Seinfeld* tapes, turned toward them. "What? What's the joke?"

But they were laughing so hard neither of them could get the words out.

Rebecca smiled and went back to the TV. When Jess moved in five days ago she was tearful, angry and confused. The change in her was palpable and much of it was due to Lipstick. Al-though Rebecca had been there with hugs, late-night talks and encouragement, it was Lipstick who had seen the cheering up of Jess as some kind of mission. OK, maybe her campaign was a tad on the unrelenting side—what with her quoting endlessly from *You Can't Afford the Luxury of a Negative Thought,* repeatedly showing her all-time favorite videos and telling rambling family anecdotes, her point usually hovering way off in the distance like a German verb—but there was no doubt it had worked, at least on a superficial level. Deep down Jess was still pretty miserable.

"I married a perv," she'd said to Rebecca, as she sat breast-feeding Diggory late last night. "The Dig-Dig has a perv for a father. It'll scar him for life."

Rebecca had almost said, "Unlike having a mother who refers to him as the Dig-Dig," but didn't.

Instead, she made the point that thousands of blokes, even those in healthy relationships, kept secret stashes of soft porn. "Come on," she said gently, "you're an agony aunt, you know all this. You also know it's no reason to walk out. OK, thirty people caught him jerking off over Miss July. Desperately humiliating for both of you, I agree, but he didn't exactly plan it."

"I know. I know. That's not the issue anymore." She went silent for a minute. Finally she took a deep breath. "When I was getting ready to come to your place that night, I couldn't find a suitcase. Finally I saw one on top of the wardrobe. I pulled it down and opened it." She paused. "It was revolting, Becks, utterly revolting."

"What was?"

"I found this...this mask thing. Black leather. Covered in studs. I think Ed's into autoasphyxiation—you know when men starve themselves of oxygen in order to heighten their orgasm."

"Blimey," Rebecca said. She asked her if she had it.

"You must be joking. I could hardly bear to touch it. I left it where it was and found another case. You know, I'm starting to think maybe Ed's willy-nilly isn't my fault after all. I mean, perhaps

I don't really know him and all these years I've been married to some sick weirdo who's into all sorts of repulsive stuff. Either that or he's gay."

A single tear streaked Jess's face. Rebecca gave her another hug and gently wiped it away.

"You know," Lipstick tutted, "you've got some right old cuticle buildup here. When was the last time you had a manicure?"

Jess took another sip of wine (since she was breast-feeding, she was limiting herself to one glass, which she did her best to make last all evening).

"Never had one," she said.

Lipstick brought a bowl of warm water onto the sofa arm and placed Jess's hand in it. "What?" she said. "Don't you even file your nails?"

"Nah, I just bite them off and throw them away."

The two of them roared. Then Lipstick suggested they put on another of the videos she'd brought with her. So far they'd been subjected to *Erin Brockovich* ("my all-time heroine after Gloria Gaynor"), Harrison's christening and the "where-are-they-now?" documentary about the children from *The Sound of Music*. "Maybe a bit later," Rebecca heard Jess say. She suspected Jess was starting to get just the teensiest bit fed up with Lipstick's videos.

Rebecca hadn't expected Jess and Lipstick to hit it off. Although she'd deny it with her dying breath, Jess could be a snob when she chose. (Rebecca had lost count of how many times she'd heard her refer to Andrew and Fergie as the Argos Royals.) Now that they were mates, she couldn't have been more pleased, especially since Lipstick was happy to spend hours entertaining Diggory and having endless heavy conversations about Ed, which took some of the pressure off Rebecca.

The only thing getting her down was the clutter and mess everywhere.

Even though they'd moved Harrison's treadmill into the hall, the living room still contained (chintz notwithstanding) Lipstick's tanning bed, Diggory's travel cot (in which he was now tucked up and sleeping soundly), a camp bed and half of the Brent Cross Early Learning Centre.

Then there was all Jess's feeding detritus lying around: the breast pads, the breast pump, the smelly muslins.

She didn't have the heart to say anything to Jess because she didn't want to upset her. Instead, she did her best to keep on top of the mess, but it was a losing battle. Lipstick tried to do her bit, but it didn't amount to much since she was leaving for the Talon Salon at the crack of dawn and wasn't getting back until well after seven.

"I've got this special twofer deal going," she explained. "Clients come in for a manicure and I throw in a special doggy claw trim and paint job. The phone just hasn't stopped ringing."

On top of all this, Rebecca was pining for Max. Although they were speaking on the phone every night, she hadn't seen him for days—not even at work, since he wasn't due back until next week. He kept asking her to come round after work, but even though Lipstick was on hand, she felt bad about leaving Jess. Ed was phoning her several times a day, desperate to talk, but she was steadfastly refusing to take his calls, maintaining she was still too angry.

So desperate was he to make contact that late one night he'd stood for half an hour in icy, teeming rain, shouting up to her and begging her to let him explain. In the end Rebecca had taken pity on him and had gone downstairs in her dressing gown carrying two mugs of cocoa, and she and a soggy, pathetic-looking Ed had sat on the floor in the lobby having this awkward conversation about the wanking episode.

He explained he'd been feeling miserable because Jess wasn't there when he got home and he assumed she'd decided they weren't going to celebrate his birthday. That day he'd also been out and bought a whole load of porn mags.

"I…you know, thought they might help with my problem."

Rebecca gave him a sympathetic nod.

"Then the bloke in the shop brought out the doll. Everybody knows those things are a joke, but he said the plastic really turns some men on. So I thought I'd give it a go. I got home, saw there was nobody about and the rest you know."

"So did you?…I mean were you able…?"

"Not a dickybird." He smiled a weak smile.

"Ed? You're not…I mean, has it occurred to you that maybe you might possibly be…you see, Jess thinks…"

"I'm gay?"

She colored up and gave a weak nod.

"Well, I'm not."

"Brilliant," she said, giving a nervous laugh. Then quickly: "Not that it would have mattered a hoot to me if you had been gay. Or to Jess, for that matter. Well, of course it would have mattered to her initially, 'cause it would have meant the two of you splitting up, but I'm sure she'd have come round eventually."

They sat in silence for a few moments.

"And…" Rebecca cleared her throat and coughed. "…the, er…the mask thingummy Jess found. What should I say that was?"

"Mask thingumy?"

"Um. Bit pervy, she said. Found it in a suitcase."

"Pervy? Becks, I haven't the foggiest what you're on about. All I bought was the doll. I swear I don't own anything remotely mask-like."

She was pretty sure he wasn't lying, but she decided not to push it. This was something Jess was going to have to sort out with him herself.

She put her arm round him and said that at least nobody had gone to *Private Eye* with the story.

"Thank God," he said. "I'd have survived, but being an agony aunt and all that, it wouldn't have done Jess's career much good."

Once they'd finished their cocoa, he made her promise to tell Jess why he'd bought the doll and the porn and even then he hadn't been able to get it up. He also wanted her to know he was desperately sorry for hurting and humiliating her and that he loved her desperately and wanted her back.

But when Rebecca tried speaking to Jess, she said it was all crap and lies, although she chose to believe the bit about him not being gay.

"Of course he could get it up with the magazines. And he lied about the mask. Why? Because he's scared shitless I'll divorce him and he'll never see the Digwig again."

"I know," Lipstick said, spraying Jess's nails with Quick Dry, "why don't I make us some more deep-fried Fritos?"

It was like talking to a brick wall, trying to explain to Lipstick that deep-frying a Frito was like waxing a candle. Having said that, they'd had them every night that week and everybody had to admit they tasted sublime.

"Oh, not more Fritos," Jess moaned, "they must have a zillion calories in them."

"Doesn't matter," Lipstick shot back, "it's a waning moon."

"Come again?" Rebecca said.

"OK, I'm reading this truly amazing book about living your life according to the lunar cycles and it says quite clearly that you can't get fat on a waning moon."

Rebecca shook her head in disbelief, but Jess—who had now allowed herself a couple of glasses of wine—declared that was good enough for her and commanded Lipstick to wheel on the Fritos.

"You know," Jess said after Lipstick had disappeared into the kitchen, "I really like her. And have you seen how wonderful she is with the Digalig? Talk about a natural. She calms him down in an instant with that massage she does. And yesterday she did an entire science lesson with him."

Rebecca made the point that Lipstick was showing him leaflets on laser hair removal. Jess said, so what were lasers if they weren't science—Golden Grahams? Then she changed the subject and asked Rebecca if she'd gotten her interview with Coco Dubonnet yet. Rebecca sat up, switched off the *Seinfeld* vid and explained.

"But there must be some way of getting in there," Jess said.

"Where?" Lipstick asked, coming back into the room. She put the bowl of Fritos and saucer of mayonnaise down on the floor.

Rebecca picked up a Frito and dipped it in the mayo. "Oh, it's just some story I'm working on."

"What sort of story?"

Rebecca couldn't really be bothered to tell it all over again, but decided it would be rude not to, since Lipstick had taken an interest. She took another handful and started to tell her about the Mer de Rêves party, Wendy and the wrinkle cream and how she'd gotten the sack.

"Come on, there has to be some mistake," Lipstick said. "MdR products are wonderful. They don't come any better. I've used them on clients for years. Why would such a successful company put its reputation at risk like this?"

"Greed," Rebecca said simply. "This new cream could be worth billions to them."

Lipstick sat shaking her head. She was clearly finding Rebecca's revelations hard to take in.

"What I need to do is get into the Mer de Rêves Paris office and steal a sample of the cream for analysis."

"God," Lipstick said, munching, "how you gonna do that?"

"Dunno." Rebecca shrugged. "I'm still working on it."

"Just shows you can't trust anybody in this world," Lipstick said. "Maybe I should give up my prize money."

"What prize money?" Jess asked.

"My MdR prize money. I sold two hundred and fifty Mer de Rêves facials this year, more than anybody else in the country. They've just named the Face Place and Talon Salon their South East Region Outlet of the Year. I was due to go to Paris in a couple of weeks to pick up my five-hundred-pound prize money. I'm not sure I'll bother now."

Rebecca leaned forward on the sofa. "Hang on. Hang on," she said, running her fingers through her hair. "Let me get this straight. You're going to Paris? To the MdR office?"

Lipstick nodded. Rebecca and Jess watched as with painful slowness, the penny dropped inside Lipstick's head.

"Oooh, ooh, wait. Don't say anything. I've got it. I've got it." She was virtually bog-eyed with excitement. "That's it, I'll go and steal the cream for you."

"That's a thought," Rebecca said diplomatically. "On the other hand, maybe we could both go."

"Brilliant. Why didn't I think of that? I'll phone the organizers tomorrow and get you in as my assistant."

"You really think you could do that?" Rebecca said.

"Don't see why not."

"Blimey, that would be brilliant. I don't know what to say." She suddenly felt guilty for all those harsh, uncharitable thoughts she'd had about Lipstick.

Lipstick waved her hand in front of her as if to say, "Don't be daft. You don't need to say anything."

"Omigod," she squealed, "this is the most exciting thing I have ever done in my life. Just the thought of all that sleuthing and skulking around brings me out in goose bumps. It's just so Erin Brockovich. Did I ever tell you, she's my number one heroine after

Gloria Gaynor? Come to think of it, I've got a micro mini and low-cut top, just like the one she wore in the film. ..."

While Rebecca sat wondering what she'd just let herself in for, Jess leaned across and switched on the TV. "*Watching Me, Watching You* is on. They're doing celebs this series. Should be a laugh." She turned up the volume. "God," she said, "that's Lucretia Coffin Mott, isn't it?"

It was. She and the other celebrity contestants were being issued their daily challenges. Lucretia's was to clean out the chickens.

"Er, sorry, people," she said haughtily. "La Coffin Mott does not do chickens."

"Brilliant," Rebecca cried, clapping her hands. "She'll last about five minutes."

The next shot was of a resigned, uncomplaining Snow wearing a boiler suit, up to her elbows in chicken shit. Every so often, the camera cut away to Lucretia in the Communication Room demanding they send in Nicky Clarke, a flotation tank and her Mer de Rêves face cream.

Rebecca pulled the duvet up over her shoulders and lay gazing at the photograph of her mother, which was sitting on the bedside table.

"Don't half miss you," she said.

She reached out and picked it up. Then she gave Judy a kiss, switched out the light and slipped the photograph under her pillow.

She was just drifting off when Lipstick's Brazilian rain forest music started. Apparently the only way she could fall asleep was if she was serenaded by waterfalls and squawking parrots. Rebecca kept asking her to turn it down. (Jess, of course, said she found the music rather soothing and couldn't see the problem.) Lipstick always apologized profusely and promised to lower the volume, but the next night's backdrop was as loud as ever.

After a minute or so, the music stopped. No sooner had Rebecca muttered "hoo-bloody-ray" than it was replaced by Lipstick's voice. She couldn't hear what was being said but it sounded like she was on her mobile. Rebecca glanced at her bedside clock. Who she could be speaking to this late? Certainly not Stan. He always made a point of telling Rebecca not to phone after half past ten. Of course it was no business of hers if Lipstick and her mates liked to chat in the early hours. Odd, though.

She was due at Max's flat at eight the next evening. Jess had gone with Lipstick to an Enya concert, leaving Diggory with Lady Axminster. She'd invited Rebecca, too, but since Rebecca would rather have submitted to an entire body wax than sit through an hour and a half of Enya, she made her excuses. Off the hook as regards counseling, she'd phoned Max and invited herself round.

The plan was she'd bring in Chinese and then he'd decide if he felt up to going out. It was just after seven now. She decided to kill an hour by going to the pub with some people from the news desk. Then, just as she was leaving, Charlie Holland collared her, wanting to know what progress she'd made on the story. She told him about Lipstick, who by now had spoken to the Mer de Rêves people.

"They seem perfectly happy for me to come to the prize giving. They're even sending an extra Eurostar ticket."

In the end, she got to the pub a few minutes after the others. She was heading over to the bar where they were all gathered, when she spotted Max. He was sitting at a table in the corner. Lorna Findlay was with him. She was wearing a long-sleeved scoop-neck top that kept slipping off her wondrously chiseled shoulders. She made no attempt to pull it back into place. She was too busy having prolonged eye contact with Max and doing an irritating, simpery thing with her lips. Every so often there was a sexy toss of the curls. They were clearly working, though, because they both had yellow legal pads in front of them and a good deal of note making seemed to be going on. Rebecca forced herself to relax and remind herself what Jess had said about jealousy destroying relationships. She made her way to Max's table.

"Hello," she said, smiling warmly at both of them. She turned to Max, whose spots had now completely cleared up. "I thought we were meeting at your place."

"Yeah, I know," he said, getting up to kiss her hello, "but there's been a really exciting development with the French story, so Lorna and I decided to meet up for a drink to discuss it. I took a chance on your being here."

He did the introductions, during which Rebecca was convinced Lorna was looking her up and down, taking in her three-seasons-old Jigsaw work jacket, which since this morning had a large dried-up patch of Diggory sick on the shoulder.

"Tell you what," Max said, "why don't I get another round of drinks?"

"Not for me," Lorna said, "I'll have to be going in a minute. I've got a dinner with Jack Straw."

Rebecca said she'd have a spritzer. Max disappeared to the bar.

"We have met. Sort of," Rebecca said, sitting down. "We passed on Max's landing the other day."

"Oh, yes, I remember," Lorna said. "You had a bowl or something." Her tone made it sound like Rebecca had been carrying Lassa fever.

"Chicken soup," Rebecca said with an uneasy laugh. "You know, Jewish penicillin."

"Sweet. Max is lucky to have somebody to make a fuss of him. He tells me you've got a makeup column."

Rebecca nodded. "Yes, but it's not what I see myself doing long term. I really want to get into investigative reporting."

"Really?" she said, a definite smirk dancing on her lips. "So what's in the column this week?"

Rebecca colored up. "Er…ten tantalizing ways to enhance your toe cleavage…but I'm also working on this really exciting, hush-hush story about corruption in the cosmetics industry. I think it's going to be really—"

"You know," Lorna said, picking imaginary fluff off her skirt, "the contents of my makeup bag could do with an overhaul. I'll have to phone you for some advice."

At a loss for a suitably caustic reply, Rebecca merely smiled weakly.

Just then Max returned with her spritzer.

Lorna began to gather up her papers and put them in her briefcase. "Have fun, you two," she said, standing up. Then she turned to Max, gave him not a double but a triple kiss and whispered directly into his ear, but so as Rebecca could easily hear, "I'll call you when I get back from Chequers."

She shot Rebecca the briefest of smiles and turned to go, her pert little bum wiggling inside its exquisitely cut Prada housing.

Max sat back on his chair, smiling and shaking his head. "Don't you think Lorna's just amazing?"

"I'll call you when I get back from Chequers," Rebecca mimicked under her breath.

"Sorry?" Max said.

"No, nothing."

Max sipped some beer. "She has this phenomenally incisive mind. Absorbs information like a sponge. Watching her come to grips with a story is positively awesome. I'm good at the legwork, but she's streets ahead planning strategy. I think we make a really good team."

"She clearly thinks so," Rebecca said icily.

"Of course, Lorna and I go way back. I've known her since we did our journalism course together. She had balls even then. Once, when Thatcher came to give a talk, she interrupted her and started tearing into her about everything from school milk to the Falklands."

"I imagine she'd have been right up Margaret Thatcher's street, though," Rebecca said.

In her head, she could hear Jess begging her not to, but she couldn't stop herself. She cleared her throat. "Max, you would tell me, wouldn't you, if anything was going on between…"

But she didn't get a chance to finish. Brian Woodhouse, the annoyingly matey fifty-something picture editor, had just come over and was busy slapping Max on the back. "So, you're over the pox, then?" he bellowed.

Rebecca grimaced. As usual, Brian had no idea his white hairy paunch was hanging out, having burst his shirt buttons.

"Always worse when you get these things as an adult," he went on. "I got mumps off the kids a few years ago. Fucking agony. Nuts swelled up to the size of potatoes." He gave Max a conspiratorial dig in the ribs and lowered his voice. "So, you and the luscious Lorna, then, eh? Way to go, mate. Way…to…fucking…go."

Rebecca hoped Max was about to make it clear he and Lorna were only working together, but before he had a chance, Brian had shot off to the men's room.

They ended up going for a curry with the news desk people. By eleven everybody was still drinking, but Max said he was feeling tired and the two of them made their excuses. Rebecca hadn't drunk much and drove them back to his flat.

"What's this?" she said as she took off her coat. On his message pad by the phone he'd written in huge letters that were impossi-ble to miss: "Parents' evening Wednesday 25th." "Why on earth would you be going to a school parents' evening?"

For the briefest of moments he looked like he'd been caught in the headlights. Then: "It's Amy's. Her mother's on her own. So I go with her to offer a bit of support."

"You are so kind, do you know that? How many other godpar-ents would do that?"

She couldn't help thinking that kindness in a man was just the sexiest thing. She put her arms round him.

"I'm not really tired, you know," he said, stroking her cheek. "I just said I wanted to get away."

She smiled back at him. "You did?" she said.

He nodded. "I've missed you, these past few days," he said.

"Mmm. Me too."

A second later they were kissing. He tasted of wine.

"Max," she said when they'd finished, "there's something I want to ask you. About…"

She was going to say "you and Lorna," but she didn't get the chance because he had started kissing her again. Before she knew it, she was kissing him back and she was getting that delicious quiv-ering feeling in her stomach that she always got when she was des-perate to be ravished.

"Come on," he whispered, taking her hand. He led her to the bedroom and began undressing her. Every so often he would stop to kiss her shoulders, her stomach, the tops of her breasts, trail his finger over the cotton crotch of her pants. When she thought her legs were about to give way, she moved toward the bed.

"I've got a better idea," he said, grinning. He pulled her toward the glass table he used as a desk. Very gently, he pushed her over.

Soon his hands were stroking her buttocks, through her knick-ers. Then suddenly, without warning he slipped his fingers under the fabric. The next thing she knew he was pushing them hard inside her.

She cried out in delight. He carried on exploring her, she letting out tiny, soft yelps. Eventually he pulled her pants down to her ankles. She shuddered as tiny cold drops of rose-scented oil fell onto her skin. He began massaging it into her buttocks. Every so often he would stop to brush his fingers between them as they got wetter. The last time he did this he carried on down toward her clitoris. The second she felt his touch, her entire body trembled. He kissed the back of her neck and whispered to her how much he wanted her. The flicking and teasing carried on until she was crying out to him to come inside her. She was vaguely aware of him undoing his jeans belt. Soon his penis was teasing the entrance to her vagina. She cried out again as he pushed himself into her. His thrusts were slow and gentle. She heard herself begging him to go harder, to make her come. He seemed reluctant at first, clearly scared of hurting her, but she kept on. In the end it was almost painful, but all the time he carried on stroking her clitoris, varying the pressure, making her gasp for more, refusing her and then finally relenting. Finally the exquisite, jerky explosion began.

Afterward Max lay on her chest, trailing a finger over her face.

"D'you know which bit of you I think is really cute?" he said.

She looked up at him and shook her head.

"Your eyebrows. They're gorgeous." He started stroking them. "Make you look like Sophia Loren."

"Not Noel Gallagher?"

"Well, maybe a bit Liam..."

He started laughing. She began thumping him playfully on his back, but he took hold of her wrists, pinned them down above her head and began kissing her again.

"So," he said, "when am I going to get to see your flat?"

"God, it's a bloody mess at the moment. And we wouldn't be alone. There's Jess, Lipstick, the baby, Harrison."

"Come on, I don't care if the place is a mess. I'd like to meet Jess and Lipstick."

"OK," she said. "What are you doing Saturday night?"

"Having dinner at your place." He started kissing the back of her neck. "Now then, what was it you wanted to talk to me about before?"

"Oh, it's not important. Work stuff. It'll keep."

"Sure?" He turned her over and began kissing her tummy. Immediately he began heading southward.

"Positive," she whispered.

There were nine e-mails altogether: one from an ambulance driver, another from a cranial osteopath, two from male
midwives and five from a prosthetic limb technician who lived in a
mobile home in Shanklin.

Not one doctor among them. Rebecca couldn't help laughing.
"Gawd. What do you do with the woman?"

"What woman?" Jess said, coming into the bedroom. She was
wearing pajamas and holding two mugs of coffee.

"My grandmother," Rebecca said, taking one of the mugs. "She's
been advertising me on dateadoctor.com."

"No."

"See for yourself."

Rebecca got up and let Jess sit down at the computer. She
started spinning through the e-mails.

"You know, False Leg guy doesn't sound so bad," she said, clearly
battling to keep a straight face. "Says he can play the theme to *The*

Deer Hunter on his teeth. E-mail him back and ask him if he can do 'Jake the Peg.'"

Jess snorted with laughter. Rebecca responded by bashing her over the head with a giant bag of cotton balls.

"Why don't you just tell Rose about Max Factor?" Jess said. "Then she'd stop all this matchmaking."

"What, and have her go on and on about how disappointed she is I'm not going out with somebody Jewish?"

"But she's been fine about Lipstick."

"Precisely. That means there's even more pressure on me not to let her down. Plus if I told her about Max, she'd want to meet him. Then she'd start cross-examining him about his prospects. He hasn't even said he loves me yet."

"He will." Jess smiled. "But you've only just met. Give him a chance." She paused. "So, what are you cooking tonight?"

"I thought I'd keep it really simple—Delia's beef in beer. I've done it loads of times and it always works. Thing is, I was wondering if it was a bit seventies—you know, too earthenware Crockpot."

"No, I think it's great. I'll dig out a Fleetwood Mac album and a wraparound dirndl skirt and we'll be well away."

Rebecca's face fell.

"I'm kidding," Jess said. "Sounds fab. Oh, by the way, I hope you don't mind, but Mum sort of invited herself over tonight."

"Fine. The more the merrier."

"She's been feeling a bit down," Jess went on. "She'd been planning this huge fund-raiser for some disease or other. Then last week, totally out of the blue, they announced a cure. I'm convinced that whenever that happens, a tiny part of her dies."

Lipstick, who had left one of her beauty therapists in charge of the salon and taken the day off, said she'd do the dinner party shopping while Rebecca made a start clearing up the kitchen.

"I've got to pop into the butcher's anyway. I thought I'd cook Harrison something really special for his supper."

Rebecca pulled on the smelly rubber gloves. (On the rare occasions Jess did any washing up, she got water in the gloves and forgot to turn them inside out to dry.) The sink was overflowing with days old, mostly unscraped plates and pans. Grimacing, she started pulling them out, dropping sodden pieces of toast, dog food and bacon fat into the bin as she went. She had just turned on the hot water tap when the phone rang. It was Wendy, sounding exceedingly jumpy.

"I've had a couple of anonymous letters," she said, "warning me off going to the press about what I overheard at Mer de Rêves."

"Have they threatened you?"

"Sort of. Whoever wrote them said I'd live to regret it if I revealed what I knew. I don't feel safe. So I've decided to go and stay with some friends in Scotland until this whole thing blows over."

They spent the rest of the conversation discussing Lipstick's plan to infiltrate the Mer de Rêves office in Paris.

"You'd need to find the lab," Wendy said. "The only problem is it's hidden in a mass of basement tunnels and almost impossible to find unless you know where you're going. I know exactly where it is because I've been there dozens of times with my boss. I'll draw you a detailed map and drop it off on my way to the station."

Wendy arrived half an hour later, pale, jittery and petrified she might have been followed. She refused to come in. She simply handed Rebecca an envelope and a slip of paper on which she'd written her phone number in Scotland. Before Rebecca had a chance to give her a hug, tell her how much she appreciated what she was doing and that she would do her best to ensure that the *Vanguard* paid her a whacking fee for all this, she was gone.

* * *

By six the whole flat was filled with a glorious meaty-boozy smell and Rebecca was lying in a bubble bath with a glass of wine. She'd just finished topping off the hot water when Lipstick knocked on the door.

"Becks, have you seen that bag of meat I bought for Harrison?"

Rebecca said she hadn't and went back to making shampoo horns with her hair.

"But it was in the fridge. You sure you haven't seen it?"

"Positive."

"It was blue plastic."

"The only blue plastic bag I've seen is the one with my braising steak in it."

"No, yours was in the white bag."

"No, it wasn't."

"It was," Lipstick insisted. "I explained when I got back from the shops. I definitely remember saying, 'Harrison's meat is in the blue bag, yours is in the white one.' "

First one shampoo horn collapsed on Rebecca's head, then the other. When Lipstick got back from the shops, Rebecca had been engrossed in Wendy's map of the tunnels underneath the Mer de Rêves offices. She'd clearly misunderstood.

"But it's all beef, right?" Rebecca could feel her heart rate rising. "I mean what difference if I cooked Harrison's meat instead of the stuff you got me?"

"Well, personally I wouldn't mind," Lipstick said. "The French eat it all the time. It's a real delicacy over there and extremely expensive, but I'm not sure how everybody else would feel."

Feeling almost numb by now, Rebecca eased herself slowly out of the bath and opened the door. She stood in front of Lipstick completely starkers, dripping all over the linoleum.

"I haven't made beef in beer, have I?"

Lipstick shook her head slowly.

"What I thought was braising steak was probably last seen running in the two forty-five at Epsom. I cooked horse, didn't I?"

"'Fraid so," Lipstick said.

"Horse in beer."

"Seems that way."

"That's not a Delia recipe, is it?"

"Not so far as I know," Lipstick said.

While Harrison demolished what the three of them were now referring to as Shergar stew, Jess stood in front of the open kitchen cupboards.

"OK," she said, "it would appear to be a toss-up between Big Soup and mandarin-flavor Jell-O."

"What about the real beef?" Lipstick said. "That's still in the fridge."

"No time to cook it," Jess came back. "Braising steak takes forever."

Rebecca asked what time Waitrose shut.

"Fifteen minutes ago," Lipstick said.

She suggested getting something ready prepared from the Italian deli round the corner, or simply ordering takeout.

"But I told Max I was going to make something. Now I've decided it's an OK time in our relationship for me to cook for him, I wanted to impress him."

Jess shut the kitchen cupboards, turned and grinned at Rebecca. "I know how you can really impress him," she said, "What about Minge?"

"Hmm, but isn't that more an after-dinner thing?" Rebecca said.

"No, stupid," Jess came back. "I mean Thick Minge."

Thick Minge, short for Araminta, was Jess's überposh best

friend from Slapton Gusset. Although not one of the brightest, she now ran a successful catering business in Notting Hill.

"But I wanted to cook," Rebecca moaned again.

"Well, you can't," Jess barked, sounding exactly like her mother. "There isn't time. And Minge is brilliant. Plus she always makes too much. She's got this chest freezer full of stuff. Why don't I phone her and see if she can let us have something?"

They were in luck. It turned out Minge was on her way to Crouch End to deliver the food for a golden wedding party. She said she'd dig a *boeuf en croûte* out of the freezer and drop it round on the way.

By eight o'clock everybody was ready and they were sitting in the living room knocking back Shiraz and smoky-bacon-flavored Doritos. Lipstick was wearing thick lip liner, and a sparkly, tassely more-is-more creation from Karen Millen. Jess was in her cargo pants because she hadn't packed any smart clothes. Rebecca had changed nine times and eventually settled on jeans and a cropped-sleeve T-shirt, because she didn't want to look like she'd tried too hard.

"What time did Minge say she'd be here with the beef?" Rebecca asked for the umpteenth time.

"Quarter past," Jess said wearily. "Stop panicking. She'll be here."

"What do you think of my napkin swans, then?" Lipstick said, nodding toward the table, which they'd brought in from the kitchen (the tanning bed and treadmill having been shared out between the two bedrooms). "I could have done teapots if you'd preferred. Or clogs."

Rebecca smiled and said swans were great.

Lady Axminster arrived first, immediately noticed *Woman*

Wanking and winced. She brightened up no end, though, when Lipstick came over and introduced herself with a deep curtsy. Lady Axminster then air-kissed Rebecca. When it was Jess's turn, her face fell again. "I know you're under a terrible strain, darling, but letting oneself go is so terribly bad for one's morale. Surely a bit of rouge wouldn't hurt. And look at you. Who wears fatigues to a dinner party? If you want to win Ed back, you have to start being more feminine."

"OK," Jess said, handing her mother a Shiraz, "how's about I grow a third breast?"

"You know, Jessica, sarcasm really is the lowest form of wit."

"Smoky-bacon Dorito, Lady A?" Rebecca cut in, sensing a situation brewing.

Her ladyship raised a polite hand in refusal.

"And what on earth makes you think I even want Ed back?" Jess went on irritably.

"Well, if you don't, you should. Diggory needs a father. And it's not as if he actually cheated on you."

Jess was clearly confused by her mother's pro-Ed stance, since Lady Axminster had never approved of her marrying outside her class, and in particular to a tabloid journalist.

"And Ed loves you," Lady Axminster went on. "You only have to look at him to see that." In a virtually unprecedented show of emotion, her voice softened. "I don't think your father was ever really in love with me." She sat down on the sofa.

"What, not ever?" Jess said, sitting down next to her.

"Well, I suppose there was that time just after we met when he lost interest in the cricket for a couple of days."

"Well, my Stan's an angel," Lipstick piped up.

"Lucky old you," her ladyship said. "My Vere is still alive."

At that moment Harrison burst in and leaped onto Lady Axminster's lap, almost knocking the wine out of her hand.

"Oh," she gasped—in delight rather than annoyance, "and who is this handsome little chap?" She immediately started nuzzling him and scratching his head.

"Harrison Ford, ma'am," Lipstick said.

"Ah," Lady Axminster laughed, "just like the actor chappy."

"Indeed, ma'am. Actually I've got his christening album. Would you like to see it?"

A couple of minutes later the two of them were off, oohing and aahing at Harrison's puppy pictures.

"And that's my dad's dog, Isaiah," Lipstick pointed out.

"Oh, after the prophet?"

Lipstick gave her a perplexed frown. "No," she said. "One eye's higher than the other."

Rebecca and Jess excused themselves on the pretext of needing to check on the dinner.

"Gawd, it's nearly nine!" Rebecca wailed. "Where's bloody Minge?"

Jess had just gone to phone her on her mobile when the intercom went.

It was Max. He came in bearing a vast bunch of lilies and white roses.

"Oh, they're wonderful," Rebecca said, taking the flowers and kissing him.

Just then Jess reappeared. Rebecca did the introductions. Jess didn't manage much more than, "Hi, pleased to meet you," on account of her mouth freezing itself into a stupid grin brought about by instant and overwhelming physical attraction.

"Phwar," she whispered into her friend's ear as Rebecca led Max into the living room to meet Lipstick and Lady Axminster.

When she found out he was the *Vanguard*'s science correspondent, Lady Axminster immediately began quizzing him about mad cow disease. Then Lipstick chipped in, saying how much the world owed to Thomas Edison because without him we'd all be watching television by candlelight. Lady Axminster roared, assuming Lipstick was joking, and asked Max what he'd studied at university. When he said radio astronomy, Lipstick countered with: "Oooh, so I bet you'll have no trouble working out what star sign I am, then."

Deciding Max was more than capable of holding his own with her ladyship and Lipstick, Rebecca went to find Jess. She was in the kitchen.

"OK, what did Minge say?"

"She'll be five minutes. Apparently there was a broken-down bus in Harlesden."

When the door went again, Rebecca assumed it was Minge. When it turned out to be Grandma Rose, she virtually keeled over.

"Omigod," she said to Jess as they waited for Rose to come upstairs, "when she finds out about me and Max, she'll have one of her strokes."

It turned out Rose had decided to pop in and say hello since she was on her way to visit her friend Milly who lived in the next road. "She's had a nasty bout of bronchitis. So I thought I'd take her some of those homophobic remedies."

Then she dug Rebecca in the ribs, winked and asked her if she'd had any interesting e-mails recently.

Before Rebecca could confront the thorny issue of dateadoctor.com, Rose heard the chatter from the living room.

"Oooh, you've got people."

She handed Rebecca her coat and trotted into the living room. Lipstick, looking surprised and delighted, offered her a huge hug and introduced her to Lady Axminster. Rose offered her commiserations about Jess and Ed and said pointedly that at least Lady Axminster had a daughter who was married. Then she let out a long sigh and said she'd virtually given up hope of Rebecca ever finding a husband.

"And this is Max," Lipstick said. "He's a journalist."

She shook his hand. Rebecca watched as she scrutinized the Paul Smith jacket and expensive shirt. (Grandma Rose understood little of modern fashion, but there was nothing the daughter of Maurice Bernstein, Ladies' Mantles and Bespoke Suits, didn't know about tailoring.)

"Max," she said finally, clearly approving of the stitching on his lapels, "you seem like a discerning young man. Do an old woman a favor."

"Oh, come on, Rose," Lipstick cut in, "you're not old."

"Listen." Rose laughed. "I can remember when Barnum and Bailey was only Barnum."

Lipstick offered Rose a glass of wine, but she declined, presumably because she needed both hands to speak.

"Now then," Rose said, turning to Max, "take a good look at Rebecca. Tell me honestly. What do you think? She's intelligent. She's pretty. You know, the ophthalmologist did wonders with her lazy eye. The only time you can see it now is when she's tired. Of course she went through a terrible time with her skin when she was a teenager, but that's all cleared up now. Don't you think she'd make somebody a lovely wife?"

Rebecca had heard enough. Crimson faced, she went back into the kitchen and poured herself more wine. When the intercom went yet again, she let Jess get it. A few moments later she came into the kitchen carrying a large silver foil parcel.

"Houston, we have food," she declared. "I told Minge we already had dessert, but she threw in an almond tart anyway. When I offered to pay, she wouldn't hear of it."

Rebecca's face lit up. She said she'd send Minge flowers on Monday to say thank you.

Just then Max came in. Rebecca apologized for Rose. "I'm sorry if she embarrassed you."

He grinned and said she hadn't. Not even remotely. "By the way, I love the painting."

"Oh, what, *Woman Wanking?*"

He laughed and colored up slightly. "Yes," he said. "That's the one."

"Glad you approve."

"So what's for dinner?" he asked.

"Oh, I did a *boeuf en croûte*," Rebecca said casually, indicating the foil parcel sitting on the counter. "I made it a couple of hours ago. Just needs a quick reheat in the oven."

Jess suggested it would crisp up more without the foil. Rebecca agreed and began taking it off.

"Can't wait to see this," Max said. "Bet it's magnificent."

Confident Max was about to be severely impressed, Rebecca pulled off the final layer of foil. "Ta-dah," she sang. But instead of wows, there was silence.

She looked down. Sitting on the counter was a huge iced cake. On top it said, "Nan and Cyril. Congratulations on your Golden Wedding."

Of course, everybody had hysterics. Rebecca did her best to join in, but she found it hard to laugh about the Shergar stew and Thick Minge. She couldn't help feeling everything was her fault and that she'd buggered up the entire evening. Domestic goddesswise, she felt about as adequate as a Voyage cardigan in a thunderstorm.

By the time they'd phoned Minge and she'd collected the cake and come back with the beef, it was well after eleven. Then, the moment they sat down to eat (minus Rose, who'd left for Milly's—laughing her head off—shortly after the cake incident), Max's mobile rang. It was Lorna to say she'd arranged a midnight conference call with the French minister for the environment and he should get over to her place straight away.

"A conference call at midnight," Rebecca said. "On a Saturday?"

"Apparently he's at some dinner," Max said, getting up from the table. "Then he's catching a plane to Mexico City. Said he'd speak to us on the way to the airport. I'm so, so sorry, Rebecca, but I really have to go. It'll take me at least half an hour to get to Lorna's."

She walked him to the door. "We'll catch up during the week, eh?"

She nodded.

"Then there's the wedding on Saturday."

Max's mate Adam, a sub on the *Independent,* was getting married to Zoe, a staff writer on the *Sunday Tribune* who was a friend of Rebecca's. It was only when Rebecca happened to mention the wedding to Max a few days ago that they worked out the connection and each realized the other had been invited.

"I'm looking forward to it," she said.

"Me too."

He apologized again for having to dash off, snogged her briefly but thoroughly, and was gone.

Rebecca was woken by the phone. She reached out from under the duvet, her hand fumbling for the receiver. "Hi, Gran," Rebecca said, sounding groggy and full of early morning nose block. "What time is it?"

Apparently it was "well after nine."

"So, you and this Max, then?"

Rebecca rolled over onto her back.

"I wasn't sure," Rose went on, "so I just rang Marjorie."

"Marjorie" was in audible italics. Rose was clearly relishing being on hobnobbing terms with the aristocracy.

"What do you think?" Rebecca said tentatively.

"I think he's wonderful."

"You do? But he's not Jewish."

"Rebecca, listen to me. The world is full of famines, wars, children dying of AIDS and you're worried because your boyfriend's not Jewish? Isn't it time to get a little perspective here?"

"Me, get a little perspective?" Rebecca gasped.

"All right, I admit I may have been a bit intolerant about the religion thing, but now I can see just how happy your dad is with Bernadette. And if anybody deserves a bit of happiness in his life, it's Stan."

Rebecca couldn't believe what she was hearing.

"And I suppose I was a bit put out when nothing happened between you and that nice Warren chap—particularly when I found out his father just died and left him forty million pounds."

Ah, Rebecca thought, chuckling to herself. So that explained how he pulled the gorgeous Fabergé.

"Anyway," Rose went on, "that's all by-the-by now. Max is a lovely boy and he's practically a doctor."

"No, he's not, he's the *Vanguard*'s science correspondent."

"Now you're just splitting hairs. What that boy doesn't know about blood pressure isn't worth knowing. He gave me an entire lecture on how I should be cutting down on salt. On top of that, it turns out one of the companies that makes those electronic blood pressure machines has just sent him one, as a freebie. Said it was mine if I wanted it." She paused. "Look, sweetie. I know it's early days yet. But if it works out for the two of you, I couldn't be happier."

"And it *will* work out," Jess said that evening as they watched an *ER* repeat—Lipstick had gone to bed early. "I've told you before, just give it time and stop worrying."

Rebecca grunted. "Bet Bloody I'll-call-you-when-I-get-back-from-Chequers Lorna doesn't cook Shergar instead of braising steak. Bet Bloody Lorna can knock up a Thai feast for thirty at the same time as running a marathon, shaving her pubes and mugging up on Labour's transport policy."

She lay on the sofa contemplating, hands under her head. Then: "She's after him. I just know it."

"Well, it's you he wants," Jess declared, without taking her eyes off the TV screen, "not Bloody Lorna. I can tell just by the way he looks at you."

"Really?"

"Really."

Rebecca smiled and went all coquettish. She sat up. "So...er... how exactly would you say he looks at me?"

"I dunno." Jess shrugged. "He just gives you these looks, that's all. When he thinks nobody can see. God, Dr. Greene's sexy. Oh, I love this episode. It's the one where they operate on his malignant brain tumor. He gets over it."

"What sort of looks?" Rebecca asked. "I mean, would you say they're sexy, affectionate or just platonic?"

"Affectionate...Oh, look, Dr. Corday really loves him. She's having their baby. I love her hair. Do you reckon it's naturally curly or she has it permed?"

"Not sexual, then? Or loving?"

Jess was glued to Dr. Greene and his carcinoma. Rebecca repeated the question.

"Loving, too," Jess said vaguely.

"So, definitely not sexual, then?"

"OK, affectionate, loving and sexual."

Rebecca went back to the TV, but only for a moment. "So, how much is sexual? I mean what would you say is the ratio of affection to sex?"

"Sixty—forty...Ooh, ooh, look. Some bloke's arresting. Come on, get out the bloody paddles!"

"What, sixty: sex, and forty: affection? Or the other way round?"

Now Jess sat up. "For chrissake, moron," she barked at the screen, "he needs a shot of adrenaline....Becks, please. A man could be dying here. Max Factor cares about you, OK?" She lay back down again.

"Really?" Rebecca said.

"Omigod, we're off again. He cares about you—really, really, really. OK?"

Satisfied at last, Rebecca watched the rest of *ER*. Afterward she picked up the newspaper and turned to the TV listings.

"It's *Watching You, Watching Me* next," she said. "We have to see how Lucretia's getting on. I can't believe she hasn't been chucked out yet."

During the break Rebecca put the kettle on and Jess went to the loo. When they got back it had already started.

Lucretia, a girl-band singer called Brie and some F-list soap actress whose name Rebecca had forgotten were sitting chatting in the girls' bedroom.

"Do you know," Lucretia said as she finished cleansing her face with a cotton pad, "I'd like Prince Charles to take me from behind."

Rebecca sat bolt upright. Jess gasped.

"Yeah," Brie said. "Wasn't that a big hit in the eighties for Frankie Goes to Hollywood?"

Lucretia laughed. "It's not a song," she said, unzipping her outsized makeup bag. "It's my secret fantasy. I've never ever told a soul until this moment."

"What on earth's going on?" Rebecca said to the screen. "Lucretia has the most almighty hang-up about sex. She wouldn't even acknowledge having a sexual fantasy, let alone talk about it."

Glued to the screen, they watched as Lucretia unscrewed a jar of Mer de Rêves face cream. Rebecca recognized the gleaming Mercedes hubcap top and the letters *MdR* picked out in tiny pretend diamonds. The *Watching You, Watching Me* people had clearly refused her request for Nicky Clarke and the flotation tank, but sent somebody round to her flat to fetch the cream she'd left behind.

"You know," Lucretia said, dotting her face with cream, "I lie in bed sometimes imagining the two of us romping in slow motion through the gardens at Highgrove. I'm completely naked. He is too, apart from gardening gloves and a pair of pruning shears...."

Rebecca and Jess squirmed as her fantasy became more and more graphic.

"Of course, it's all wondrously dangerous because neither of us knows when Camilla or the boys might appear. The bit I like best is when he fondles my lobelia ..."

Snow, who had walked into the room at that second, stopped and did a confused double take. Then, clearly assuming she'd misheard, she placed a neatly folded pile of laundry on Lucretia's bed.

"There's another load still in the dryer," she said. "I'll iron it later."

Lucretia nodded.

Then Snow said that Billy Piper and Ainsley Harriott had just made cocoa if anybody wanted it.

Jess turned to Rebecca. "How could she humiliate herself like that on national TV—in front of millions of people? Charlie Holland is going to be furious. Wouldn't surprise me if he gave her the boot. What is the woman on, risking her career like that?"

"God knows," Rebecca said. "God only knows."

As it turned out, she didn't see Max at all that week. When he wasn't meeting secret contacts in greasy diners off the A1, he was in late-night meetings with the people at Channel 6—which of course included Bloody Lorna. He'd only phoned her twice and each time he'd seemed distracted and distant. She kept telling herself he was working on the most important—not to mention lifeendangering—story of his career and had every right to be distracted and distant. But a huge part of her couldn't help wishing he was working on the most important, life-endangering story of his career without the help of Bloody Lorna.

Jess kept up the pep talks, though, and by Friday, knowing she was going to see him the next day at the wedding, she'd cheered up no end.

By now she was in no doubt that she'd fallen in love with Max. She wasn't sure exactly when it happened. During that daft Kit Kat row maybe. All she knew was that when she was with Max she was overwhelmed by the feeling that she'd come home. She could say anything to him. He made her laugh. He was her warm place. When she was with him, she could shut out the rest of the world.

Hardly a night went by when she didn't fantasize about him taking her in his arms and telling her he loved her too. Maybe it would happen tomorrow, she thought, when he saw her in her wedding outfit.

Another one of her girlfriends had gotten married last spring and she'd splurged on a gorgeous sixties-style pale pink woolen dress and jacket. The dress was a dead straight shift, but it managed to cling in all the right places. The tiny boxy jacket had big buttons and three-quarter-length sleeves. She'd set it off with a row of chunky pearls, and a low-brimmed hat. Everybody had said she looked "sooo Audrey." She didn't actually pick anyone up, though. All the decent blokes had been in couples, but she'd felt their eyes on her. The only chap who'd made a move was the toastmaster, who had a handlebar mustache and a beach hut at Swanage. Even so, she couldn't remember ever having felt quite so sexy. Max wouldn't be able to keep his hands off her when she walked into that church tomorrow.

She stayed up late, getting her clothes ready and (for once in her life) planning her route. The wedding was being held at Zoe's parents' place—a vast manor house somewhere in the wilds of north Yorkshire. Max and Rebecca weren't driving up together because Max was spending the night with Adam and some friends in Leeds, where they were having Adam's stag night.

* * *

By half past seven, she was ready to go. Lipstick was still asleep, but Jess, who was up feeding Diggory, gasped when she saw her and said the moment they got to the reception Max was bound to cart her off to one of the bedrooms to ravage her. "Hope you've got decent underwear on."

Then she told her to go and have a wonderful time and forget all about Bloody Lorna.

Despite pelting rain and several sets of roadworks on the M1, she reached Leeds just before eleven. Kettlesthwaite was a good forty miles farther north. Even on minor roads it couldn't take more than an hour. The service was at twelve. She should make it with a few minutes to spare.

Soon the city gave way to glorious Yorkshire countryside. The rain had stopped and patches of denim blue were beginning to break through the February sky. She stuck *Abba Gold* in the cassette player and began singing along, belting out the lyrics for all she was worth.

The first time she sensed the car was losing power, she thought she was imagining it. When she looked at the speedo and realized she wasn't, she started pressing down harder on the gas. The aged Golf merely shuddered and continued to slow down. She pressed the accelerator again. Then again. Nothing. Just before the car came to a complete stop, she managed to pull into a muddy recess next to a five-bar gate.

"Oh, terrific," she muttered, bashing the steering wheel.

She reached under the dashboard and tugged the hood lever. Although her underhood skills were limited to filling the windscreen fluid dispenser, she felt she should take a look. An obvious bit of wiring may have come loose that she might just be able to shove back. She opened the car door. After the downpour, the road was awash with liquid mud. Tentatively, she lowered a pink suede sling-back. Then she reached across to the passenger seat and picked up her mobile. (Her dad was a brilliant mechanic. If she couldn't find anything obviously wrong under the hood, she would phone him for advice.)

She got out of the car and stood surveying the narrow lane for muddy puddles, roadkill and anything else that could put her precious Manolos at risk. Looking back, she supposed she must have heard the cattle truck coming. But she'd clearly been too preoccupied with her road stakeout to notice. By the time she saw the truck bearing down on her, it was too late to get back in the car. She pinned herself to the side of the car, managing to drop her mobile in the process and watched in silent horror as it thundered by, spraying her jacket, skirt and shoes in thick, sand-colored mud. For a few moments she was too numb to move. All she could do was stand there, staring at her ruined clothes. Finally a single tear streaked her face. Like Max would want to ravage her now.

She bent down and picked up her phone. The back of the case was cracked and coming off. She tried turning it on. Nothing. "Marvelous. Now I can't even phone the AA."

Her only consolation was that Kettlesthwaite could be no more than a few hundred yards round the next bend. The last signpost had said it was half a mile off and that had been a fair way back. Since she couldn't possibly turn up to the wedding covered in mud, she had no choice but to phone the AA from a phone box and get them to tow her back to London. She'd stop off en route to explain everything to Max. A second tear now followed the first. Of course he'd be dead sympathetic, but deep down he'd be thinking she had about as much point as an ejector seat in a helicopter. Then he'd dump her for Bloody Lorna.

She got back in the car, took off her hat and sat staring at it. Unless, of course, she did go to the wedding. Maybe there was a little boutique in the village where she could buy a new outfit. She laughed at her stupidity. Kettlesthwaite would possess nothing more than a pub and a manky general store selling Kraft cheese slices, Vicks and Instant Whip. Then again the place might be larger than she'd thought. It could well have a vaguely trendy clothes shop. Nothing designery maybe, but she was in no position to quibble. A high street label would be fine.

She picked up her bag and the Habitat table light she'd gotten Adam and Zoe as a wedding present. Then she locked the car and set off, a mud-splattered Audrey in search of an oasis in the style desert of rural England.

Apart from a motorbike roaring past, splashing her in even more mud, there was no traffic.

With its immaculately restored stone cottages scattered around a white chain railing-enclosed duck pond, Kettlesthwaite was a positively candy box English village. As she'd predicted, there was a general store and a pub. The church was at the far end. She could see the morning suits and big hats filing in. Even if she found something to wear—the chances of which were remote—there was no way she was going to make the service now.

Then she spotted it on the other side of the pond, a second tiny shop set back from the pub. After a few paces she was near enough to read the swirly gold lettering above the window. Refusing to be deterred by the fact that it said "Miss Nob," she carried on walking. Miss Nob's bow-fronted window frame was painted white and filled with small, square panes of glass. Some of these had bull's-eyes. Any minute now, she expected to see the Bennet sisters come filing out, giggling and clutching new bonnet ribbons.

The closer she got, the harder she prayed there would be something vaguely suitable on Miss Nob's racks. A French Connection jacket and trousers, maybe. A skirt and blouse would do. Anything. So long as the chest didn't shout Giorgio or Tommy.

What she found made her heart sink into her muddy Manolos, but didn't even remotely surprise her. The mannequin in the window was wearing a Miss Marple tweed suit and matching trilby with two pheasant feathers sticking out. At her feet was a blue and mauve mohair shawl and a substantial tan leather handbag, its front flap embossed with the image of a shire horse and cart. Rebecca pushed the door anyway. It was locked. The handwritten postcard stuck behind the glass said: "Closed due to slipped disk." Saddened as she was by Miss Nob's incapacity, Rebecca couldn't help feeling relieved.

There was nothing for it. She would go back to her original plan of phoning the AA and getting them to tow her back to London. As she couldn't see a phone box, she headed for the general store.

The woman behind the counter was plump and bosomy—pushing seventy at a guess. Rebecca positioned herself next to a pyramid of El Paso refried beans, which were on special offer, and waited while the woman cut four slices of streaky bacon for a doddery old bloke in a cap. After the first two, she stopped to consult him about the thickness. He waved a frail hand in approval. She returned to the machine, her pink nylon overall making swishing sounds as she went. While she wrapped the bacon they chatted about the weather, her saying it had been so cold last night her teeth hadn't stopped chattering.

"Which was a bit disconcerting, I can tell you," she said, "seeing as they were sitting in a glass." She roared. He smiled a frail smile to indicate he'd gotten the joke.

"OK, see ye Wednesday, Horace, petal," she said, handing over the bacon. "Yer veal and ham should be in by then."

"Ay, right you are, Val."

Horace turned to go. Noticing Rebecca, he touched his cap by way of greeting and then tottered off.

"Sorry about that, petal," Val said, turning to Rebecca. "Poor soul only buried his Thelma last week. Got took sudden. Kidney failure."

"God," Rebecca said, shaking her head, "losing a wife must be devastating when you've been together all those years."

"Wife? Oh, no, Horace never married. Thelma was 'is whippet. Now then, what can I do you for?"

Rebecca was about to ask if she could use the phone, but Val, who had suddenly noticed her muddy clothes, came back before she'd even opened her mouth. "Eee, now then, petal. Whatever happened to you?"

Rebecca smiled sheepishly and explained.

"So you've nowt to wear for t'wedding? Be a shame to miss it after you've come all this way. And it's going to be a belting do by all accounts."

"Haven't got much choice really. I can't walk in looking like this."

Val stood there, looking Rebecca up and down.

"You know our Cheryl's about your size. Well, she was until she moved to Pudsey. Size eighteen she is now. Of course, I blame the water. They get different water down there. You see up here, we get north Yorkshire water. They get west Yorkshire water. Must make a difference. I've always said a change in water can play havoc with your system. Takes time to adjust."

"How long's she been there?"

"Our Cheryl? In Pudsey? Ooh, must be getting on for seventeen year." She paused. "Anyway I've still got the dress she wore when she was maid of honor at my sister's wedding in 1978. I've never been able to part with it. She looked like a duchess in it. And what with it having a three-quarter sleeve it covered up nearly all of her psoriasis. Why don't you come upstairs and take a look? There's nowt wrong with it and it's just your color."

Rebecca made all the excuses she could think of not to try on our Cheryl's ancient psoriasis-infested bridesmaid creation, but Val refused to take no for an answer. A few moments later, she was following her out through the back of the shop and upstairs.

Val's bedroom consisted entirely of loud, clashing florals. The only relief was provided by a man's maroon dressing gown that was hanging on the back of the door, suggesting there was a Mister Val.

Val opened the melamine wardrobe and pulled out a full-length, Empire-line dress in shiny nylon chiffon. In tangerine shiny nylon chiffon. With an equally tangerine rose at the cleavage.

"Now then, I know it seems a bit limp on the hanger, but don't be put off. It looks better on."

Better on what? Rebecca thought. On fire?

"Wow, it's lovely," Rebecca said, fingering the nylon and assuming full-on gush mode, "but I'm not sure it's quite me."

"'Course it is, petal. Come on, take your things off and try it on."

Rebecca went to wash the mud off her hands. When she came back, Val had disappeared and the dress was on the bed. She began taking off her clothes. A few moments later there was a tap at the door.

"Coo-ee, you decent?"

"Just about," Rebecca said, sliding her arms into the sleeves.

"Oh, my word," Val said, zipping Rebecca up the back. "Now then, don't you look grand. Fits like a glove. I think I got the beer stain off the front." She examined the skirt and confirmed that she had. Then, taking Rebecca by the hand, she led her to the full-length mirror.

"Now then, petal. What do you think?"

"Omigod," Rebecca blurted, her face etched in pain.

"See, I said you'd be amazed at how fabulous you'd look."

"Yeah, fabulously orangina," Rebecca muttered under her breath. She was just about to reach for the zipper when a thought occurred to her. OK, the dress was cheap, nasty and positively hideous, but at the same time she had to admit there was something distinctly retro about it. It screamed platforms, Abba and flicky hair. And vintage was very in at the moment. She reached inside her bra cups and hoisted up her bosom. It did give her a wonderful cleavage. And the skirt was long enough to hide her muddy shoes. Maybe, just maybe, she could get away with it. She did a half twirl and then another.

"All right," Rebecca said. "I'll give it a go."

They both agreed that since the mud looked like it contained a fair amount of oil, Rebecca's suit was beyond saving. Val said she'd toss it. Rebecca promised to dry-clean the dress and send it back the following week.

It turned out Zoe's parents' house was only a few hundred yards from the church.

"It's set back in its own grounds," Val said. "You can't miss it. Huge marquee thing in the garden."

With a hug from Val and wrapped in a white crocheted shawl she'd managed to dig out, Rebecca set off for a second time.

"Oh, my God," Guy Debonnaire bellowed, waving his champagne flute. "Look, everyone, the divine Miss Fine has come as a tangerine."

A dozen or so people turned to look at her, but it felt like hundreds. She hadn't felt this embarrassed since she was eighteen and did her first postcoital pussy fart. She might have known Guy would be there. Zoe said she was inviting practically everybody from the *Tribune*.

"And what have you come as, Guy?" a woman's voice piped up from the crowd. Whomever it was had clearly spotted Guy's emerald brocade jacket with flared cuffs. "A gay leprechaun?"

Everybody hooted, which made Rebecca feel much better. Then they turned back to their conversation and champagne.

A moment later, Guy came lurching across. "Sorry, Becks. I didn't mean it. Honest. Please forgive me. I only said it because you won't go out with me. Come on, have dinner with me. Please. You know you want to."

"Sorry, Guy," she said, her eyes darting round for Max, "I'm actually seeing somebody at the moment."

"Ah, yes, I've heard all about you and the illustrious Mr. Stoddart. The last time I saw him he was standing by the bar, talking to some people from the *Tribune*."

She thanked him and began easing her way through the crowd. It was then that she spotted Bloody Lorna, standing a couple of feet away, chatting with another group. Rebecca had no idea what Lorna was doing at the wedding. Of all the people she didn't want to see her in the tangerine dress, Lorna had to be on top of the list. She stared into the distance, determined not to make eye contact.

"Rebecca, hi! Lovely to see you. Mind you, it would be hard to miss you in that absolutely glorious color."

Lorna was wearing a stunning black suit with magenta buttons and matching turned-back cuffs. On her head was a black and magenta feathery creation, which on anybody else would have looked comical, but on her looked so Kate Moss.

"Hello, Lorna," Rebecca said, greeting the woman as if she were a recurring bout of cystitis. "Not at Chequers this weekend, then?"

"No, Tony and Cherie are at Balmoral," Lorna said, coming over to air-kiss her. At one point their cheeks collided. Lorna's cheekbones were protruding and sharp. Rebecca felt like she was being air-kissed by Yorick.

"This is Rebecca Fine, everybody. She works for the *Vanguard*—as their toe cleavage correspondent."

Rebecca wondered how much champagne Lorna had put away, since she was being even more bitchy than usual.

There was a round of polite, rather awkward smiles. Then some guy appeared whom everybody seemed to know apart from Rebecca. While the kissing and handshaking was going on, she slipped away.

She spotted Max standing at the bar with three blokes in morning suits. She recognized one as Ben, Adam's best man.

"Hiya," she called out, waving. Max broke away from the group and came toward her.

"Rebecca, I was worried about you. What happened? Why are you so late?"

She said it was a long story and she'd tell him after she'd had a drink.

Then he noticed what she was wearing.

"Wow," he said, clearly taken aback, "great dress."

"You hate it, don't you?"

"No…" She could see he was fighting not to laugh.

"Yes, you do. You're laughing."

"No, I'm not. Honest." He coughed a couple of times. "I love it. It's, erm, very…"

"Orange?"

"Well, yes, I would have to agree it is just a tad orange. But I was going to say it's very different from your usual style. But different is good. That's the problem with the world today. Not enough diversity. Dead boring."

"Liar," she said, smiling. "Look, I know the dress is vile, but it was either this or not come."

"How d'you mean?"

As she told him about the breakdown, the cattle truck and Val, he finally burst out laughing.

"I suppose it is pretty funny," she said, "but it wasn't at the time." He stroked her cheek.

"Oh, by the way," she said, trying to sound not in the least put out, "I just bumped into Lorna. I didn't know she was going to be here."

"No, nor did I until yesterday. Turns out she's Zoe's cousin."

"Oh, right."

"Anyway, the dress looks brilliant," he said. "You look fantastic. Now come here and give me a proper kiss. I've really missed you."

"So, how's the story going?" she said as they pulled away.

"I'll tell you about it in a minute. Look, do you mind if I abandon you for a bit? Something really important's just come up and I have to make a couple of phone calls. You grab a drink and mingle. I'll come and find you. It won't take long. Promise."

"Make sure it doesn't," she grinned, running her hand over his behind before he disappeared.

Rebecca took a glass of champagne from the bar and looked round for Zoe, the bride, to wish her congratulations. Rebecca adored Zoe. She was one of the sweetest, most positive and jolly people Rebecca knew. The only problem was she'd been cursed with a size eighteen body and tits to match. Until a few months ago, the whole world had been convinced she would never find a bloke. Then Adam joined the *Tribune*. He was pushing forty and a bit of a porker himself (hence his nickname, Fat Boy Fat). The two of them hit it off immediately, having discovered a mutual love of haiku and barbecued food. Six weeks later the wedding had been booked.

After a few minutes, Rebecca decided to go upstairs to the bathroom to check her makeup. She was standing at the basin rinsing foundation off her fingers when Zoe came sailing in. Her floaty dress was gathered tight under her bust. On her head she was wearing a garland of fresh gypsophila and ivy. Rebecca could just hear Guy Debonnaire saying something cutting like: "Ooh, darling, don't tell me—Weight Watchers is putting on *A Midsummer Night's Dream.*"

The two of them exchanged excited kisses and hugs and Rebecca told Zoe how wonderful she looked.

"Yes, but look at you," Zoe came back. "That dress is just so seventies. You are clever. I wish I was brave enough to do something like that."

Deciding Zoe probably didn't have the time or the inclination on her wedding day to listen to the cattle truck tale, Rebecca smiled and accepted the compliment.

They walked downstairs together.

"Oh," Zoe said, "I must introduce you to my cousin Lorna. You know, Lorna Findlay from Channel 6 News. I know how much you're trying to break into investigative stuff. She'd be a brilliant contact."

"Actually, we know each other—through Max Stoddart at the *Vanguard*. They're working on a story together. In fact he and I have just started seeing..."

She realized Zoe wasn't listening. She'd stopped outside the drawing room and was peering in.

"Between you and me," Zoe whispered, "I think it's probably a bit more than a story they're working on."

She giggled and jerked her head, indicating that Rebecca should take a look. The room was empty apart from Max and Lorna, who were standing by the French doors gazing out onto the cheesy postcard English garden and hills beyond. Lorna was resting her head on his shoulder. He was holding her, whispering into her ear and stroking her hair. They looked so intimate, like lovers sharing secrets. Rebecca felt herself starting to shake. She was certain her legs were about to give way.

"Becks, you OK?" Zoe said. "You've gone ever so pale."

Rebecca swallowed hard. "No, yes. No, I'm fine. Really. I just need a drink, that's all."

They carried on walking toward the marquee.

"And Lorna and Max are so well suited, don't you think?" Zoe carried on. "Both absolutely gorgeous. And she's dead brainy. Plus she's so organized and the perfect hostess. I mean, a man like Max, highly intelligent, ambitious, needs a consort, don't you reckon?"

Zoe was the kind of old-fashioned, unliberated girl who used words like *consort* in conversations about marriage.

"Maybe we should fix him up with the duke of Edinburgh," Rebecca muttered.

Zoe burst out laughing. "You know what I mean, though. She always looks so poised, elegant and in control. Don't you wish you were more like her? I know I do."

Rebecca carried on staring. By now she was choking back tears.

"Now, come on, Becks, chin up. There's somebody out there for you. You just need to get out more. Have you thought about learning to salsa? Adam and I have just started lessons. It's such a giggle and great exercise."

Then she said she really ought to go and mingle.

Without thinking, Rebecca headed straight back to the drawing room. She was just about to burst in on Max and Lorna and demand to know what the bloody hell was going on when she saw the wedding photographer, followed by half a dozen bridesmaids, heading her way. Probably about to take some photographs in the drawing room, she thought. She couldn't possibly make a scene. As she stood there wondering what to do, she heard somebody behind her. She turned round. It was Guy.

"Poor old Becks," he said, seeing Max and Lorna. "Trouble in Camelot, is there? You know you can always come and cry on my shoulder. Or any other bit of me you fancy."

"Oh, just bugger off, Guy," she said, pushing past him. She realized all she wanted to do was leave. She picked up her dress and started running down the hall.

"I'll take that as a maybe, then, shall I?" he called after her.

As she reached the front door she pulled Val's shawl out of her bag. "God, this won't be enough," she said. "I'll get frostbite out there."

Then she noticed an ancient battered Barbour hanging on the coat stand. She hesitated for a moment, then grabbed it up and threw it on over her dress.

A couple of minutes later she was standing at the end of the gravel drive, staring at the empty lane. In the freezing half light the countryside looked as bleak as she felt. She pulled the Barbour round her and felt the drizzle falling on her face. Only then did she realize that on top of being dumped by Max, she had no car, no mobile and no idea how she was going to get back to London. She stood there wondering whether to go back into the house and call a taxi. But she couldn't face the thought of seeing Max and Lorna again. Then, quite miraculously, she saw it, putt-putting toward her. It couldn't have been doing more than fifteen miles an hour. She held out her arm as if she were stranded in the rain at Oxford Circus.

"Tractor!" she yelled. "Tractor!"

13

Rebecca came into the kitchen and put the phone down on the table.

"Who was that you were speaking to?" Jess said, grating cheese onto the beans on toast she'd just made for Rebecca.

"Darren. He made me promise I'd phone to let him know I got home OK."

Darren was the crooked-toothed young tractor driver who had taken Rebecca back to her car, lifted up the hood and immediately diagnosed her problem as damp in the electrics. As luck would have it, he just happened to have a can of WD-40 in his overall pocket because the tractor was always playing up the same way. He'd sprayed it over the engine and the car had started immediately. It had been all she could do not to hug him. Instead, she offered him a tenner for his trouble, but he wouldn't hear of it.

Jess put the beans on toast down on the table. "Come on," she said, "you'll feel better once you've had something to eat."

Rebecca fell heavily onto a kitchen chair and began toying with a few beans. "Where's Lipstick?"

"Gone to see her builder and nag him about how long everything's taking."

Rebecca carried on toying. "I'm not really hungry."

"Eat," Jess commanded. "It'll do you good."

"Anybody ever told you you'd make a great Jewish mother?" Rebecca smiled.

As she shoved a forkful of food into her mouth she suddenly realized how hungry she was. A moment later she was scooping up beans like a famished cowboy taking a pit stop in the middle of a corral.

"I just can't believe Max could behave like such a slimy bastard," Jess said, taking a bottle of white wine out of the fridge.

"Tell me about it. I mean, you think you know somebody. Then something like this happens."

"On the other hand," Jess said thoughtfully, "there is a possibility—slim, I'll grant you—that Lorna and Max might not be having an affair."

"Yeah, right," Rebecca said, her mouth stuffed with food "That's why they were draped in each other. I don't get it. A few minutes before we'd been snogging. How could he two-time me like this? And with me there, in the same house, right under his nose. What sort of a person does something like that? When was he going to tell me, when their kids started university?"

Jess put two glasses on the table, sat down and began pouring the wine—a full glass for Rebecca, a splash for herself. "OK, it's a long shot, but maybe they were just being affectionate."

"Affectionate," Rebecca repeated.

"Think about it. You said yourself they've known each other for ages and it's not as if he had his tongue down her throat."

"He didn't have to," Rebecca said, picking up her wineglass. "Look, you weren't there. You didn't see how they were together. I told you the other night, it's her he wants. I reckon he just saw me as some bird to have a bit of fun with. Come on, why would a bloke like Max Stoddart want to get serious with a woman who turns up at a wedding dressed like Peggy Bundy's matron of honor?"

"Easy," Jess came back. "You were brave. Dead brave. And that's why he loves you."

Rebecca grunted.

"Look," Jess said, "I'm not saying he definitely isn't having an affair with Lorna—all I'm suggesting is that you may have read too much into what you saw. After all, you were feeling pretty vulnerable today. You'd had the breakdown, then the dress thing. Max is a decent bloke. He wouldn't string two women along like this. Plus, from what you've told me, Lorna is vile. What can he see in her? I bet the phone goes any minute and it's him worried sick about you and wanting to know why on earth you ran off."

"You reckon?" Rebecca said, allowing herself to believe for a moment that Jess could be right.

When eleven o'clock came and the phone still hadn't gone, she decided the idea that Max and Lorna weren't shagging was utterly preposterous. How she could have even considered it, she had no idea. Then Jess discovered the phone had been off the hook for hours.

"Probably Harrison," she said.

Irritated with Harrison, but at the same time vaguely cheered up because there was a credible explanation for Max's silence, Rebecca went to soak in the bath. Afterward, she took the phone to bed with her. Just in case. She tried to read, but couldn't concentrate. Finally, around midnight, she fell asleep sitting up, the phone still in her hand. Then, a few minutes later it rang, jolting her awake. In a flash she pressed the connect button.

"Hello? Max? Is that you?"

"OK," the unfamiliar, jolly male voice came back, obviously from a room full of people, "I'd like to order one chicken tikka masala, two lamb passanda, a prawn rogan josh and four stuffed paratha…"

"Sorry, you've got the wrong number," she mumbled.

A second later it rang again.

"Look, will you stop phoning me. This is not the Star of India."

"Rebecca? That you?"

"Max?"

"Oh, thank God. I've been trying to get you for hours."

"You have?" she said, her face brightening. "Sorry about just then. I thought you were a wrong number."

"I think I must have tried forty times." There was genuine panic and concern in his voice. "And look, before you say anything, I know what you saw. That Guy creep told me. But it's not what you think. I can explain."

She almost laughed. He sounded like the guilty lover in a bad Hollywood romance.

"Don't tell me," she said sarcastically, "you were comforting her."

"Yes, actually."

"Oh, Max. Come on. Do you really expect me to believe that?"

"But I was. Honest. You have to believe me. Lorna's godfather had just died that morning. Lord somebody or other. Apparently they were very close. She hadn't wanted to come to the wedding, but because Lorna and Zoe are cousins, Lorna's mother had put pressure on her to be there. She'd had a couple of drinks and she just broke down. All I did was give her a hug."

"Looked like a damned sight more than a hug to me."

"Rebecca, it was a hug. I promise. There is absolutely nothing going on between me and Lorna. Why on earth did you run off like that instead of waiting to talk to me?"

"The two of you were all over each other. I had all the information I needed."

"But you didn't. You got it all wrong."

"And it wasn't just me who thought there was something going on. Zoe did too."

"I'm sorry," Max said. "It must have looked awful, but it was all completely innocent. Her godfather had just died. Honest. There is nothing going on."

She let out a long, slow breath. "Really?"

"Promise."

"Jess said there might not be."

"Well, she was right. I'd come round now, to show you precisely how much there isn't going on between me and Lorna, but I'm actually in a taxi on my way to Waterloo to catch the Eurostar."

He explained that a meeting with one of his French contacts that had been planned for Monday had been brought forward to Sunday morning. Apparently the chap was off to South America for a conference. On top of that several people he had lined up to go on the record about the nuclear story were getting cold feet and having second thoughts about taking part in the film. As a result he was going to have to work on them all over again.

"I'm busy all day tomorrow, so I may not get a chance to phone you."

She told him that was no problem and asked him how long he was going to be away.

"Probably until the end of the week."

"I'll miss you," she said.

"I'll miss you, too. And I'm sorry I upset you."

"I'm sorry I overreacted and ran out like that." She smiled and snuggled down in the bed. "Speak to you soon. Take care."

She fell asleep almost immediately, the smile still on her face.

She was woken briefly at seven by Lipstick slamming the front door (she was going to Manchester for the day to see Stan) and slept until just after nine. She wouldn't have woken then, if it

hadn't been for all the shouting. Half asleep and petrified something had happened to Diggory, she leaped out of bed. She ran into
the hall, her head spinning because she'd stood up too quickly. She
saw Jess crouched by the front door, yelling through the letter
box.

"Get away from me, you depraved sicko. If you don't go away
right this second, I'm calling the police. How could you come
round here, wearing that … that THING?"

"But it's not what you think," Ed's slightly muffled voice came
back. "Just open the door and take another look."

"No. I've seen enough. Look, Ed, I'm past caring what you get
up to on your own, but don't start drawing me into your sordid little half life."

"Jess," Rebecca said, frowning. "Do you mind telling me what's
going on?"

"It's him. Autoasphyxiation Man."

"What?"

"OK, if you don't believe me, take a look."

Rebecca bent down and peered through the letter box. Two
eyes were staring back at her out of a hideous black mask. It was
made of molded rubber and covered in silver studs—sort of
Village People meets Hannibal Lecter.

"Eeeew," Rebecca said, suddenly noticing the anteater snouty
bit and screwing up her face. "Scareee."

"What did I tell you?" Jess cried, half hysterical, half tri-
umphant. "It's the thing I found in his suitcase."

Rebecca looked a second time. The mask was like nothing she'd
seen before. She felt the hairs stand up on the back of her neck.

" 'Morning, Ed," she said, deciding the willy-nilly had sent him
mad and the only approach was to humor him. "All right?"

"No, I'm not bloody all right. I want to come in and talk to my
wife."

"I can hear you're upset, Ed," she soothed, sounding like some "please lay your anger on the table and share it with the group" shrink.

"Well, then bloody open the door."

"I'm not sure I can do that just now. You see, Jess is a bit perturbed by your—er—face furniture."

She asked Jess how Ed'd gotten into the building. Apparently one of the neighbors had let him in on her way out.

"OK, I agree it was a mistake to put it on," Ed said. "I just thought if she saw me wearing it here, in broad daylight, she'd realize it wasn't what she thought. Right, I'm taking it off."

There were a few seconds of silence after which they heard Ed move away from the letter box and begin a whispered conversation.

"Who's he talking to?" Jess snapped. "Omigod, I bet it's one of his perv cronies from the autoasphyxiation club. Christ, there could be dozens of them out there."

Rebecca looked through the letter box, but Ed and his companion were outside her field of vision. The conversation went on for a couple of minutes. Then: "'Mornin', ladies." It was another male voice—older and vaguely familiar. "This is Tony, your milkman, speaking. I would just like to say that after giving the matter careful consideration, I have come to the conclusion that the gentleman here is definitely not a perv." Before buying his milk round, Tony had spent donkeys' years as a barrister's clerk and always spoke as if he were giving evidence in court. He cleared his throat. "While the article in question would appear to be somewhat unusual in design, I have looked at the label and can confirm it is in fact a Japanese cycle mask."

"A cycle mask?" Rebecca said.

"No doubt about it," replied Tony, "and a very fancy one it is, too." She heard him pick up the empties and clink off down the hall.

"Don't believe him," Jess said to Rebecca. "I'm telling you, it's some pervy sex toy my husband puts on before hanging himself from the door frame and shoving gerbils up his arse."

Ed cried out in frustration. "For Christ's sake. How many more times do I have to go over this? The shop threw it in when I bought my bike, but I never wore it. Will somebody just listen to me when I say I'm not a perv? You can phone the shop and ask if you don't believe me."

"Don't you dare open that door," Jess hissed, as Rebecca reached for the catch. But she was too late. It was already open.

"Hiya," Rebecca said with a nervous smile. She couldn't help worrying that Tony had been lying as Jess had suspected and really was a fellow perv. "Come on in."

"Thank you. Now then," he said, handing the mask to Jess, "look at the label."

"Nippon Cycle Corp," she read. She looked at him, a distinctly hangdog expression on her face. "OK, promise me you don't stick gerbils up your arse."

"I promise you, I do not stick gerbils up my arse. Now then, come and give me a kiss."

Reluctantly, looking back at Rebecca for approval, she moved toward him. A second later they were in each other's arms.

"Actually, I stick budgies up it," he said, grinning.

Rebecca went back to bed with the Sunday papers while Jess and Ed sat in the living room, making up and playing with Diggory. After an hour or so, she poked her head round the living room door to offer Jess and Ed coffee and bagels.

"It's OK," Jess said, her face full of smiles. "I'll think we'll have something when we get home."

An hour later amid tears, thank-yous and I'll-miss-yous, they'd loaded up the car.

"By the way," Rebecca said, "you were right. Max rang late last night. There wasn't anything going on between him and Bloody

Lorna." She explained about Bloody Lorna's godfather dying. "I made a bit of a fool of myself."

"Doesn't matter," Jess said. "So long as the pair of you are back on track." Then she gave Rebecca a hug.

Rebecca began folding up Jess's camp bed. Despite the overcrowding and Jess's slovenliness, she was going to miss her and Diggory.

She spent the afternoon cleaning the flat. By six the kitchen and bathroom were positively gleaming. Then she put on her PJs, opened a bottle of Penfolds and settled down to watch *Antiques Roadshow*. About eleven she took herself to bed with one of her *Seinfeld* vids. She was woken in the small hours by Lipstick letting herself in, yakking loudly on her mobile. Rebecca's bedroom door was open and it was impossible not to hear what was being said.

"If I play my cards right," she was saying, "I should have the money pretty soon."

Rebecca frowned. What money?

"No, I don't know exactly when, but the whole thing's been a total breeze up till now. It shouldn't be much longer. You should have seen me in action, babe. He was a total pushover. Talk about putty in my hands. No, I don't think there'll be any problems. I'm so excited, babe. I just can't wait for us to be together again. It's been so long. But we have to think where to go. D'you know where I've always fancied? Brazil."

By now the color had drained from Rebecca's face and her heart was racing.

So, Lipstick really was out to fleece Stan. She was even planning to do a runner with some lover—to a South American country that had no extradition treaty with Britain. The ditsy lovable airhead thing, the new blinds, the cushions, sucking up to everybody was all an act—a ploy to gain their trust, making it easier for her to pounce. She must have done it today, while she was with Stan in Manchester. She'd probably asked him for money—claiming it was for some new business venture. Or perhaps she had per-suaded him to put some of his investments in her name. Rebecca was on the point of barging into the room and confronting her, but managed to stop herself. It would only end in a massive row and Lipstick running off with Stan's money. What she needed to do was warn Stan. It was up to him to confront her. She thought about phoning him straight away, but decided a call from her at three in the morning would frighten him to death. She would leave it until the morning.

God only knew how she was going to break it to him.

She lay in bed until Lipstick had gone to work. Then she tried Stan, but there was no answer. She dialed his mobile, but it was switched off. As soon as she got to the office she tried him again on the shop number. He picked up immediately.

"Hi, sweetie. Look, can I call you back? I'm just about to start interviewing prospective managers. I'll be busy all morning. Then I'm going off to see if I can find Bernadette an engagement ring. She told me yesterday she'd like a solitaire. So I thought I'd get her a cluster of solitaires. What do you think?" He burst out laughing.

She felt sick. Poor Stan. Here he was joking as usual, without even the remotest idea of what was going on.

"Very funny, but look, Dad, this is very important. I really do need to talk to you."

"Oh, look, the first interviewee has just walked in. I really have to go. By the way, great news about you and this Max chap. Your gran told me."

"But, Dad..."

He was gone.

Realizing she needed somebody to talk to, she dialed Jess. Her line was busy so she decided to try Max. She didn't like disturbing him while he was working, but she assumed he'd have his mobile switched off if he was in the middle of something important. He picked up almost immediately.

"Hi, Max, it's me. Listen, something terrible's happened..."

"OK, Monsieur Volaile," Max came back, "if you could just fax those details to me at my hotel I'd be grateful."

She realized what was going on. "Whoops. Sorry," she said. "You're in an important meeting and can't talk?"

"*Exactement*, monsieur."

She was just about to hang up when she heard a woman's voice in the background. "Max, come on. Get off the phone. The minister is starting to get impatient. He has to leave for the airport in a few minutes."

Rebecca put down the phone. There was no mistaking that haughty tone. Lorna was with him in Paris.

"OK, OK," she said, doing her best to calm down, "Max and Lorna are working on the French story together. It's perfectly reasonable she should be in Paris with him." And by the sound of it they'd clearly been working rather than shagging. But why hadn't Max told her she was going to be there? If there was nothing going on between them, why keep it a secret?

Her thoughts were interrupted by Charlie, who'd come over to get an update on the Mer de Rêves story. She didn't have the heart to tell him about Lipstick being a liar and a cheat who had undoubtedly been conning her about the Mer de Rêves award and that for the moment, at least, she now had no idea how she was going to infiltrate the MdR lab.

At lunchtime, her head bursting with worries about her dad, Max and Lorna and the Mer de Rêves story, she popped out to get a sandwich. Then, when she got back, she couldn't eat it. Instead, she decided to try Max again. She had to find out once and for all what was going on between him and Bloody Lorna. She was just about to dial his number when she heard Bryony, the news desk assistant, shouting across the room.

"OK, people—Lucretia alert. Lucretia alert."

So obsessed was everybody in the office with Lucretia's Prince Charles confession, that Bryony had been unofficially relieved of all news desk assisting duties. Instead, she spent the day glued to her computer screen, monitoring *Watching You, Watching Me* live online, with instructions to yell if it looked like Lucretia was about to drop another ball. A moment later, thirty people, minus Charlie Holland, who was writing a lead in his office with the door closed, had gathered round Bryony's desk. Lacking her colleagues' enthusiasm, but curious nonetheless, Rebecca joined them. She got there just in time to hear Lucretia confess that she'd always fancied a threesome with Willard Scott and Barbara Walters. The snorts and guffaws were deafening.

Rebecca had tried to join in the fun, but her mind was taken up with imagining what was going on between Max and Bloody Lorna. She could just see them strolling arm in arm by the Seine, sipping Pernod in some little bar in the Latin Quarter. Each night they would climb the steps to Sacre Coeur and stand there looking out over the city. She could see it now, lit up like a box of jewels. Then he would take her in his arms and tell her how much he loved her.

She dialed his mobile again. When she got no answer she decided to try the hotel.

"Ah, Monsieur Stoddart et Mademoiselle Findlay," the chap on the desk said. "Oui. Room 213. I weel put you through."

A sharp intake of breath from Rebecca. "*Non, monsieur, un moment, s'il vous plaît.* Er, Monsieur Stoddart and Mademoiselle Findlay—they are in the same room?"

"*Mais oui. Bien sûr.* I connect you now."

The phone was picked up on the third ring.

"*Allo?*" Perfectly accented French, but once again, there was no mistaking the voice.

It was as much as Rebecca could do to get the words out. "Er, is Max there?" It came out as a hoarse whisper.

"Sorry, he's in the shower. Can I take a message?"

"No. No message."

"Hang on, I'll find out how long he's likely to be....Honey, you almost finished in there?"

Honey. She called him honey. A single tear streaked Rebecca's cheek. She could see it all now. Max had clearly been in two minds about whether he wanted her or Lorna. Paris, with all its magic and romance, had intoxicated him and he'd chosen Lorna. All she could think about was the pair of them shagging in some sumptuous *fin de siècle* hotel room overlooking the Seine.

It wasn't long before the hurt turned to anger, not to mention an overwhelming desire for revenge. Before she knew what she was doing she'd picked up the phone and was dialing the Channel 6 switchboard. Her voice perfectly calm and steady, she asked to be put through to Lorna's office. A woman she took to be her personal assistant answered almost immediately.

"Oh," Rebecca said innocently, "is Lorna Findlay there?"

"No, I'm afraid she's in Paris all week."

"Oh, dear. Well, may I leave a message?"

"Certainly. Go ahead."

"It's a rather delicate personal matter. I'm phoning from the clinic."

"Clinic? What clinic would that be?"

Rebecca cleared her throat. "The, er ..." She lowered her voice. "The special clinic."

"Special? How is it special?"

"No, no. You misunderstand. I'm phoning from the STD clinic. It's with reference to Ms. Findlay's anal warts...."

* * *

"Ooh, ooh," Bryony was calling out for a second time. "Rumpus."

Everybody, including Rebecca, who was feeling positively cathartic after her phone call, leaped up and rushed over to the screen.

"OK, I have had it," Snow was yelling at Lucretia. They were alone in the girls' bedroom. "It's about time you learned to look after yourself."

"Snow, darling, please calm down," Lucretia was saying. She looked genuinely taken aback. "All I did was remind you to use the thermometer I gave you to check my bathwater was precisely sixty-seven degrees. I can't see why you lost your temper."

Lucretia put a placating hand on Snow's shoulder. Snow snatched it away.

"I lost my temper because I'm fed up with being treated like your servant," Snow snarled. "From now on you can run your own bath, do your own washing and ironing, put your own ice in your drinks and rub anticellulite cream into your own bloody arse. I am out of here. Do you understand? Out of here!"

As Snow stomped off into the communication room—presumably to arrange her exit from the house—the entire office broke into cheers and applause.

"Blimey," somebody said through the din, "who'd have thought Snow would finally find the balls to stand up to Lucretia?"

The catharsis starting to wear off, Rebecca thought about going home. But she knew she'd only mope and eat. Plus she just had to find some way of getting into the Mer de Rêves offices. She decided to put in another call to the senior PR in Paris and have another go at buttering him up. She rang his extension, but there was no reply. She would try again later.

In the meantime she had a column to write. She opened her desk drawer and went trawling through her freebie samples, looking for inspiration.

By five o'clock—between the occasional blub and worrying about Stan—she'd managed to research and write what she considered to be a spectacularly focused and well-argued piece in favor of cheek stains as opposed to traditional powder blushers.

Starving now, because she'd had no lunch, she rewarded herself with a cappuccino and an apricot Danish from Salvo's. As she sat sipping and chewing, she thumbed through the *Daily Mail*. A picture on the Dempster page caught her eye. An elderly tweedy type who looked like she had spent her life mustering hounds had been photographed at the Harrods delicatessen counter beating another woman round the head with a large vacuum pack of smoked salmon. The beatee was in her fifties, Rebecca guessed. She was tall, slim and exquisitely dressed—or had been. At the precise moment the photograph was taken, her face, hair and suit were covered in coleslaw. Rebecca burst out laughing, but stopped almost immediately.

"Bloody hell." The elderly tweedy type doing the beating was Lady Axminster.

She didn't bother to read the text. Instead, she got straight on the phone to Jess.

"Oh, God," Jess groaned. "It happened weeks ago. Mum made me promise not to tell anybody because she's so ashamed. She hoped it wouldn't get out, but some paparazzo just happened to be in the Food Hall, photographed them and sold it to Dempster."

Rebecca asked her what had caused the fracas.

"It was terrible. This woman she'd never met in her life, but who clearly knew her, came up to her and announced she'd slept with Dad while he and Mum were on honeymoon."

"On honeymoon? My God. Bitch."

"Mum thought she knew everything there was to know about

Dad's philandering, but this came as a real shock and she just lost it."

"I'm not surprised," Rebecca said. "But why would this woman have told her now—after all these years? It's such an unnecessary and spiteful thing to do."

"I know, but as you can imagine not a lot of discussion went on. Once Mum had finished bashing her up, she vamoosed. If you look, they've named her in the piece. Mum feels she ought to phone her to apologize, but at the moment she's still too angry."

Rebecca made her promise to tell Lady A how sorry she was.

"So," Jess said, "you and Max Factor still on track?"

Rebecca said there had been an unforeseen derailment, but when she got to the bit about the anal warts, Jess screamed with laughter.

"I don't get it," Jess said finally. "All you're looking for is a man who's sensitive, caring and good-looking. Why can't you find one?"

"I'll tell you why. Because they all have boyfriends."

Jess gave a half laugh. "Come and have dinner," she said. "You'll only sit at home and get miserable."

Rebecca explained about the Lipstick situation and said she couldn't come because she really needed to be at home to keep an eye—or to be more accurate, an ear—on things. It took Jess a few minutes to process what Rebecca had told her.

"I'm sorry, I just don't see it. There has to be some mistake. Lipstick's kind, generous—a bit of a ditz brain, I grant you, but she's not a crook."

Rebecca grunted and said there was no mistake. "The ditsy thing is just a brilliant act, a cover. We've all been taken in."

Jess let out a slow breath. "I still can't believe it," she said. "Look, just promise me one thing—that you'll discuss all this with Stan and not do anything daft like go charging round to the Talon Salon to confront her. If you're wrong, you will make such a fool of yourself."

Rebecca said she had no intention of confronting Lipstick and that she was fully aware this was her father's problem, which he had to sort out for himself.

Rebecca put down the phone and found herself returning to the photograph of Lady Axminster.

"Blimey, she really went for this woman," Rebecca said, noticing the contents of the woman's posh carrier bags lying strewn all over the floor. Among the clothes and shoes was a large jar. Rebecca only noticed it because the shop lights had caught the diamond letters on the lid, brilliantly illuminating the MdR logo.

She still hadn't made contact with Stan. Apparently as soon as he'd finished interviewing prospective managers he'd had to drive over to Sheffield to sort out some emergency with his French knicker supplier. She'd been trying his mobile, but it was switched off. She looked at her watch and decided to call him again, but all she got was his voice mail. When she phoned the shop, the girl who answered said that they hadn't heard from him since he left and that as far as she knew he was still in Sheffield.

As Rebecca put down the phone, it began to dawn on her that something could have happened to him. Maybe he'd broken down. Or, God forbid, had an accident. A bad accident. She started to think the unthinkable. He could be lying dead in a ditch. And maybe it wasn't a genuine accident. Maybe Lipstick had caused it on purpose. Could she have persuaded him to change his will in her favor and then ...?

"Omigod," Rebecca cried out, "she's cut his brakes."

She realized the moment she'd said it that the idea was preposterous. She'd clearly become so obsessed with the Max and Bloody Lorna thing that she wasn't thinking straight. Lipstick might be a cheap con artist, but she wasn't capable of murder. And

the overwhelming likelihood was that Stan hadn't had an accident. He'd probably gone out for a drink with the French knicker
bloke in Sheffield and simply forgotten to switch his mobile on.
On the other hand, Lipstick was clearly out to ruin Stan financially.
For all Rebecca knew, she might have done it already. She suddenly
realized that with Stan out of contact, she had no option but to
take matters into her own hands. Totally forgetting her promise to
Jess, she decided she had to confront Lipstick now, before she took
off for Brazil.

She charged to the lift, putting on her jacket as she went.

Of course, the rush hour traffic had to be particularly night-
marish that evening, and it was well after six by the time she
reached the Face Place and Talon Salon. She wasn't sure if it would
still be open. Then she saw Lipstick's BMW—registration: K9
GAL—parked outside and realized she was still there. She came to
a cartoon halt in front of it and leaped out of the car, totally unaware her rear end was sticking miles out into the road.

As she opened the door and stepped into the empty reception
she was convinced she'd stumbled across the Muswell Hill annex
of the Palace of Versailles. The walls were covered in floor-to-
ceiling mirrors with swirly gilt edging. Against the window was a
matching gilt table with a mirror top. At one end of it was a pile of
glossies. At the other sat a gold cherub playing a lyre. The carpet
was mauve with a gold scroll design. More cherubs were sus-
pended from the ceiling along with a vast crystal chandelier. Tiny
gilt chairs with mauve velvet seats lined one wall. A second gilt
table identical to the first, although minus the cherub, served as
the reception desk. Rebecca walked over to it, picked up a tiny
brass bell shaped like a lily and shook it so that the stamen inside
tinkled. She wasn't sure who would appear, Lipstick or Marie
Antoinette's PA.

But it was Lipstick, carrying Harrison on her front in a baby sling. "Becks," she said, looking both surprised and delighted. "I was just about to lock up. What are you doing here?"

"I think it's time you and I had a talk," Rebecca said icily.

Lipstick looked taken aback for a moment. Then: "Ooh, I think we've been rumbled, Hawwie," she giggled. "Becks is a bit cwoss with us because we've been keeping an ikkle seecwit."

"Ah, so you admit there is an ikkle seecwit, then?"

Lipstick pulled a fake long face. "Guilty, your honor," she said. "Look, I know I should have told Stan, but I was holding back until everything had been finalized. I wanted it to be a surprise."

"Oh, it'll be a surprise all right," Rebecca said, wondering what, precisely, "it" would turn out to be.

"You know, Becks," Lipstick said, scratching the top of Harrison's head, "this has to be the best day of my life."

"I bet," Rebecca muttered.

"I've got your dad and now all this. So how did you find out? Did the council try and reach me at the flat this morning?"

Rebecca frowned. "The council? What's the council got to do with it?"

Now it was Lipstick's turn to look confused. "But they must have told you. The council's just given me planning permission to extend the salon into the empty shop next door. I've been waiting months for a decision and suddenly there's a letter waiting for me on the mat when I got in this morning."

So that was it. She'd convinced Stan to give her money to expand the business. Now she would simply dump him and move on to the next unsuspecting sucker.

"Must be costing a fortune," Rebecca said pointedly.

"Tell me about it. But you should have seen me with my bank manager last week. I was magnificent. I charmed the pants off him....Didn't I charm the pants off him, Hawwie? Putty in my hands he was. Anyway he said if I came up with half the money, the bank would probably lend me the rest. The only problem was the loan had to be approved at the bank's head office. Then, would you believe it, just before you arrived the manager rang to say it had all gone through. So everything's come together on the same day. I can hardly believe it."

"And the rest of the money—where's that coming from?"

"Oh, that's not a problem. I've got some savings and my gran died last year and left me a fair bit." She paused. "I know I haven't shown it, but the last few weeks have been pretty tense. I don't know what I would have done if I hadn't had my oldest friend to talk to, in Australia."

"You have a best friend in Australia?" Rebecca said, swallowing hard. That would explain the late-night calls.

"Yes, Mandy. Can't believe I haven't mentioned her. Lives in Brisbane with a what d'you call it … a pederast."

"A pederast? Your best friend is married to a pederast?"

"Oh, maybe that's not it. But it's definitely ped something."

Rebecca thought for a moment. "You don't mean a podiatrist, do you?"

"Yeah, that's it. Anyway I've been discussing everything with her—usually in the middle of the night because it's the only time I can get her. Hope I didn't disturb you."

"Good God, no," Rebecca said, laughing too loudly. "Didn't hear a thing."

"Anyway," Lipstick went on, "I haven't seen her in years because she could never afford the fare back home, but her cake-making business is really picking up, so we've decided to meet up in the summer. We thought somewhere a bit unusual, maybe. I've always fancied Brazil."

"So, Dad isn't involved in the business expansion?"

"Stan? Absolutely not. Listen, Becks, when your father asked me to marry him I made sure he understood one thing. I have my own money and I make my own way. I've never been a kept woman and I've no intention of becoming one now."

Just then the phone went on the reception desk.

"Hiya," Lipstick said. She covered up the mouthpiece. "It's your dad," she mouthed to Rebecca.

So he hadn't had an accident, thank God.

"Says he's been wandering round bookshops in Sheffield all afternoon looking for more bizarre titles."

"Say hi from me and ask him if he found any," Rebecca said.

Lipstick asked and then burst out laughing. "Two," she came back. "*Truncheons, Their Romance and Reality* and *What to Say When You Talk to Yourself.*"

"Brilliant," Rebecca said, moving over to the window to give Lipstick some privacy.

By now she was consumed with guilt. Stan trusted Lipstick: why hadn't she been able to do the same? There was no doubt in her mind that her chances of being reincarnated as Jennifer Aniston had been well and truly dashed. The best she could hope for was to be brought back as one of Bloody Lorna's anal warts.

Lipstick told Stan she missed him and loved him and put down the phone.

"So, was that all you wanted to talk about?" she said to Rebecca. "You looked a bit stressed when you came in."

"I know. Sorry. It's Max. He's dumped me for Bloody Lorna."

"Oh, Becks, I'm really sorry." She put her arms round Rebecca and hugged her. Harrison, trapped between the two bodies, started to yelp.

"There you are, even Hawwie's upset. Aren't you, baby?" She chucked him under the chin. Then she looked back at Rebecca and smiled. "I've got some news that'll cheer you up. The Mer de Rêves people have brought forward the date for the awards ceremony." She reached into her overall pocket and with a dramatic flourish produced two first-class Eurostar tickets.

"They sent these. We're off on Friday."

"Ooh, *formidable!*" Rebecca cried in her best French accent.

"No," Lipstick said, frowning. "They're not for anybody else. They really are for us."

 **14**

...and you know what I'd love? Some cock-a-leekie soup."

" Hang on, Gran," Rebecca said, switching her mobile to her other ear. "Let me get this straight. You want me to bring you back cock-a-leekie soup? From France?"

Rebecca had been sitting drinking coffee in the Eurostar departure lounge at Waterloo—Lipstick had gone for a pee—when Rose rang to wish them bon voyage.

"What's wrong with that?" her grandmother came back. "But don't go mad. It's heavy. A couple of tins will do."

"But it's not French."

"What isn't?"

"Cock-a-leekie soup."

"Don't be daft. How can it not be French?"

"Because it's Scottish."

"Scottish," Rose mocked, laughing. "Didn't they teach you any French at school? Look, cock's French for chicken. Coq au vin is chicken in wine. Cock-a-leekie is chicken in leeks. Lez leekies. I mean, if that doesn't sound French I don't know what does. All you can get here is the Baxters version, but I've always meant to try the real thing."

Rebecca sighed. Seeing there was no way she was going to convince Rose that cock-a-leekie soup wasn't French, she decided to give up trying. When she got back from Paris she would simply say the workers at the cock-a-leekie plant were *en grève* and attempt to placate her with a jar of bouillabaisse.

"And a couple of French sticks would be nice," Rose continued.

Rebecca made the point that it was a waste of time buying baguettes since there were so many bakers in London these days that made wonderful French bread. "And it'll be stale by the time I get it home."

"I can freshen it up in the oven," her grandmother insisted. "If you ask me, French bread from France still tastes more authentic. But if you can't be bothered…."

"No, it's OK," Rebecca said kindly. "I don't mind."

She did really. Nursing a baguette home on the train would be a total *pain* in the arse. On top of that, all the other passengers would think she was some unworldly Eiffel-tower-snow-dome-buying McPleb who'd never eaten French bread before and had been so overwhelmed by the taste and sophistication that she was taking it home for all her McPleb friends to try. Then she'd be forced to have very loud pretend conversations on her mobile, in her best A-level French—about charcuterie and Jacques Derrida's theory of deconstructionism—to prove how utterly au courant she really was with French culture. Maybe it would be a good idea to have a bottle of absinthe sticking out of her bag as well, she thought, to shove the point home.

"So," Rose said. "I heard about what happened with you and Max. Your dad told me. I'm so sorry, sweetie." She paused. "Still, you have to be positive. There are plenty more *poissons* in the *mer*. You never know, you might come back with a gorgeous Frenchman.

Like that Julio Iglesias chappie. Bit old for you, maybe, but I think he's lovely."

"But Julio Iglesias is Spani—" Gawd. What was the point? "Yeah, you never know. Maybe I will."

"You loved Max, didn't you?" Rose said gently.

Rebecca closed her eyes. "Yes," she said, swallowing in an attempt to get rid of the lump in her throat. "Yes, I did."

"I take it he hasn't been in touch?"

"He's phoned a few times, but when I see his number come up I ignore it. Look, I really have to go. They'll be announcing our train in a sec."

Rose said she loved her and told her to have a wonderful day shopping. (Rebecca hadn't revealed the real reason they were going to Paris on the grounds that Rose would have been scared witless.)

"We will," she said. "Love you too."

As Rebecca was putting her phone back in her bag, Lipstick reappeared and sat back down. She was thumbing through the French dictionary she'd bought for the trip.

"What you looking up?" Rebecca said.

"The French for *penis*."

"Fair enough," Rebecca said casually, as if Lipstick had said she was looking up the French for umbrella. She picked up the copy of the *Independent* she'd just bought and started reading.

"It's for Harrison," Lipstick went on. "I can't go all the way to France without bringing him back a little pressie."

"And you thought a penis would make the perfect gift," Rebecca said, without looking up from the paper. "I didn't realize he needed a new one. So what are you thinking? Dior? Balenciaga? Comme des Garçons?"

But Lipstick was too busy concentrating and hadn't heard her. "Oh, here it is. *Le pénis*. That's easy enough. Now, then, what's the French for *horse butcher*?"

Lipstick began flicking through the pages again.

"*Boucherie chevaline*," Rebecca said vaguely. Then, coming out from behind the newspaper: "Oh, God. Not more bloody horse meat."

"It's just that it's so easy to get out there and one of my clients told me that in France dried horses' willies are a really popular doggy treat."

Rebecca stared at her in disbelief, then burst out laughing. "I think she may have been having you on."

"No, it's true. Apparently they're full of vitamins and iron."

"Yeah, right," Rebecca came back, still giggling. "Well, I dare you to go into a *boucherie chevaline* and ask for a horse's willy."

They arrived at Gare du Nord just before one. As they crossed the concourse, dodging a large yellowish puddle, Lipstick began sniffing the air. "You know that smell gets me every time," she said.

"Yeah, me too," Rebecca replied wistfully. She inhaled deeply. "Suddenly you're transported back to some little left-bank bar in the fifties, and there's André Gide and Jean-Paul Sartre debating some moot philosophical point or other over a bottle of Pastis. Then in walks Picasso, arm in arm with Simone de Beauvoir."

Lipstick looked confused. "Funny," she came back. "It never has that effect on me. All I know is, it's very different from our smell."

"That's because they use different tobacco," Rebecca explained.

"Would that affect it, then? I never thought of that."

"Definitely. What else could it be?"

"I dunno," Lipstick mused. "I've often wondered if it's got something to do with all the wine they drink. I thought that over the centuries maybe their kidneys had evolved differently from ours. You get the same smell in Spain and Italy. They're heavy wine drinkers, too. But in America it's the same as ours. They're more into beer, like us. I've made quite a study of it over the years."

Rebecca blinked. "We're not talking about French cigarettes, are we?" she said.

"Cigarettes?" Lipstick replied. "No, I'm talking about how French stale pissy smell is totally different from Brit stale pissy smell."

Since the awards ceremony didn't start until three, they had booked lunch at a Michelin-starred restaurant a few streets away from the Mer de Rêves offices on rue du Faubourg St-Honoré. Lipstick had made it clear she thought it was far too expensive, but Rebecca had dismissed her objection on the grounds that a) the *Vanguard* was picking up the tab and b) they were about to embark on a highly dangerous mission, which if it went wrong could mean their being thrown in the Bastille for fifty years and the least they deserved was a decent lunch.

They decided to take a cab. Their grumpy, monosyllabic driver, who had clearly graduated *avec honneurs* from the *misérablist* school of French taxi driving, spent the journey swearing under his breath and driving as though he were auditioning for a part in *Wacky Races*. They assumed he'd been hoping to pick up a fare who wanted to go to the French equivalent of Newport Pagnell and was pissed off they only wanted to be taken to the eighth arrondissement.

"I hope you didn't bloody tip him," Lipstick said as he screeched off.

"I did, but only one euro. I told him he should be thankful for small *mercis*."

La Cloche d'Or was set in a row of haughty white buildings with chichi wrought-iron balconies and canopies. Along with the A-list restaurants and boutiques, they housed exquisite antique shops, *chocolatiers* and *parfumeries*, each interior more intimidatingly rococo than the last.

As they walked toward the door, a wondrously coutured woman in her sixties swanned by.

"Look," Rebecca whispered, "even her eye bags are Prada. God, I wish you hadn't made us dress up in all this gear. We look like we escaped from a brothel in Tirana."

She was referring to their Erin Brockovich outfits. Just when Rebecca had thought Lipstick had forgotten all about her mad plan for them to "dress the part" for their sleuthing expedition, she'd arrived home last night with two PVC bomber jackets (almost new from the Oxfam shop round the corner) and two plastic carrier bags. One of these she'd handed to Rebecca. It contained a see-through leopard-print blouse, a cheap black satin miniskirt with a Liz Hurley safety pin thing going on down each of the side seams and impossibly high stilettos. The other bag contained Lipstick's outfit, which was similarly Kings Cross at midnight, only in red. At first Rebecca had categorically refused to wear her outfit, but Lipstick had gone on and on about how much she wanted to act out her Erin fantasy.

"And you never know, a bit of leg and cleavage might come in handy for softening up some security guard at Mer de Rêves."

Rebecca had grunted and finally given in.

The restaurant's faded maroon velvet drapes and matching banquettes were perfectly accessorized by the formal, almost reverential atmosphere.

"Gawd," Lipstick whispered, "has this lot come to eat lunch or pay it their last respects?"

They stood there, desperately trying to control their giggles.

Suddenly *la patronne* appeared from behind a gargantuan vase of white lilies, sitting on the bar. "*Bonjour, mesdames,*" she sang, offering them an obsequious smile. She was bulky. Matronly. In a plain navy woolen shift with buttons down the front. An Hermès scarf was tied loosely at her neck. It took her a moment or two to take in what they were wearing. Suddenly the smile froze on her face and her entire body stiffened. Without offering to take their jackets, she beckoned one of the waiters and whispered into his ear. A few moments later he was leading them to their table.

"In the corner, right next to the bleeding *lavabos*," Rebecca hissed. "She thinks we're on the bloody game."

Lipstick told her to stop overreacting and ordered two glasses of champagne. "You're just nervous about this afternoon. You'll feel better when you've had something to drink."

Rebecca smiled and admitted she was beginning to feel a bit scared. "I mean, what if they catch us trying to steal the cream? Tomorrow we could be up before some French judge, charged with attempted robbery."

Lipstick reached across the table and took Rebecca's hand. "It's going to be fine," she soothed. "I promise."

When Rebecca asked her how she knew, she said she'd had a sign that morning.

"What sort of a sign?"

"It was amazing. This white feather came floating down in front of me. Just appeared out of nowhere. I've been reading this book on angels and apparently a white feather is a sign that your guardian angel is looking after you and everything's going to be OK."

"What, and it materialized just like that—from nowhere?"

Lipstick nodded. "From nowhere."

"What were you doing?" Rebecca asked.

"Nothing. I was in the bedroom, just plumping up the pillows."

They sat in silence for a few minutes, observing the groups of snooty women like Prada Eyebag, the somber gray-suited business-men lunching decorously with their girlfriends, the sycophantic waiters delivering their flowery lectures about the foie gras and the lapin.

"And just look at those two biddies over there," Lipstick giggled. "I hope I'm still coming out to eat in posh restaurants when I'm that old."

Rebecca looked. A pair of shrunken old ladies with faces like car tires were sharing a banquette by the window. Neither spoke as they slowly and meticulously scraped their fish from its bones.

Lipstick picked up the giant brown leather menu. "I can't understand any of this," she said. "What's that?"

"*Andouillette avec bulots*? It's sausage made from pig's offal with whelks."

Lipstick winced. "What about this?"

"*Cervelles*? That's brains."

"I think I'll just have a green salad followed by the salmon cutlet."

Rebecca said she'd have the onion soup to start and would think about her main course while she went to the loo. She stood up.

"Ooh, look," Lipstick said. "What about a steak? Can't go wrong with a nice French filet steak. Have some chips with it and we can share them."

"OK, sounds great," Rebecca said, "order me that. Can you manage?"

"No problem. I'll just point."

Exactly as Lipstick had predicted, the moment the champagne kicked in, Rebecca started to relax. As she sat spreading her roll with the most delicious Normandy butter, she realized she was rather enjoying herself. She had finished the bread and had resorted to eating lumps of butter off her knife, when two waiters approached their table. Each was carrying a plate covered by a huge silver dome. These were placed, with great solemnity, in front of the two women. Then, with a magnificently camp flourish, and at precisely the same second, the domes were lifted. In perfect unison, the waiters wished them *bon appétit* and retreated. They had another fit of the giggles and Lipstick said she felt like the queen.

"Wow, just taste this vinaigrette," Lipstick said, inviting Rebecca to try the salad.

Rebecca stabbed some leaves with her fork. The dressing was tangy, slightly sweet and heavy with garlic and mustard. Truly magnificent.

Rebecca's onion soup was equally divine. If Stan had been there, he would have said it was "like angels pissing on your tongue."

They'd just finished their first course when two particularly snooty-looking middle-aged women walked in. One had a gray chin-length bob that looked like it had been cut with the aid of a set square. She was dressed from head to toe in baggy black Yohji Yamamoto. The other one was wearing an ankle-length fur coat over a beige trouser suit. Poking out from under her arm was a yippy chihuahua.

"Ah, cuuute!" Lipstick squealed. "Mind you, it looks a bit anorexic, even for a chihuahua."

"Probably lives on crudités and Evian," Rebecca declared.

La patronne clearly knew the pair and greeted them with double kisses. Not London or New York mwahhs, but proper puckered-lipped smackers on the cheek. She led them to a table, two down from Rebecca and Lipstick.

"Look, she's pointing in our direction," Rebecca whispered. "I'm sure she's apologizing for having to put them so close to us. God, they look really pissed off."

"Well, they'll just have to get pissed on again," Lipstick said with a shrug.

Just then, the Rosencrantz and Guildenstern waiters reappeared to give their synchronized dome lifting, act two.

The moment they'd exited, Rebecca's face dropped like a mudslide.

"What on earth's that?" Lipstick asked, looking at Rebecca's plate.

"That," Rebecca announced, "is steak tartare."

Lipstick poked it with her fork. "It's raw," she said. "I'd send it straight back if I were you."

"It's meant to be raw," Rebecca said. "That's what steak tartare is—raw minced beef mixed with garlic and herbs. People adore it, but I've never quite been able to develop a taste for it."

Lipstick screwed up her nose. "Oh, Becks, I'm so sorry. I thought it was a piece of steak."

"No, it's my fault," Rebecca said. "I should have looked at the menu. I was so desperate for the loo, I wasn't concentrating."

They decided to share Lipstick's salmon and the chips. These had just arrived, crispy and golden and sans dome. The problem was Rebecca couldn't face the embarrassment of letting Rosencrantz and Guildenstern see she hadn't touched the beef. She forced herself to try a couple of mouthfuls but couldn't get it down.

"I know," Lipstick said excitedly. "The dog. Put some meat on a napkin and leave it on the floor. I bet it comes to have a sniff around."

Looking anxiously to check nobody could see, Rebecca began forking up steak.

They watched the dog's nose start to twitch. Soon it was padding toward them. It was Lipstick who noticed the dog was dragging a tiny, string-handled carrier bag along the floor.

"Oh, poor ikkle thing," she whispered, picking up the pooch. She rubbed her nose against its wet snout, ignoring Rebecca's eye rolling. "Did the naughty string tie itself round your paw, den?" She unwound the handle. The dog jumped onto the floor and made a beeline for the meat.

"That's it, you tuck in," Lipstick said, patting its bony flank.

"So, come on," Rebecca said, "what exquisite little bauble is in the bag? Bound to be doggy related. A Lalique food bowl? A bottle of 'Chanel pour Chien'?"

Lipstick glanced round, placed the bag beside her on the banquette and took a peek. "Oh…my…God," she said, "Talk about ironic. It's only a jar of Mer de Rêves face cream."

"Which one?" Rebecca said.

Lipstick opened the carrier again. "Revivessence—Antirides, Super Intensif," she read. "Umm. That's not one I've come across before."

Rebecca dropped the chip she was just about to put in her mouth. "Revivessence?" she said in a whispered shriek. "That's it. That's only bloody it."

"What is?"

"That. In the bag."

"No."

"Yes."

"What, this? This is the stuff we've come to steal?"

"Quick," Rebecca said, hands shaking, "pass it to me. Under the table so's nobody can see."

Lipstick passed it. Rebecca turned so that she had her back to the two women. Then she opened the bag and pulled out the jar with its trademark diamond-studded lid.

"But it's not on the market yet," Lipstick said. "That's why we've come to steal it."

Rebecca trailed her fingers over the glass diamonds and shrugged. "Maybe one of them works for the company or they know somebody on the inside. Quick, I need some kind of container with a lid."

"What?" Lipstick said. "You're going to steal it?"

"Not all of it. Just enough to give to a lab for analysis."

Lipstick went searching in her bag and came up with a tiny round plastic pot. She opened it and took out a pair of foam earplugs.

"Sometimes Harrison sleeps on my bed and snores," she explained. "It's OK, they're new. The box is perfectly clean."

By now Rebecca had unscrewed the lid on the jar of cream. She took the earplug container and, using her dessert spoon, scooped a dollop of the thick rose-scented glop into it.

"This is just so brilliant," she said, screwing the lid back on. "Now we don't have to go to the prize giving. Let's just pay the bill and get out of here. Then you, me and the cream can catch the next train home."

Rebecca was about to summon one of the waiters when the funereal quiet was ruptured by the two snooty women.

"*Salope,*" Beige Woman cried.

Rebecca and Lipstick turned to look, along with all the other startled diners.

Yamamoto Woman's hand flew to her mouth.

"*Salope! Salope! Salope!*" Beige Woman came at her again.

"What? What? What?" Lipstick whispered to Rebecca.

"It means 'dirty bitch.'"

"Blimey."

The *"salope"* was followed by a list of insults, which Rebecca couldn't even begin to translate. Against this tirade the woman in black started crying.

"*Je vous déteste,*" Beige Woman carried on furiously. "*Toujours je vous ai detestée.*"

Around the restaurant people were busy exchanging embarrassed glances. Rebecca sat glued to the two women, translating for Lipstick as best she could. "Apparently she's always hated her. Now she's saying how much she hates her clothes, her house, her dog and her children. Oh, my God, now she's telling her that her husband's got a gay lover."

Yamamoto Woman's eyes were bulging out of her head. She threw some notes down on the table, got up and headed for the door. The other woman began rummaging irritably for her purse, clearly intending to do the same. It was only when she stood up that she realized she didn't have her dog. She bent down and lifted the edge of the tablecloth.

"Hortense," she cried, her voice softening. "Hortense, *ma petitie, ou es tu? Viens ici, bébé. Viens ici.*"

Hearing the voice, Hortense went scampering off toward her owner. The woman picked her up, admonished her gently and nuzzled her. Holding the dog under one arm, she began gathering up her bags.

"*Oh là là, ma crème!*" she gasped, clearly panic-stricken. "*Ou est ma crème?*"

"*Ici,* madame," Rebecca trilled.

The woman came tearing across, snatched the cream from Rebecca and immediately began accusing both of the women of trying to steal it. Rebecca did her best to explain that the dog had brought it over, but her usually excellent French hadn't just deserted her, it had abandoned her and gone off to join the Foreign Legion. Lipstick carried on in her best Franglais.

"*Non, non. Calmez-vous* down, madame. It's not what you *pensez. Nous* do not want to steal *votre crème.*" She turned to Rebecca. "This French lark's easy. *Pièce de gâteau.*"

By now *la patronne* and Rosencrantz and Guildenstern had come over to investigate the brouhaha. Beige Woman demanded to know why they had allowed English prostitutes into the restaurant. Then she turned back to Rebecca and Lipstick.

"Zee Engleesh women are all whores and thieves," she shouted, sending gobbets of spittle flying onto Rebecca's face. "And your men, wiz their earrings and shaved 'eads—*ils sont* barbarians, hooligans, philistines. Go back home to your stinking country with eets turnips and ze queen wiz ze face like an 'orse."

Then she turned and teetered off toward the door, glaring at *la patronne* as she went.

At that moment *la patronne* rushed across and offered her profound apologies. "Pleese forgeev this. These women, zey are all crazy lately."

"So there have been other incidents like this?" Rebecca said.

"*Mais, oui.* Not here, but at other places—gallery openings, at the new Tracey Emin exhibition at the Pompidou. Then at the opéra last week, in ze middle of ze *Fledermaus* two women zey nearly kill each other. It is *la cocaïne, n'est-ce pas.*"

Gradually everybody calmed down and turned back to their food.

Rosencrantz, or it could have been Guildenstern, came over with a bottle of champagne. "On zee 'ouse," he said.

Rebecca said it was very kind, but they had a train to catch and could they just have the bill.

While they waited, Rebecca's mind went back to the Lady Axminster piece in Dempster. She remembered the photograph. She was positive there had been a Mer de Rêves jar lying on the floor. And in that edition of *Watching You, Watching Me,* the one when Lucretia confessed to wanting to be taken from behind by Prince Charles, hadn't she been scooping cream from the distinctive jar?

"Oh, my God," she said eventually. "It's not cocaine that's been sending these woman doolally, it's face cream."

"What?" Lipstick shot back.

She reminded her about Lucretia Coffin Mott.

"Then there was this piece in Dempster." She explained. "Each time, Mer de Rêves has been the common factor. I think this mystery chemical Wendy was talking about is affecting their brains."

Lipstick gave a doubtful frown. "Oh, come on," Lipstick said, laughing. "I can imagine it damaging the skin—causing some dreadful allergic reaction, but the idea of it sending them bananas…it's a bit…" She sat trying to conjure up an appropriate metaphor. "It's a bit Batman, isn't it?"

"Batman," Rebecca repeated.

"Yeah. I saw this episode once where the Joker drugs the dough at the Oreo cookie factory, and the entire population of Gotham City falls asleep and he goes round stealing their money. Of course, the mayor is unaffected because he's allergic to Oreos. He tells Batman and Robin what's been happening and—"

"What are you saying?" Rebecca cut across her. "That we should bring the caped crusaders in on the Mer de Rêves case? It's a thought, but Adam West must be seventy by now. Don't you think he might have lost his crime-fighting edge a bit?"

"Ha, ha. All I'm trying to say is that your theory is a bit far-fetched."

"Well," Rebecca said with a determined expression, "I think it's pretty near-fetched actually."

They stood outside looking at the map, trying to work the way to the nearest Metro, Lipstick singing: "Dinna, dinna, dinna, dinna—dinna, dinna dinna, dinna—BATMAN!"

"OK, this way," Rebecca said eventually, "toward the church."

"You sure you've got the cream?" Lipstick said.

"Yeah, it's in my pocket."

She put her hand inside her jacket, just to check. It was empty. She tried the other pocket.

"Omigod, it's not there."

Lipstick told her to calm down and try her bag. It wasn't there either.

"Maybe I left it on the table."

Leaving Lipstick on the pavement Rebecca charged back into the restaurant. Unaware of the stares, she ran back to where they'd been sitting. She looked on the seats, the table. She even got down on her knees and crawled underneath. Nothing.

One of the waiters came over.

"*Excusez moi,*" Rebecca said, getting back onto her feet, "*est-ce que vous avez trouvé un petit*..." Shit, what was the word for *con-*

tainer? Boîte was the best she could come up with. "*Oui, est-ce que vous avez trouvé une petite boîte?*"

"*Une boîte? Non, nous n'avons rien trouvé.*"

A moment later she was back outside.

"OK," she said, running her fingers through her hair, "there's nothing for it. Back to the original plan. We'll just have to go to the awards ceremony. We should be OK. It doesn't start for another fifteen minutes."

The pair consulted the map again and started walking.

They'd been going a couple of minutes when Lipstick noticed the shop sign, complete with gilt horse's head, on the other side of the street.

"Ooh, look, a horse butcher. Quick, we've just about got time."

"Don't be daft," Rebecca screeched, "we can't walk into Mers de Rêves carrying a horse's willy."

But Lipstick was already crossing the road. By the time Rebecca caught up with her she was inside the shop, standing at the counter.

"Ah, *bonjour, monsieur,*" she was saying to the butcher, "*avez-vous un pénis de cheval?*"

So you really reckon," Lipstick said breathlessly, trying to keep pace with Rebecca, who was somehow managing to stride out despite the stilettos and tight skirt, "that when he invited me into the back, it wasn't his horses' willies he was going to show me?"

"For the umpteenth time, French butchers do not sell horses' willies. He could see how you were dressed. He thought you were doing business."

Rebecca glanced down at the map. "Next left," she said. "God, we are so late."

After leaving the restaurant, they'd walked for ten minutes in the wrong direction before realizing they were reading the map upside down.

"OK, this is it."

With its smooth white stone thirties façade and tall arched windows in bronze frames, the Mer de Rêves building was by far the most elegant and imposing in the street. They pushed open the even taller arched door and stepped into a perfectly preserved Art Deco interior. The floor and walls were cream polished marble. There was a sweeping Fred and Ginger staircase with a chrome balustrade and pink frosted lights for newels. Lipstick said the place looked like the Stoke Newington Odeon before they turned it into a ten-screen multiplex.

The girl at the reception desk was wearing a sludge-colored woolen sack thing with an asymmetric neck. Her black hair, which was streaked with scarlet Crazy Colour, had been wound into dozens of worm cast curls. Each was held in place next to her scalp by a miniature wooden clothes peg with a plastic rose on top.

"Bonjour, mesdames?" she said with a perky smile.

Rebecca explained they were there for the awards ceremony.

"Ah, you are a leetle late."

Rebecca explained about the upside-down map.

"Well," the girl said, "zee others are upstairs listening to Coco's speech of welcome. Zey will come down in about five minutes on the way to ze conference room for ze champagne reception. You can join zem zen."

She invited them to take a seat in one of the leather and walnut armchairs.

Rebecca picked up a copy of French *Vogue*, flicked through it for a few seconds and put it down again. "I'm getting the jitters again," she said.

"Come on, we'll be fine," Lipstick soothed. She offered Rebecca a mint. Rebecca shook her head and said she felt too sick. Lipstick took one for herself and sat chewing and looking about the place. After a bit she leaned forward and tapped Rebecca on the knee.

"What's that, then?"

Rebecca looked up. "What?"

"That. Over there at the bottom of the staircase."

Lipstick nodded toward a square table made of pink mirrored glass, supported by glass Doric-columned legs. On it stood a very large glass dome—the kind of thing that might sit on a grand mantelpiece, covering an antique clock or a much-treasured stuffed badger.

By now Lipstick was leaning forward in her chair, squinting.

"It can't be," she said.

"What can't be what?"

"Under the glass—I think it's a pot of Mer de Rêves cream."

"And this is the Mer de Rêves office," Rebecca came back. "What would you expect to find on display—a nice piece of halibut?"

"But suppose it's—you know—the Revivessence?"

"Don't be daft. They wouldn't leave a pot of the new stuff out for one of their rivals to nick."

Lipstick shrugged. "They might," she whispered. "Come on, let's take a look." She stood up and wiggled her skirt down to her lower thighs.

The deliberate, self-conscious saunters that followed made them look like a couple of incompetent baddies from a vintage cops-and-robbers caper.

Sitting under the dome, its diamond-encrusted lid cleverly illuminated by the light from the pink frosted newels, was a jar of Revivessence.

"Bloody hell," Rebecca said.

"I knew that white feather meant something," Lipstick said. "I just knew it."

They stood staring at the cream, their noses virtually pressed against the glass. Just then a uniformed security guard approached. He was a beefy, nightclub bouncer type. Definitely more Peckham than Paris, Rebecca thought.

"*Il est interdit de toucher,*" he said in a languid, un—security guard sort of a way. He adjusted his hat on his close-cropped, mousy-colored head.

"Can't touch," Rebecca translated.

"Oh, *pardon, excusez-nous,*" Lipstick said.

"Hey…*pas de problème.*" The guard smiled. Then he started humming Bob Marley's *Buffalo Soldier.*

As the guard took up his position next to the dome, they went back to their seats.

"So near and yet so far," Lipstick mused wistfully, as if she were stating a proposition from Hegel. "I mean, the cream's sitting here right in front of us and we've got to go searching for more in the basement."

Rebecca grinned. "No, we haven't," she whispered. "Come on, you remember our plan—the reason we dressed up in these daft outfits. All you have to do is chat up the guard for a few minutes. Then you make out you've got something in your eye. You ask him if he can help get it out. You take him to the window and while he's doing the business with a sparkling white handkerchief, I lift up the dome, nick the cream and we do a runner."

"S'pose there's an alarm?"

"If there is we grab the cream and make a run for it."

"OK, and what about the girl at the desk?"

"Bugger," Rebecca muttered. "I'd forgotten about her."

Then, as if by magic, two monster-arsed American tourists—a man and a woman—walked in asking for directions to "Nodah Daime."

"Ah, Notre Dame, *oui,*" the receptionist trilled. "Come wiz me. I will direct you to ze Metro."

She stood up and led the arses to the door.

Lipstick looked at Rebecca. "The angels sent them," she said. "What else can it be?"

"Whatever." Rebecca shrugged. "Right on your bike, Erin. Coco Dubonnet is going to be here any moment."

Lipstick took off her coat and undid another button of the red blouse. "God," she said, swallowing hard. "What am I going to say to him?"

"I don't know. You'll think of something." Rebecca couldn't believe that Lipstick, of all people, was getting nervous about chatting up a bloke.

Lipstick ran her tongue over her lips, threw her hair forward, then back, and set off toward the table—a definite Erin wiggle in her walk. A second later she stopped and turned, an anxious expression on her face. "Stan will forgive me for flirting with another man, won't he?"

"Don't worry," Rebecca said, "I'll explain."

She dug Lipstick between the shoulder blades. Lipstick hesitated for another moment or two. Then she hoisted up her skirt and sashayed off again. Rebecca positioned herself nearby, pretending to be studying a particularly stunning arrangement of tropical flowers.

"*Bonjour,*" she heard Lipstick say to the guard, a definite hesitation in her voice. Then she put her hand in her jacket pocket. "*Voulez-vous un Rolo?*"

The guard looked round to check nobody was watching. As he took the Rolo he looked Lipstick up and down a couple of times, a definite leer on his lips.

"Yesss," Rebecca murmured, spotting the leer as she peered between a couple of birds of paradise. "Yes."

"*Vous êtes anglaise?*" he asked.

Lipstick nodded. His eyes were locked on her cleavage. Rebecca could see she was feeling uncomfortable.

"Come on, Lipstick," Rebecca muttered, "what's gotten into you? In the third year you used to snog anybody for a bite of their Marathon."

Lipstick cleared her throat. "So," she said to the guard. "Er, has anybody ever told you that *vous êtes* le spitting image of Grant Mitchell?"

He gave a confused frown. "*Tante Michelle? Je n'ai pas une tante Michelle.*"

"Non, non. Grant Mit-chell. *Il est un acteur dans* EastEnders. *C'est un opéra de savon que nous avons en Angleterre."*

By now Rebecca's head was in her hands.

"Opéra de savon?" the guard said.

"Oui. Vous must *avez les savons en France. Nous avons beaucoup—Emmerdale, Corrie, Brookside.* Anyway, Grant *etait* married *avec* Tiffany, *mais malheureusement, elle est morte.* Run over by her father-in-law. *C'est beaucoup, beaucoup tragique. Il habite en* Spain *maintenant, avec* their little girl, Courtney—so he's not actually in it anymore, as such. But his *maman,* Peggy, gets the occasional *carte postale."*

"Oh, for Chrissake," Rebecca murmured, "show him a bit of leg, drape yourself on him. Do something."

"Je suis Pierre."

"Bernadette."

"Tu es très jolie, Bernadette," he said. "Very pretty. Yes?"

"Merci." Lipstick's face had turned the same red as her blouse.

By now his body was virtually touching hers. He trailed his finger slowly over her cheek.

Right, Rebecca thought. At last they were getting somewhere.

She turned toward the door to check on the Americans. They were fiftyish at a guess, wearing identical denim jackets and jeans that were stretched taut over their blubber. The husband was asking the receptionist if there was a House of Pancakes near Nodah Daime.

At the same time she could hear Pierre asking Lipstick if she'd like to have dinner with him.

"Er, *non.* I don't think so," Lipstick shot back. "*Je suis* very busy."

"But you 'ave to eat, *non?"* He stroked Lipstick's cheek again. She flinched.

Rebecca gave a yelp of frustration from behind the flowers.

"So you are busy zees evening?" Pierre said dreamily.

"Oh, yes, I'm definitely busy. *Très, très* busy."

Rebecca raked her fingers through her hair. They'd blown it. Lipstick had panicked and they'd lost their best chance of getting hold of the cream.

Outside the Americans were now fretting about foot-and-mouth disease.

"Back home in Fish Creek, Wisconsin—where the cheese comes from," the wife was saying—"they told us to get to a hospital if we started getting blisters on our hands or foaming at the mouth. But apparently there's not much they can do because pretty soon you go mad and die."

The receptionist did her best to explain that it was the British, not the French, who'd had foot-and-mouth, that it was over now, humans couldn't get it and anyway it didn't send people mad. "You are confusing it wiz zee mad cow disease."

The woman in particular didn't seem convinced and began muttering about it being brought over on the Eurostar.

"But animals, zey do not use ze Eurostar."

"Yes, they do," the chap said, elbowing the receptionist in the ribs. "They're called the Briddish." Then he roared, long and loud. He laughed so hard, he was bent double.

"You know, that's really funny, Murray," his wife giggled. "Really funny." She turned to the receptionist. "Back in Fish Creek, my husband is known for his wit. In the eighties, he won the Monterey Jack Wittiest Cheese Maker award, three years running."

"And, you know, everything's so expensive over there in England," Murray went on. "When we left our hotel two days ago the guy on the desk said 'Come back again' and I said, 'What for? To visit my money?' "

Murray could barely contain himself. He straightened, threw back his head and doubled over again. Up and down he went. Up and down. Finally, as he stood there slapping his thigh and shaking his rear like Baloo in *The Jungle Book*, a loud rip rent the air. The seat of his jeans had burst open down the middle to reveal a bare, quivering sumo bottom four feet across, covered in tufts of sweat-matted black hair.

"*Mon Dieu!*"

"Omigahd, Murray—your pants!"

"Son of a bitch! For crying out loud, Marcie, do something!"

Marcie handed him her street map, which he slapped to his rear.

"Pierre—*vite.!*" the receptionist cried out to the security guard. "*Ton veston.*"

"Quoi?" Pierre said dozily, turning away from Lipstick.

"*Ton veston. Ton veston,*" the receptionist repeated.

Seeing what had happened to the American, Lipstick's hand shot to her mouth. Then she started to giggle.

"I think she wants you to lend him your jacket," she said to Pierre. "*Ton veston—pour l'homme. Il a splitté* his *pantalons.*"

"Quoi?"

"God, what are you on?" Lipstick said. "*L'homme—là bas.* His *pantalons sont* kaput."

Pierre looked. Finally, the Euro dropped.

"*Ah, oui,*" he said. Slowly, he began taking off his jacket.

"So, your 'usband," the receptionist said to Marcie, " 'e like to go commando, *non?*"

Marcie reddened. "Oh, yes—always has." She giggled. "He does it for me. I just find it so darned sexy knowing he's buck naked under that denim."

Pierre strolled over to the door, the receptionist yelling, "*Vite, vite!*"

"You know," Lipstick said to Rebecca, who was standing beside her now, "when I was doing my beauty therapy training we were always taught that men never got cellulite. Shows how wrong you can be, doesn't it? I mean, here it is, firsthand evidence right in front of us that men get cellulite, just like women. Maybe I should write to somebody."

"Brilliant idea," Rebecca said. "Perhaps we should sit down and compose the letter right now. On the other hand, seeing as we're standing alone in front of a jar of Revivessence, maybe we should steal that instead."

"Oh, God. Shit. Sorry. Right."

Just then they heard voices and footsteps on the stairs.

"Fuck," Rebecca muttered, "it's Coco Dubonnet and the prize-winners. You lift the glass, I'll grab the cream."

Gingerly, Lipstick touched the dome, testing to see if it was alarmed. Nothing.

"Brilliant," Rebecca whispered. "Right, tilt it back."

As Lipstick lifted the glass dome, Rebecca slid the jar into her handbag. As she closed it, she looked up to see a blonde thicket of English beauty salon managers coming down the stairs, dressed for a slightly upmarket hen night in Cheadle. Rebecca had never seen a picture of Coco, but she was renowned for monochrome, minimalist style and it was quite clear that she wasn't here, among the Donatella knockoffs. Then from the first landing came the sound of a mobile ringing.

"*Oui?*" The woman's voice echoed off the marble walls.

"Must be Coco," Rebecca said. She looked up. All she could make out through the chrome balustrade was a straight gray bob and the back of a long black coat.

"Who cares? Come on, we've got to get out of here."

"Ah, *Madame N'Femkwe,*" Coco continued, "*c'est toujours un plaisir.*"

"She's the wife of that African dictator," Rebecca said.

"Fine, whatever. Let's go." Lipstick pulled on her friend's sleeve, but Rebecca was suddenly curious and refused to budge.

"You adore zee gel *pour les yeux?*" Coco chirruped. "Zee under-eye puffiness 'as completely gone? *Magnifique.* What did I tell you? Madame Gaddafy, she swear by eet....*Mais naturellement*—of course I can let you have a free sample of our new *crème*. I will send eet by special courier tonight."

"Probably go in the same batch as Mrs. Saddam's depilatory cream," Rebecca sneered.

"Whatever," Lipstick said. "Now come on."

As Rebecca turned to go, she saw Coco Dubonnet coming down the stairs. "Look! Look!" she whispered to Lipstick. "It's the woman from the restaurant. The one who was insulted by her friend. She's Coco Dubonnet."

"OK, right. Brilliant. So what?"

"Well, it means she can't know how harmful the cream is."

"Why?"

"Because she's been dishing it out to all her friends. She'd have to be an evil cow to do that, knowing it was dangerous. This all points to her executives pulling the wool over her eyes."

"Look," Lipstick said, utterly exasperated by now, "sorry as I am for her, do you think we can possibly get out of here now?"

They did another of their self-conscious saunters to the door. Murray now had Pierre's jacket hanging down over his behind, the sleeves tucked into the waistband of his jeans. The receptionist was giving Marcie directions to the Monoprix.

"Your 'usband can wait in an empty office until you get back."

As Rebecca and Lipstick approached, the receptionist turned round. "But, *mesdames*, you cannot possibly leave. Look, Coco, she is coming now. You must stay to collect your prize, *non*?"

"Already got it," Rebecca said as she and Lipstick began to squeeze past Murray.

Pierre looked at Lipstick. "You 'ave my phone number, *oui*?" he whispered.

She nodded.

* * *

Outside they were met by a blast of icy wind and sheeting rain.
"I think the Metro's this way," Rebecca said. They linked arms.
Heads bowed against the wind, they half ran, half tottered down
the road, past all the big-name fashion houses. They'd been going
for a few seconds when they heard Pierre shouting at them to
come back.

"Shit, he's after us."

"Oh, God," Lipstick squealed. "What do we do?"

"Just keep running."

Suddenly Lipstick tripped on an uneven paving stone. Rebecca
just managed to stop her falling.

"I can't run in these," Lipstick said as she stood, trying to get her
breath. "I know, let's go into Versace. It's Italian. Maybe we could
claim political asylum."

"Funnee. Come on. You have to keep going."

"Bernadette, give eet to me." It was Pierre again. "Pleez, you give
eet to me. I must have it."

"Gawd," Rebecca said between puffs, "sounds like he's gaining
on us."

They turned round. In fact, Pierre hadn't moved more than a
few feet from the Mer de Rêves building.

They slowed to a brisk walk.

"Pleez." It was Pierre again, arms outstretched, begging them.

Lipstick looked at Rebecca. "Do you think he'll get the sack?"

Rebecca said it was possible.

"Sorry, Pierre," Lipstick shouted. "I'm truly sorry, but you'll understand soon."

They watched him shrug and amble back inside.

They were booked on the seven o'clock Eurostar, but managed
to get seats on the five. Rebecca just about had time to pop into a
deli round the corner from the station and pick up two baguettes
and a jar of bouillabaisse for Rose.

"I'm sorry I got cold feet about chatting up Pierre," Lipstick said as the train pulled out of Gare du Nord. "I just kept thinking about Stan. I know it sounds pathetic, but it felt like I was cheating on him."

"You really love him, don't you?"

"You have no idea," Lipstick said.

Rebecca squeezed her hand.

"Come on," Lipstick said after a few moments, "I'm curious. Let's take a proper look at the cream this time."

Rebecca reached into her bag and put the jar on the seat, between them. She unscrewed the lid.

Lipstick blinked. "What on earth is that?" she said.

Rebecca prodded the dried planty bits with her finger. Then she picked up the jar and sniffed.

"That," she said, "if I'm not mistaken, is Moroccan Super Skunk."

Lipstick, petrified they would get caught at customs
with Pierre's stash, insisted on getting off the train briefly
when it stopped at Calais to dump it in a waste bin.

Rebecca was feeling too fraught about the Mer de Rêves debacle to care what happened to the stuff. Plus she had no use for it, since she didn't smoke dope. She'd done it a bit at university and when she first started working—enough to recognize Moroccan Super Skunk when she saw it—but it always gave her a double helping of the munchies with paranoia topping. She'd finally given up after downing three tubs of chocolate chip cookie dough in one sitting and spending the entire night accusing Ben and, to a lesser extent Jerry, too, of having it in for her.

She sat gazing out the window, waiting for Lipstick to get back, wondering what she was going to say to Charlie Holland. How could she have been so naive as to think there was cream in the Revivessence jar? If there had been, it would have been kept in a locked and alarmed display case. Pierre and the glass dome were simply for show. From now on, Charlie would never let her loose on anything more challenging than the beauty column. When Nat, the regular cosmetics columnist, came back after maternity leave, she wouldn't even have that. As for getting serious work on other newspapers, she could kiss that good-bye once word got round about what a cock-up she'd made of the Mer de Rêves story. There was no doubt in Rebecca's mind that her career as an investigative journalist was over.

She opened her bag and went rummaging for her packet of Wrigley's. Chewing gum always helped her think.

"I know there's some here," she said irritably, pulling stuff out of her bag and putting it on the table. It was then that she saw it. The hole in the bag's lining. First she pulled out the packet of Wrigley's. Next came the earplug box.

"Omigod, it's here!" she squealed. "I didn't lose it." She couldn't have been more excited if George Clooney had walked up to her and announced he wanted her for his sex slave. She pressed the earplug container to her chest. "Thank you, God. Thank you. From now on I will dedicate my life to being a good, kind human being who thinks only of the needs of other people." She paused. "Well, maybe not actually *dedicate*. I have a life. But you know what I mean."

Just then Lipstick reappeared, back from her dumping mission.

"You'll never guess what I've found," Rebecca singsonged.

"What?"

"Ta-dah!" Rebecca cried, holding out the pot.

Lipstick's face lit up. "My God, you found it. I can't believe it. Where was it?"

She explained about it having gone through a hole in the lining of her bag.

"Right," Lipstick said, "now for Chrissake put it away somewhere safe. Listen, I don't mean to rain on your parade. But you'll never guess who's sitting back there."

Rebecca frowned. "Who?"

"Max."

"What?"

Lipstick nodded.

"You are kidding, right?"

"Wrong."

"Shit."

"And he's got a woman with him. I assume it's that Lorna Findlay, not that I've ever watched her program. And they seem pret-ty cozy together."

"What am I going to do? He *cannot* see me in this getup."

She'd been determined that the next time she saw Max, she would exude elegance and serenity; an air of easy, but aloof self-confidence, which said: "I am so over you and back in control of my life." Assuming he'd be back in the office on Monday she'd even sent her powder-blue Whistles suit to the cleaners and booked a blow-dry with Camp David before work.

She looked down at her leopard-print blouse, the nasty micro-mini with the safety pins down the sides; felt her hair hanging round her face like soggy tagliatelle. The only thing she exuded right now was knackered hooker caught in a downpour and a faint whiff of stress-induced underarm BO.

"OK," she said to Lipstick, "we have to move into another carriage."

Lipstick said she had to be joking. It was Friday evening and the train was packed.

"Then we need some kind of disguise."

Lipstick's eyes widened. "Ooh, ooh," she squealed. "I know, chadors. I saw a whole thing about them on the Discovery Channel."

"Brilliant," Rebecca said. "I'll ask one of the stewards, shall I? I'm sure that along with the miniature packs of hickory roasted peanuts and hot towels, they always carry an emergency supply of heavy black robes favored by fundamentalist Muslim women."

"Stop taking the piss," Lipstick said. "You haven't just seen what I've seen."

"Don't tell me, the next carriage is full of women on their way to a fundamentalist hen night in London."

"Yes."

"What?"

"Well, I don't know about the hen night bit. They've got their husbands with them. But the point is, I just saw a couple of chadors in dry-cleaning bags. They were draped over a suitcase in the luggage rack outside."

"And your idea is we steal them?"

"Not steal them, exactly," Lipstick said. "Borrow them. The suitcase had a label tied to it with a London address. We can get them cleaned again and return them with a big bunch of flowers."

"Don't be daft. If we get caught, who's going to believe we were going to return them? We'd be done for theft."

"OK, what do you suggest? Any minute now, Max or Lorna could come down the carriage."

Rebecca sat there dithering, drumming her nails on the table. "I don't know."

"Come on," Lipstick urged.

Rebecca stopped drumming. "OK," she said, her face breaking into a smile. "Let's do it."

They decided they would take it in turns to go outside, "borrow" a chador and put it on in the loo. Rebecca couldn't get over how hot and cumbersome the thing was. On top of that, wearing something that covered most of her face was making her feel decidedly claustrophobic. She looked at herself in the mirror, peering out of the wide cotton mesh, which covered the eye slit.

"God, I look like a pepper grinder in mourning."

She came out of the loo and shuffled toward the automatic compartment door, praying she wouldn't catch the hem on one of her stilettos and trip. As she sat down opposite Lipstick, who was already in her chador, a couple of the men in suits sitting at the table on the other side of the aisle stared at her. They were clearly wondering what had happened to the original two women. But they didn't seem too bothered and quickly returned to their papers and laptops.

"Do you mind telling me," Lipstick whispered to Rebecca, "how Muslim women flirt wearing this gear?"

There they sat for the rest of the journey, two strict Muslim women swathed in black—one reading *The National Enquirer,* the other with her head buried in *Cosmo,* engrossed in an article entitled "We Reveal the Truth About Anal Orgasm."

As the train neared London, people started getting up to put their coats on and retrieve bags from the overhead lockers.

Then, she saw him, coming down the aisle toward the loo. Her heart lurched along with the train, which had just taken a bend a bit quickly. He was wearing Paul Smith jeans and a long-sleeved black T-shirt. He looked tired, she thought. Yeah, probably from all the shagging. But much as she tried to hate him, she couldn't. It was as much as she could do to resist leaping out of her seat and throwing herself at him.

As he drew level with the table, he stepped on a piece of her chador hem, which was sticking out into the aisle.

"Oops, sorry," he said.

"Oh, no, it's my fault." She snatched at the black cloth.

He looked shocked and startled at the sound of her voice. For a second, maybe less, their eyes locked through the chador's eye mesh. Then, still looking mildly bewildered, he carried on down the aisle.

"Gawd, you nearly blew it there," Lipstick said.

"I know. I know," Rebecca came back, her heart still racing from wanting him and the fear of being discovered.

As the train pulled in, Rebecca whispered to Lipstick not to move until everybody had gotten off. "Then we go to the loo and get out of these things. By the time we've finished, Max and Lorna will be well away."

It was a good ten minutes before they left the train. As they stepped onto the platform, they saw a Eurostar steward a few yards in front of them, surrounded by a dozen or so chador-clad women and their bearded husbands. The heavily accented men were waving their arms and shouting, demanding the police be called to investigate the theft of two robes. The hapless steward, who couldn't have been more than twenty, was trying to calm them down by saying he would go and fetch a more senior member of staff, but the men had formed a tight cordon round him and were refusing to let him go.

"Quick, hand me your chador," Rebecca said to Lipstick. "I think I've found a way to save on postage and flowers."

A few seconds later she'd carefully folded both robes and put them back, exactly where Lipstick had found them. "If it's a couple of those black robe things you're looking for," she called to the steward, over the din, "they're on the luggage rack."

In a second one of the men had climbed back onto the train and retrieved the garments. His wife moved forward, took Rebecca's hand in both of hers and said she would remember her to Allah in her prayers.

"Me too," murmured the steward, wiping his forehead.

"Oh, it was nothing," Rebecca said, offering the woman a smile to melt an ayatollah. "Nothing at all."

Still giggling, they reached the main concourse. Rebecca looked round for any sign of Max and Lorna. Nothing. Probably got picked up by a limo, Rebecca thought.

"Come on," Rebecca said, "let's go and find a cab."

They headed toward the stand. The queue for taxis was long, but it seemed to be moving at a decent lick. They were almost at the front when Rebecca heard somebody calling her name. She froze.

"My God, tell me this isn't happening," she said to Lipstick. "It's Max. After everything we've done to avoid him."

"Rebecca! Please! We need to talk."

She turned to see him half walking, half trotting toward the cab stand. He couldn't go any faster because he was weighed down by the huge leather holdall he was carrying.

"God, why can't this queue move any faster?" Rebecca muttered.

Suddenly she felt a hand on her shoulder. She turned round. "Max. What a surprise."

"I know. I know," he panted, putting his bags down. "I can't believe you're here. I was buying a paper and as I looked up I caught this glimpse of you, disappearing into the crowds. I've been looking for you everywhere."

She could feel his warm breath on her face. He seemed fraught. Guilt, she assumed.

"So, what are you doing here?" he said.

"Lipstick and I have just gotten back from Paris."

Lipstick gave him a tentative wave and said hi.

"Really? We must have been on the same train."

She could tell he was desperate to talk about what was going on between them, but was holding back because Lipstick was there.

By now he had noticed her clothes. A smile began to hover on his lips. "You look very … very …" He ran the flat of his hand over his head as he searched for the right words. "I mean, the skirt, it's not very …"

"Nice?"

"I was going to say, long. It's not very long. Looks, you know—like it might be a bit drafty."

"I've been working undercover," she heard herself say. "Charlie asked me to write a color piece on the Union of Working Women's annual conference. They don't allow the press in, so I had to pretend to be a delegate. Lipstick came with me—for moral support."

Just then a taxi pulled up.

"I'll get in and ask the driver to wait," Lipstick said to Rebecca. "'Bye, Max, nice to see you again."

"Yes, you too," Max said. He turned back to Rebecca. "So, sounds like an exciting trip."

"It was. And how's your story going?"

"Great. Look, can we go somewhere and talk?"

"I don't think there's much point, do you? I've found out all I need to know."

"Look, I know it was you who phoned my room when I was in the shower. Lorna told me it was somebody from the office, but I knew just by looking at her that she was lying. I really can explain everything."

"Oh, come on, Max. I've heard it all before."

"But I can." Suddenly his eyes shot to his jacket pocket. Inside his mobile was ringing.

"Shit. What now? I'm sorry, but I have to answer it." He flipped the phone open. "Who?" he barked. "Monsieur who? Look, I'm in the middle of a very important meeting. Can this wait? Can I call you back?....*Ah, pardon Monsieur le Premier Ministre...non, ce n'est pas une problème. Non, non, pas du tout.*"

A look of urgent concentration came over him. He turned and took a few paces back from the road, his finger stuffed in his ear against the traffic noise.

Rebecca stood watching him. If he hadn't been on the phone to the French prime minister, she might have given in to the impulse to jump up at him, fling her arms round him and beg him to stop loving Lorna.

"Come on, sweetheart. Let's get you home."

She felt Lipstick take her hand.

* * *

"What you need is a night out," Lipstick declared, once they were in the taxi. "Tell you what, my cousin Donal's over from Ireland for a couple of weeks. He's a real laugh. You'll love him. Why don't you, me and Jess meet up with him for a drink this week?"

"Great," Rebecca said, but her heart wasn't really in it. She didn't say anything for a minute or so. Then: "Lipstick?"

"What is it?"

"Thanks for coming today. I couldn't have done it without you."

"My pleasure."

"You know," Rebecca went on, "it's funny the way things have worked out—particularly after the way we hated each other in school."

Lipstick looked down at her nails. "You know, I really am sorry about the way I bullied you," she said. "I've been expecting you to bring it up. I can't believe you waited this long. I should have said something myself, but I was frightened it would open old wounds and you'd get angry. Then I suppose another bit of me thought maybe you'd forgotten."

"So what was it about? Why were you so horrible to me?"

Lipstick shrugged. "Jealousy, I suppose. You were clever. I wasn't and I couldn't stand it. My dad used to say my mum could study for a blood test and fail. I suppose I inherited my brains from her."

"But you're not stupid. Look how you've built up the Talon Salon."

"Oh, come on, I was. I never understood anything. I remember I had these total blank spots. Like Roman numerals. You weren't in my history group. You never saw me make a fool of myself the day I started going on about Britain fighting in World War Eleven. You know, I'm still haunted sometimes by the sound of those kids laughing at me."

"Yeah, I know what you mean. Do you remember the night of the fifth-year prom when you called me Spot and said you had no idea why I'd come because nobody would dance with me? People pissed themselves laughing."

"I know. God, you must still hate me."

"Don't be daft. How can you possibly think I still hate you?" Rebecca took her hand.

"I know I shouldn't have taken out my feelings of inadequacy on you," Lipstick said, "but you and your gang were pretty up yourselves, you know—putting on that Waiting for Whatnot thing in the lunch hour."

"Oh, blimey, Godot," Rebecca said. "Did we really do that?"

Lipstick smiled and nodded. "But it was no excuse for the way I behaved. I was a total cow. Forgive me?"

"Of course I forgive you....You know I'm so glad you're marrying my dad. When I first found out, I thought you'd take him away from me, but I know now that's never going to happen."

"Oh, Becks, I wouldn't do that. Not ever."

"I still think it would feel pretty weird if you and Dad had a baby, though."

"Well, that could be a long way off," Lipstick said. "He still hasn't found out if his vasectomy reversal worked. But you know, sometimes when we're cuddling up on the sofa we can't resist thinking up baby names."

"Really? Come on, what's on the list?"

"We thought maybe Madonna Enya Lourdes if it's a girl and Declan Eamon Fergal if it's a boy. What do you think? I mean, they're not very Jewish-sounding, are they?"

"Not very, no," Rebecca said.

"The thing is," Lipstick went on, "I'm a bit worried about how Rose will react."

Rebecca said that assuming Rose's newfound religious tolerance continued, she was sure she would be fine with the names.

She thought it best not to mention that once Rose discovered a grandchild of hers was to be given not just one, but a string of Catholic names, she would revert to her former self quicker than you could say circumcision brunch.

Nor did she say that she could see it all now: the two women in the hospital together—Lipstick recovering from having a little Madonna or Declan and Rose recovering from having a little heart attack.

So, you heard anything from Max Factor?" Jess said, coming back into the kitchen. She'd been to check on Diggory, who was sitting in his car seat in Rebecca's living room. He was listening to the CD of eighteenth-century organ music his mother had brought with her, and which sounded to Rebecca like it had been composed by Morticia Addams.

"He's phoned two or three times," Rebecca said, pouring coffee into Jess's mug. "But when I see his number come up on the caller display, I ignore it. Plus, I've switched off the answer machine."

"You're going to have to face him eventually," Jess said.

"I know. I forced myself to go into the office for a few hours this morning—all dolled up, like I planned, to show him I didn't give a damn. But he wasn't there. Snow—you know Lucretia's gofer from *Watching You, Watching Me*—is back on the news desk and said he's viewing film rushes all this week."

"You know what would make you feel better?" Jess said, a smile creeping over her face.

"What?"

"To have Max see you out with another bloke. Talk about getting your own back."

Rebecca laughed and made the point that as an agony aunt, Jess was meant to tell her to take up a fulfilling hobby and get on with her life, not behave like a jilted sixteen-year-old.

"I know," Jess said, "but it could be fun. Childish, but fun."

She suggested hiring an escort to come and pick Rebecca up from the office after work one evening. Rebecca said they cost a fortune and she couldn't afford it because she'd just replaced her broken mobile with a brand-new one with a personal organizer and Internet access.

"Blimey, what on earth do you want all that for?"

Rebecca said she didn't and that she had no idea how to make it do anything more complicated than dial out. She hadn't even worked out how to access her messages. It was just that the cute, twenty-something sales guy in Carphone Warehouse had spent twenty minutes flirting with her. This having gone some way at least to reaffirming her desirability as a woman, even though she knew perfectly well it was only a ploy to make a sale—she hadn't been able to say no to the phone.

"Plus, it's such a waste," Rebecca said regarding the escort suggestion, "if you don't have sex with them."

"Don't worry about that," Jess said. "He could have sex with me." She laughed, but Rebecca could tell she was only half joking.

"So, Ed still not getting it up?"

Jess shook her head. "I even gave him this brilliant hand job the other night, you know, with loads of oil—nothing. In the end we both got so bored I started doing my Cartman impression."

She sipped some coffee. "Anyway," she went on, "he finally went to the doctor. He did some blood tests. We're still waiting for the results, but he thinks there's probably nothing wrong with him physically. In the meantime, he's seeing a hypnotherapist. She thinks the willy-nilly might be due to some kind of sexual rejection from when he was young—most likely in adolescence. God knows why it's coming out now. Plus, he didn't start sleeping with women until he was twenty. I'm like, who rejected you before then? Your hand?"

Just then the phone rang. Rebecca looked at the caller display, saw it wasn't Max and picked up.

"You can?" Rebecca said, her face beaming. "That's brilliant. I'll be there in an hour or so." Rebecca explained she'd located an analytical chemist in Epsom and asked them to take a look at the cream. "When I rang this morning, the girl at the desk said they were really busy and she wasn't sure if they could fit it in. Turns out they can, so I need to get over there right away."

An hour and a half later she was pulling up outside the lab, a single-story concrete building on an industrial estate. She wasn't in there more than a minute. She simply handed over the cream to a white-coated receptionist, signed an order form and that was it.

Although she'd found the lab easily enough, doing the journey in reverse was much more difficult. This was partly due to there being virtually no signposts and partly because she hadn't eaten and was starting to lose concentration. The upshot was, she managed to get spectacularly lost. She started rummaging in the door compartment—among the Biros, sticky, hairy tampons and maps of Belgium—for a toffee or a couple of squares of stale chocolate. Nothing. Then she spotted the banana lying on the dashboard. She hadn't had time for breakfast this morning and had grabbed a banana on her way out. In the end she hadn't fancied it, as it was speckled and brown and had seen better days. She reached over and undid the skin with her teeth. She'd only taken one bite of it and grimaced at how stale and manky it tasted when her mobile rang. Muttering to herself, she put the banana down on the passenger seat and picked up the phone.

"Oh hi, Gran," she said. "How are you?" She shoved the mobile between her shoulder and chin and put the banana down on the passenger seat.

"I'm on this diet Estelle recommended. She reckons losing a few pounds might help bring my blood pressure down. The thing is with it, there's not enough to eat. So, I've decided to go on another one at the same time. Anyway, I was just phoning to say how much I enjoyed the bouillabaisse. It was wonderful and I've still got loads left."

"But it's full of fat, you know, Gran." Rebecca said, spotting a rest area and deciding to pull in to look for her map book. "You should do some exercise to work it off."

"Exercise, schmexercise. So, I'll eat briskly."

Rebecca slowed down and pulled into the rest area.

"Look, sweetie," Rose went on. "I've been trying to think of some way to help you get over Max."

"Gran, that's really kind of you, but I don't need any help. Honest."

"I hate the idea of you sitting and moping. You know I heard Warren, the nice town planner chap, has finished with that model he was seeing. She ditched him for some actor. Maybe you should give him a call. Or, better still, I could."

Rebecca let out a yelp of panic. "No! No, Gran. Please. Promise you won't do that."

"But you need cheering up."

"I'm cheered. Really, I'm perfectly cheered. Never felt cheerier."

"But you need to get out and meet new people."

"I am. I'm out all the time. I'm never in. Try me any night on my home phone. You'll never catch me. That's because I'm out being extremely cheery with men. Lots of men. Hundreds of them. All the time."

"Well, if you're sure you're all right."

"I'm sure. Couldn't be surer."

"OK, sweetheart. Love you. 'Bye."

"Yeah, love you too. 'Bye, Gran."

Rebecca threw back her head, put the phone down on the seat next to her and let out a loud sigh. Noticing a litter bin, she unwound the window, leaned out and lobbed in the banana. Then she searched the glove compartment and under the seats for her map book. Eventually she remembered Lipstick had it. She'd borrowed it when she drove to Manchester to see Stan.

She'd been back on the road for less than a minute when she looked in her rearview mirror and noticed a dark Mercedes with blacked-out windows directly behind her. She vaguely wondered who might be in it and decided it was a toss-up between Iraqi secret agents and some naff D-list celeb. She thought no more about it until she'd been twice round the same roundabout, trying to decide which exit to take, and noticed it was still there. It struck her as a bit odd, but she assumed the driver must be lost too and carried on. When the car was still with her a mile down the road, she started to feel distinctly uneasy and it occurred to her that she was being followed. But it was ridiculous. Why would anybody want to follow her?

After another few hundred yards, she noticed her petrol gauge was registering low. There was a garage up ahead. She decided to pull in and fill up. As she slowed down, the Mercedes slowed down behind her. When she indicated left, it did the same. By now she was feeling really scared. She pulled in. So did it. Suddenly she realized what was happening.

"Omigod. It's the Mer de Rêves people. They've already threatened Wendy; now they're on to me."

Instead of stopping at one of the pumps, she sped through the forecourt. As she waited at the exit for a break in the traffic, the Mercedes was behind her. She put her foot down on the accelerator and pulled out into a woefully inadequate gap in the traffic. There was a screech of brakes and a bloke in a Mondeo started hooting and waving at her. Ignoring him, she pulled into the outside lane and kept her foot down. She looked in her mirror. Shit, the Merc was still on her tail. By now her heart was galloping and she was beginning to shake.

"God. What do I do? They're going to kill me."

As she swerved in and out of traffic, doing her best to lose the Mercedes, cars were hooting and flashing all over the place. No matter how fast she went, the Mercedes stayed with her, feet from her rear bumper. She decided she had two choices: she could drive on until her car ran out of petrol, after which she would no doubt be dragged from it and bundled into the Merc by a couple of sawed-off-shotgun-wielding hoodlums. They would drive her, gagged and blindfolded, to a breaker's yard in Essex, where they would throw her into a car crusher and she would end up as a small cube. On the other hand, she could pull over now, sit with her hazards and horn going and phone the police on her mobile. She decided to pull over. Cutting off a Fiesta on the inside lane, she slowed the car onto the side of the road and began leaning on her horn. In her panic and confusion she couldn't find the hazard light switch and ended up with her heated rear window and windscreen wipers going.

She watched the Mercedes pull up and a guy get out—six foot six, black suit, dark glasses, gold hoops in both ears. Adrenaline surging through her, she ran her hand over the seat looking for her phone. Where the fuck was her phone? Where was it? The guy's face was peering in through the window. Shit, she was dead. She was so dead. He motioned for her to unwind it. Yeah, right, like she was about to open the window so that he could blow off her face. He tapped on the glass.

"Miss?"

She ignored him and carried on honking.

"Miss, please."

If he was a hired hit man, he was an exceedingly polite one. Another tap. She hesitated, then opened the window half an inch.

"Wow, I thought I'd never catch you," he said, smiling. "That was some driving back there."

She swallowed. Behind her, her hand was still scrabbling frantically over the passenger seat, looking for her phone.

"Miss, is this what you're looking for?"

He held up her phone.

She unwound the window fully.

"Where did you get that?"

"I saw you at the rest area. I was standing a few feet away and saw you drop it into the litter bin by accident. Well, I assume it was an accident. I can't imagine anybody throwing away a brand-new Ericsson T39 with built-in organizer and Internet access."

She turned and saw the manky banana lying on the seat in a brown speckled smile.

A few hours later, she was sitting in a bar in Soho telling the story to Jess, Lipstick and Lipstick's cousin Donal from Ireland.

"Anyway, after I'd apologized to the driver and explained how I'd got so cross with my gran that subconsciously I'd probably chucked the phone away on purpose, we got chatting and it turns out he works for a posh limo company and he's got some celebs in the back of the car."

"God," Jess said. "So, you're thinking is it Madonna and Guy? Michael and Catherine?"

"Eddie," Lipstick piped up.

"Eddie?" the rest of them said as one.

"You know, the dog. From *Frasier.*"

"So, come on," Donal said when everybody had stopped laughing. "Who was it?"

Rebecca giggled. "Four of the children from *The Sound of Music,*" she said.

They all laughed, apart from Lipstick, who sat looking offended. Rebecca had forgotten it was one of her favorite films and that she'd been four times to *Singalong—Sound of Music.*

"How can you not like it?" she said. "It's got everything—love, adventure, politics, comedy, music..."

"...all those ridiculous song lyrics," Donal said.

A second later he and Jess had linked arms and were singing "adieu, adieu to yieu and yieu and yieu" at the tops of their lungs.

Looking defeated, Lipstick got up to buy another round of drinks. Jess went with her to help her carry the glasses.

"So, Donal," Rebecca said, "whereabouts in Ireland are you from?" He was thirty-six, intelligent, witty, good-looking, she supposed. Not that she fancied him. She couldn't work out why, but there was something distinctly asexual about him. She was sure he wasn't gay. Try as she might, she couldn't work him out. In the end she'd put it down to his fringe—a complete turnoff as far as she was concerned in any male over the age of thirteen.

He told her he lived in Skibbereen, a small town south of Cork.

"And what do you do in Skibbereen?"

"Well, actually, I'm..."

But she wasn't listening. Out of her peripheral vision, she'd seen Max coming down the stairs into the bar. Of course, she thought, they were in Soho. Max was viewing his film rushes all this week at Channel 6. The office was a couple of blocks down the road. He was probably meeting up with Bloody Lorna.

Suddenly she could hear Jess's words echoing in her head about having Max see her with another bloke. Talk about getting your own back. He was getting closer. He was going to spot her any moment now.

She looked at Donal and cleared her throat. "Er, Donal, look, I know we hardly know each other, but do you think you could do me a huge favor?"

"If I can."

"OK—would you please kiss me?"

"Kiss you?" He looked distinctly uneasy. "Why?"

"I'll explain later."

"Well, to tell you the truth, it's not really something I feel very comfor—"

But before he had a chance to finish, she'd clamped her hand onto the back of his neck and was pulling his head toward hers. A moment later they had locked lips. She could feel his entire body going rigid. Then he started to struggle. By now, both her arms were round his neck. When she finally let him go, his face was crimson and he was gasping for breath. She glanced up to see Max retreating toward the stairs.

"Yesss," she muttered to herself. "Yesss."

Just then Jess and Lipstick appeared with the drinks.

"OK," Jess said, "the Jack Daniel's is for Becks."

She leaned across the table, toward Donal. "And the Grolsch is for you, Father."

The next morning, Rebecca was still cringing with embarrassment. "But I don't understand," she said to Lipstick, who was sitting at the kitchen table with Harrison on her lap, feeding him lightly poached egg off a teaspoon. "How could you forget to tell me he was a priest?"

"I'm sorry. I just did, that's all. Anyway, once you'd explained why you'd snogged him, he didn't seem to mind. Between you and me I think he secretly enjoyed it. I bet he went to bed last night and broke a fairly major vow."

She cackled and turned back to Harrison. "Come on, baby," she said. "One more bit of eggy for Mummy. It'll bind you up. I'm afraid Hawwie's got a bit of a runny tum this morning. But he was a good boy. He did it all in his tray, didn't you, baby?"

Rebecca grimaced and pushed away her bowl of Weetabix.

"So," Lipstick said, "how does it feel, getting your own back on Max?"

Rebecca shrugged. "Great for a bit. Now I feel pretty rubbish, to tell you the truth."

"That's because you still love him. Even though he hurt you, you can't bear the thought of hurting him back."

"He deserved it, though. After the way he behaved."

"Maybe he did, but in my experience tit for tat behavior never makes you feel better. Best to let go. Isn't that right, Hawwie? Isn't it best just to let it go?" She picked up Harrison's Burberry mac from the table and started pushing his paws into it. "Right, we've got a vet's appointment in fifteen minutes. I'll take Hawwie into the salon today to keep an eye on him."

Rebecca had just gotten out of the bath when the phone rang. It was the chap from the lab.

"I have run this test over and over and I have to say, it's a very odd result. Basically, it's a standard skin preparation. They're all pretty much the same and none, if I may tell you, as effective as Vaseline. But this cream does contain an unusual ingredient: Kenbarbitol Cyclamate."

"What's that? It sounds like something that reduces you to a nine-inch-high plastic figure with a miniature moped."

"Hmm, yes, well, I know this is going to sound a bit James Bond, but believe it or not it's a very powerful truth drug. It was invented by the Germans during the war. They used to inject it into suspected spies. People squealed almost immediately, apparently. Afterward psychiatrists used it for years to help patients lose their inhibitions and open up about their problems, but it disappeared in the sixties when drug therapies went out of fashion."

Of course, it made perfect sense. Lucretia confessing all her sexual fantasies, the Harrods customer telling Lady Axminster she'd slept with her husband, the woman in the restaurant in Paris telling her friend how much she hated her and that her husband was gay. It wasn't that Revivessence simply sent people loopy—it was a truth drug.

"But why put it in a face cream?"

"I had the same thought, so I dug out some of the literature. Apparently it has a fairly major side effect. It plumps up aging skin and fills out wrinkles. Nobody knows how it works, but somehow it boosts the body's ability to produce collagen."

"So is it dangerous?" She was especially worried about Lucretia.

"Not in the short term and with the relatively small amounts being used. I'm also pretty sure that the truth-telling effect isn't permanent. The likelihood is, it wears off an hour or so after using the cream. But there's no way of knowing what the long-term effects might be. I'd hate to think what could happen if this stuff were ever sold over the counter."

She put down the phone.

"Yesss! Oh, yesss!" She punched the air and did a little dance round the living room in her bath towel. At last something in her life was going right. She'd pulled it off—her first major investigative story. Pretty soon job offers would be flooding and she'd be able to kiss the makeup column good-bye. All she needed to do now was to phone Charlie, who was in Nigeria. A peace deal was about to be signed by two warring African states and Charlie, who had a special interest in African affairs from his days as a correspondent in

South Africa, had insisted on covering the story himself rather than sending a reporter.

She would tell Charlie about her sensational truth drug discovery and find out how he saw the story being written. She looked at her watch. They were only an hour ahead in Lagos. If she was lucky she might catch him before he left his hotel for the day.

He picked up almost immediately.

"Sorry, Rebecca, can't talk for long. All hell's broken out here."

He explained that he'd just gotten back from an all-night sitting of the peace conference. Apparently the parties were on the point of reaching a peace settlement, when Madame N'Femkwe, the wife of T'chala N'Femkwe, one of the warring leaders, burst into the compound occupied by the rival delegation screaming that the wife of the enemy leader was a bitch whore daughter of Satan who couldn't grind cassava to save her life and, more to the point, was having a passionate affair with T'chala's brother.

"Oh, my God," Rebecca gasped, her mind shooting back to Paris and Coco Dubonnet's conversation with Madame N'Femkwe. "She uses Revivessence. Madame N'Femkwe uses Revivessence. Coco sent her a freebie sample."

"Fascinating cosmetic detail, Rebecca," Charlie said dismissively, "but the point is the peace agreement here's in absolute tatters. I tell you we could be looking at a major African conflict unless Bush or Blair steps in a bit sharpish with some fancy diplomatic footwork."

"Charlie, Charlie, you don't understand. This is relevant. I know why this has happened. The Mer de Rêves cream contains…"

But the line was beginning to crack up.

"Charlie, can you hear me?"

Nothing. She tried ringing back, but the line seemed to be down.

"Fuck!"

She started pacing. What did she do now? A story that had begun as a fairly straightforward investigation had suddenly acquired ridiculous significance, and with her bizarrely at the epicenter. The whole of Africa was about to descend into war and she alone knew what had caused it and had the power to stop it. She, Rebecca Fine, makeup columnist, held the future of the African peace deal in her hands. The news had been full of stuff about how, unless the deal was signed, oil prices were going to skyrocket and the economy would be plunged into recession.

It was up to her to find a way of convincing the African heads of state that Madame N'Femkwe had only behaved the way she did because of the truth drug.

Sod the bloody Press Awards, she thought to herself. If she pulled this off, we could be talking Nobel Peace prize here. Her face formed a smug smile. Bloody Lorna would be so jealous she'd eat her own head.

In the end it didn't take her long to work out her next move. Mad, who'd painted *Woman Wanking*, had a friend, Ruby, who was the editor of *Anne-Marie*, a fashionable women's magazine with intellectual pretensions to a social conscience. And Ruby was huge mates with the Blairs. She and Cherie had done a nanny share years ago, when the Blairs lived in Islington. She picked up the phone.

"Mad, listen. Can you phone your mate Ruby and get me an urgent five-minute appointment with the prime minister?"

Mad said she was happy to phone Ruby, but felt she needed to be able to tell her why Rebecca wanted to speak to the prime minister.

"OK, but this is top, top secret, right? Apart from Ruby, you cannot tell another living soul."

Mad agreed.

When Rebecca got to the end of explaining that the entire African peace deal had been scuppered, not because Madame N'Femkwe was an evil warmonger, but because there was a truth drug in her antiwrinkle cream, Mad burst out laughing.

"A truth drug in her antiwrinkle cream. Oh, come on."

"Look, I know it sounds a bit unlikely."

"You think?"

"No, really. It's true. You have to believe me. I've even had it analyzed."

It took some time, but somehow Rebecca convinced her to phone Ruby. Five minutes later, she was back on the phone.

"Sorry," Mad said, "Ruby's reaction was much the same as mine. But she did say her magazine was doing a feature on women who suffer from poisoning fantasies, and were you up to being interviewed?"

Terrific.

She tried Charlie again—all newspaper editors had access to Number 10—but there was no reply from his hotel room. Then she tried the *Vanguard*'s news and political editors, but they were both in meetings. She had just put the phone down, when Lipstick and Harrison appeared. Lipstick looked white.

"I couldn't go in to work. I feel dreadful. Really nauseous. I think I may have caught Harrison's tummy bug."

"Come on, let's put you to bed," she said. "I'll make you a nice hot-water bottle."

"Thanks, but I think I'd prefer to keep upright. Oh, by the way, I saw Max as I came out of the vet's."

Rebecca's heart skipped a beat. "Really? Did you speak to him?"

"No, he was on the other side of the road. Seems like he's ditched Lorna because he had his arm round some girl. Looked like a student. I wasn't sure whether to tell you, but I thought I should just in case you saw them one day and got upset."

"Don't worry, that's Amy, his goddaughter. They're really close. She must have the day off school for some reason. He was probably taking her shopping."

"Oh, right. I have to say he didn't strike me as the type who went for young girls." A beat. "So, what you been up to?"

"OK," Rebecca said, "do you feel up to hearing some amazing news?"

"Go on."

She told her about Madame N'Femkwe and the truth drug. "The thing is I really need to speak to Tony Blair—or at least speak to somebody who can speak to him on my behalf."

Lipstick told her not to worry and that she was bound to reach Charlie Holland eventually.

"You know," she said, standing up. "Suddenly I'm starving. I could murder an M&M McFlurry."

Rebecca tried to tell her all that fat on an upset stomach probably wasn't a good idea, but she wouldn't listen.

"No, it's what I fancy," Lipstick said. "I've just got to have it."

The moment she disappeared with Harrison, the phone rang.

"Er, hello—is that Rebecca?" It was a male voice. Not one she recognized.

"Speaking."

"God. This is really embarrassing. Look, you don't know me and I don't quite know how to put this, but I appear to have bought you."

"Bought me?"

"Yes. In an auction."

"Sorry, I haven't got time for jokes—"

He interrupted her, begging her not to hang up until she'd heard him out. "It was organized by the Hendon and District Synagogue Ladies' Guild. I think your grandmother, Rose, is a member. Anyway, they've been raising money for Romanian orphans and your grandmother suggested all the members should bring in photographs of their single children and grandchildren and auction them."

Rebecca pressed her eyelids with her fingers. She would throttle Rose when she got hold of her.

"So, let me get this straight—sorry, what's your name?"

"Alex."

"OK, Alex. So, right, you're under the impression you now own me?"

He laughed. "No, not quite. My mother saw your photograph and thought you looked just my type. So, she decided to bid for you and won. The upshot is, I now have a date with you. I was furious with her at first, but then she showed me your picture and you looked, well, absolutely gorgeous, really. So I thought I'd risk phoning you to see if you fancied meeting for a drink. Look, I'd totally understand if you told me to get lost."

Absolutely gorgeous. He thought she looked, what was it?— absolutely gorgeous.

"So, er ... how much did your mother bid for me?"

"Seven pounds fifty."

"Wow, as much as that?"

"No, apparently that was brilliant. The bids only went up fifty pence each time. I think the most they got was a tenner for a girl who's been in *Emmerdale*. So would you like to meet up?"

He sounded pleasant enough and it wasn't as if blokes were queuing up to take her out. They arranged to meet that evening, at the All Bar One round the corner from Rebecca.

"Oh, by the way," she said, "as a matter of interest, which photograph did my grandmother choose? Was it the usual bridesmaid one with the teeth? Or the one of me aged sixteen about to throw up on the Wall of Death at Alton Towers?"

"I think it may have been the throwing up one. But you still looked cute."

"I did?"

"God, yes."

Wow, a man who thought she looked cute, even when she was about to puke. She couldn't wait to meet him.

By the end of the day, she was still no nearer getting an appointment with the prime minister, and Charlie still wasn't answering his phone. She tried his mobile, but that was permanently on voice mail, and she doubted he would be able to pick up messages in Nigeria. By six o'clock she was feeling so frustrated and miserable she decided to cancel her date with Alex. It was Lipstick who persuaded her to go because it might cheer her up and take her mind off things.

When she arrived he was already there. Her spirits sank almost immediately. He was beaky, and had the overironed look of a man who lived at home with his mother. When he stood up to shake hands she saw he was no more than five four. On top of that his voice was too loud. He began the conversation by announcing so as it could be heard three tables away that he didn't drink.

"Alcohol gives me palpitations, so I stick to soft drinks," he boomed. "But only caffeine free. I think it was caffeine that did in my bowel last year. Have you ever had a barium enema?"

"Don't think so."

"Oh, you'd remember if you had. They stick this tube up your rectum and then turn you upside down. Humiliation doesn't even begin to describe it. Having said that, you get to see your colon on TV, which is fun."

"I can imagine."

He looked embarrassed. "My God," he said, "what a subject to be talking about on a date. I can hear you saying to your friends tomorrow: 'This guy was incredibly good-looking, but the first thing he asked was, have you ever had a barium enema?' "

"Well, certainly one of the above." Rebecca smiled.

"So, I'll get the first round, shall I?" he said. Rebecca detected a definite reluctance.

"Or we can go Dutch," she replied. "I'm fine with that. Tell you what, why don't I make it my treat?"

"Really? Oh. OK, then. I'll have a diet Coke, no ice...sensitive teeth."

"Of course."

As she went through her bag to find her purse, she took out her phone and put it on the table.

"My God," he said, "you've got the Ericsson T39. Great phone."

"It is? I don't know. I talk into it. People talk back. I guess that makes it great."

"But don't you find the WAP browser awesome?"

"I have a WAP browser?"

"Oh, do you so ever have a WAP browser." He leaned across the table. "You must let me browse your WAP sometime."

"I'll ... er. I'll get the drinks, shall I?"

When she got back they talked about jobs. He was impressed she worked for a left-wing newspaper. (She didn't mention the makeup column. She had the feeling he was the type who would have views about that sort of thing.)

It turned out he was a senior manager at Muswell Hill General Hospital. She felt she should show an interest, just to be polite. As a result, he spent the next forty-five minutes explaining the intricacies of public-private partnership in the National Health Service. When he eventually went to the loo, a woman who was sitting with some friends at the next table patted Rebecca on the shoulder.

"I don't know what effect that bloke's having on you," she said, "but he's boring the pants off us."

She decided to make an excuse and leave, but in the end it wasn't necessary.

"Look," he said as he got back to the table, "I'd really like to do this again, but I really should get home early tonight. Big day tomorrow."

"Oh?"

"Yes. Tony Blair's coming to the hospital to open our new obstetrics wing. Although it's really a chance for him to make a speech about the government's commitment to the NHS."

She put down her drink, barely able to conceal her excitement. "Tony Blair is coming to your hospital? Tomorrow?"

He nodded.

She thought it best not to appear too desperate.

"God, I've never seen Blair in the flesh," she said, running her finger across the rim of her wineglass. "The Downing Street press office only allows a limited number of reporters to go to these things. I don't suppose there's even the remotest chance you could get me in, is there?"

"Don't see why not." He shrugged.

At this point she lost it, leaped out of her seat and threw her arms round him. "Thank you, thank you, thank you!" she squealed. "You have no idea how much this means to me."

He gave her a look of startled bemusement, as did the women at the next table. Then she felt his arms round her. She screwed up her face. Omigod, she thought, starting to panic. He thinks he's scored. She moved away, gently removing his arms. Then she took his hand and began shaking it vigorously. Now he looked really confused.

"Well, it's been great meeting you, Alex."

"Yes, you too," he said. "See you tomorrow. Come into the main building and ask for me at reception."

Then he said he hoped she didn't mind if he didn't drive her home, but he had to pick up his mother—whom he lived with—from her bridge night. Rebecca said she didn't mind at all.

When she arrived at the hospital, there was a press pass waiting for her, identifying her as a representative of *Health Service Management Today* magazine. There was also a note from Alex saying he'd been called away to a meeting, that he was still hoping to make the PM's speech and maybe he and Rebecca could get coffee afterward. She groaned inwardly when she got to the coffee bit. She would meet him and then let him down gently.

She headed off across the parking lot to the new obstetrics wing. As she opened the door she was confronted by a thicket of reporters, photographers and TV crews—all standing round chatting and drinking coffee from polystyrene cups. As she eased her way through, a woman she knew slightly from the *Tribune* waved and shouted hi. Finally she made it to the reception area, where the crowd had thinned out a bit. Behind the desk, a gang of nurses were passing round the lipstick and giggling nervously, while at the same time, daring each other to have a go at Tony about the way the government was neglecting the National Health Service.

It was only then that Rebecca realized something she ought to have known from the outset: with the huge press presence, not to mention all the hospital high-ups, patients and minders in attendance, she didn't stand a cat in hell's chance of having a private word with the PM.

Cross with herself for not thinking straight and desperately trying to think up some way of rescuing the situation, she wandered into the corridor that led off from the reception area. One side was glass, overlooking the parking lot. The other was made up of a series of tiny four-bed wards—all of which had been in use for a couple of months, even though the building hadn't been officially opened. She poked her head round one, taking in the NHS's best attempt at creating a home away from home—the mock mahogany dado rail (varnish chipped), the baby-blue, bow-motif wallpaper frieze (riding up at the edges) and the dusky pink nylon floor covering that was already covered in stains and ash from illegal ciggies.

Most of the mothers were gathered at the window in their dressing gowns and full makeup, watching excitedly for Tony's car. A few were carrying babies over their shoulders. She carried on down the corridor toward the dayroom. Here, half a dozen women, in slightly more upmarket dressing gowns, were sitting drinking tea and looking defiant. Definitely the Tory mums, Rebecca decided.

She wandered back. There had to be some way of getting the prime minister on his own. She knew the drill. He would come in, full of smiles, shake patients' hands and coo over a few babies. The mums would ask him about little Leo. He would smile, come over all proud dad and deliver some bland sound bite like: "Oh, he's getting to be a real rascal. Into everything. You need eyes in the back of your head." And that would be it. In a few minutes he would be heading back to the main hospital to make his speech. She had to think of some way to get his attention before he left.

Then it hit her. The solution was staring her in the face. Virtually all the mothers were up, leaving dozens of beds empty. Why not take one and pretend to be a patient? It was risky. The mother whose bed she chose could come back at any time. But it was either that or go home. She walked into the ward on her left. None of the mothers were there, although the babies were in their cribs next to the beds. Rebecca marched over to the nearest bed, took off her coat and shoes and jumped in.

A few moments later she heard footsteps coming toward her. A nurse, she presumed. She pulled the covers up over her head and turned on her side, pretending to be asleep. She prayed the nurse would carry on down the corridor. But she didn't. She stopped. At Rebecca's bed.

"All right, Mrs. Hollingsworth," she singsonged, "if you'd like to pull up your things, I'll quickly pop in your suppository. If this doesn't have your bowels open by teatime, nothing will. Mrs. Hollingsworth—you awake?"

"No."

"Oh, come on, don't feel embarrassed. It'll only take a moment. And you'll feel much better."

She reached for the bedcovers, but Rebecca's hand got there first. A tug of war followed, with Rebecca squealing and the nurse scolding her for being such a baby.

In the end, it was the prime minister who came to Rebecca's rescue. There was a commotion in the reception area. Apparently Tony's car had just pulled up outside.

"All right, Mrs. Hollingsworth," the nurse said. "Perhaps I'll leave it until Mr. Blair's gone. Don't want you to have an accident in front of the prime minister, do we?"

Rebecca lay there listening to the prime minister's greetings, cooings and the clicking of cameras getting closer. She sat up, grateful she was wearing a plain white T-shirt, which she decided could just about pass for a pajama top. Suddenly he was standing in front of her surrounded by a posse of hospital bigwigs and press.

"Hi, I'm Tony Blair." He beamed at her from the end of the bed. He looked pleasant enough, she thought. He held out her hand. She took it.

"Hello. I'm Rebecca," she said, desperately trying to disguise her nerves.

"So," he said, moving round to the crib, "what did you get—boy or girl?"

"Er … boy," she said.

He looked at the baby's wristband. "Bronte Louise. Quite an unusual name for a boy."

She sat there squirming. "Er, Prime Minister, I wonder if I could have a word with you about something."

She saw him exchange an uneasy glance with Alastair Campbell.

"Of course."

"In private."

Another glance.

"Well, I do have a really tight schedule. You can always write to me at Number 10."

"Please. It'll take two minutes of your time. I promise. It's really important."

He shot Alastair Campbell a look and the press and hospital bods disappeared.

She cleared her throat. "Look, I'm here on false pretenses. I'm not actually a patient. I'm a journalist."

His face darkened. "If there are questions you want to put to me about the NHS," he said brusquely, "you'll have to wait until after my speech. Now if you'll excuse me ..."

He turned to walk away.

"No, Prime Minister, wait. Please. This has nothing to do with the NHS. It's to do with the situation in Africa. Does the name Mer de Rêves mean anything to you ...?"

She had never told a story as fast or succinctly in her life.

"And here," she said, taking a plastic bag out from under the bed, "is the cream, together with a copy of the test results to prove it contains Kenbarbitol Cyclamate. Have your own people check it if you don't believe me."

He smiled a kind, sympathetic smile and put his hand on her shoulder. He was looking at her as if she were raving. It didn't help that just then her mobile went off in her bag. She grabbed it. She thought she'd pressed the off button, but instead she'd pressed connect. Not only that, but she'd fumbled with it so that it was blasting out on speakerphone and she had no idea how to turn it off.

"Hello, sweetie, it's me, Grandma. So, what did you think of Alex? Isn't he a wonderful boy?"

"Gran, I can't talk now, I'm with Tony Blair," she said, desperately stabbing at every button she could in an effort to shut the thing up.

Instead of taking the chance to get away, the prime minister stayed rooted to the spot, smiling. He was obviously finding the whole thing very funny.

"Sorry, darling, the line's cracking up. You're with Lionel Blair, you say? I love him. What a dancer. Lionel Blair and Anita Harris— the best dancers this country's ever produced. Tell him I saw him in pantomime a few years back. Wonderful Dick ... No, tell a lie. Maybe that was Anita Harris. Anyway, give Lionel a kiss from me."

"No, Gran, I'm not with Lionel Blair, I'm with TONY Blair."

"What? The prime minister?"

Tony Blair was now convulsing with laughter.

"Yes." Rebecca looked up and gave Tony a sheepish smile back.

"Oh, I don't like him. New Labour? What a joke. Two years Estelle's Harry has been waiting for his prostate operation. They wouldn't have done that to the Queen Mother. Anyway, I'll get off the line and leave you to it. Speak to you later. 'Bye."

Rebecca apologized profusely to the PM then tried to engage him again. "Please, you have to explain to the African heads of state that Madame N'Femkwe just couldn't help herself."

Another smile. Another shoulder pat. Another look of abject pity. Then he said good-bye.

She heard him outside with one of the consultants, discussing the misery of postnatal depression.

"And certainly in its severest form, it can lead to psychotic delusions," the doctor was saying.

Rebecca picked up her pillow and screamed into it. At which point Bronte Louise began yelling for a feed.

She was walking back to her car, having completely forgotten she was meant to be meeting Alex later, when she saw him coming toward her, waving.

"Aren't you staying for the PM's speech?" he said. "I thought that was your reason for coming."

"Yeah, I know, but ..."

"You OK? You look a bit flushed."

"I'm not feeling so good," she lied. "There's this stomach bug going round."

"So you don't fancy a coffee, then—after the speech. Thought we could have a bit of a chat."

Gawd, he was going to say he really liked her and ask her out on another date.

"Alex, I think perhaps I gave you the wrong—"

"Oh, I may as well come straight out with it," Alex interrupted. "Look, Rebecca, I do like you, but the thing is, I've just come out of a really heavy relationship. I thought I was ready to move on, but I'm not. Please don't take this as a rejection."

She looked down. "Oh, I don't. I don't," she said, desperately hoping the relief wasn't showing on her face. "So, you still love her?"

He nodded. "Daft, isn't it? Loving somebody who's in love with somebody else."

"Not at all," she said. "Take it from me, it happens all the time."

As soon as she got home, she tried again to reach Charlie. On the third attempt she got through, but they could barely hear each other.

"Look, if it's urgent, e-mail me," he said through the shooshing and crackles.

She couldn't see much point. Nobody bloody believed her about Madame N'Femkwe and the truth drug. It was Lipstick who revved her up again.

"Look, Charlie Holland knows you're not mad. E-mail him. I told you before, I'm certain he'll have a quiet word with Tony Blair."

Even though she didn't even remotely share Lipstick's optimism, Rebecca bashed out the e-mail.

Afterward Jess rang to see if Rebecca and Lipstick fancied coming over for spaghetti Bolognese. Lipstick said she would pass, since she was starting to feel sick again, so Rebecca went alone. When Ed went into the kitchen to open some wine, Rebecca asked after his willy-nilly.

"Well, I was going to talk to you about that actually," Jess said.

"You were? I'm not sure there's much I can do about it."

Jess giggled. "No, it's just that the hypnotherapist isn't making much progress with Ed and she suggested doing some past-life regression. She thinks the willy-nilly could have come about centuries ago."

"What, when he was Garibaldi? Or Anne of Cleves? My God, two intelligent people. I cannot believe you are into this kind of stuff."

"We wouldn't be normally, but we're desperate. We're prepared to try anything. Anyway, Gwen, that's the therapist, wants to do it here because she thinks Ed will be more relaxed and as Ed wants me to sit in, I was wondering if you could come round and keep an eye on the Dig-Twig. I'd ask Mum, but that woman she attacked in Harrods pressed charges and she's due at West End Central in the morning to be bound over to keep the peace."

"I still think the pair of you are bonkers," Rebecca said, "but OK, of course I'll come."

She got home just after midnight. Lipstick was still up.

"Hey, Becks, you missed the final *Watching You, Watching Me.*"

"Bugger. I knew it was tonight. I take it Lucretia won?"

"Oh, yes."

Lipstick told her how Lucretia had sashayed out of the house in a short, strapless pink chiffon number, blowing kisses to the crowd.

"Of course they're cheering and waving like mad. Then suddenly some twenty-year-old bloke catches her eye and before you know it, she's down in the crowd snogging and groping him. Of course then all the blokes want a turn. It was at least ten minutes before the telly people could get her away."

"So, she's clearly been on the cream again," Rebecca said. "You know, it's all my fault she's made such a fool of herself.

I should have gotten a message to her about the truth drug. This can't wait any longer. I've got to tell her."

She picked up her coat.

Lipstick suggested Rebecca gate-crash the after-show party, but she didn't know where it was being held.

"I'll wait for her until she gets home."

"But that could be hours," Lipstick said.

"I know, but I won't sleep unless I tell her what's been happening."

She reached Lucretia's flat in Notting Hill just after one. She parked outside, prepared for a long, cold wait. Then almost immediately, a taxi pulled up and Lucretia virtually fell out, swigging from a bottle of Baileys and singing *I Want to Sex You Up, Baby*. After a minute fumbling in her bag, she eventually found her purse and paid the driver.

Rebecca got out of the car and walked toward her. It was only then that she noticed the back of Lucretia's dress was tucked into her knickers.

"Roberta!"

"It's Rebecca," Rebecca said.

"Ah, yes. Rebecca who thinks we should run articles undermining our biggest advertisers. So, what are you doing here?"

"Lucretia, we have to talk. There's something I need to tell you."

"Talk away." She took another swig from the Baileys bottle and dug Rebecca in the ribs. "Never had the guts to drink this in public before now." She offered the bottle to Rebecca. She shook her head.

"Could we go inside?"

"OK."

Lucretia fumbled for her door key and led her up to the first-floor flat. Inside, it was exactly as Rebecca had imagined: expensive, elegant, not an ornament or curtain tassel out of place.

"Charlie sent you, didn't he?" Lucretia said. She kicked off her shoes and lay down on one of the feather-backed cream sofas. "To tell me I went too far—saying all the stuff I did. I don't know what came over me. I couldn't help it."

"I know. It's the Mer de Rêves Revivessence cream you've been using."

Lucretia snorted and took another swig of Baileys. "Don't be ridiculous, dahling. How could a silly pot of face cream make me share my most intimate sexual fantasies with the world?"

Rebecca started to explain, wondering how much Lucretia would take in, bearing in mind how drunk she was.

"And you've really had it analyzed?"

"Yep." She handed her a copy of the report.

Lucretia sat up and put the Baileys bottle down on the coffee table. "Good God. But Coco's a friend. She wouldn't do anything to hurt me."

Rebecca said there was a good chance Coco didn't know, since she was handing it out to all her friends and best clients.

"I don't care, you know—about what it did to me."

"You don't?" Rebecca said.

"Nope. I don't know how it works, but for the first time in years, I'm being true to myself. It's sort of—how can I put this—made me get back in touch with my whore within, I suppose. You know I keep thinking back to that time God spoke to me and I'm wondering if I misunderstood. It's only now that I realize what my true mission is."

"You mean the Lord wants you to become a hooker?"

"Good heavens, no," Lucretia said, positively aghast at the suggestion. Then her face broke into a smile. "God wouldn't want me to spend all day giving head. Terrible view, dahling. No, I know precisely what he wants me to do. I'm meant to leave the *Vanguard* and write a porn movie."

"Very Christian."

"But it is, dahling. It is. We have a moral duty to provide pathetic saddos with porn. It comforts them in their loneliness. But, you see, God doesn't mean me to write the usual naff stuff where the characters look like they live on benefits in an Argos catalogue. Mine is meant to be tasteful, high class and, more to the point, infinitely more stylish."

She opened her bag and took out her notebook.

"I started jotting down notes while I was in the *Watching You, Watching Me* house," she said, handing the book to Rebecca. "What do you think?"

Rebecca started reading.

"*Coming along the Catwalk—Runway Romps,* by Lucretia Coffin Mott

"Sophia, a dazzling eighteen-year-old Italian supermodel—as yet to be deflowered—is alone in her Philippe Starck kitchen, sipping iced tea. She is wearing a classic Armani shift dress (fabric swatches to follow). The doorbell rings. Enter Eduardo, the plumber, in a granite (or possibly taupe) Comme des Garçons boiler suit.

" 'Ciao, bella,' he says, admiring her facings."

"So what do you think?" Lucretia said when Rebecca had finished. "I think it's definitely got something, don't you?"

"Oh, absolutely," Rebecca said. "Absolutely."

19

Rebecca was in Jess's kitchen making herself a cup of coffee. Jess and Ed were in the living room with Gwen, the hypnotherapist from Osterley who had come to do Ed's past-life regression. She was a warm, bustling woman in her sixties—utterly unremarkable, apart from her bottle-black, waist-length braids. Apparently she'd been Pocahontas in a past life and the plaits were a tribute. Diggory was asleep in his pram—just as Rebecca had predicted he would be. Jess really hadn't needed anybody there to mind him.

Rebecca brought her coffee over to the table, pulled out a chair and picked up the *Vanguard*.

"Bugger," she said, looking at the headline running across the bottom of the front page: "African Peace Deal in Tatters." She carried on reading.

"War in Africa seemed inevitable last night, as hopes for a resumption of peace talks faded. The president of Nigeria also said at a press conference in Lagos that the British government's continued support of T'chala N'Femkwe could lead to Nigeria's cutting off oil supplies to Britain. . . ."

"Why didn't you listen to me, Tony? Why didn't you bloody listen?"

Just then, Diggory began to whimper. She went over to the pram and rocked it gently. She couldn't remember any lullabies so she sang him *I Will Survive*—Lipstick's Gloria Gaynor CDs had started to get to her. He seemed to enjoy it and settled after a few minutes. But as soon as she stopped he was off again. She decided to push the pram up and down the hall. As she went past the living room door, she could hear everything going on inside. She knew she shouldn't eavesdrop, but she couldn't help herself. She was desperate to find out who Ed had been in a past life. Perhaps he was famous. He could have been Picasso, Sartre or Michelangelo—not that she could imagine any of them being rejected sexually. But the way these things usually went, Ed would probably turn out to have led some pretty ordinary, humdrum life as Shakespeare's stationery supplier or Julius Caesar's pool guy.

"So, Ed," she could hear Gwen saying softly. "As you get more and more relaxed, you are going even farther back in time . . . farther and farther. So where are you now?"

"I'm not sure," he said, sounding completely spaced out. "Not that far back. The sixties, maybe. I can see this huge hall and there are people—rich, glamorous people I think, sitting at tables in evening dress. A celebration of some kind."

"Oh? What are they celebrating?"

"I think it's got something to do with me. It's my birthday. I'm forty-five."

"And you're happy?" Gwen asked.

"Fairly, but I've got all this stuff, important stuff on my mind. I'm worried about Kew. There are Russians in Kew."

"What?" Jess interrupted. "There are Russian tourists in Kew Gardens in the sixties?"

Gwen shushed her.

"And pigs," Ed said. "There are definitely pigs involved."

"OK, right," Jess came back. "So now there are Russian tourists and pigs in Kew Gardens."

"No," Ed said. "The Russians aren't tourists. They're soldiers. There's some kind of military bases in Kew. I've just gotten off the phone from Khrushchev. 'Come on, Nikita,' I'm saying, 'we're both civilized men, the future of the planet is at stake here. Can't we do a deal? But he won't listen. That bastard refuses to listen.' "

"Omigod," Jess piped up. "Don't you realize who he is? He's—" Another shush from Gwen.

"Let him get there on his own," she whispered. Then: "It's all right, Ed. Calm down. Just relax again. So, tell me, where is all this military activity?"

"It's not Kew Gardens. But it's Kew something. Kew … ba. Cuba. That's it. The military bases are in Cuba. And I can still see the pigs. There's this whole pig thing going on. Shit, if we don't do something, these motherfucking commie bastards are going to nuke the whole fucking world."

"All right," Gwen said, "take me back to the party. What's happening now?"

"I can see this woman. Stunning. Blonde. Fabulous figure. Huge red lips. She's standing up. She's shimmying over to the microphone. She's wearing this amazing dress that makes her breasts look like two torpedoes. OK, she's starting to sing."

"What's she singing?"

"Listen to that voice. My God, you could pour it on a pancake. Can you hear it?"

Ed started to sing softly: "*Happy birthday, Mr. President, happy birthday to you.* That's me. I'm Mr. President. I'm John Kennedy. And I'm watching her and listening to her sing. Jackie's sitting next to me, but it's Marilyn I want."

"So what do you do?"

A couple of beats.

"OK, it's later, much later. We're in her hotel suite. I'm unzipping her dress. Shit, you should see these breasts."

"Oh, God," Jess said. "I'm starting to feel weird, here."

"Ditto." Rebecca muttered to herself, but her embarrassment didn't stop her listening.

"She's unbuttoning my shirt," he went on. "Now she's undoing my fly. She's on her knees and she's—oh, my God. Oh, my God. She's...she's...No, wait."

"What?"

"She's stopped."

"Thank Christ for that," Jess said.

"Why? What's happened? Can you tell me what she's doing now?"

"She's giggling like a little girl. She can't stop giggling and she's saying...she's saying, 'Gee, Mr. President, it's real cute. But would you be a li'l less embarrassed if we skipped straight to the cigarette?'"

"Omigod!" Jess squealed. "JFK had a small willy and he never slept with Marilyn after all because she rejected him."

Ed sounded close to tears.

"Marilyn's laughing. She's still laughing."

"It's all right, Ed," Gwen soothed. "I'm going to bring you back now."

She asked Jess to hold his hand.

"It's OK, baby," Jess was whispering to him. "It's OK. You've got a lovely willy. It's perfect. Honest. Just the right size."

"Euuuch. Too much information," Rebecca muttered, pushing the pram back to the kitchen.

"God," Jess said to Rebecca (Ed, who wasn't quite sure what to make of it all, had gone for a walk to think and clear his head). "So at last we know how the willy-nilly started."

"You reckon?" Rebecca said doubtfully.

"Of course. You realize this information about Kennedy's willy could be worth millions."

"Oh, absolutely," Rebecca replied. "Go to any newspaper and explain that your husband thinks he was JFK in a past life and that he had a small willy and they're bound to believe you. Probably offer you half a mil on the spot."

"OK, no. You're right." A faraway look came over her. "But, Becks, just think. I'm married to the man who saved the world from nuclear disaster—to the man who was king of Camelot. The Diggydumpling is the son of the president of the United States. What a legacy. What a legacy."

"Jess, get a grip. I always thought agony aunts were sensible, grounded people. It's so unlike you to get carried away like this. Read my lips. You are married to Ed. Ed is not JFK. The only thing he's ever saved is money off coupons."

"But he *was* JFK," Jess protested. "He was."

Rebecca rolled her eyes. "Oh, come on. This Gwen is clearly a quack."

"All right, I admit it's possible. But you weren't in that room with him, Becks. You didn't see the look on his face. He was Kennedy. I know it....So, tell me honestly, do you think I could carry off a little pink suit and a pillbox hat?"

After she left Jess, Rebecca drove to the *Vanguard*. If she was grateful for one thing, it was that Max hadn't been in for ages. In fact, she hadn't seen him since their meeting at Waterloo.

After he'd finished working on the documentary, he'd taken some time off. Then last Monday his piece revealing how only a lucky accident had saved London and Paris from being nuked finally appeared in the *Vanguard* (the TV program aired on the same night). The next day, all hell broke loose politically, on both sides of the Channel. There was talk of the French prime minister resigning. In Britain, the government was fielding awkward questions about the safety of British nuclear installations. All that week it seemed like every time Rebecca switched on the TV or the radio there was Max, with John Humphrys or Jeremy Paxman purring all over him about his stupendous scoop.

Rebecca never watched for long, though. It was too painful. (She hadn't watched the documentary for the same reason.) Then, on the weekend, he'd left for France to give evidence at the inquiry that had hastily been set up into the near-explosion at the French nuclear plant.

The moment Rebecca walked into the office, people started clapping and yelling congratulations.

She gave an uneasy smile. Why on earth would they be cheering her? She had nothing to do with Max's story.

"OK, what's going on?" she demanded.

"News just in from Reuters," Snow said. "The peace deal in Africa is back on again. The oil crisis is over and according to Charlie, it's all due to you."

"Charlie's back?" God, she thought, he must have spoken to Tony Blair.

"He got back a few minutes ago, and he hasn't stopped going on about your Mer de Rêves story. Said he wanted to see you the moment you came in."

Rebecca started heading toward Charlie's office. She'd gone a few paces when she turned round. Excited as she was about what Charlie might be about to tell her, she felt she had to say a few words to Snow.

"By the way," she said, "welcome back. Everybody thought it was brilliant the way you stood up to Lucretia."

"Thing is, I didn't do it completely alone. I had a bit of help."

"How do you mean?"

Snow looked round to check nobody was listening. "Well, the night before, I nicked some of Lucretia's Mer de Rêves cream when she wasn't looking. You see, I've got definite beginnings of crow's-feet at the corners of my eyes and I thought it might help."

"And did it?"

"Not really. But that's probably because I only tried it the once. What it did was force me to tell Lucretia the truth about how I felt about her. It was the oddest sensation. I just couldn't help myself."

"I bet it felt fantastic, though."

"Did it ever. I still can't believe I actually did it. But what was even odder was that after I walked out, she wrote me this long rambling letter saying she'd been given this mission from God to write a porn movie and how sorry she was for the way she'd treated me. She said she'd been so miserable not being herself all these years and that she took her frustrations out on the people who worked for her. I don't know if it's the aftereffects of the cream or God, but do you know it's the first time I've ever known Lucretia to apologize for anything? She even sent me these." She nodded toward the bunch of white lilies sitting on her desk.

"Those have to be a first," Rebecca said, shaking her head.

"Anyway, you've no idea what standing up to her has done for my confidence. I've even told Justin I'm happy to marry him, but there's no way on this earth I'm about to become Mrs. Snow Ball. God, do you know, Rebecca, the way I'm feeling at the moment, I could take on the world."

When Rebecca poked her head round his office door, Charlie was on the phone. He beckoned her in. "Speak of the devil, Prime Minister. The woman responsible for all this has just walked in... All right. Will do. 'Bye."

Charlie stood up, his face full of smiles. Then, in a unique, rather stiff display of affection, he came over, put his arm round her and gave her a squeeze. "What can I say, Rebecca? What a result. Do you realize that without you, the country would now be facing a desperate economic crisis? Blair is over the fucking moon. Says he'll be in touch soon to thank you personally."

"So, what happened? Did you phone the prime minister after I e-mailed you?"

"I had a quick word. I managed to persuade him to send the cream for a second analysis. You see, it made a certain amount of sense to me. My father was parachuted into enemy territory during the war and was captured and tortured by the Gestapo. They held on to him for months before sending him off to a POW camp. At one stage they injected him with Kenbarbitol Cyclamate. My mother always used to wonder how a man could have suffered so much and yet have a completely line-free face—even in old age. But the thing about what's happened now is that you did all the hard work. I just tied up a few loose ends."

Charlie said the plan was to run a news story on the front page the next day that would carry the headline: "*Vanguard* Reporter Saves Peace Deal."

"I'll get somebody on the foreign desk to do that. What I want you to do is tell the full Mer de Rêves story, which we'll run over pages two, three and four. Do you think you can have it ready by ten?"

She had it ready by eight. In many ways it was the easiest piece she'd ever written. All she had to do was tell it the way it happened. Charlie had told her to try and get a comment from Mer de Rêves.

"But leave it until the last moment. That way it'll be too late for them to get an injunction to prevent the piece appearing."

As Charlie had predicted, their senior press officer in France went into orbit when Rebecca phoned him at home to say the newspaper was about to accuse Mer de Rêves of using a potentially harmful drug in their face cream.

"OK, they're trying for an injunction," Rebecca said, tearing into Charlie's office.

Charlie had his feet up on his desk. "It's past eight," he grinned, looking at his watch. "Some hopes."

The rest of the week, it was Rebecca's turn to do the rounds of the TV and radio news programs. Her desk was filled with flowers—from her dad and Lipstick, Rose, Jess and Ed. One bunch came without a card. She assumed they were from Charlie, but he categorically denied having sent them.

When the Mer de Rêves lawyers announced they would be suing the *Vanguard,* Rebecca started to panic. But Charlie said the scientific evidence against them was overwhelming. Meanwhile, every last jar of Revivessence had been confiscated by the French police.

A day later, Coco Dubonnet and her board of directors were arrested and charged with an assortment of offenses that sounded like Marie Antoinette's rap sheet.

"But Coco is innocent," Lucretia insisted when she phoned Rebecca in a panic that night. "Her directors sanctioned the making of this cream, behind her back, I just know it. I must do something to help her. I must."

She was as good as her word. The next day the editors of British and American *Vogue* flew into Charles de Gaulle. They were followed by the editors of *Elle, Tatler* and *Harper's.* Very soon every editor from every glossy in Europe, along with most of Hollywood and hundreds of Coco's clients (including Madame N'Femkwe), had arrived. The city was almost forced to declare a state of emergency, such was the run on Perrier, green salad and egg whites. Lucretia chaired a tactics meeting at the Georges Cinq, at which it was decided each of them would submit a written testimonial to the police, attesting to Coco's good character.

What was more, the following three nights, as the world's press looked on, two hundred of the planet's most glamorous women (with their makeup artists, publicists and personal chefs) held a candlelight vigil outside the Mer de Rêves building, to protest the charges brought against Coco and sing "We Shall Overcome."

By the end of the week Coco's name had been cleared and all charges against her dropped. She was also free to carry on trading under the Mer de Rêves name, since all the truth cream had been impounded. The decision appeared to have less to do with the protest rally and more to do with the police being unable to find any evidence to prove Coco had known about the dangerous effects of the cream. What was more, her managing director, together with half a dozen members of the Mer de Rêves board, confessed to having masterminded the entire affair entirely on their own. (*Le Figaro* claimed to have evidence that the confession had been extracted under duress. Apparently the police had stripped the men, tied them down and smeared their naked bodies with Revivessence.)

The next day Rebecca was able to phone Wendy and tell her that Lucretia had put her case, and that of the other members of staff who'd been sacked by Mer de Rêves, to Coco. She immediately offered them substantial financial compensation as well as their jobs back. The others opted to take the money and find new jobs. Wendy decided to stay on. Coco had been so impressed by Wendy's courage and determination that in addition to a cash payout, she had offered her an executive position at Mer de Rêves, a six-figure salary and a seat on the board. Despite everything that had happened, Wendy decided it was far too good an offer to turn down.

"I don't know quite how to thank you for all you've done," Rebecca said to her, "other than to say there will be a sizable check from the *Vanguard* on its way to you soon. You know this is far and away the best story I've ever had."

"Well, let's hope it leads you to bigger and better things," Wendy said.

* * *

"You know," Charlie said, "a French lawyer mate of mine reckons the guys at Mer de Rêves responsible for the antiwrinkle cream could go down for ten years."

He had come over just as she was getting ready to leave for the day and was now sitting on the edge of her desk, winding up one of her sushis.

"Wow, so we're in the clear. Nobody's suing anymore."

"Correct." He put the sushi down and watched it *click-clack* across the desk. "You know," he said, "taking on you and Max was the best thing I ever did."

He hesitated for a moment. "I'm so sorry, you know—about the two of you splitting up. For what it's worth, I thought you made a great pair."

"Yeah, so did I. But you know ..."

Just then the sushi fell on the floor. Charlie instantly bent down and picked it up. The plastic prawn halves had come away from the slab of rice.

"I am so sorry. Tell me where you bought them and I'll get you some more."

Rebecca laughed, said they'd cost virtually nothing and she had no idea where she bought them.

"Don't worry," she said, taking the broken sushi from him and dropping the pieces into her bag, "I'll stick it back together with some superglue."

"Anyway," Charlie said, smiling, "the pair of you are going to walk away with God knows how many press awards this year."

"What, me too?"

"Don't look so astonished. Of course, you too. This is a major story. Believe me, nobody will better it this year. Now then, I've been thinking about how best to show you my appreciation. How do you fancy heading up a small team dedicated to investigative stuff?"

"Me?"

He looked around. "I don't see anybody else sitting at this desk."

"What about the makeup column?"

"Well, since Nat who did the column before you has decided not to come back because she wants to be with her baby full time, I think the reinvented Snow will jump at the job. Next objection."

Her face broke into a broad smile. "I don't have one," she said.

"Right, let's have lunch tomorrow to celebrate. One o'clock at Drake's."

Rebecca sang *I Will Survive*, complete with gestures, all the way to the multistory parking garage. It had happened. She'd done it. She'd landed her dream job. Apart from waking up and discovering she was Julia Roberts, life couldn't get much sweeter than this.

Just as she was about to put the key in the car door, she stopped singing and stared up at the concrete ceiling.

"Thanks, Mum," she whispered. "I love you."

On the way home she phoned her dad, who couldn't stop telling her how proud he was of her. Then he got choked up, the way he had the night she played the lead in *Toad of Toad Hall* in junior high school.

"And Charlie's even taking me out to lunch tomorrow," she said.

"Wow. My baby being wined and dined by a Fleet Street editor. Your mother would be so proud of you."

She could feel tears welling up.

"Yeah, I know."

"And I have news, too," he said, "I'm coming home tomorrow. I've finally found a manager for the Manchester shop."

It would be great to have her dad back. She'd missed him. On top of that, the work on Lipstick's house was finished, which meant she would be moving out in a few days. Much as she was go-

ing to miss Lipstick, she couldn't wait to have the flat to herself
again.

By the time she got home, Lipstick (who had by now spoken to
Stan) had been out and bought champagne.

"Here's to a brilliant future," Lipstick said, handing her a glass.
"So what are you going to wear tomorrow?"

Rebecca shrugged. "Lipstick, this is Charlie we're talking about
here. I could turn up dressed as a Morris dancer and he wouldn't
notice."

"I know," Lipstick said, "but you want to show him you can
dress the part for this new job. It doesn't hurt to make a good
impression."

Rebecca was puzzled. "I don't get it," she said. "Why are you so
concerned about what I wear tomorrow?"

"I care about you, that's all, and I just want to see you looking
your best. Is that such a crime?"

Lipstick shuffled uneasily and started examining her cuticles.

Rebecca said she supposed it wasn't.

They ordered Chinese takeout. Still high on excitement and
adrenaline, Rebecca ate tons. She couldn't help noticing Lipstick
barely touched a thing. This bug of hers was certainly dragging on.

Rebecca arrived at Drake's bang on time. She was wearing her
posh powder-blue suit. Her choice of outfit had little to do with
the fact that she was meeting Charlie and everything to do with
Drake's being the kind of place where women wore posh powder-
blue suits.

An unsmiling, surly waiter told her Charlie hadn't arrived yet
and led her to a table by the window. The restaurant was famous
for its sublime food and cold, aloof—to the point of downright
rude—service. Martin Drake, the tantrum-throwing owner-chef,
whose turnover of kitchen slaves rivaled the Gulag at its height,

readily admitted that the possession of two Michelin stars gave him the right to treat his customers like ignorant rabble. The more often stories appeared of him forcibly ejecting some poor punter who'd had the temerity to suggest his quenelles were a tad on the heavy side, the more impossible it became to get a table for dinner inside six weeks. (Although like most publicity junkies, he made exceptions for media supremos, including Charlie, for whom a table could always be found.)

Rebecca ordered a glass of mineral water.

"Still or sparkling?"

"Sparkling."

"We have a choice." He proceeded to reel off a list of names she'd never heard of.

"Glen Morag," she said. It all tasted the same to her.

"Can I bring you some bread?"

"Yes, please," she said.

"What sort of oil?"

"Er, olive, I think."

The waiter rolled his eyes.

"Of course, olive. But we have a choice. First there is the Adapte, a rich fruity oil from the western slopes of mount Ida, overlooking the Aegean Sea and Lesbos. Then there is Romeu, which is a little more full-bodied, from the Tras Os Montes region of Portugal. My personal favorite, however, is the Da Vero, which comes from a 350-year-old farm in Segromigno, overlooking the Tuscan plain. It has an unusually delicate flavor and stands in sharp contrast to the more assertive oils from Umbria and Chianti."

"Does it?" she said. She was more than a little confused by now and couldn't remember any of the names.

"So, which is it to be?" he said, tapping his pad with his Biro.

"I'm not sure. Would you mind going through them again?"

He let out an irritable sigh. "Adapte, a rich fruity ..."

"OK, yes, the Adapte. That would be fine."

"Not the Romeu?"

"Or the Romeu, if that's what you recommend."

"Rather than the Da Vero?"

"Ah, yes. From the 350-year-old farm, overlooking the Tuscan plain."

"It is particularly good today," he said.

"Let's go with that, then."

"The Da Vero. An excellent choice if I may say so."

"Glad you approve," she said.

As she sat wondering how much longer Charlie was going to be, she couldn't help eavesdropping on a couple of American businessmen giving their order to a different waiter.

"And perhaps we could offer you a little amuse gueule, with the chef's compliments."

The pair exchanged confused glances.

"Sure," they said.

"So, what's with the amuse girl thing?" one of them said to his companion, after the waiter had gone. "What do they do, bring in a hooker before the entrée?"

Rebecca looked at her watch and began smoothing out nonexistent creases in the tablecloth. Anxious to find something to occupy herself, she picked up her bag and took out her Filofax. She began flicking through the pages, pretending she was checking her appointments. After a minute or so she got bored. As she put the Filofax back in her bag, she noticed the pieces of broken sushi. She took them out and put them on the table. Somewhere she had some superglue.

Without stopping to consider how ridiculous she would look, sitting in the middle of one of the smartest restaurants in London, doing a spot of DIY on a piece of windup sushi, she started rummaging through her bag. Eventually she found the glue and unscrewed the top. She picked up one of the halves of plastic prawn and squeezed the tube. Nothing. She squeezed again, harder. The superglue shot over the tablecloth. Without thinking she wiped at it with her fingers. Then, with the same hand she picked up the two pieces of plastic prawn and the rice slab.

Suddenly, she was aware of somebody standing over her. Assuming it was Charlie, she looked up and smiled.

"Max." Her shock at seeing him instantly gave way to profound discomfort.

"Hi," he said, returning her unease.

"I thought you were in France," she said.

"Got back last night."

"Oh, right."

Silence.

"So," she said, "who you meeting for lunch?"

"Charlie."

"Charlie? But I'm having lunch with Charlie—to celebrate my new job. He didn't say anything about ..."

The waiter, who had been hovering at a discreet distance moved forward. "Er, Mr. Holland has just phoned to say he is caught up in an urgent meeting and that he isn't going to be able to make it. He sends his apologies and hopes you and Mr. Stoddart enjoy your lunch."

Rebecca and Max looked at each other.

"I think maybe I should go," Max said.

"Yes, me too." She started to get up.

"On the other hand," he said, "we could stay. It seems a shame to waste a freebie lunch."

She thought for a moment, then nodded.

"OK." She extended her hand toward the seat opposite.

"Ah, Edward Sushihands," he said, smiling.

Her face turned crimson. The two halves of prawn and plastic rice were stuck to her fingers.

The waiter glowered.

"It's OK," she said anxiously, "I think I've got some nail polish remover in my bag. That usually gets glue off."

"Not in here, please, madame. The smell."

"It's OK, I'll go outside."

She picked up her coat.

"I'll come with you," Max said.

Outside, the sky was heavy with rain, but it was holding off for the time being.

He took the bottle of nail polish remover from her.

"OK, hold out your hand," he said.

The liquid was ice cold on her skin. He began pulling gently at the pieces of plastic.

"Tell me if this hurts," he said.

"It's fine."

But it wasn't fine. The pain of wanting him and knowing she couldn't have him was unbearable.

"So," he said, "I *think* we've been set up here. Looks like old Charlie's been playing cupid. Funny, he doesn't seem the type."

She gave a nervous laugh. "No, he doesn't. By the way, I thought your French nuclear piece was brilliant. I haven't watched the film yet. But I taped it. And you were great with Paxman on *Newsnight*."

"Thanks, I was shitting bricks. Your story was pretty amazing, too. Did you get my flowers?"

"They were from you? Oh, God, Max. I had no idea. They came without a card. That was a sweet thought. Thank you."

"You're welcome. And congratulations on this new job. Charlie told me. Sounds amazing."

"I know. I can't wait to start. So, how's Lorna?"

"Lorna? I couldn't tell you. Haven't seen her for ages."

He stopped dabbing at her fingers and looked at her.

"Just for the record, there was never anything going on between me and Lorna—at least not on my part."

"Oh, come on, Max, don't try and pretend the pair of you weren't sharing a room in Paris. The bloke on the desk was in no doubt about it. Then when I got through, I heard her call you *honey.*"

"OK, I admit she booked a double room, but the moment I found out, the penny dropped, I realized she was trying to split us up and I unbooked it. Clearly the bloke on the desk hadn't caught up with that. She only managed to get in because I'd been stupid enough to leave my door unlocked."

"So, why didn't you tell me Lorna was going to be in Paris, too?"

"Because I didn't know."

Rebecca looked distinctly doubtful.

"It's the truth," Max came back. "When I arrived at the hotel, Lorna and the film crew were already there."

He explained that the Channel 6 people had panicked after he'd told them that various interviewees were getting cold feet, and as a result they'd decided to bring the filming forward.

"She spent the entire week coming on to me. I made it clear nothing was going to happen, but she wouldn't take no for an answer. After you phoned we had a huge row and I slung her out, but it still didn't make any difference."

"And you really expect me to believe all this?"

"Ask any of the crew—they'll tell you what a hard time she was giving me. I bored them all stupid going on about it. When I wasn't doing that or fending off Lorna, I was trying to reach you."

By now his face had taken on a strained, almost desperate expression. She was starting to believe him.

"By the way," he said. "You know that story she told me at the wedding about her godfather dying? Complete nonsense. I found out the old boy made a speech in the House of Lords the following Monday. It was just a ploy to get me away from you. Even on the train coming back she was all over me and refused to take no for an answer."

"But you and Lorna are still working together?"

"Good God, no. When we got back to Waterloo, I got really heavy and told her there was no way we could carry on working on the film project together. If you'd watched it you'd see how the editor recut it in such a way as to get rid of her and I ended up doing all the voice-overs."

He began trying to dislodge the slab of rice, which was being particularly stubborn. "So, you still seeing this bloke I saw you with?"

"Father Donal?"

He grinned. "A priest? You're seeing a priest?"

"No, I er..." She was starting to feel embarrassed. "I snogged him to make you jealous. He's Lipstick's cousin, but I didn't know he was a priest then."

"So, that means you're not actually seeing anybody."

She looked up at him.

"Not as such. No." She paused. "Max. Have you spoken to Lipstick recently?"

"Why?"

"Oh, I just thought that us getting together like this may not be entirely down to Charlie Holland."

"I spoke to her yesterday. I asked her if she thought there was any chance you'd agree to see me."

"And what did she say?"

"Well, she was pretty cool with me until we'd gotten this Lorna business sorted. Then she said she'd see what she could do."

By now it was perfectly clear to Rebecca that Lipstick had gotten together with Charlie and orchestrated the meeting with Max. *That's* why Lipstick had been so unusually interested in what Rebecca was planning to wear.

The slab of plastic rice finally came away, but he carried on holding her hand.

"The thing is," he said, "I've really missed you. I haven't slept for ages for thinking about you."

"Really?"

"Really."

"I've been thinking about you a bit, too," she said.

"You have?"

She nodded.

"You see," he said. "What I'm trying to say is that I love you and I'd like us to try again."

"I don't know," she said. "I'd have to think."

"Fine, take as long as you need."

"OK, I've thought," she said. "I'd like us to try again, too."

"What, you've decided, just like that?"

"Yes," she said, beaming.

"How come?"

"Because I love you too, you dope."

He came toward her, swept her fringe out of her eyes and kissed her.

"I've lost my appetite all of a sudden," he said.

"Me too."

"So, do you want to come back to my place?" he said. Then he lowered his voice. "If you like, I'll show you my . . ."

"Max, I have seen it before."

He grinned at her. "I was going to say, I'll show you my documentary."

I'm not sure I've got anything in for breakfast," Max said, trailing his finger over her breasts. "How's about I nip out and get some croissants?"

"Great," she mumbled, still half asleep. She pushed his hand away and began scratching her breasts, as if some tiny insect had been crawling over her and left her skin itching.

"Or *pains au chocolat?*"

" 'K."

"Or I could get bacon and eggs—do us a fry-up."

He leaned across and began sucking at her nipples.

"Gerroff." She tried to turn over but he pulled her back and began planting tiny kisses all over her stomach.

"Or kippers?" he said between kisses. "I know, croissants and kippers."

"Fine."

He kissed her again. On her cheek this time.

"And when I get back," he said softly, stroking her hair, "there's something I really need to talk to you about."

She turned back onto her side, barely registering what he was saying. "OK, whaddever."

"Right," he said, pulling on his jeans, "I'll be twenty minutes."

She woke up slowly. The bright winter sun was pouring in through the window. She lay there, eyes still closed, feeling its warmth on her face. Just when she thought life couldn't get any better, it had. She couldn't remember a time when she'd been this happy. And it was Lipstick she had to thank. She felt another pang of guilt as she remembered how suspicious she'd been of her in the beginning.

Eventually she pulled on Max's dressing gown and headed for the shower. A few minutes later, she was sitting on the sofa wrapped in a towel, reading the newspaper TV listings. She wondered if there was a Saturday matinee they could watch in bed later—preferably one of those made-for-TV tug of love courtroom weepies where the rich white liberal parents adopt a baby, only to have the dirt poor, black, ex-druggie birth mother reappear eight years later, claiming to have gotten her life straight and demanding the child back. She would start blubbing at the bit where the birth mother—having won the case—finally realizes how cruel she's being depriving the child of the only parents he's ever known. Max would comfort her, marvel at how sensitive and caring she was, fall in love with her even more and then they'd shag until it was time to order takeout, which they would eat while watching Cilla's *Moment of Truth*. (Then again, maybe she should drop the *Moment of Truth* idea. She wasn't absolutely certain her relationship with Max had reached a level where she felt comfortable confessing to a nonironic passion for Saturday night TV game shows.) But there weren't any films she fancied. Maybe they'd go for a walk in Highgate Woods and get tea somewhere.

She put down the paper and picked up the copy of *Spin*, which was lying on the coffee table. Assuming it belonged to Amy, she began flicking through it, smiling to herself as she realized virtually none of the band names meant anything to her.

She'd just finished getting dressed when she heard a loud clanking sound from the kitchen.

"Max? You back?"

No answer.

Still thinking it was Max making the noise, she stood up and headed toward the kitchen.

"Max, that you?" She opened the kitchen door and gasped. A girl, fifteenish at a guess, was rummaging through the bread bin. She looked up at Rebecca and slammed the bread bin shut.

"There's never anything to bloody eat in this place," she said sullenly.

Rebecca blinked. Then her face broke into a smile. "Of course. You must be Amy."

"That's me."

"Max'll be back soon. He's gone out for kippers."

"Yuk. I hate kippers."

"I'm not sure you were being offered any," Rebecca said brightly, while at the same time thinking this was one stroppy teenager.

She was, nevertheless, exquisite. Smooth alabaster skin, shoulder-length red hair, wide dark blue denim jeans, which were so long that the bottoms were frayed and grubby. A crocheted cloche hat with candy stripes going round it was pulled down to her eyes.

Amy turned and opened the fridge. The back of her hooded top said, "I hate my life and want to die."

"Empty," she groaned. "It's always bloody empty."

"I think there's some bread in the bread bin," Rebecca ventured. "Might be a bit stale, but I could make some toast."

Amy shrugged. Rebecca took that as a yes and opened the bread bin.

"I'm Rebecca, by the way."

"I know," Amy said, sitting down at the kitchen table.

"Oh, Max has told you about me, then?" Rebecca dropped a couple of slices of bread into the toaster.

Amy stared hard at Rebecca.

"He tells me everything."

Rebecca frowned. "He does? So, Amy, where do you live?"

"Islington."

"I love Islington. Loads of trendy shops."

"So, how long have you two been going out?"

Ah, so he didn't tell her absolutely everything.

"Oh, you know," Rebecca said. "A while."

"So, is it serious?"

Rebecca was beginning to feel a tad uncomfortable being cross-examined by Amy. Why was she so interested in her relationship with Max?

"Could be," she said.

Amy turned away and opened her rucksack. She took out a stick of strawberry-flavored lip balm and began coating her lips. Rebecca noticed a CD sticking out of the bag.

"Oh, you're into Papa Roach, then. I saw his new album got a great review in *Spin*."

A definite look of disdain from Amy. "He's crap. The CD belongs to a friend. She left it at my house. I'm into Tupac."

"Tupac?" Rebecca came back tentatively.

"Tupac Shakur."

"Oh, right."

"But only the albums since he died."

"Of course."

The toast popped up. Rebecca took it out and began buttering. Just then Max's key turned in the door.

"Hi, Dad," Amy said as he walked in with the shopping.

Rebecca's arm froze in midbutter. Dad? Did Amy say Dad? She turned round slowly.

Max looked like he'd been caught nicking the cutlery at a royal garden party.

"Hi, sweetheart," he said to Amy. "I...er, I wasn't expecting you until this afternoon."

"I know," she said, "but I just wanted to check out where we're going tonight. I really fancy seeing the new Coen brothers movie. Then we could get Chinese afterward." She stared pointedly at Rebecca, shoving the point home that she intended this to be a date for two, not three.

"Listen, Ames," Max said, his eyes still fixed on Rebecca, "do you think maybe you could go in the living room and watch TV for a bit? Rebecca and I need to talk in private."

"What about my toast?" she said grumpily.

Rebecca held out the plate of toast. Amy took it and trudged off.

"A child?" Rebecca hissed. "You have a child? And you didn't even bother to tell me? Did you think I wouldn't notice this third person coming to visit? And not only do you keep her a secret, but you tell me she's your goddaughter. Max, what is going on here? How could you lie like that?"

"Look, I know it was wrong, but it's complicated. I wanted to be sure about us before I said anything." He was standing inches from her now, his hands gripping the tops of her arms. "I'd planned to tell you today. Amy was the big thing I wanted to talk to you about over breakfast."

Rebecca stood, shaking her head. "Max, last night you told me you loved me and still you didn't tell me about Amy. Tell me, just tell me, what sort of a future have we got if there's no trust between us?"

Just then Amy walked back in. Max's hands shot into his pockets.

"Forgot the honey," she said. She went over to one of the cupboards. "Oh, and Dad, I've seen these brilliant Bolt jeans. I could really do with some new ones. These are totally shot."

"Look, Ames," Max said, looking down at the floor and running his hand over his forehead, "this really isn't a good time."

"No, you two carry on," Rebecca said, picking up her coat from the back of the chair. "'Bye, Amy. Nice to have met you."

She virtually ran to the front door. Max came after her and took hold of her wrist.

"Rebecca, I know this whole thing has come as a shock, but please don't go."

"Max, just leave it. I need to think." She pulled her wrist away.

Amy had come out of the kitchen and was hovering in the hall. "'Bye," she said, her smile smug and victorious. "And thanks for the toast."

Back home, Rebecca lay on her bed staring into space. Part of her was still reeling with shock. He had a child. She still couldn't believe it. But why lie about it? He'd said it was complicated. But what could be so complicated he couldn't tell her? Why hadn't he trusted her? Maybe there were other things he'd lied about, too. His relationship with Bloody Lorna, for example. The hairs stood up on the back of her neck.

Just then the intercom went.

"OK, Max, I think it's time we got this thing sorted."

"It's not Max, it's Amy."

"Amy?" She was the last person Rebecca expected. "Come on up."

The girl's sweatshirt was soaked. The sunshine had been shortlived and it was now bucketing outside. Rebecca offered to dry it on the radiator.

"Thanks," Amy said, peeling it off to reveal a sleeveless T-shirt. Rebecca offered to fetch her a sweater, but she said she was fine.

Rebecca led her into the living room.

"Wow," she said, glancing round the room, "this place is fantastic. So much cooler than where my dad lives. His flat is totally tragic, with all that ancient pine."

Rebecca thanked her and offered her a seat.

"So." Rebecca smiled, inviting her to explain the reason for her visit.

"I found your address on Dad's PalmPilot."

Rebecca nodded.

"He doesn't know I'm here. I mean he didn't send me or anything. Probably kill me if he found out. I said I was going to Camden Market."

"Did you get the jeans money out of him?"

"No way. When I left him he was in no mood to be gotten round. Look, he told me everything. About how he lied. He knows he shouldn't have done it. And I was pretty pissed off, too. It's not very nice knowing he couldn't bring himself to tell you about me. But it isn't all his fault."

"How come?"

"Because I can be a total cow. Every time Dad gets a new girlfriend I get jealous and play up."

"Like you did back at the flat?"

"Oh, that was nothing," Amy said brightly. "I can be much worse than that."

"Really?"

"Absolutely. There was this one time when Dad was just about to leave on a weekend trip to Venice with this woman he really liked and I pretended to break my arm. By the time we got home from the hospital he'd missed his flight."

"Wow, I bet Max loved you when he found out what you'd done."

"Mum and Dad grounded me for a month."

"And what happened to Max and the woman?"

"They had a huge row about me and she left him. It's the same every time. I get jealous of his girlfriends. They get jealous of the time he spends with me and it ends. Mum keeps telling me I have self-esteem issues and that I have to stop sabotaging his life. She talks like that. She's training to be a psychotherapist."

Rebecca looked at Amy. "So," she said, "what's made you change your tune all of a sudden? Why are you telling me this?"

"Because when you left him I saw what a state he was in. I've never seen him like that. I could see how much he loves you and now he thinks you've gone for good. Anyway, I rang Mum because he was so upset. She said Dad had been a prat. Actually she said he'd lied about me because he'd panicked and ignored his inner adult voice, but she meant he'd been a prat. Then she said if I didn't acknowledge my part in all this, I would be putting my relationship with Dad at risk. She also said I should come and apologize to you." She paused. "So here I am. I'm really sorry for being so rude back at the flat."

"That's all right," Rebecca said. "I think it was very brave of you to come and talk to me. And your mum sounds like a really sensible woman. I'd like to meet her."

"Yeah, she's great. You need a psychobabble-to-English dictionary when you have a conversation with her, but basically she's OK."

Just then the buzzer went again. It was Max.

He stood in the doorway, his hair plastered to his forehead, rain streaking down his face. He looked more fanciable than ever, she thought.

"You're wet," she declared, a smile hovering at the corners of her lips. She let him into the hall.

"Couldn't start the car. Dead battery. Had to get a jump start." He paused. Then: "Rebecca, I am so sorry I lied. It was unfair to you and it was unfair to Amy, but she gets so bloody jealous whenever I have a girlfriend. Then, whoever I'm seeing gets jealous of her and the whole thing falls apart…"

"I know," Rebecca said. "Amy's just explained."

He looked taken aback. "What? Amy's here?"

"In the living room. She's just been telling me how she sabotages your life."

Max gave a half laugh. "That's her mother talking. So has Amy actually accepted how difficult she can be?"

"Totally."

"I can't believe it. Her mother and I have spent months trying to get through to her. She's not a bad kid. You'll love her when you get to know her. She's great with animals. She's got this white rat called Plague."

"Nice," Rebecca said. "You should have trusted me, Max. I wouldn't have run away."

"I know that now, but I was so scared of frightening you off. It was bad enough convincing you I wasn't seeing Lorna. I thought this would have been one strain too much. So, do you forgive me?"

"Not sure," she said, arms folded. "You've made a puddle on the floorboards."

She wiped the rain off his forehead with her sleeve. "'Course I forgive you."

She hung up his wet coat and they went into the living room. The moment they walked in, Amy jumped off the sofa.

"Dad, please don't be angry. I didn't mean to interfere, honest."

He put his arms round her. "I'm not angry. This is my fault. I should have been straight from the start."

Rebecca suggested she cook them all breakfast while Max went to the bathroom to dry off. Amy followed Rebecca into the kitchen.

"You know," Rebecca said as she stood frying bacon and eggs, "I had my dad to myself for years after my mum died. He's getting married soon and even at my age I was really jealous for a bit. So I know how you feel."

"Thing is," Amy volunteered, "I try not to be jealous, but I just can't help it."

"Tell me about it," Rebecca said with a half laugh. "But now that I've gotten to know my dad's girlfriend, we've become really close."

"Really?" Amy didn't look entirely convinced.

"I don't want to take your place with your dad, you know," Rebecca said gently. "You'll always be his little girl....Listen, how do you fancy some hot chocolate and whipped cream? I think I might even have chocolate sprinkles somewhere."

The moment she got the words out, Rebecca's face fell. Christ, how patronizing was it possible to get? The girl was fifteen. She was probably into crowd surfing and skinning up and here she was offering her bloody hot chocolate—with sprinkles.

"Great," Amy said. "I love hot chocolate." She even said she'd whip the cream. "You know," Amy went on, "I really do love your flat. Dad's is so sad with all that pine and crap. It'd be great if he moved in with you."

"You think so?" Rebecca said, feeling there might yet be hope for her relationship with Amy.

"Yeah, then I could bring all my friends back here. God, we could have a great party."

"What?" Rebecca almost dropped the spatula.

"Don't worry, Dad doesn't allow any booze."

"Well, we'll have to see."

"About the moving in or the party?"

"Both," Rebecca said.

Amy was distracted by Harrison, who came wandering in, snout twitching at the bacon smell. "Omigod," she squealed, bending down to stroke him, "doggy surfer shorts. Those are just so cool."

After breakfast, Amy took Harrison into the living room and the pair of them sat curled up on the sofa while Amy gossiped to her friends on her mobile. Max and Rebecca began clearing plates and loading the dishwasher. He asked her what she thought of Amy.

"Well, I admit she's a bit of a handful. But I like her. With a bit of time, I can really see us getting along. Mind you, she's nothing like me when I was that age. I was a timid little thing in braces."

"Funny, I had you down as a right moody cow."

Rebecca went for him with a wet dishcloth, but he dodged her.

"So, how did you come to have a child so young?"

"Jo—that's Amy's mum—and I met on holiday when I was twenty-one. We fell in love, got married and had Amy a year later. A year after that the marriage was over. We realized we'd been way too young. The split was never acrimonious, though. In fact, when Jo got married again a couple of years ago she invited me and my mum and dad.

"So, Amy doesn't make any difference?" he said. "To us, I mean?"

She had to admit that now that Max came as a package deal, she'd been wondering when they would have time for each other. With her new job, which was bound to involve long hours and trips away, all they'd have was weekends. How would she cope with a morose teenager hanging around? She suddenly realized how her relationship with Max now mirrored Lipstick's relationship with Stan—except of course Rebecca wasn't a pain-in-the-arse fifteen-year-old. On the other hand, she could see Amy's point of view, too. The poor kid was feeling precisely the same emotions she'd felt when Stan announced he was marrying Lipstick.

She came over and put her arms round him. "Does this answer your question?" she said. Then she kissed him.

"I love you," he said.

"Oh, by the way," he said. "There's something I want to show you that might cheer you up. It's in my coat pocket."

He went into the hall and came back with a slightly damp copy of the *Standard*.

"It's yesterday's," he said, handing it to her. "I meant to show you last night. Page five."

She turned the pages and started reading.

" 'Lorna Findlay sacked after Cabinet Caper.' Lorna Findlay has been dramatically dropped from the Channel 6 flagship news program *Tonight* after reportedly being found in a compromising sexual situation with a married man, rumored to be a senior government minister. According to a statement from Channel 6, she will now cohost an afternoon homes and lifestyle program with the *Sunday Tribune* journalist Guy Debonnaire."

Rebecca slapped the page and burst out laughing. "Bend down and kiss my toe cleavage, Findlay," she crowed. "That's put paid to your trips to Chequers."

"Poor woman. You have to feel a bit sorry for her. Apparently she's also been suffering from these disgusting warts." He lowered his voice. "Apparently they're up her bum."

"Oooh. God, how awful," she said.

"Yeah. Everybody's talking about it. I assumed you knew."

"No," she said, looking the picture of innocence. "Haven't heard a thing."

Just then the door buzzer went.

"God, who is it now?" Rebecca sighed.

It was Rose.

"I was on my way to see Jack," she said, kissing Rebecca. "You know—my friend with the colostomy bag who lives round the corner—the one we all call Semi Colon. Anyway, I couldn't pass by without popping in to say well done on the new job. I'm so proud of you. Plus you never told me how it went with Alex, the hospital administrator. You seeing him again?"

She'd barely finished her sentence when Max came into the hall.

"Ah," Rose said, clearly taken aback. "So, you two…?"

Rebecca nodded.

"Who's Alex?" Max said.

"Oh, he bought me in an auction. Or at least his mother did. For seven and a half pounds."

Max looked confused.

"I'll explain later," Rebecca said.

They all headed to the kitchen, then Rose decided she needed the loo. Rebecca had just finished filling the coffeepot when Amy walked in to say she'd decided to go and meet some friends.

"Where?" Max said.

"Well, we said Camden Market. I thought I might buy those jeans. Thing is I've only got a fiver on me."

Max turned to Rebecca.

"Not enough allowance left at the end of the month," he explained. Then to Amy: "Look, I am not a bottomless pit. You'll have to save up."

"Oh, Max." Rebecca gave him a pleading look.

He hesitated for a few seconds and then took his wallet from his pocket. "Oh, all right, then," he said, handing her three tenners. "Off you go."

"Thanks, Dad. Love you."

She mouthed a thank-you to Rebecca. Just then, Rose reappeared.

"Gran, I'd like you to meet Amy. Amy is Max's daughter."

Rose's eyes couldn't have gotten any wider.

"A daughter?" she whispered to Rebecca. "He has a daughter?"

"Hi," Amy said, holding out her hand to Rose.

"Hello, Amy. I'm Rose, Rebecca's grandma. My, what a beautiful girl you are. I can see you're going to break a few hearts. Now then, why don't you come and sit down?" She patted the seat next to her. Amy shot her dad an uneasy glance and then sat.

"So, tell me, sweetie, how old are you?"

"Fifteen."

"Ah, wonderful age. What I wouldn't give to be fifteen again. And, do you have a boyfriend yet?"

Rebecca rolled her eyes. Max said he'd pour out the coffee.

"No, not yet," Amy said.

"Gran," Rebecca hissed.

"Listen, Amy, I have a friend with a grandson about your age—maybe a year or two older. Lovely boy. Tall, very good-looking. He's into that singer. Oh, you know...what do they call him, Enema, is it?"

They were saved, quite literally, by the bell. This time it was the telephone. Rebecca picked up. Her face fell almost instantly. "What?...What's happened? No, don't worry, we'll be there as soon as we can."

Rebecca could hardly breathe, let alone speak.

"OK, OK, take it easy," Max said, putting his arm round her and helping her to a chair.

"No, I don't want to sit down. We have to go. That was Lipstick phoning from the salon. I couldn't make out what she was saying, she was in such a state, but Dad seems to have collapsed. She's called an ambulance."

Rose's hand flew to her chest. The color drained from her face. "My God," she whispered.

"OK," Max said, taking charge, "where do you want to go, the salon or the hospital?"

"I'm not sure where they'll take him. Let's go to the salon."

Max turned to Amy. "You going to be all right?"

"Yeah, after Camden I'll go back to Mum's. We'll go out to eat another night."

He nodded.

She got up and gave Rebecca a quick, rather awkward hug. "I hope your dad's OK," she said.

"Thanks," Rebecca said, managing a weak smile.

Max drove like a lunatic to the salon. Nobody spoke for the entire journey.

The door was opened by a woman whose entire body was swathed in white bandages. She looked like she'd escaped from some ancient B movie about mummies. Nobody bothered to ask why.

"My dad, is he OK?"

"He's fine," the woman said. "He's in one of the beauty treatment rooms at the far end."

Rose and Rebecca charged to the back of the salon. Max had said that since he wasn't family, he would wait in reception with Mrs. Tutankhamen.

Stan was lying on the couch, looking pale, but otherwise OK. Lipstick was standing on one side of him. A young woman paramedic was standing on the other side, taking his blood pressure.

"Dad? You OK? What happened? We've been frantic."

"My God," Rose said. "Look at him. My friend Cissie had a better color when she'd been dead for two days."

Lipstick moved out of the way, so that the two women could kiss him.

"It's nothing. Really," Stan said, taking his mother's hand. "I choked, that's all. And I stopped breathing for a few seconds."

"A few seconds?" Lipstick piped up. "It was over a minute. I thought I'd lost him. Then one of my clients heard me screaming and came rushing in."

"What, the Mummy's Curse woman?" Rebecca said.

"Her name's Maggie and she's wearing a seaweed wrap. Anyway, thank God she knew how to do that Heimlich maneuver thing and was able to clear his windpipe."

Rose turned to the paramedic. "Is he going to be all right?" she said. Her voice trembled and she was gripping Stan's hand so tight, his fingertips were bright red.

"I'm sure there's no permanent damage," she said. "But I think he should come along to the hospital anyway, just to let the doctors take a look at him."

"I should think so, too," Rose said. "And if you ask me, he should have a CAT scan. Oh, and if he needs an anesthetic at any stage, don't give him a local. My son can afford imported."

The paramedic wrapped her stethoscope round her neck and smiled. "I'm sure a CAT scan won't be necessary. They'll just want to check that his heart is all right."

"Mum, I'm OK. Really," Stan butted in.

Rose shrugged as if to say, "Well, I've said my piece. If you drop dead, don't come crying to me."

The paramedic said she would wait outside to give Stan a couple of minutes with his family, but then they really should get to the hospital.

"So what were you doing to choke?" Rose said, sweeping back his hair to cover his bald patch.

"Sucking on a Fisherman's Friend," Stan said.

"You're lucky he didn't hit you," Rose chuckled.

"So did you just choke by accident," Rebecca said, "or did something specific cause it?"

Stan and Lipstick exchanged a look.

"Will you tell them?" Stan said. "Or shall I?"

"You," Lipstick said.

"OK, I'd just popped into the salon to let Bernadette know I was back from Manchester. Straight away she drags me in here to tell me her news. First she tells me about the shop extension. Then she drops the real bombshell. I'm so shocked, I choke on the sweet."

"What bombshell?" Rebecca and Rose said in unison.

"I'm pregnant," Lipstick declared, her face beaming.

"Can you believe it? I'm going to become a father again. At my age."

Rose was speechless.

"But," she spluttered eventually, "I thought you had a tracheotomy."

"You mean a vasectomy, Mum. I had it reversed."

"What? They can do that?"

The hugging and the kissing seemed to go on for ages.

"I should have guessed," Rebecca said to Lipstick. "That's why you were off your food. You had morning sickness."

"Yeah and I have to say, it's not getting any better."

She took Rebecca to one side. "So, you and Max, you're OK again, then?"

"Yes, we're OK," Rebecca said. "He's outside. The only thing is, I just found out he's divorced with a fifteen-year-old daughter."

"What? You are kidding."

"No. I'll tell you about it later." She paused. "Thanks, Lipstick. For Paris, for getting me back with Max, marrying Dad—everything."

Lipstick laughed. "My pleasure," she said. "Now, why don't you bring Max in and introduce him to Stan?"

Rebecca walked Stan to the ambulance. Lipstick said she'd catch up to him. As she was leaving early for the day and the girls in the salon would be on their own for the rest of the day, she wanted to make sure they remembered how to set the salon burglar alarm.

"I like Max," Stan said. "He's clever, good-looking. Your mother would have adored him."

"You reckon?"

"I know." Then he put his arm round her and gave her a squeeze. "I think she would have approved of Lip—"

She stopped herself. As far as she knew, Stan had no idea about Lipstick's nickname from school.

He smiled. "It's OK, I know about Bernadette being called Lipstick. And she's told me all about how horrible she was to you at school. I can't tell you how sorry she is. I've met her mum and dad. They're lovely people. They'd have to be to approve of her marrying an old fart like me. But they spoiled her, gave her no discipline when she was growing up. She was a pretty mixed-up kid."

"I know. We talked."

"And you don't hold it against her?"

"Not anymore. I really like Lipstick. I have a strong feeling the two of you are going to be really happy."

"You know something?" he said. "I do too."

Max and Rebecca dropped Rose at Semi Colon's.

"You know," Max said later, as they lay beside each other on Rebecca's pink sofa, "that could be us one of these days."

"What, with colostomy bags?"

"No, you dope. Pregnant. After we get married, of course."

"Oh, of course." She was giggling quietly to herself.

He turned toward her. "You do want to get married, don't you?"

"I can think of nothing I'd like more," she said, snuggling up to him and kissing him on the cheek.

"Good. That's settled, then. And babies? You want them, too, don't you? I mean ideally I'd like three."

"O-kaaay," she said. "Would that be all at once or one at a time?"

"All at once would be more convenient. I mean, then you get all the grotty baby stuff out of the way in one go, but if you can't manage it, one at a time would be fine."

"Right, just so long as I know."

He was sitting up. "Oh, God, I'm not assuming too much, am I? I wouldn't dream of forcing the baby issue. After all, I have got Amy."

She looked at him. The truth was she'd never given babies more than the occasional thought until this moment. "Well, it won't be easy with my job and everything, but, yes, a couple of years from now, I can definitely see us with a baby. Mind you, I think Amy will have a few words to say about it."

"Nah. Even though she plays up whenever I get a girlfriend, she's been desperate for a baby brother or sister for ages. Her mother doesn't want any more, so it's down to me."

He began stroking her hair and planting tiny kisses on her face.

"I am so in love with you," she said, bringing her lips toward his.

Just then the door buzzer went.

"God, what now?" Rebecca groaned, pulling herself up. She left Max on the sofa and went to the door.

It was Jess, bubbling over with excitement. "Look, I just had to come round. I'm desperate to hear all about you and Max. Lipstick told me how she got the two of you back together. God, was the makeup sex brilliant? I want all the details."

She hadn't seen Max standing in the hall.

"Hi, Jess."

She jumped. Then she turned bright red. "Max. Hi. I don't know why, but I didn't think you'd be here. Look, if you guys want some privacy, perhaps I'd better..."

"Don't be daft. Come on in," Rebecca said, leading her into the living room.

"Oh, and guess what?" Jess said, "We've sorted out Ed's willy-nilly once and for all. We know what really caused it."

"But you already know," Rebecca said. "Ed was JFK and got rejected by Marilyn Monroe."

"Come again?" Max piped up.

The two women ignored him.

"No, Ed was never JFK. We both think you're right about that Gwen woman. She's just a charlatan who messes with people's heads. The thing is, Ed went back to the doctor this morning and got the result of his blood test. And it turns out he's got an underactive thyroid. Isn't that just *the* best news?"

"Terrific," Rebecca said. "Assuming something can be done about it."

"He's got some pills to take. It's only ever-so-slightly underactive, but it explains the willy-nilly. And the doctor says he should be back to normal in a few weeks."

"Wow," Rebecca said, "you'll have to take a second honeymoon."

"Yes," Max said, "you could come with us."

"What? You two? You're ...?"

"Yep," Rebecca said. "We're getting married."

"Oh, guys." Jess's eyes were full of tears. "Come here and give me a hug."

"You know," Rebecca said after Jess had gone, "I think my ribs are actually bruised from all the hugging that's gone on today."

Max was barely listening. "You don't think Jess thought I was serious about her and Ed coming on honeymoon with us, do you? I mean, I love Jess and I'm sure I'd like Ed, but it will be our honeymoon."

"Too late," Rebecca said. "As she was leaving she said she'd send off for some brochures. She fancies the Maldives."

"Shit."

"Joking," Rebecca said, bashing him with a cushion.

"Thank God for that."

"No, she really fancies the Caribbean."

They were in the middle of the most fantastic snog when the phone rang.

"Leave it," Max commanded.

"I can't. Something could have happened to Dad."

She picked the phone up off the coffee table.

"Sorry? Who?" she said, sitting up and frowning. "Omigod, Prime Minister. Yes, Charlie mentioned you might phone. . . . Yes, it did work out well . . . yes, I'm delighted too . . . what, this evening? Yes, I think I can make it. No, it's not a problem. I'll look forward to it."

"Jeez," Max said. "That was the PM?"

She nodded.

"He was phoning to thank me for saving the African peace deal and now I've got to go and pack an overnight bag."

"Why, where are you going? I had plans for tonight. I thought we'd go to bed with a curry and a bottle of wine and watch *Millionaire*."

She burst out laughing. "Max Stoddart watches game shows? I don't believe it."

"Yeah, but only in an ironic way," he said, clearly embarrassed. "Plus, if we're getting married there are things to talk about. Honeymoon destinations to decide on."

"Sorry," she said, getting up off the sofa. "It'll have to wait. Don't worry, though—I'll call you when I get back from Chequers."

Nine months later, at the British Press Awards lunch in London, Rebecca and Max won the Journalist of the Year and Investigative

Story of the Year awards, respectively; at the Golden Rain Porn Film Awards in Las Vegas, *Coming Down the Catwalk* walked off with Willies for best screenplay and best costumes; and at Muswell Hill General Hospital, Lipstick gave birth to Madonna Erin Rose O'Brien-Fine.